ELVES

VOL. 1

WRITTEN BY JEAN-LUC ISTIN

ILLUSTRATED BY KYKO DUARTE

COLORS BY SAITO

INSIGHT COMICS

San Rafael, California

ELVES

PART 1
THE CRYSTAL OF THE BLUE ELVES

BY ISTIN AND DUARTE

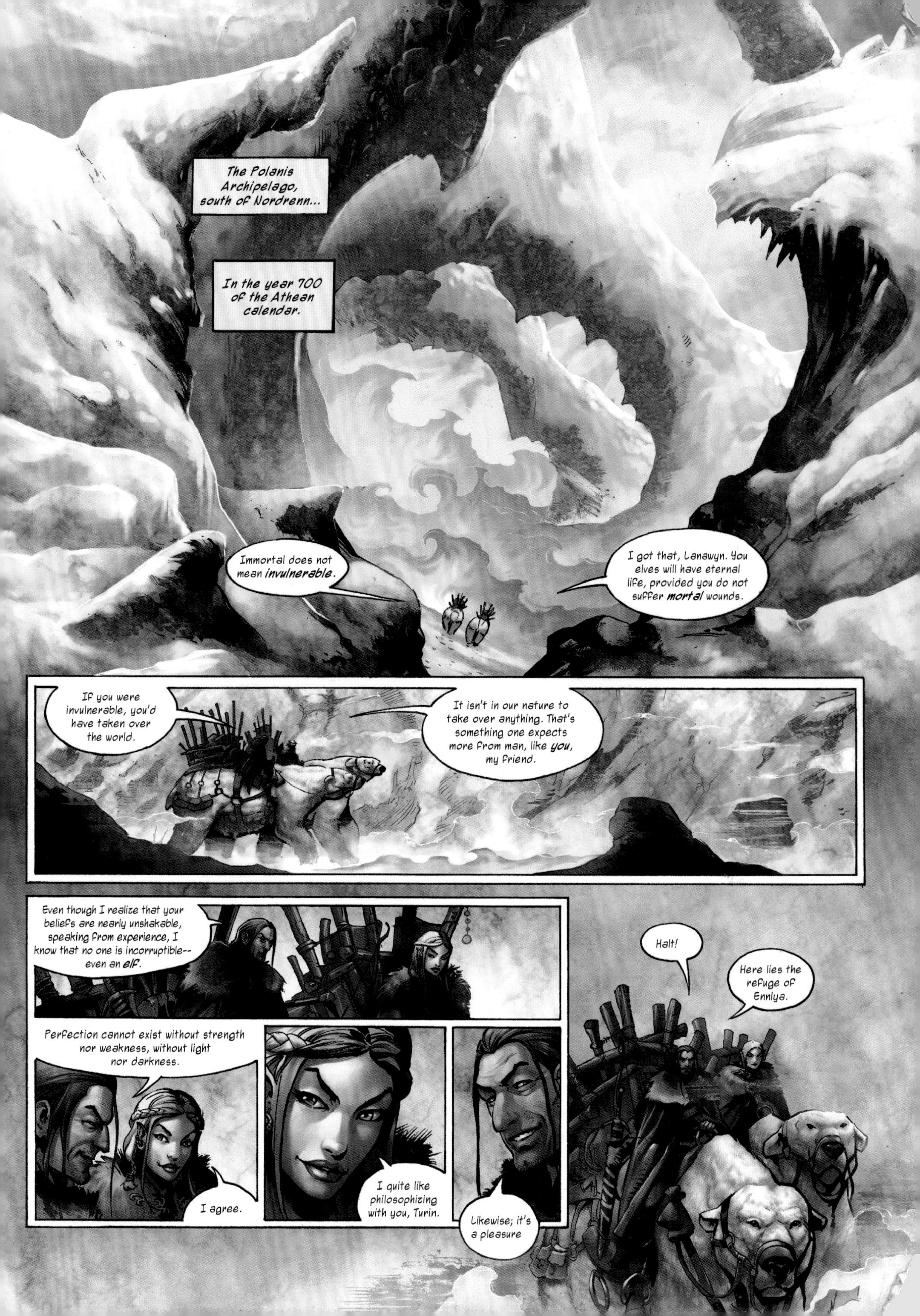
The Polanis Archipelago, south of Nordrenn...
In the year 700 of the Athean calendar.
Immortal does not mean *invulnerable*.
I got that, Lanawyn. You elves will have eternal life, provided you do not suffer ***mortal*** wounds.
If you were invulnerable, you'd have taken over the world.
It isn't in our nature to take over anything. That's something one expects more from man, like ***you***, my friend.
Even though I realize that your beliefs are nearly unshakable, speaking from experience, I know that no one is incorruptible-- even an ***elf***.
Halt!
Here lies the refuge of Ennlya.
Perfection cannot exist without strength nor weakness, without light nor darkness.
I agree.
I quite like philosophizing with you, Turin.
Likewise; it's a pleasure

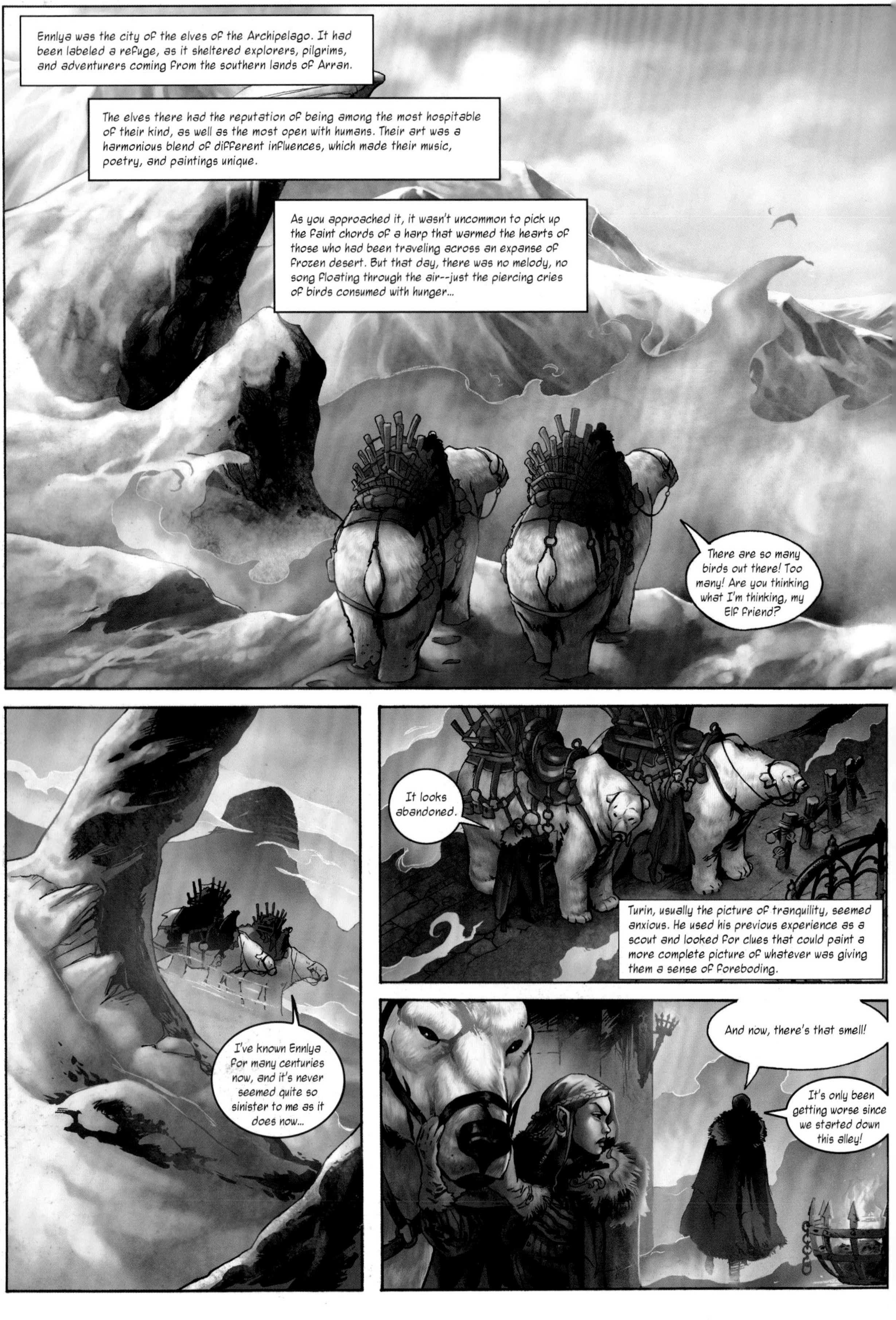
Ennlya was the city of the elves of the Archipelago. It had been labeled a refuge, as it sheltered explorers, pilgrims, and adventurers coming from the southern lands of Arran.
The elves there had the reputation of being among the most hospitable of their kind, as well as the most open with humans. Their art was a harmonious blend of different influences, which made their music, poetry, and paintings unique.
As you approached it, it wasn't uncommon to pick up the faint chords of a harp that warmed the hearts of those who had been traveling across an expanse of frozen desert. But that day, there was no melody, no song floating through the air--just the piercing cries of birds consumed with hunger...
There are so many birds out there! Too many! Are you thinking what I'm thinking, my Elf friend?
I've known Ennlya for many centuries now, and it's never seemed quite so sinister to me as it does now...
It looks abandoned.
Turin, usually the picture of tranquility, seemed anxious. He used his previous experience as a scout and looked for clues that could paint a more complete picture of whatever was giving them a sense of foreboding.
And now, there's that smell!
It's only been getting worse since we started down this alley!

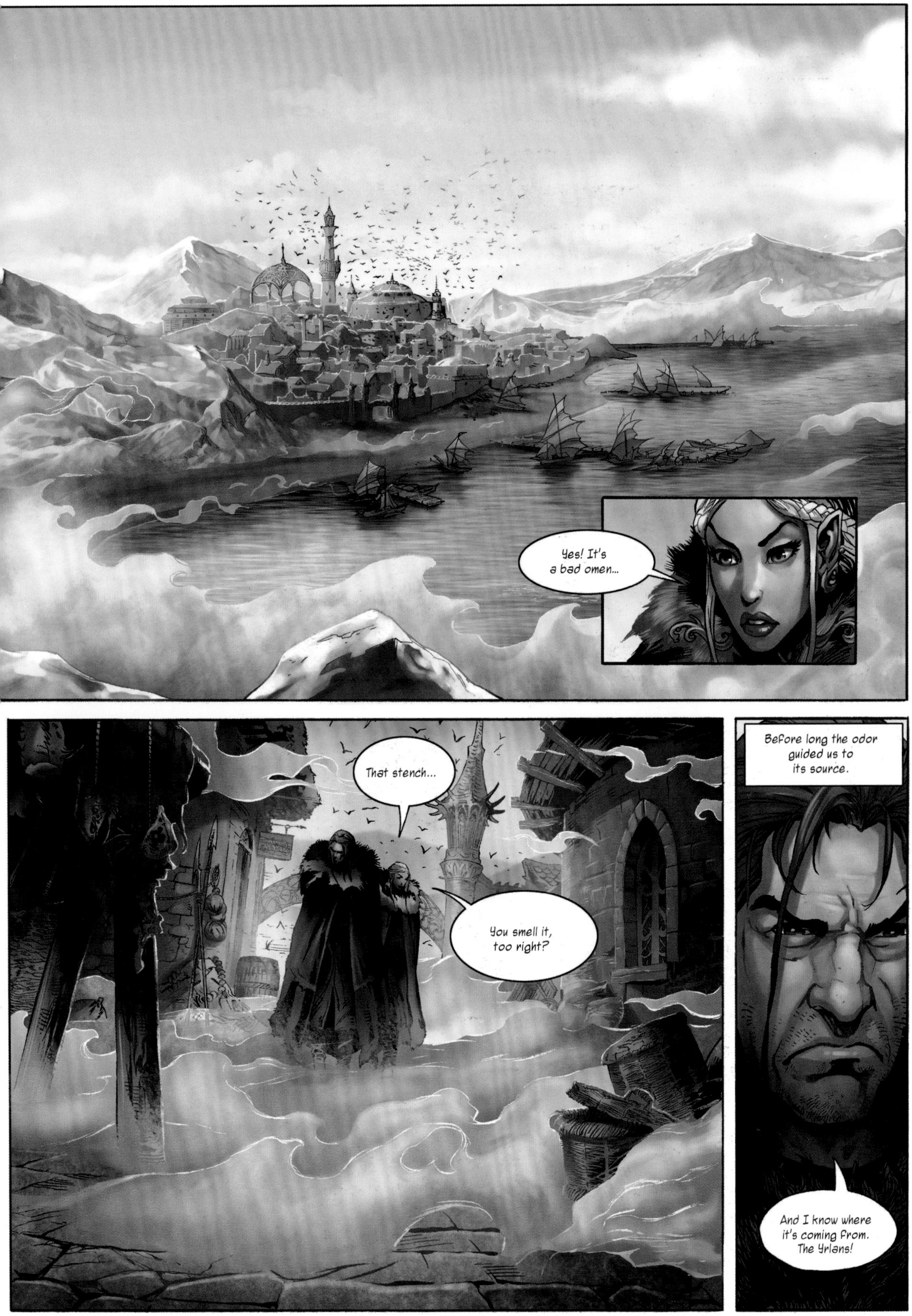
Yes! It's a bad omen...
That stench...
You smell it, too right?
Before long the odor guided us to its source.
And I know where it's coming from. The Yrlans!

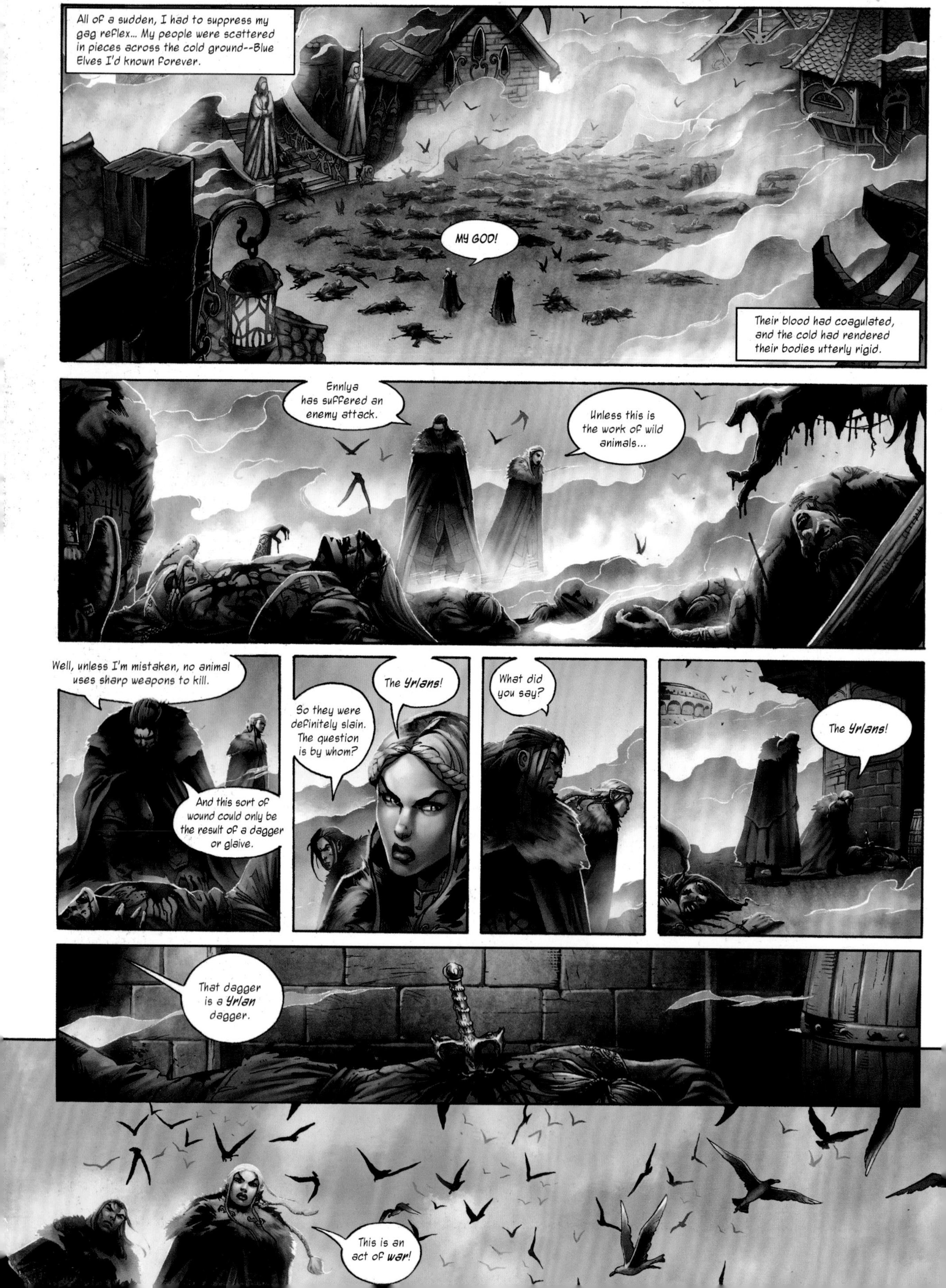

All of a sudden, I had to suppress my gag reflex... My people were scattered in pieces across the cold ground--Blue Elves I'd known forever.
MY GOD!
Their blood had coagulated, and the cold had rendered their bodies utterly rigid.
Ennlya has suffered an enemy attack.
Unless this is the work of wild animals...
Well, unless I'm mistaken, no animal uses sharp weapons to kill.
And this sort of wound could only be the result of a dagger or glaive.
So they were definitely slain. The question is by whom?
The Yrlans!
What did you say?
The Yrlans!
That dagger is a Yrlan dagger.
This is an act of war!

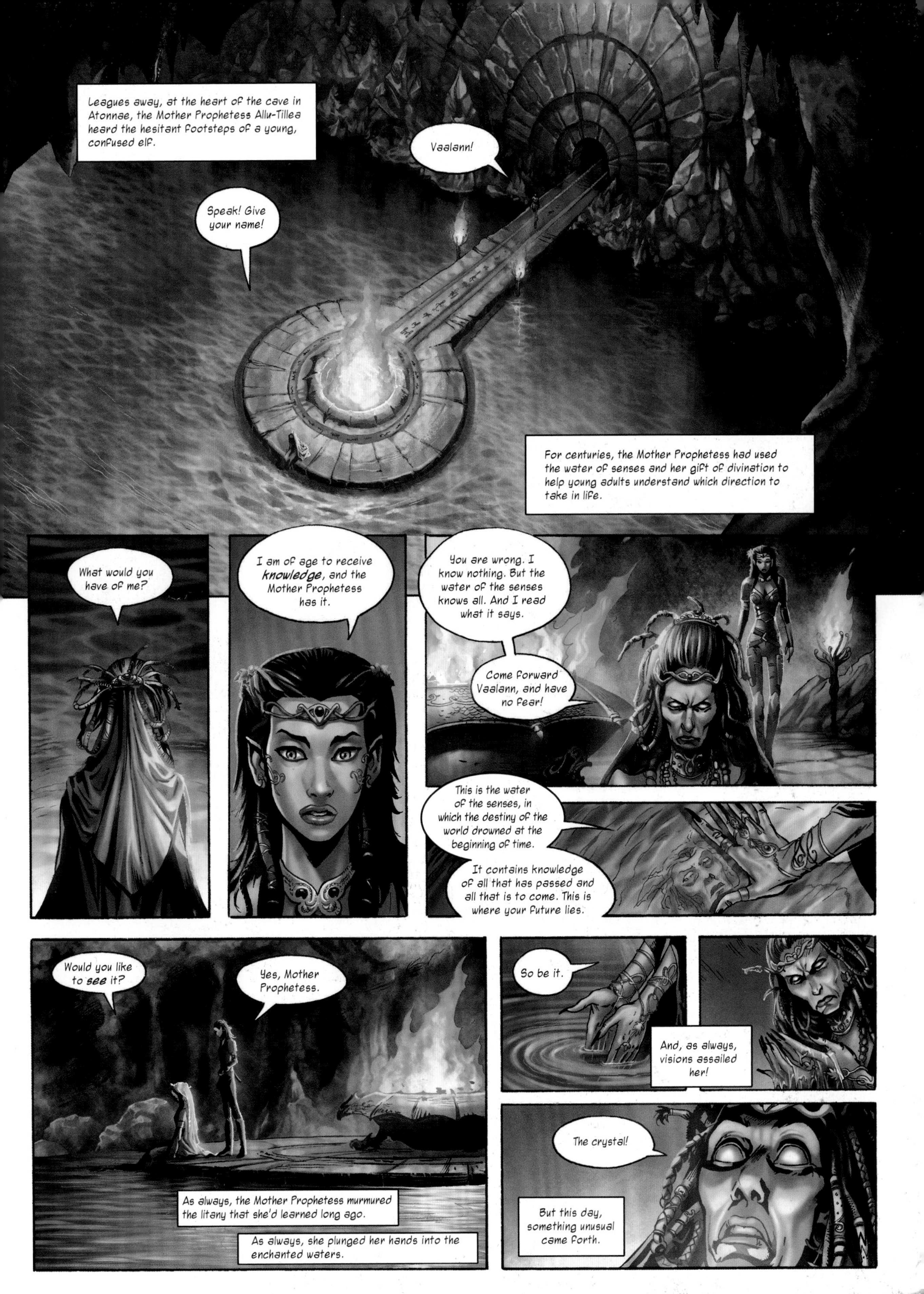
Leagues away, at the heart of the cave in Atonnae, the Mother Prophetess Allu-Tillea heard the hesitant footsteps of a young, confused elf.
Speak! Give your name!
Vaalann!
For centuries, the Mother Prophetess had used the water of senses and her gift of divination to help young adults understand which direction to take in life.
What would you have of me?
I am of age to receive knowledge, and the Mother Prophetess has it.
You are wrong. I know nothing. But the water of the senses knows all. And I read what it says.
Come forward Vaalann, and have no fear!
This is the water of the senses, in which the destiny of the world drowned at the beginning of time.
It contains knowledge of all that has passed and all that is to come. This is where your future lies.
Would you like to see it?
Yes, Mother Prophetess.
As always, the Mother Prophetess murmured the litany that she'd learned long ago.
As always, she plunged her hands into the enchanted waters.
So be it.
And, as always, visions assailed her!
The crystal!
But this day, something unusual came forth.

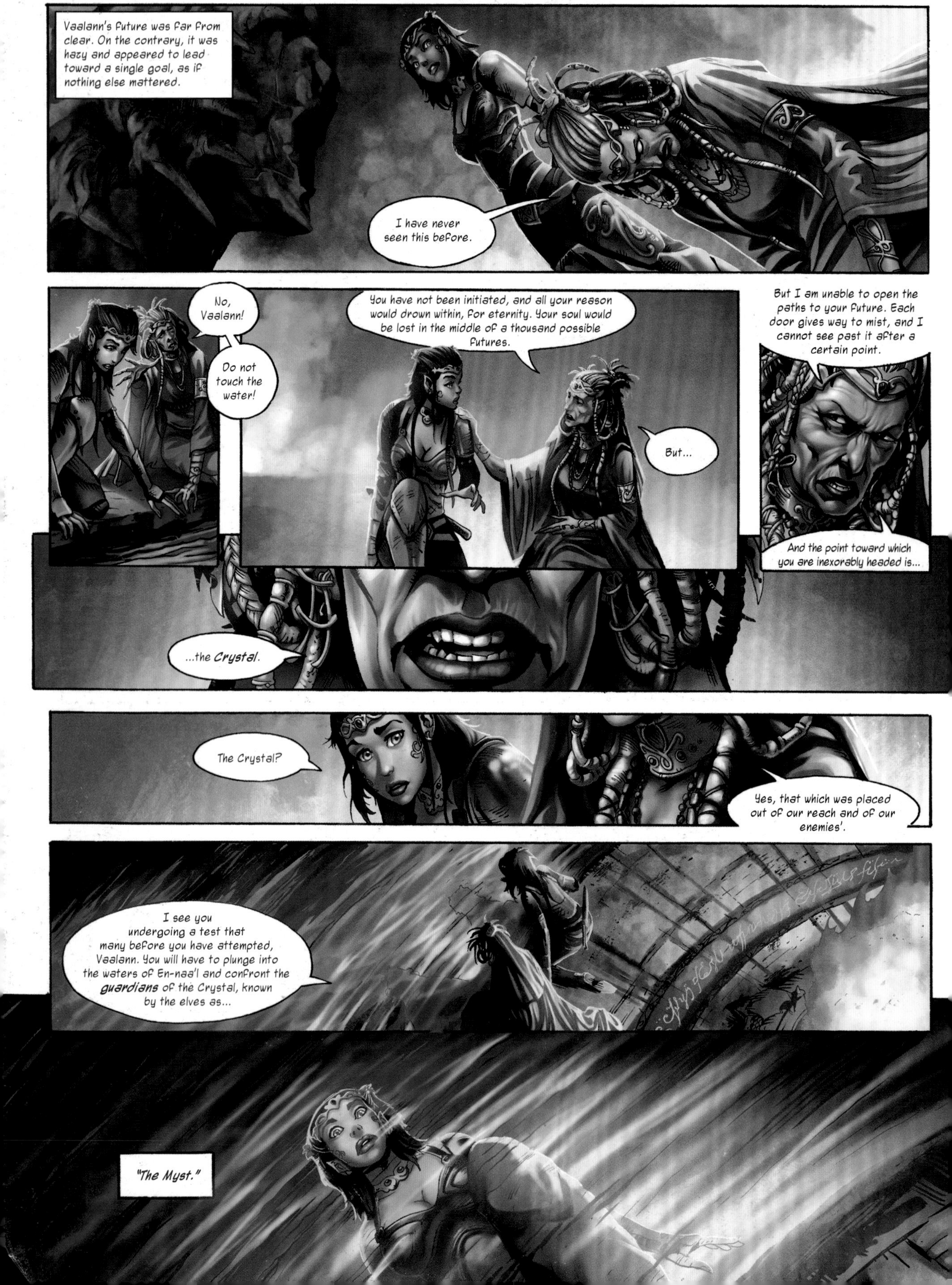
Vaalann's future was far from clear. On the contrary, it was hazy and appeared to lead toward a single goal, as if nothing else mattered.
I have never seen this before.
No, Vaalann!
Do not touch the water!
You have not been initiated, and all your reason would drown within, for eternity. Your soul would be lost in the middle of a thousand possible futures.
But...
But I am unable to open the paths to your future. Each door gives way to mist, and I cannot see past it after a certain point.
And the point toward which you are inexorably headed is...
...the Crystal.
The Crystal?
Yes, that which was placed out of our reach and of our enemies'.
I see you undergoing a test that many before you have attempted, Vaalann. You will have to plunge into the waters of En-naa'l and confront the guardians of the Crystal, known by the elves as...
"The Myst."

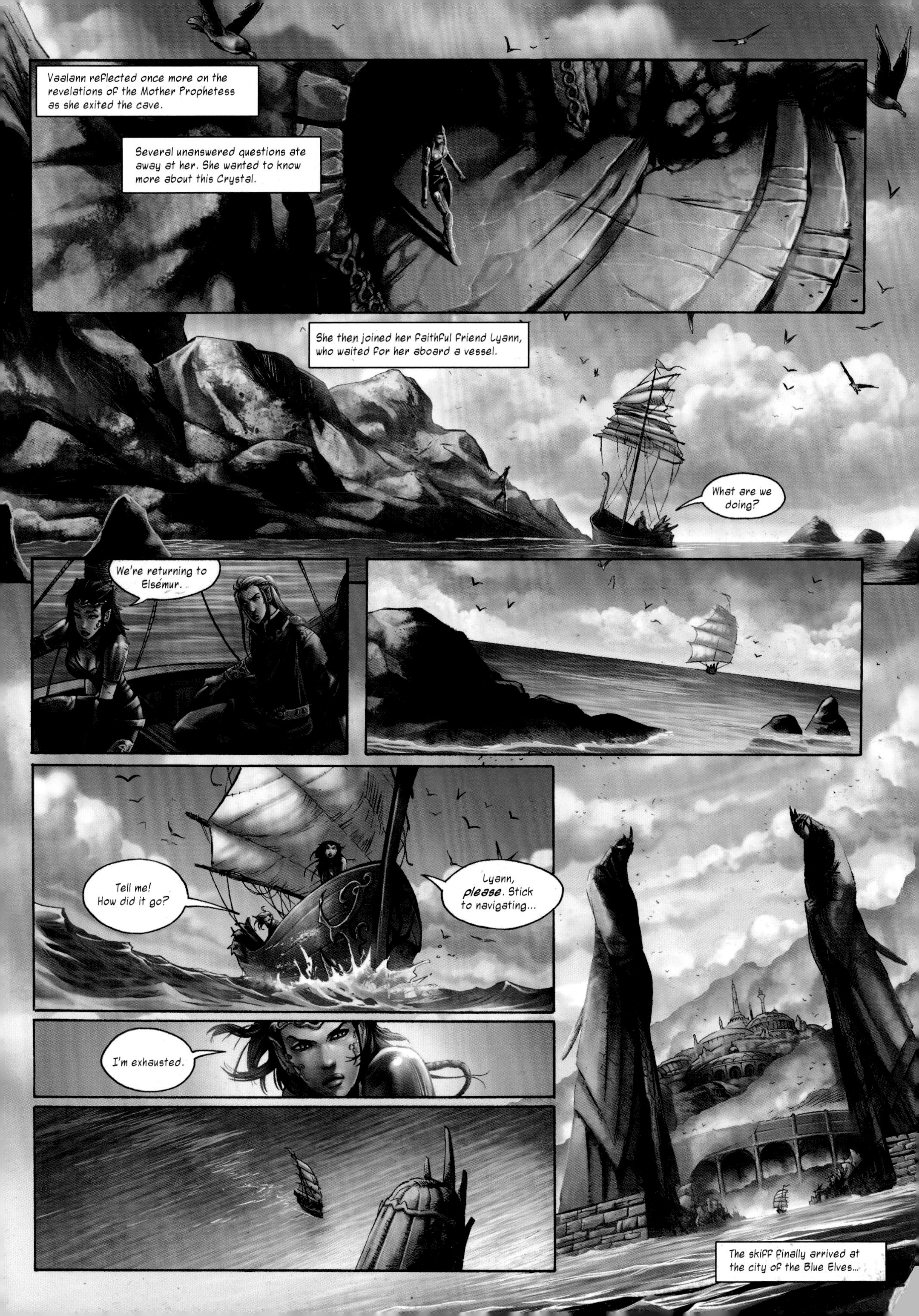
Vaalann reflected once more on the revelations of the Mother Prophetess as she exited the cave.
Several unanswered questions ate away at her. She wanted to know more about this Crystal.
She then joined her faithful friend Lyann, who waited for her aboard a vessel.
What are we doing?
We're returning to Elsemur.
Tell me! How did it go?
Lyann, please. Stick to navigating...
I'm exhausted.
The skiff finally arrived at the city of the Blue Elves...

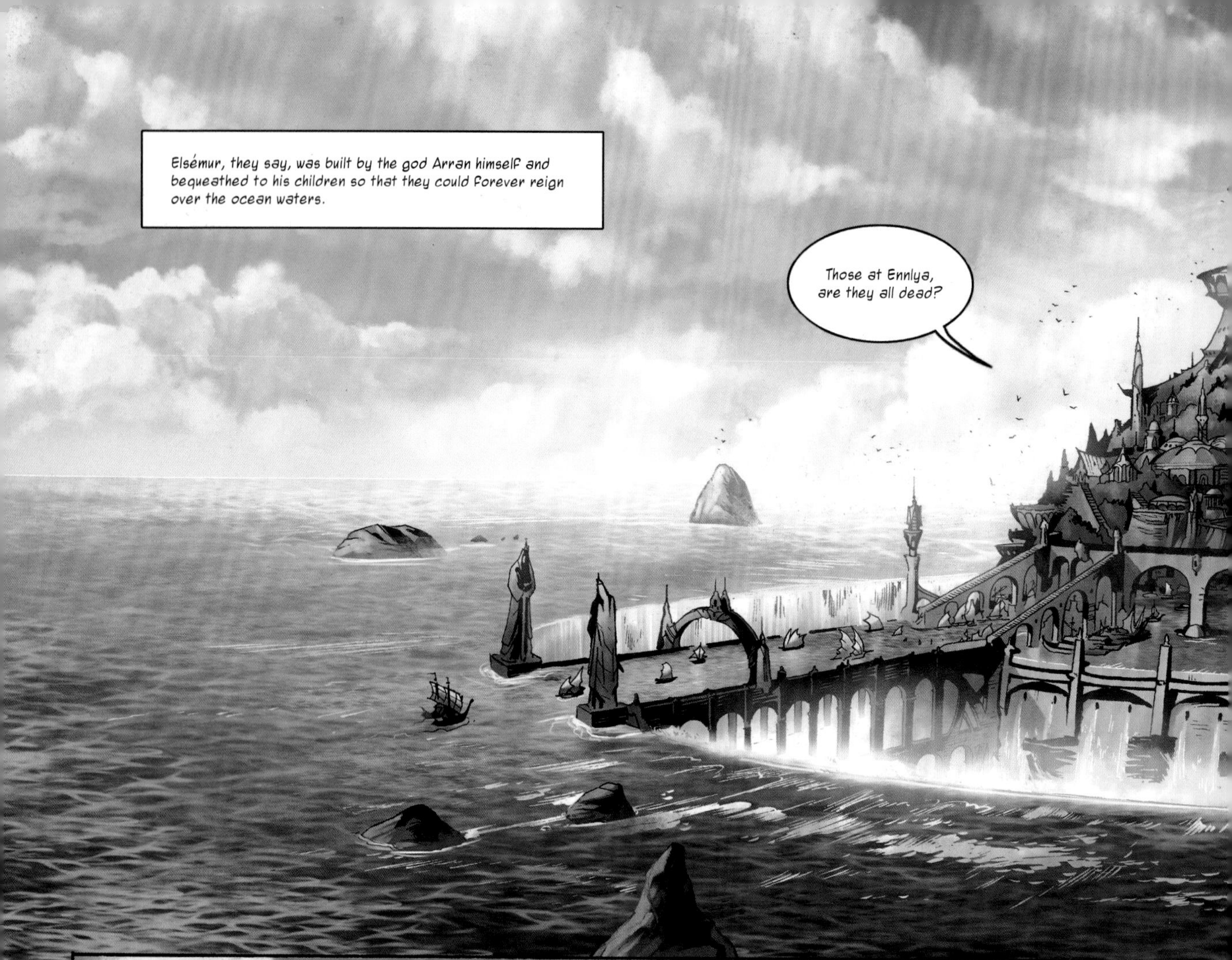
Elsémur, they say, was built by the god Arran himself and bequeathed to his children so that they could forever reign over the ocean waters.
Those at Ennlya, are they all dead?

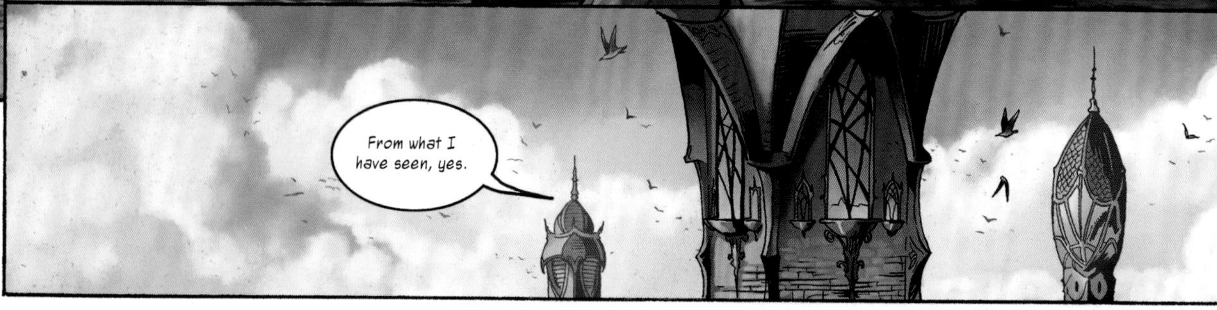
From what I have seen, yes.

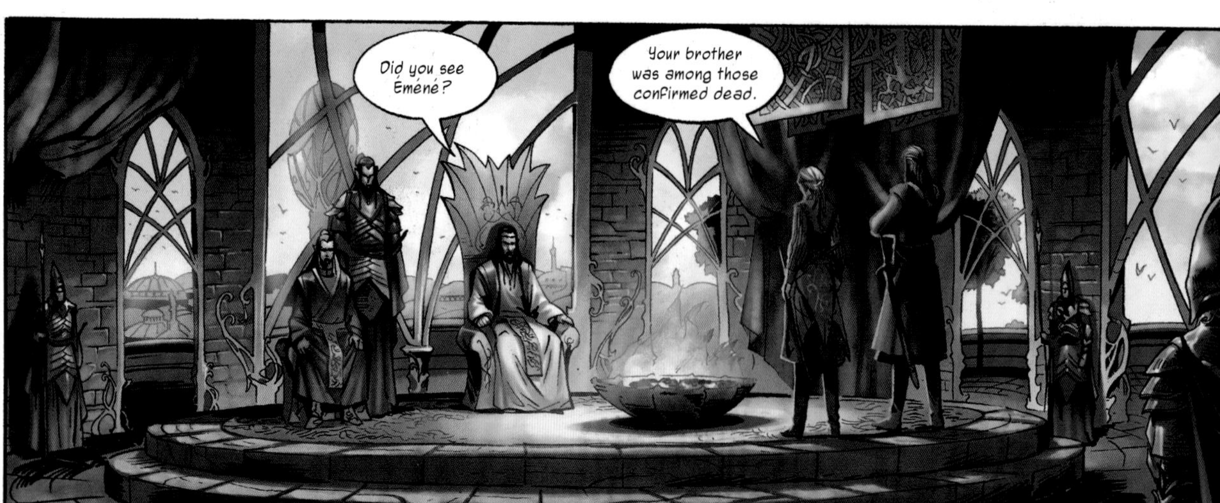
Did you see Éméné?
Your brother was among those confirmed dead.

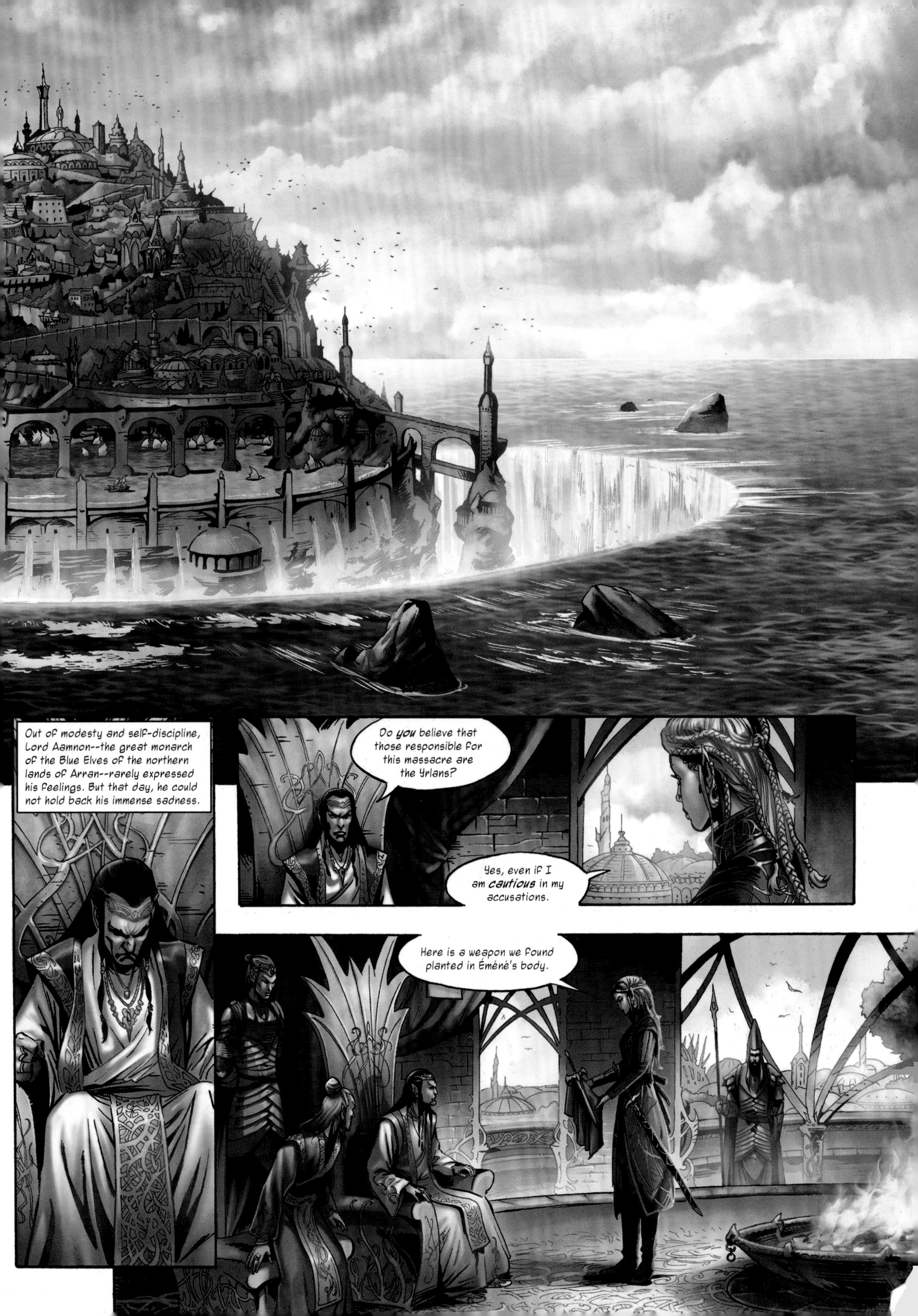

Out of modesty and self-discipline, Lord Aamnon--the great monarch of the Blue Elves of the northern lands of Arran--rarely expressed his feelings. But that day, he could not hold back his immense sadness.
Do *you* believe that those responsible for this massacre are the Yrlans?
Yes, even if I am *cautious* in my accusations.
Here is a weapon we found planted in Éméné's body.

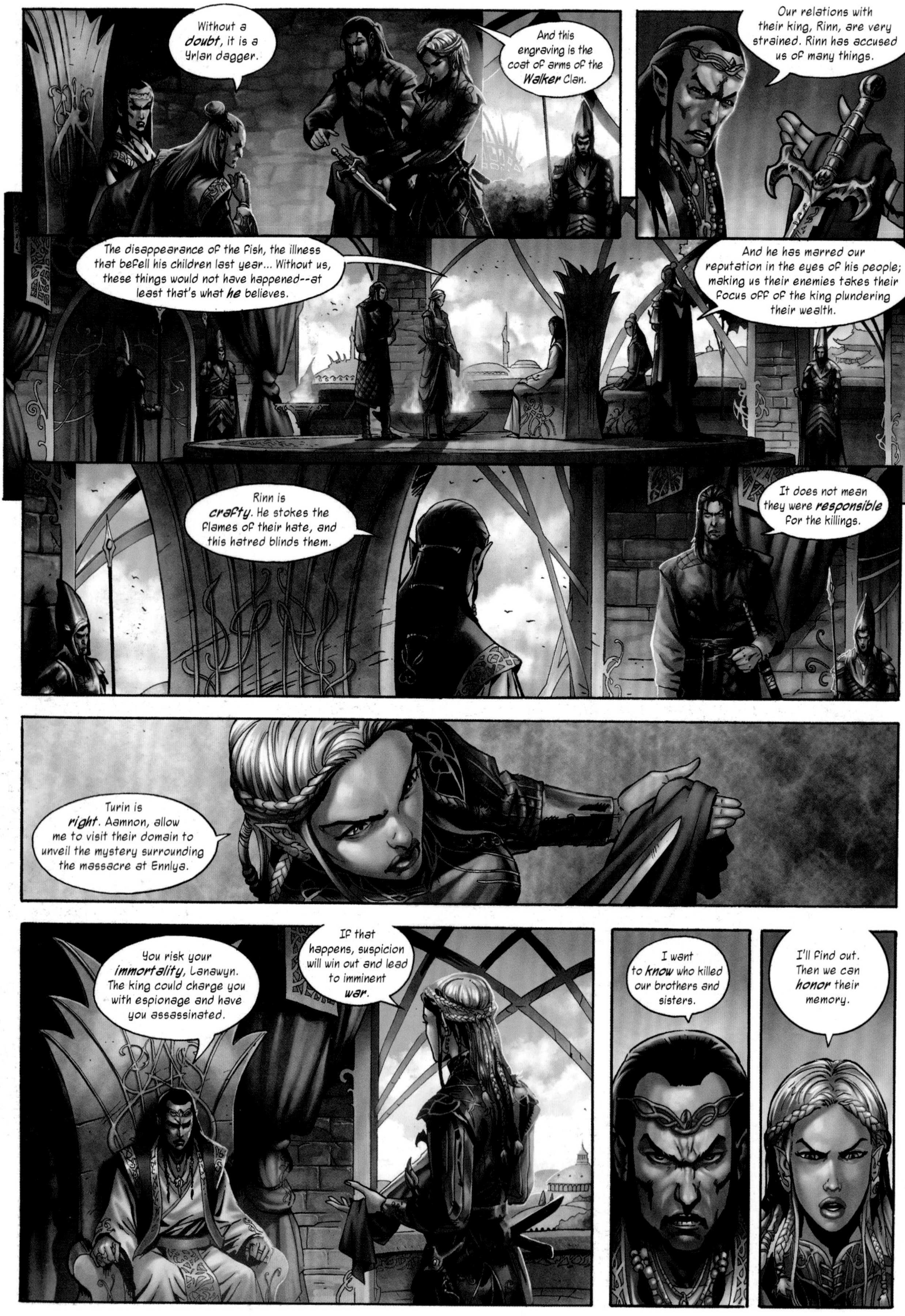
Without a doubt, it is a Yrlan dagger.
And this engraving is the coat of arms of the Walker Clan.
Our relations with their king, Rinn, are very strained. Rinn has accused us of many things.
The disappearance of the fish, the illness that befell his children last year... Without us, these things would not have happened--at least that's what he believes.
And he has marred our reputation in the eyes of his people; making us their enemies takes their focus off of the king plundering their wealth.
Rinn is crafty. He stokes the flames of their hate, and this hatred blinds them.
It does not mean they were responsible for the killings.
Turin is right. Aamnon, allow me to visit their domain to unveil the mystery surrounding the massacre at Ennlya.
You risk your immortality, Lanawyn. The king could charge you with espionage and have you assassinated.
If that happens, suspicion will win out and lead to imminent war.
I want to know who killed our brothers and sisters.
I'll find out. Then we can honor their memory.

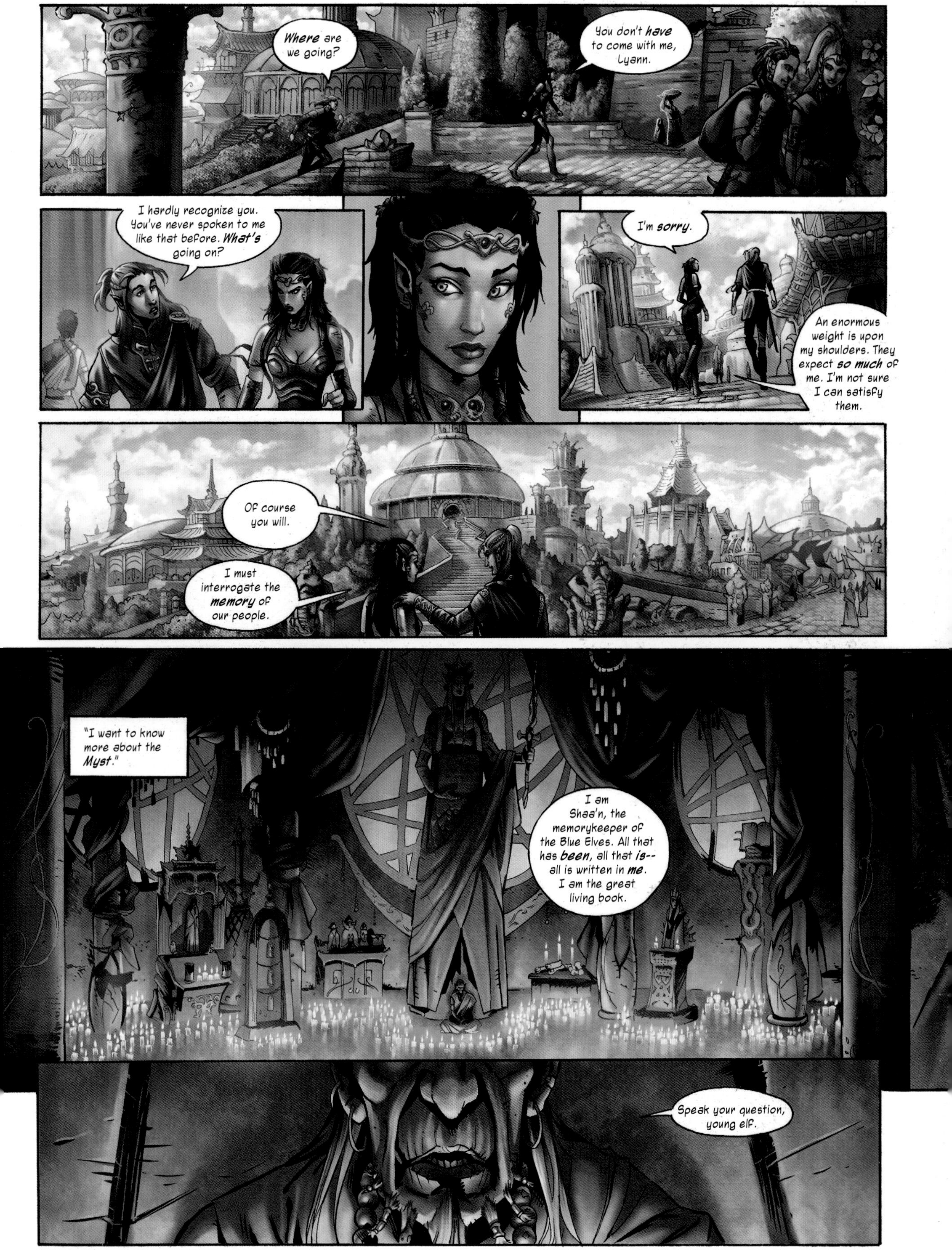
Where are we going?
You don't have to come with me, Lyann.
I hardly recognize you. You've never spoken to me like that before. What's going on?
I'm sorry.
An enormous weight is upon my shoulders. They expect so much of me. I'm not sure I can satisfy them.
Of course you will.
I must interrogate the memory of our people.
"I want to know more about the Myst."
I am Shaa'n, the memorykeeper of the Blue Elves. All that has been, all that is-- all is written in me. I am the great living book.
Speak your question, young elf.

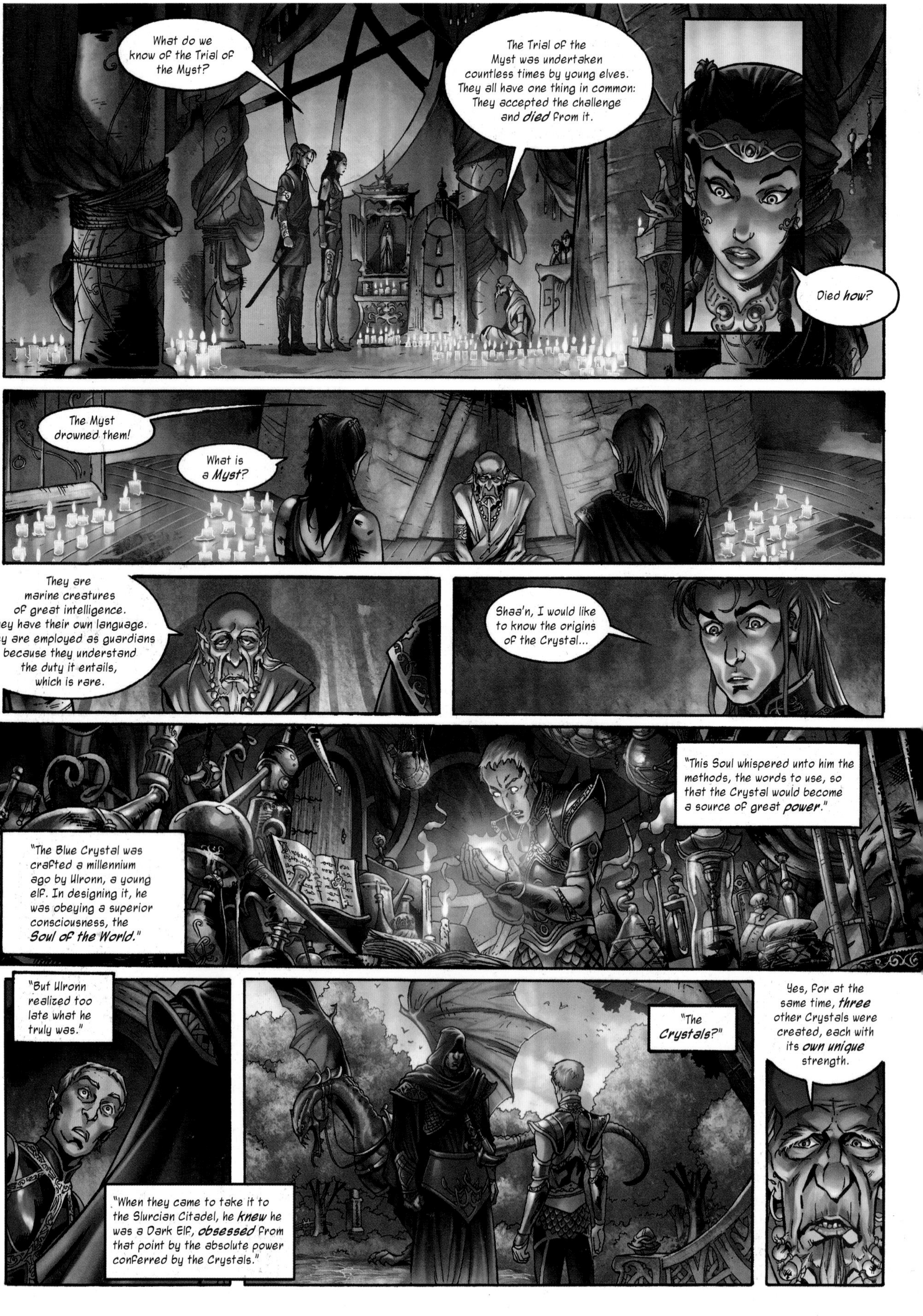

What do we know of the Trial of the Myst?
The Trial of the Myst was undertaken countless times by young elves. They all have one thing in common: They accepted the challenge and *died* from it.
Died *how*?
The Myst drowned them!
What is a *Myst*?
They are marine creatures of great intelligence. They have their own language. They are employed as guardians because they understand the duty it entails, which is rare.
Shaa'n, I would like to know the origins of the Crystal...
"The Blue Crystal was crafted a millennium ago by Ulronn, a young elf. In designing it, he was obeying a superior consciousness, the *Soul of the World.*"
"This Soul whispered unto him the methods, the words to use, so that the Crystal would become a source of great *power*."
"But Ulronn realized too late what he truly was."
"When they came to take it to the Slurcian Citadel, he *knew* he was a Dark Elf, *obsessed* from that point by the absolute power conferred by the Crystals."
"The *Crystals?*"
Yes, for at the same time, *three* other Crystals were created, each with its *own unique* strength.

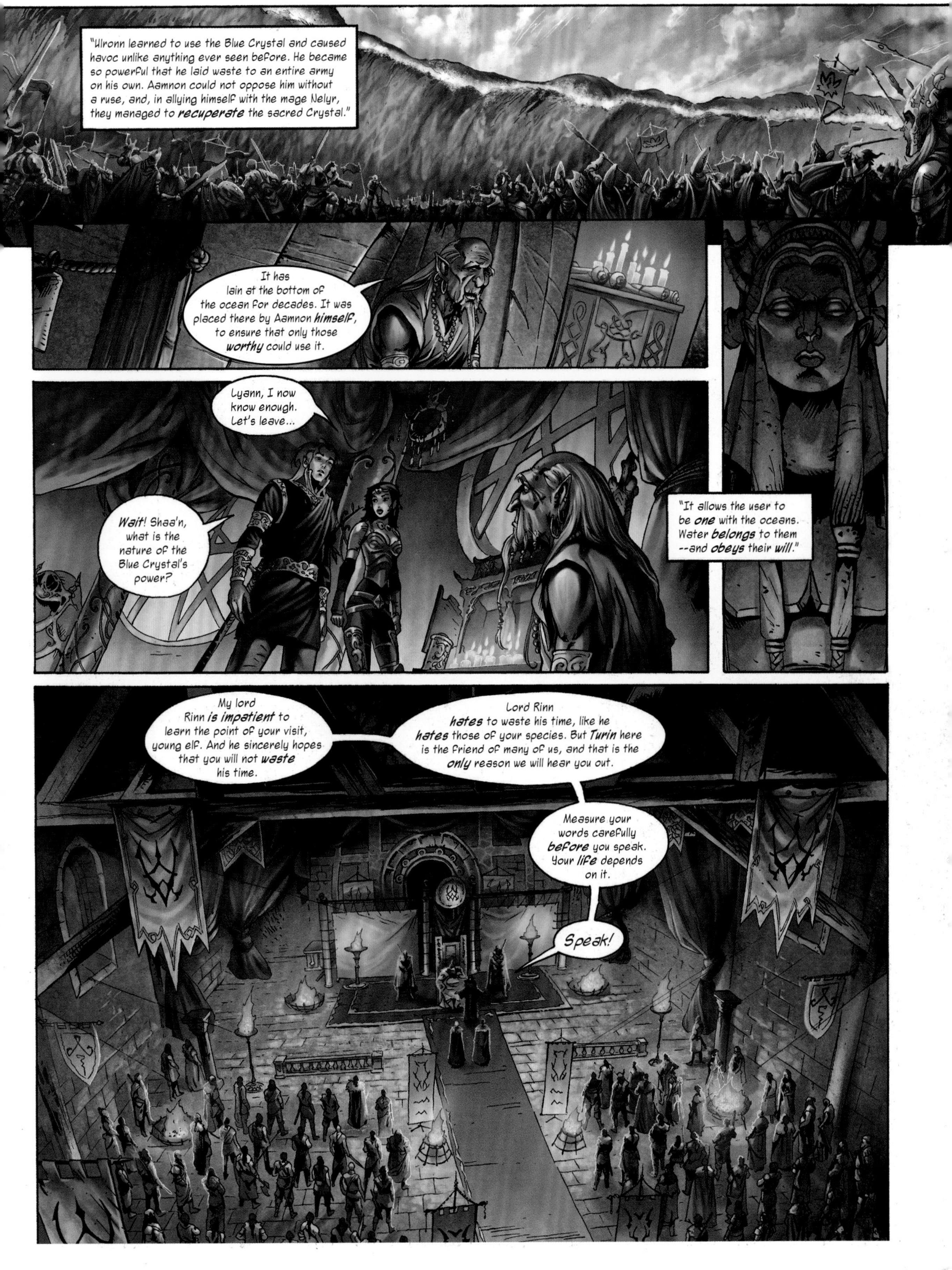
"Ulronn learned to use the Blue Crystal and caused havoc unlike anything ever seen before. He became so powerful that he laid waste to an entire army on his own. Aamnon could not oppose him without a ruse, and, in allying himself with the mage Nelyr, they managed to recuperate the sacred Crystal."
It has lain at the bottom of the ocean for decades. It was placed there by Aamnon himself, to ensure that only those worthy could use it.
Lyann, I now know enough. Let's leave...
Wait! Shaa'n, what is the nature of the Blue Crystal's power?
"It allows the user to be one with the oceans. Water belongs to them --and obeys their will."
My lord Rinn is impatient to learn the point of your visit, young elf. And he sincerely hopes that you will not waste his time.
Lord Rinn hates to waste his time, like he hates those of your species. But Turin here is the friend of many of us, and that is the only reason we will hear you out.
Measure your words carefully before you speak. Your life depends on it.
Speak!

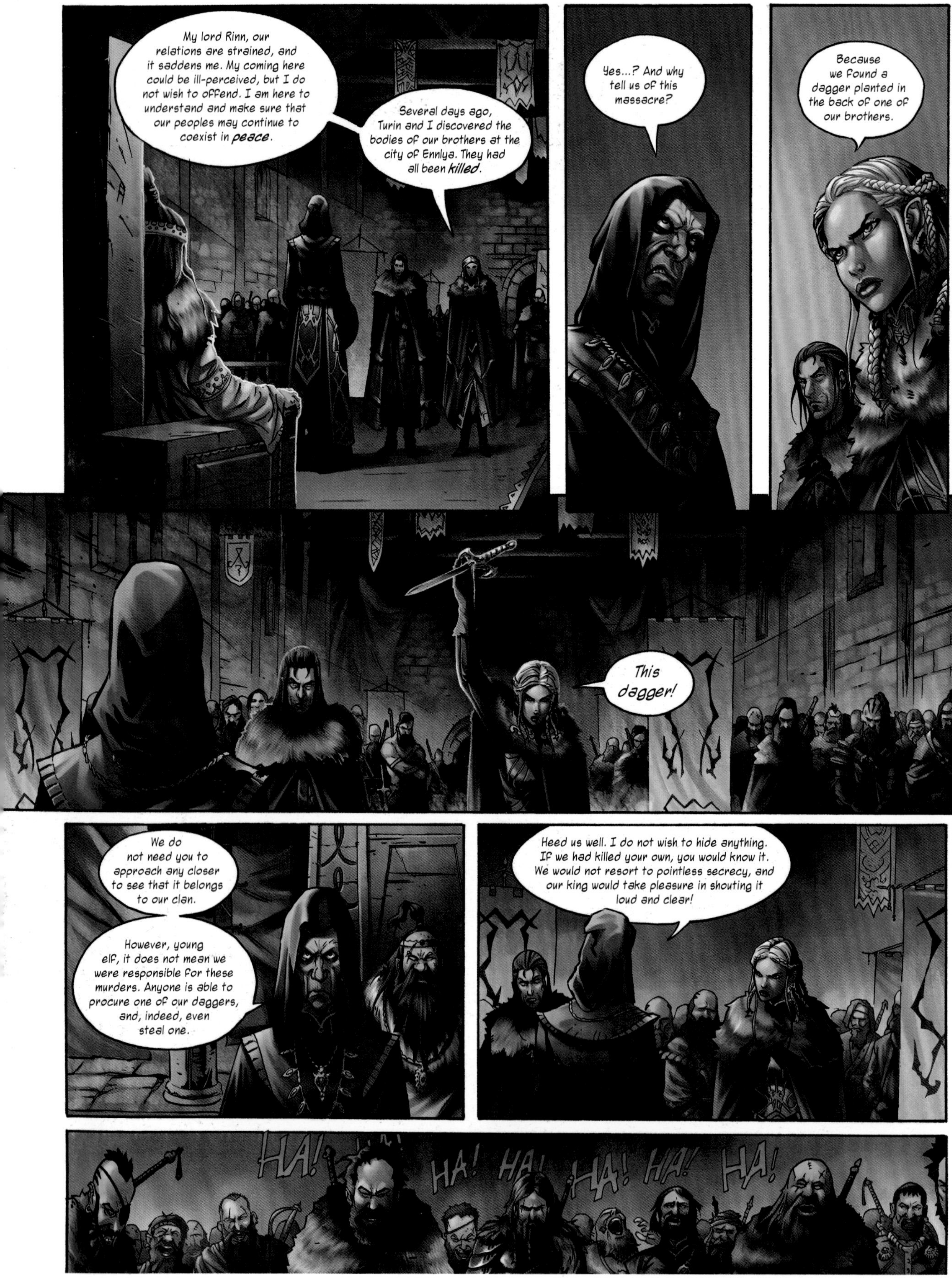
My lord Rinn, our relations are strained, and it saddens me. My coming here could be ill-perceived, but I do not wish to offend. I am here to understand and make sure that our peoples may continue to coexist in *peace*.
Several days ago, Turin and I discovered the bodies of our brothers at the city of Ennlya. They had all been *killed*.
Yes...? And why tell us of this massacre?
Because we found a dagger planted in the back of one of our brothers.
This dagger!
We do not need you to approach any closer to see that it belongs to our clan.
However, young elf, it does not mean we were responsible for these murders. Anyone is able to procure one of our daggers, and, indeed, even steal one.
Heed us well. I do not wish to hide anything. If we had killed your own, you would know it. We would not resort to pointless secrecy, and our king would take pleasure in shouting it loud and clear!
HA! HA! HA! HA! HA! HA!

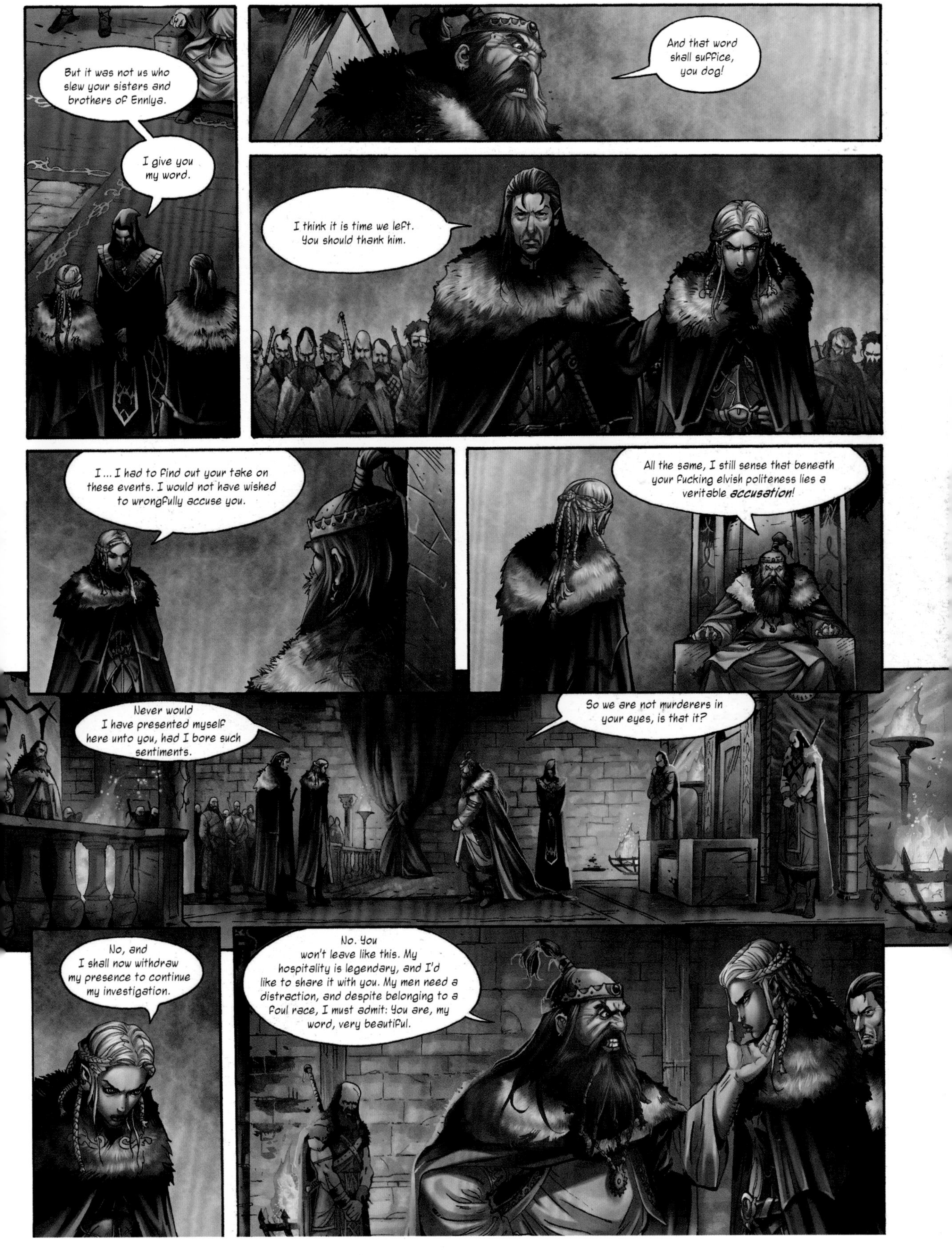
But it was not us who slew your sisters and brothers of Ennlya.
I give you my word.
And that word shall suffice, you dog!
I think it is time we left. You should thank him.
I ... I had to find out your take on these events. I would not have wished to wrongfully accuse you.
All the same, I still sense that beneath your fucking elvish politeness lies a veritable accusation!
Never would I have presented myself here unto you, had I bore such sentiments.
So we are not murderers in your eyes, is that it?
No, and I shall now withdraw my presence to continue my investigation.
No. You won't leave like this. My hospitality is legendary, and I'd like to share it with you. My men need a distraction, and despite belonging to a foul race, I must admit: You are, my word, very beautiful.

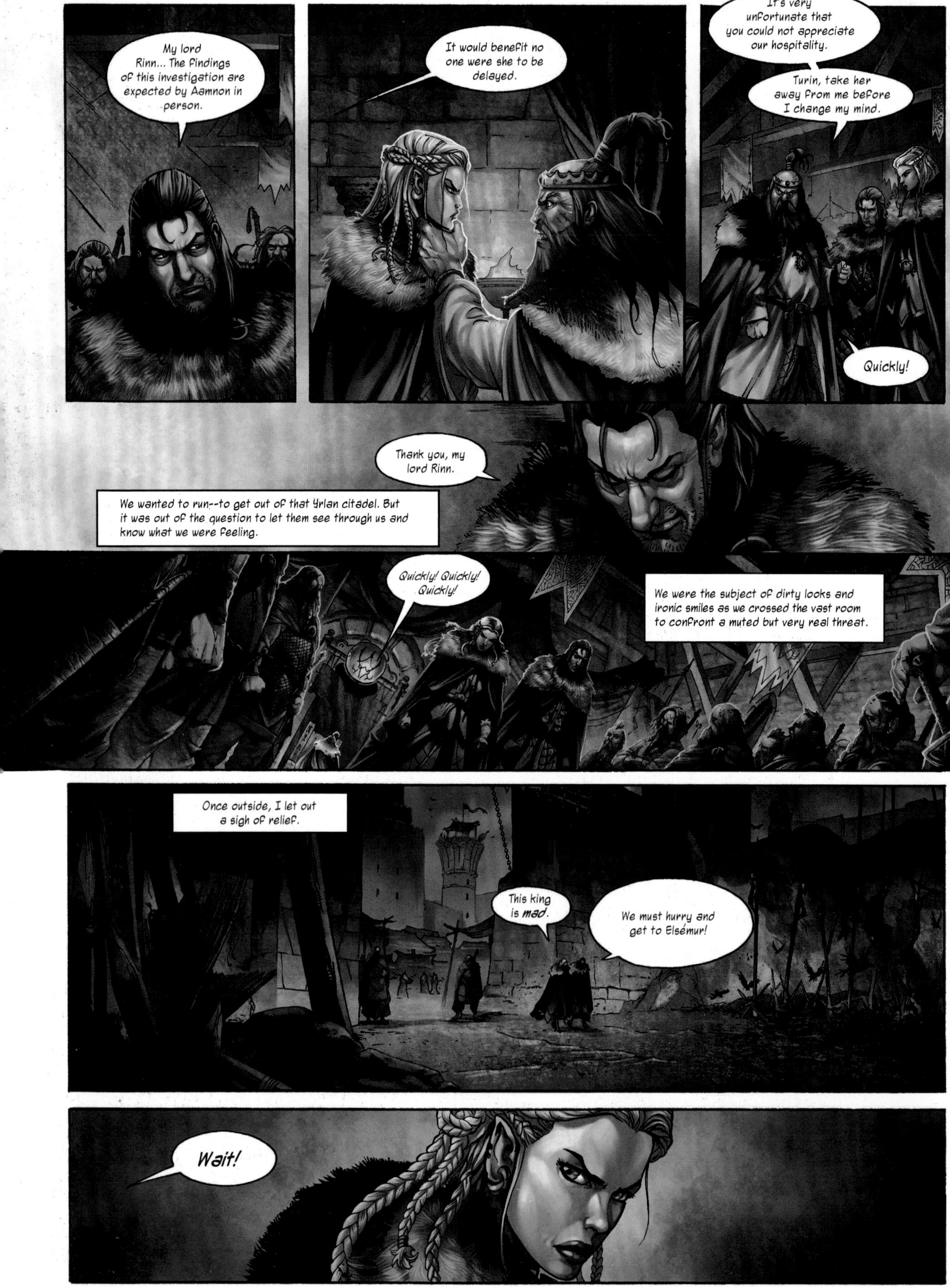
My lord Rinn... The findings of this investigation are expected by Aamnon in person.
It would benefit no one were she to be delayed.
It's very unfortunate that you could not appreciate our hospitality.
Turin, take her away from me before I change my mind.
Quickly!
Thank you, my lord Rinn.
We wanted to run--to get out of that Yrlan citadel. But it was out of the question to let them see through us and know what we were feeling.
Quickly! Quickly! Quickly!
We were the subject of dirty looks and ironic smiles as we crossed the vast room to confront a muted but very real threat.
Once outside, I let out a sigh of relief.
This king is *mad*.
We must hurry and get to Elsémur!
Wait!

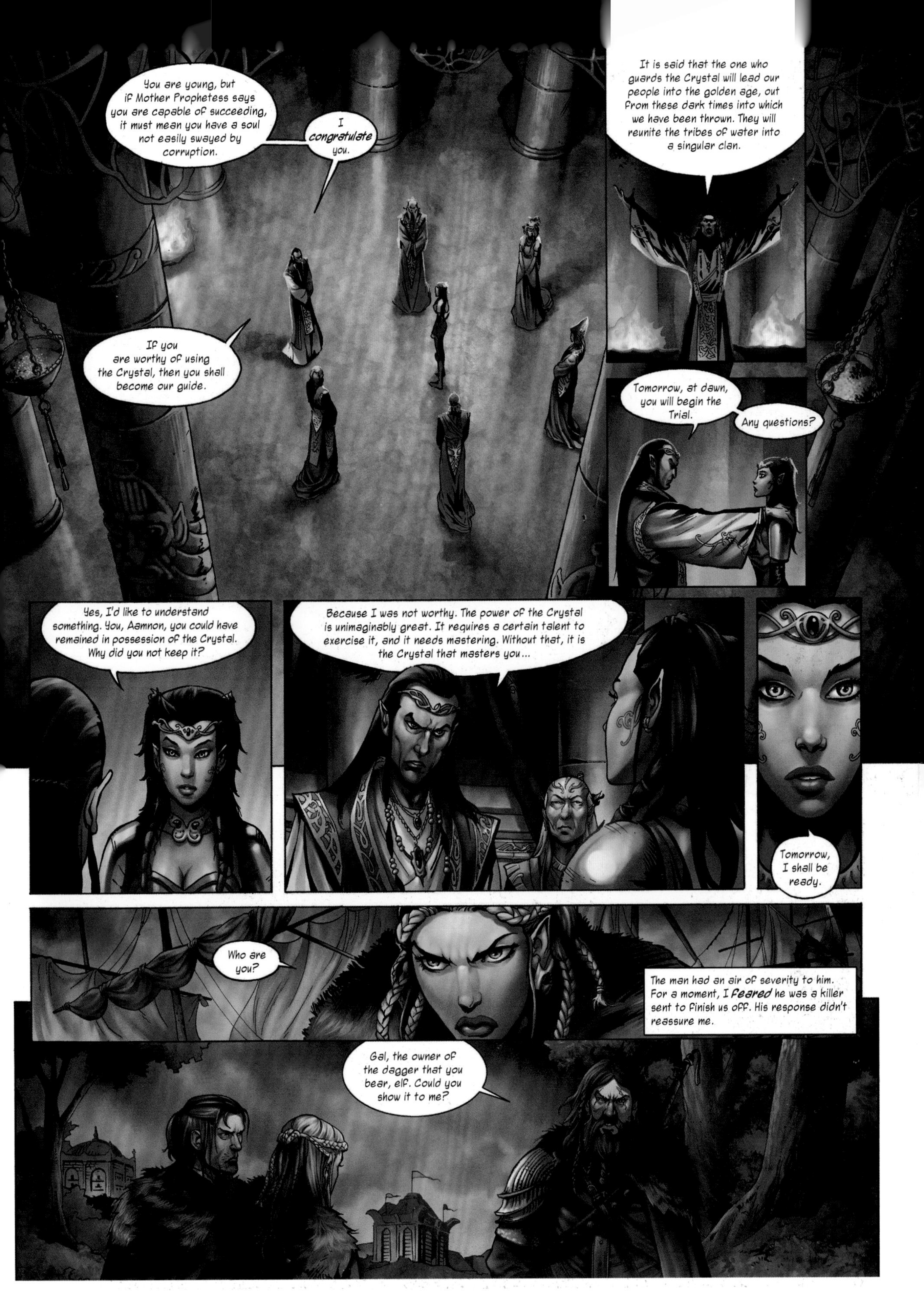
You are young, but if Mother Prophetess says you are capable of succeeding, it must mean you have a soul not easily swayed by corruption.
I congratulate you.
If you are worthy of using the Crystal, then you shall become our guide.
It is said that the one who guards the Crystal will lead our people into the golden age, out from these dark times into which we have been thrown. They will reunite the tribes of water into a singular clan.
Tomorrow, at dawn, you will begin the Trial.
Any questions?
Yes, I'd like to understand something. You, Aamnon, you could have remained in possession of the Crystal. Why did you not keep it?
Because I was not worthy. The power of the Crystal is unimaginably great. It requires a certain talent to exercise it, and it needs mastering. Without that, it is the Crystal that masters you...
Tomorrow, I shall be ready.
Who are you?
The man had an air of severity to him. For a moment, I feared he was a killer sent to finish us off. His response didn't reassure me.
Gal, the owner of the dagger that you bear, elf. Could you show it to me?

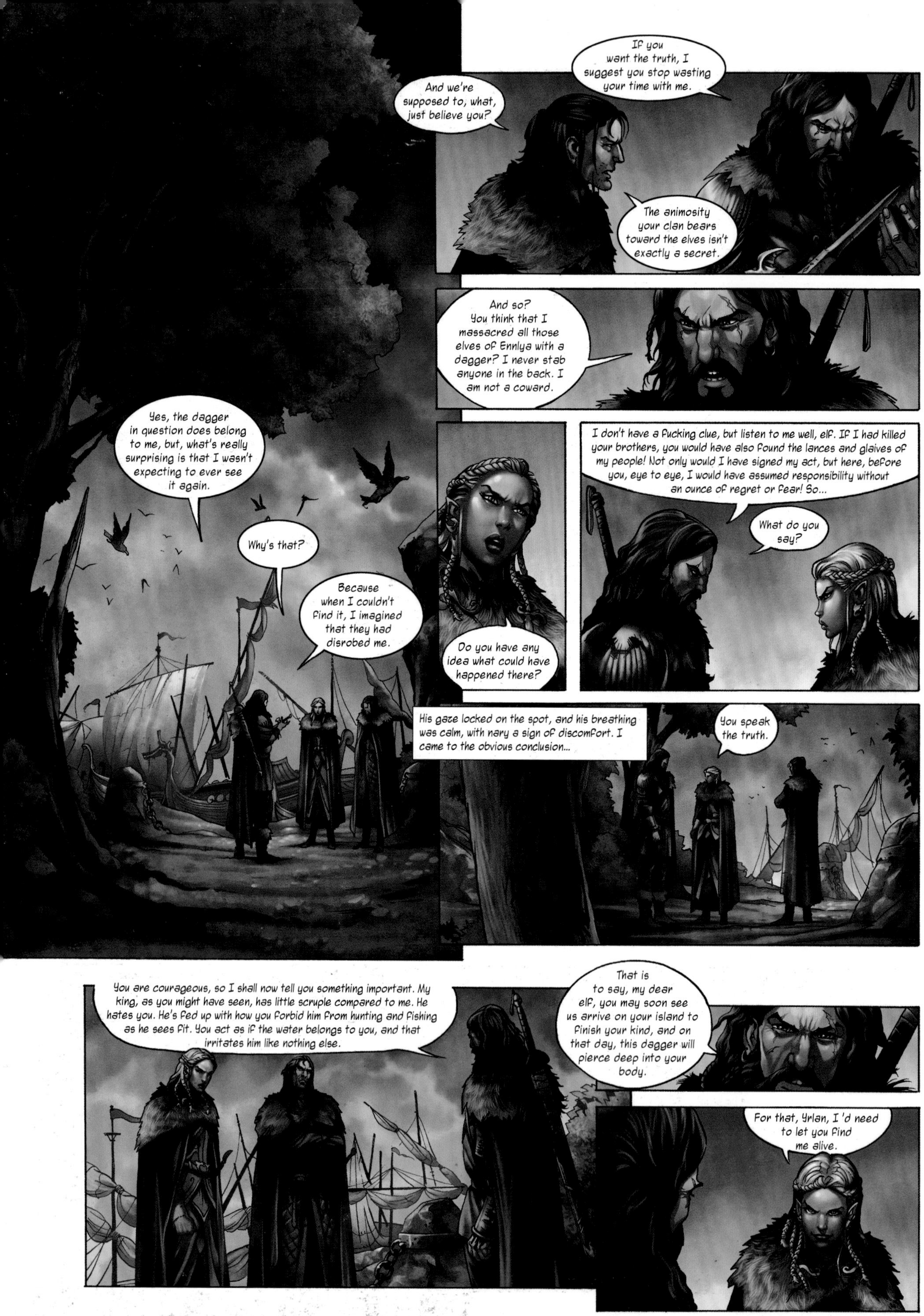
And we're supposed to, what, just believe you?
If you want the truth, I suggest you stop wasting your time with me.
The animosity your clan bears toward the elves isn't exactly a secret.
And so? You think that I massacred all those elves of Ennlya with a dagger? I never stab anyone in the back. I am not a coward.
Yes, the dagger in question does belong to me, but, what's really surprising is that I wasn't expecting to ever see it again.
Why's that?
Because when I couldn't find it, I imagined that they had disrobed me.
Do you have any idea what could have happened there?
I don't have a fucking clue, but listen to me well, elf. If I had killed your brothers, you would have also found the lances and glaives of my people! Not only would I have signed my act, but here, before you, eye to eye, I would have assumed responsibility without an ounce of regret or fear! So...
What do you say?
His gaze locked on the spot, and his breathing was calm, with nary a sign of discomfort. I came to the obvious conclusion...
You speak the truth.
You are courageous, so I shall now tell you something important. My king, as you might have seen, has little scruple compared to me. He hates you. He's fed up with how you forbid him from hunting and fishing as he sees fit. You act as if the water belongs to you, and that irritates him like nothing else.
That is to say, my dear elf, you may soon see us arrive on your island to finish your kind, and on that day, this dagger will pierce deep into your body.
For that, Yrlan, I'd need to let you find me alive.

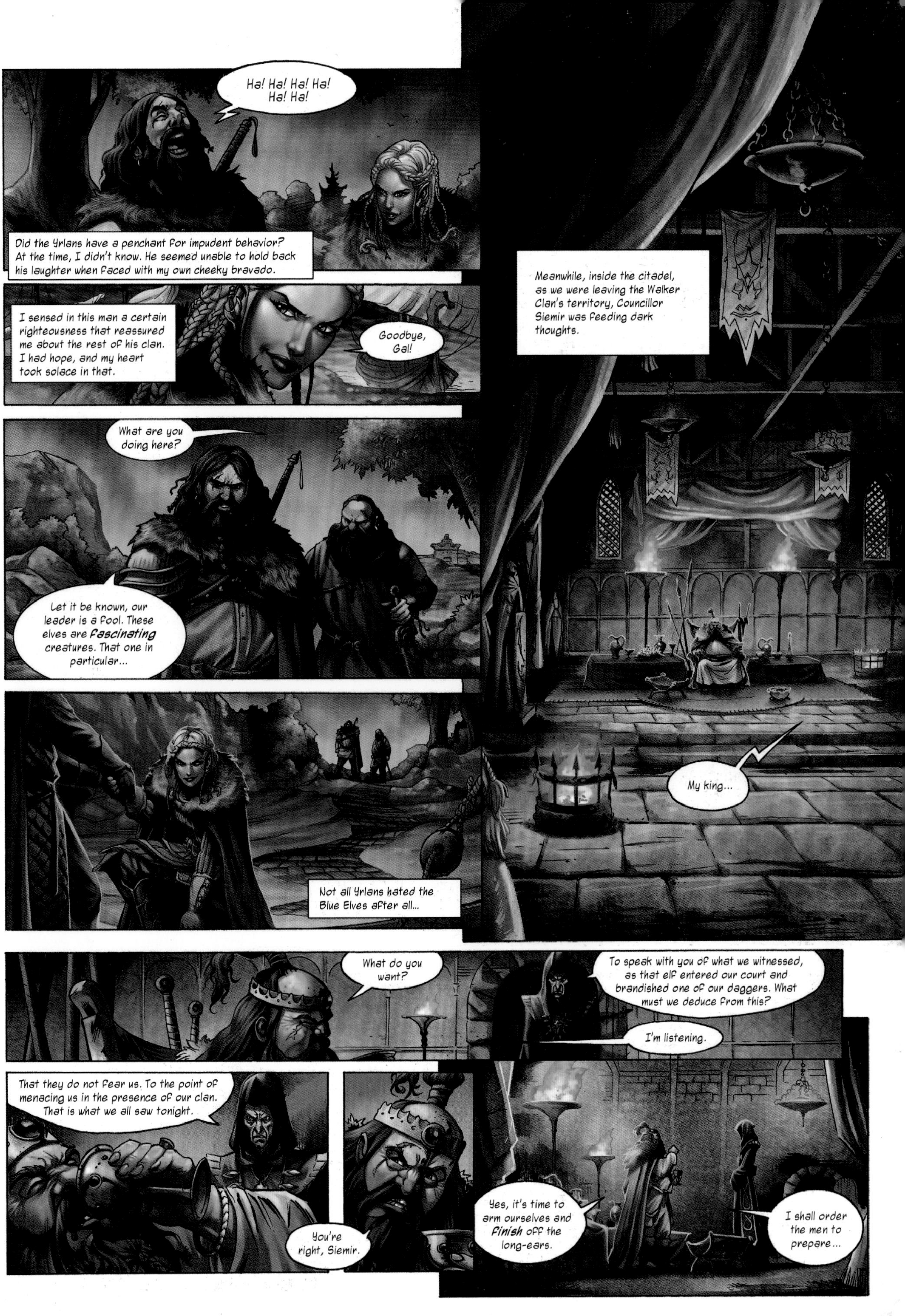

Ha! Ha! Ha! Ha! Ha! Ha!
Did the Yrlans have a penchant for impudent behavior? At the time, I didn't know. He seemed unable to hold back his laughter when faced with my own cheeky bravado.
I sensed in this man a certain righteousness that reassured me about the rest of his clan. I had hope, and my heart took solace in that.
Goodbye, Gal!
What are you doing here?
Let it be known, our leader is a fool. These elves are *fascinating* creatures. That one in particular...
Not all Yrlans hated the Blue Elves after all...
Meanwhile, inside the citadel, as we were leaving the Walker Clan's territory, Councillor Siemir was feeding dark thoughts.
My king...
What do you want?
To speak with you of what we witnessed, as that elf entered our court and brandished one of our daggers. What must we deduce from this?
I'm listening.
That they do not fear us. To the point of menacing us in the presence of our clan. That is what we all saw tonight.
You're right, Siemir.
Yes, it's time to arm ourselves and *finish* off the long-ears.
I shall order the men to prepare...

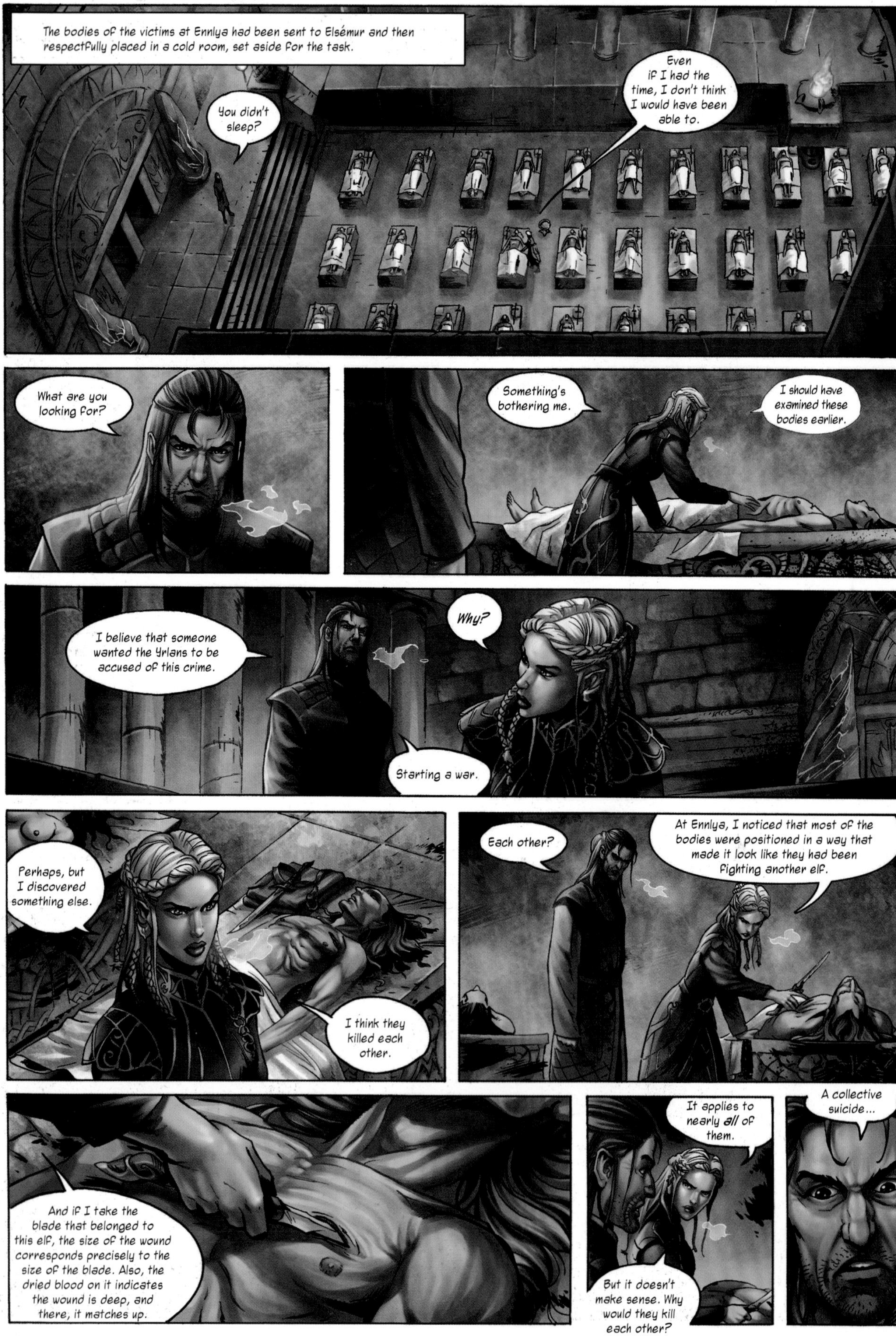

The bodies of the victims at Ennlya had been sent to Elsémur and then respectfully placed in a cold room, set aside for the task.
You didn't sleep?
Even if I had the time, I don't think I would have been able to.
What are you looking for?
Something's bothering me.
I should have examined these bodies earlier.
I believe that someone wanted the Yrlans to be accused of this crime.
Why?
Starting a war.
Perhaps, but I discovered something else.
I think they killed each other.
Each other?
At Ennlya, I noticed that most of the bodies were positioned in a way that made it look like they had been fighting another elf.
And if I take the blade that belonged to this elf, the size of the wound corresponds precisely to the size of the blade. Also, the dried blood on it indicates the wound is deep, and there, it matches up.
It applies to nearly *all* of them.
But it doesn't make sense. Why would they kill each other?
A collective suicide...

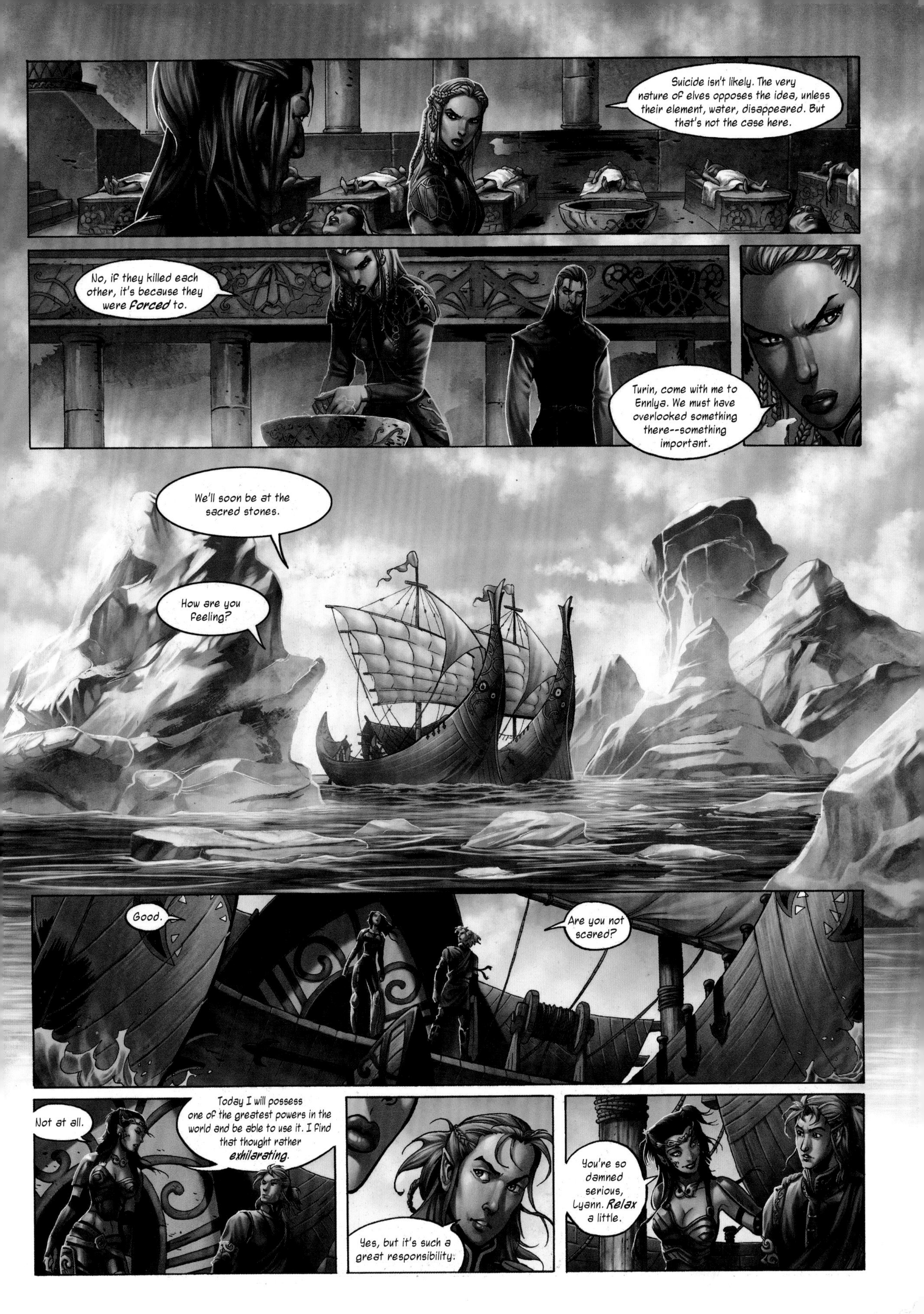
Suicide isn't likely. The very nature of elves opposes the idea, unless their element, water, disappeared. But that's not the case here.
No, if they killed each other, it's because they were *forced* to.
Turin, come with me to Ennlya. We must have overlooked something there--something important.
We'll soon be at the sacred stones.
How are you feeling?
Good.
Are you not scared?
Not at all.
Today I will possess one of the greatest powers in the world and be able to use it. I find that thought rather *exhilarating*.
Yes, but it's such a great responsibility.
You're so damned serious, Lyann. *Relax* a little.

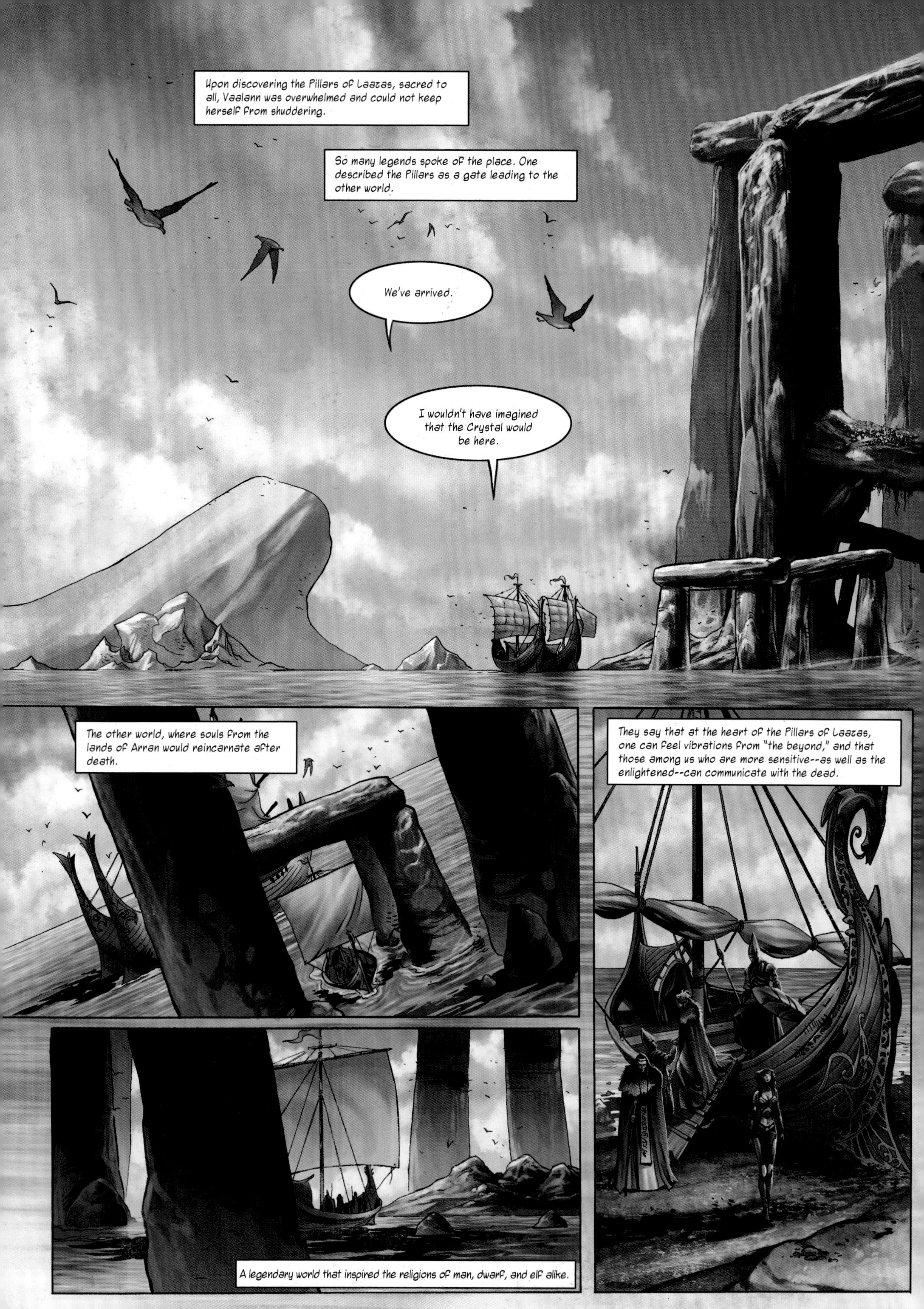
Upon discovering the Pillars of Laazas, sacred to all, Vaalann was overwhelmed and could not keep herself from shuddering.
So many legends spoke of the place. One described the Pillars as a gate leading to the other world.
We've arrived.
I wouldn't have imagined that the Crystal would be here.
The other world, where souls from the lands of Arran would reincarnate after death.
They say that at the heart of the Pillars of Laazas, one can feel vibrations from "the beyond," and that those among us who are more sensitive--as well as the enlightened--can communicate with the dead.
A legendary world that inspired the religions of man, dwarf, and elf alike.

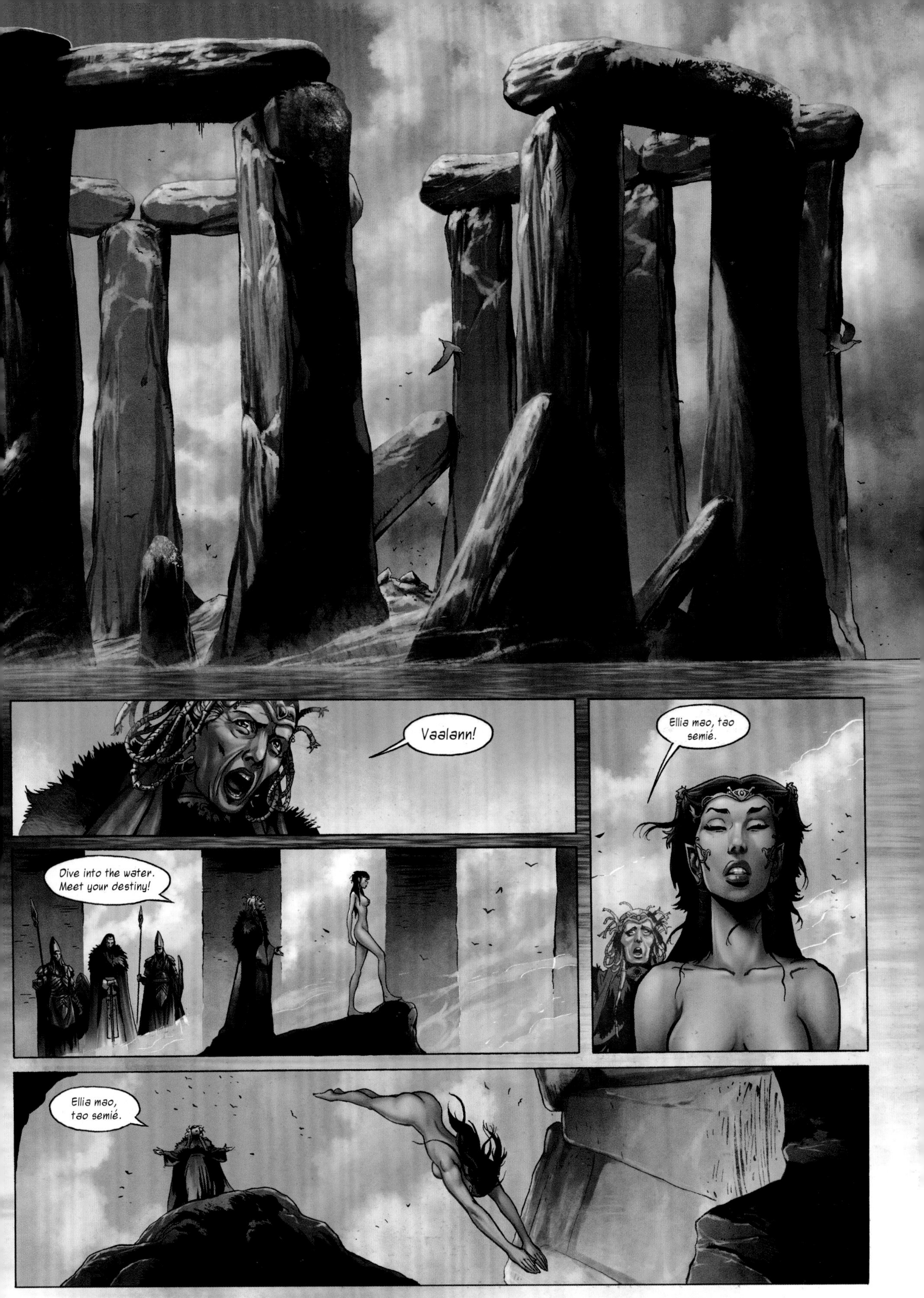
Vaalann!
Ellia mao, tao semié.
Dive into the water. Meet your destiny!
Ellia mao, tao semié.

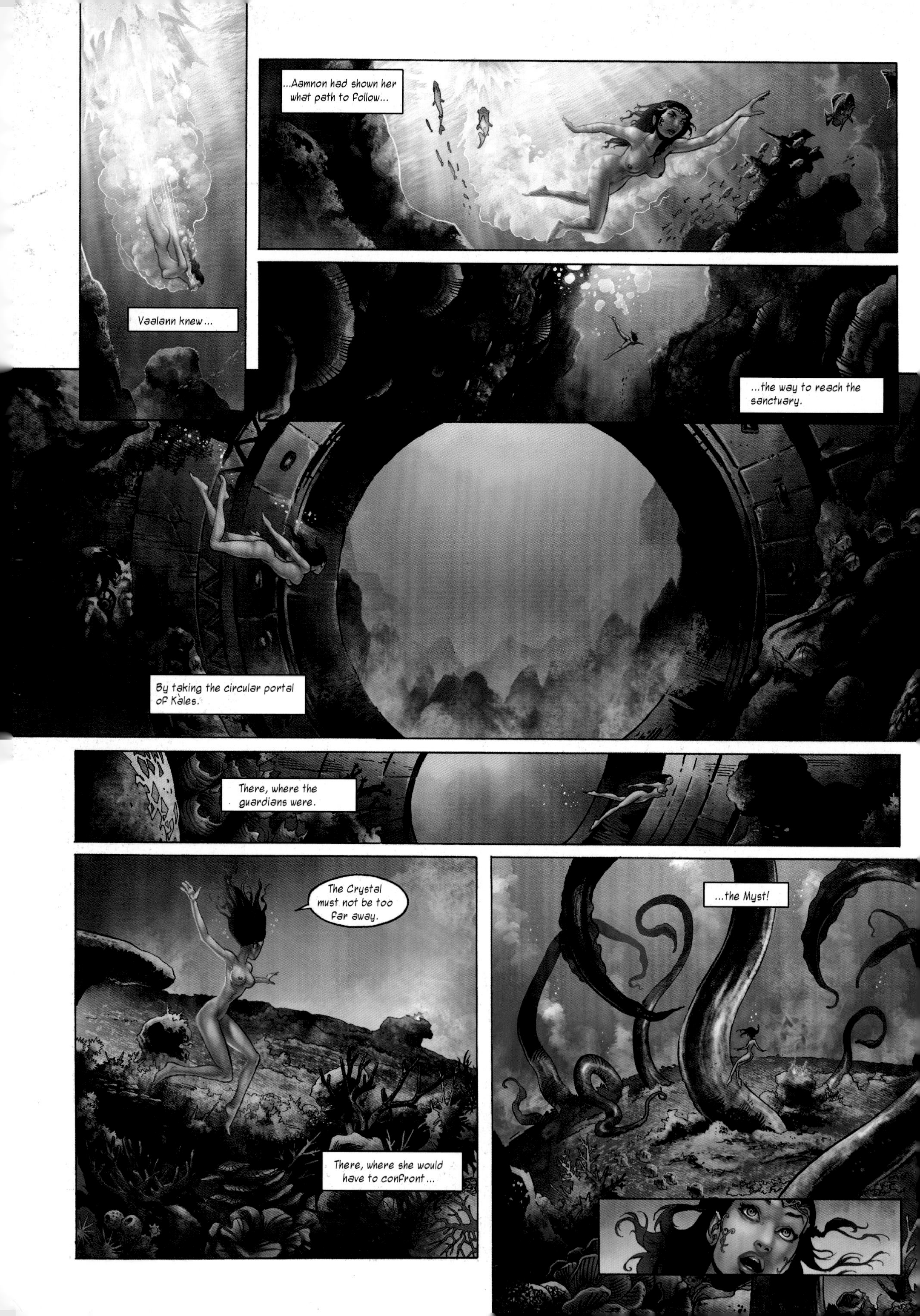
Vaalann knew...
...Aamnon had shown her what path to follow...
...the way to reach the sanctuary.
By taking the circular portal of Kàles.
There, where the guardians were.
The Crystal must not be too far away.
There, where she would have to confront...
...the Myst!

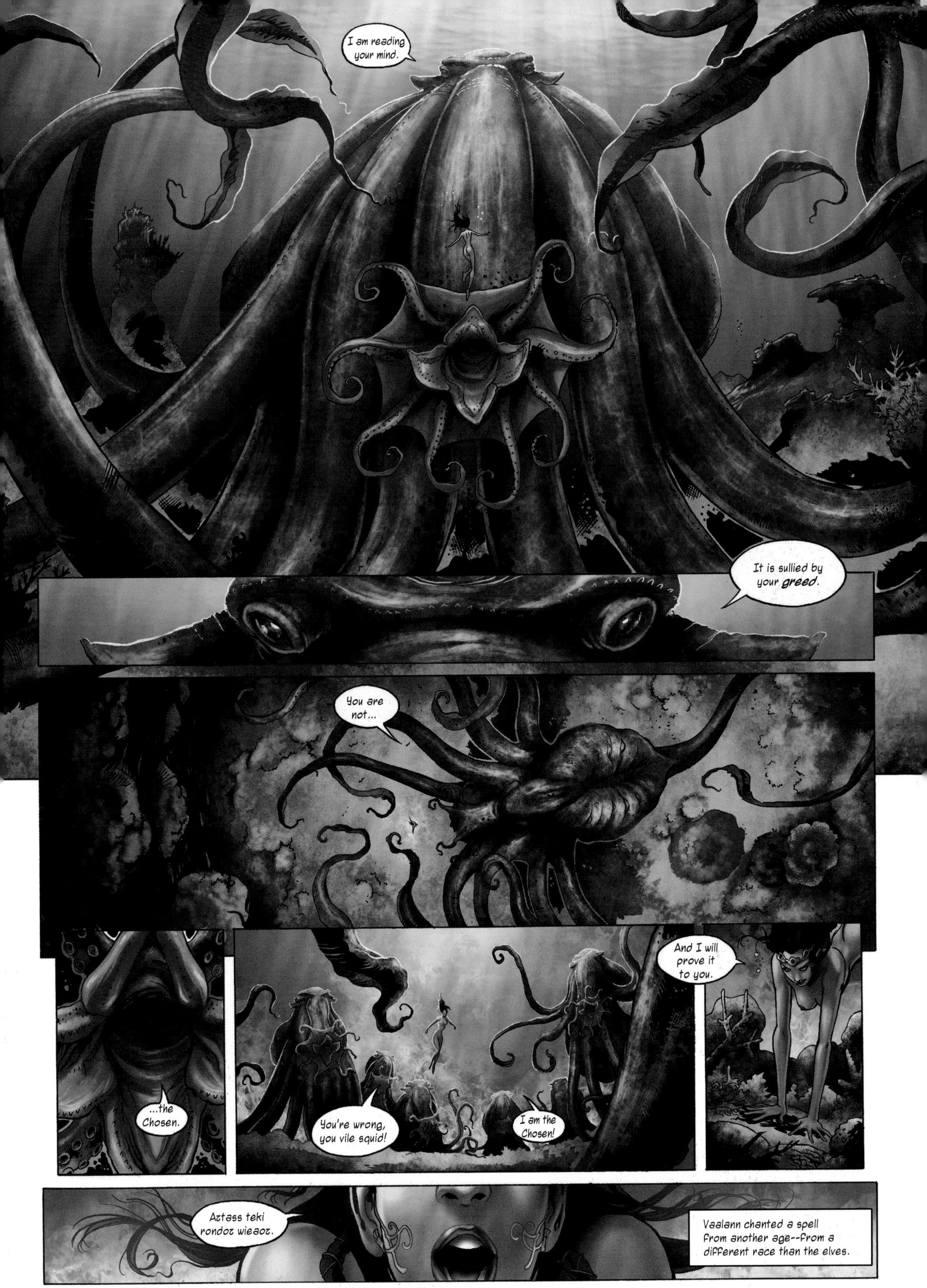

I am reading your mind.
It is sullied by your ***greed***.
You are not...
...the Chosen.
You're wrong, you vile squid!
I am the Chosen!
And I will prove it to you.
Aztass teki rondoz wieaoz.
Vaalann chanted a spell from another age--from a different race than the elves.

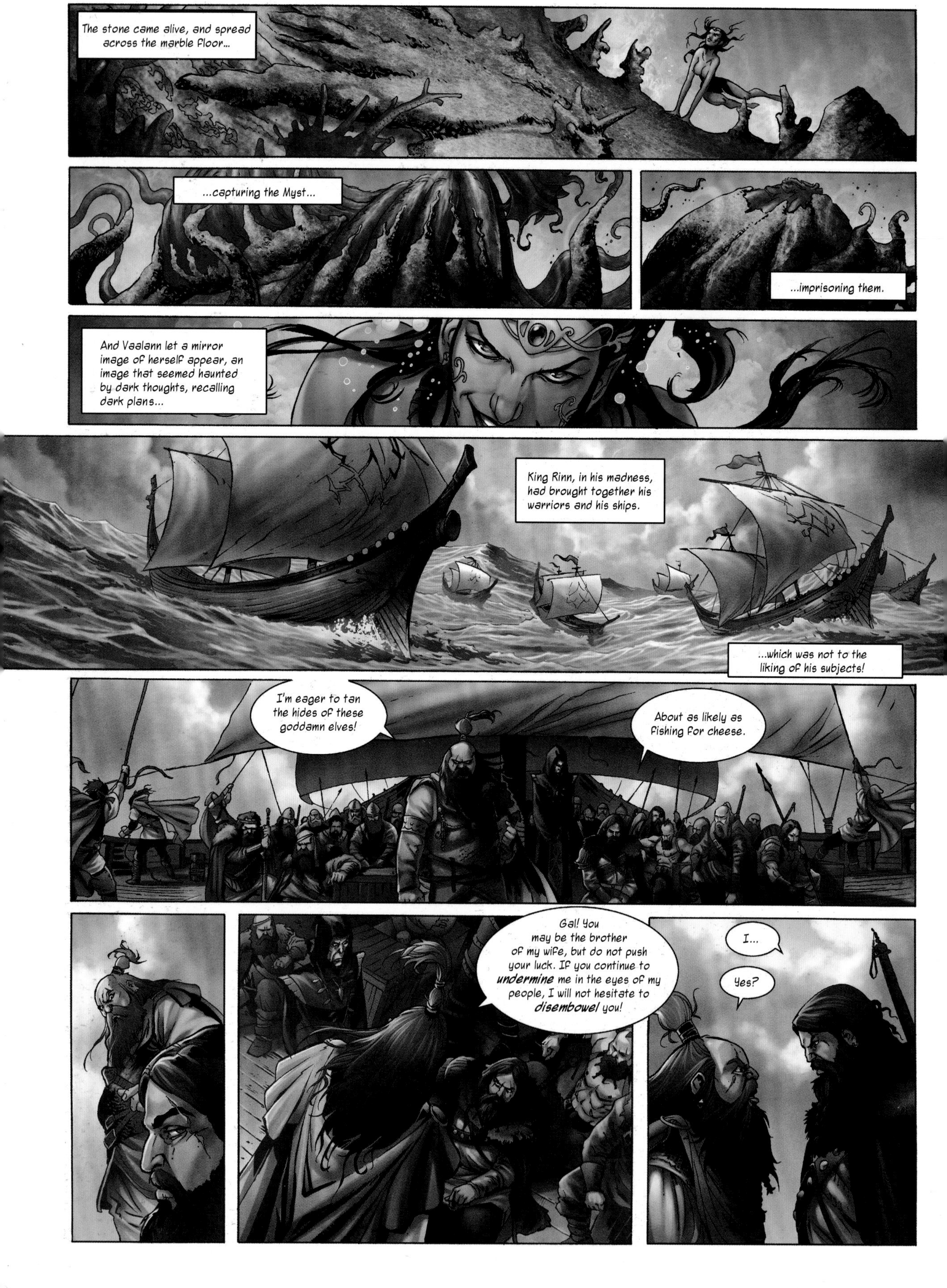

The stone came alive, and spread across the marble floor...
...capturing the Myst...
...imprisoning them.
And Vaalann let a mirror image of herself appear, an image that seemed haunted by dark thoughts, recalling dark plans...
King Rinn, in his madness, had brought together his warriors and his ships.
...which was not to the liking of his subjects!
I'm eager to tan the hides of these goddamn elves!
About as likely as fishing for cheese.
Gal! You may be the brother of my wife, but do not push your luck. If you continue to **undermine** me in the eyes of my people, I will not hesitate to **disembowel** you!
I...
Yes?

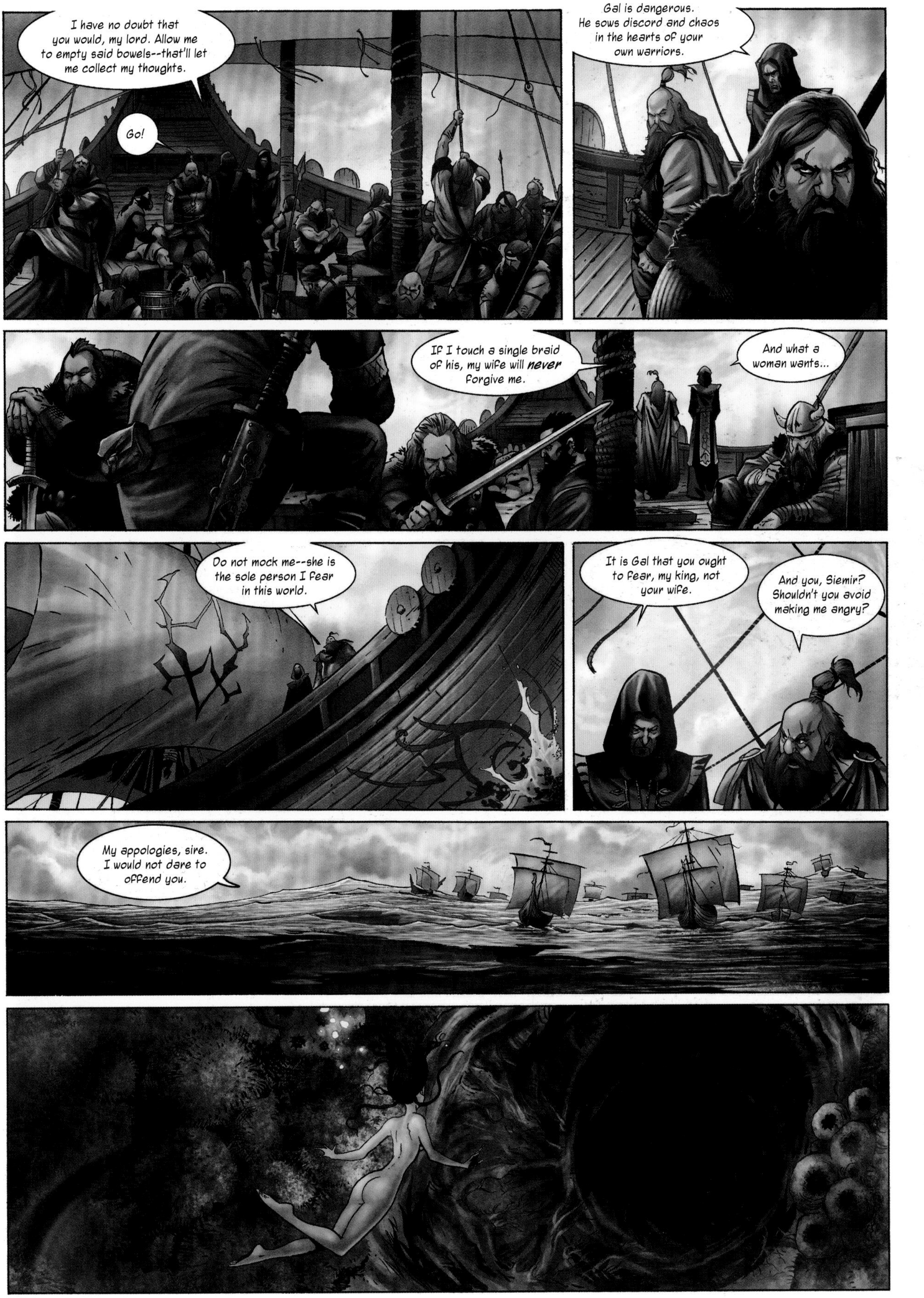

I have no doubt that you would, my lord. Allow me to empty said bowels--that'll let me collect my thoughts.
Go!
Gal is dangerous. He sows discord and chaos in the hearts of your own warriors.
If I touch a single braid of his, my wife will *never* forgive me.
And what a woman wants...
Do not mock me--she is the sole person I fear in this world.
It is Gal that you ought to fear, my king, not your wife.
And you, Siemir? Shouldn't you avoid making me angry?
My appologies, sire. I would not dare to offend you.

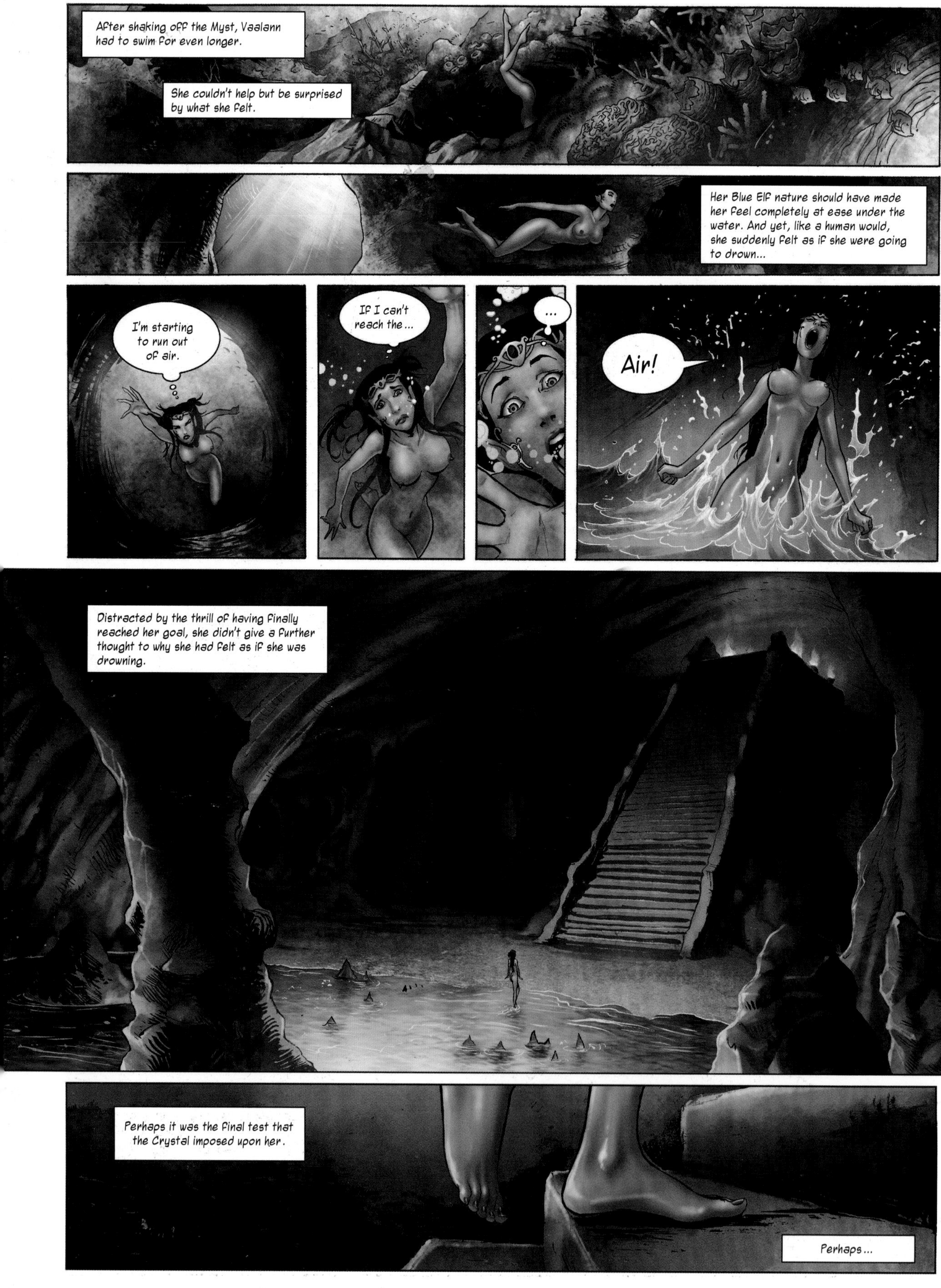
After shaking off the Myst, Vaalann had to swim for even longer.
She couldn't help but be surprised by what she felt.
Her Blue Elf nature should have made her feel completely at ease under the water. And yet, like a human would, she suddenly felt as if she were going to drown...
I'm starting to run out of air.
If I can't reach the...
...
Air!
Distracted by the thrill of having finally reached her goal, she didn't give a further thought to why she had felt as if she was drowning.
Perhaps it was the final test that the Crystal imposed upon her.
Perhaps...

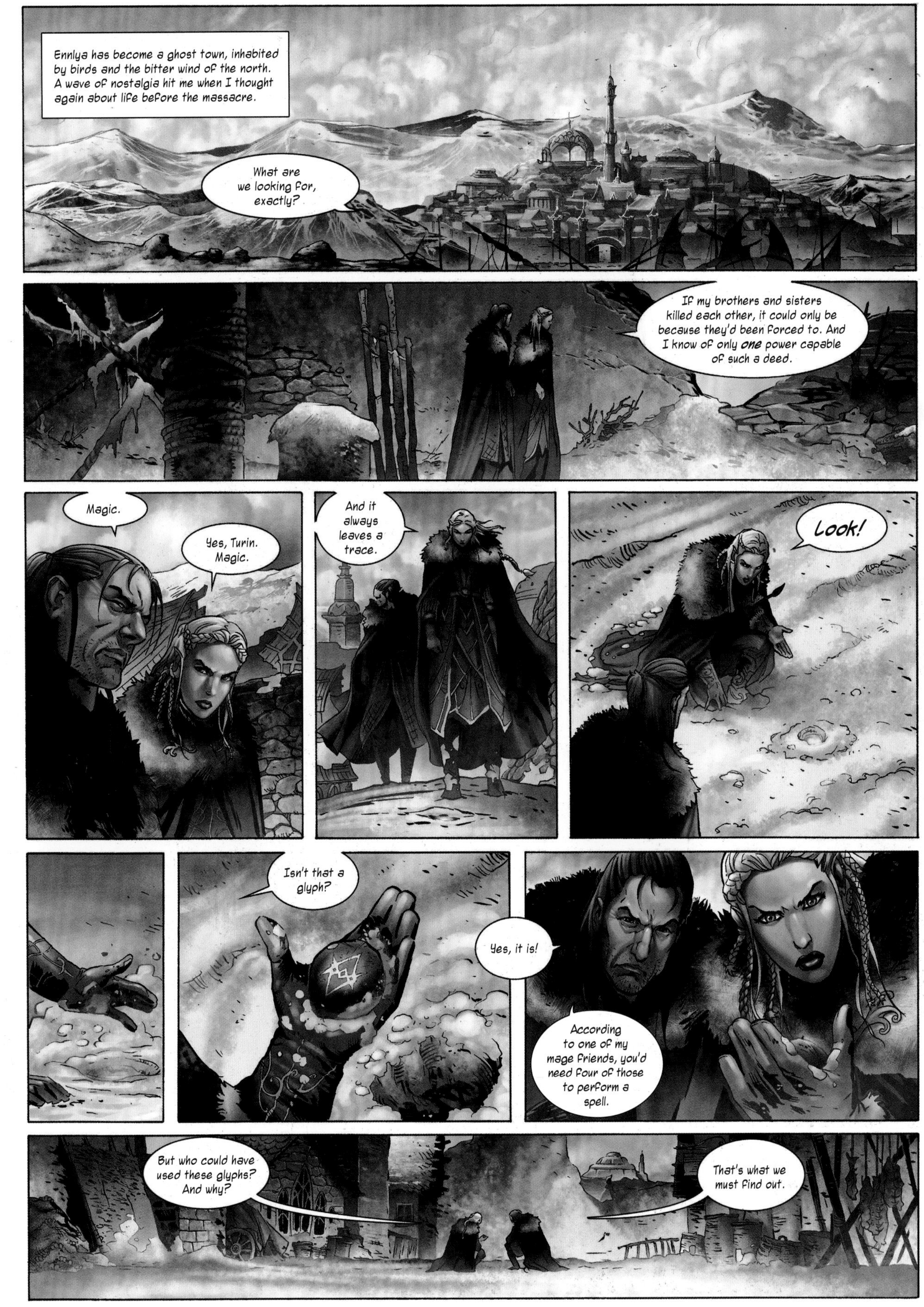

Ennlya has become a ghost town, inhabited by birds and the bitter wind of the north. A wave of nostalgia hit me when I thought again about life before the massacre.
What are we looking for, exactly?
If my brothers and sisters killed each other, it could only be because they'd been forced to. And I know of only *one* power capable of such a deed.
Magic.
Yes, Turin. Magic.
And it always leaves a trace.
Look!
Isn't that a glyph?
Yes, it is!
According to one of my mage friends, you'd need four of those to perform a spell.
But who could have used these glyphs? And why?
That's what we must find out.

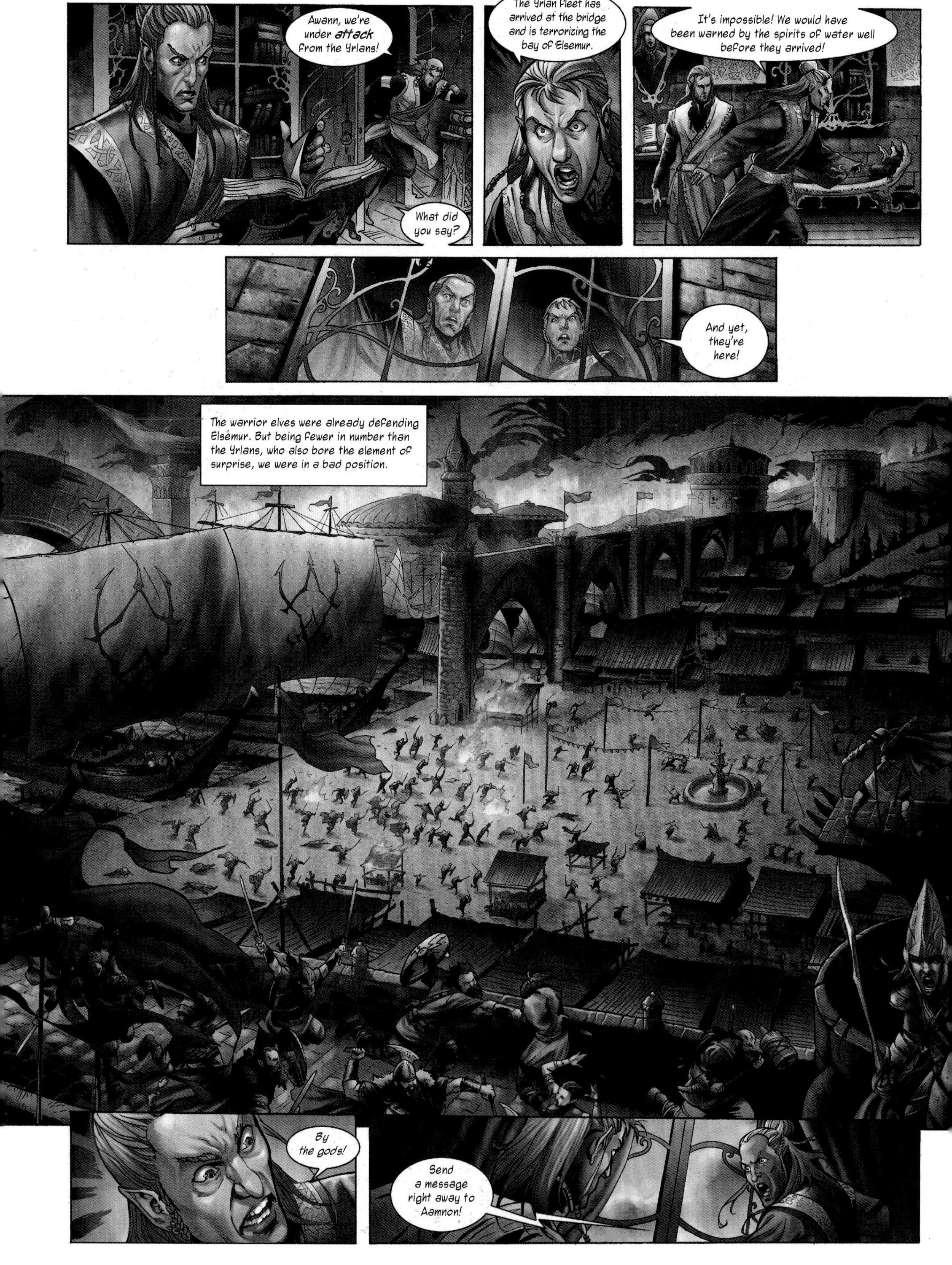
Awann, we're under attack from the Yrlans!
What did you say?
The Yrlan Fleet has arrived at the bridge and is terrorizing the bay of Elsemur.
It's impossible! We would have been warned by the spirits of water well before they arrived!
And yet, they're here!
The warrior elves were already defending Elsémur. But being fewer in number than the Yrlans, who also bore the element of surprise, we were in a bad position.
By the gods!
Send a message right away to Aamnon!

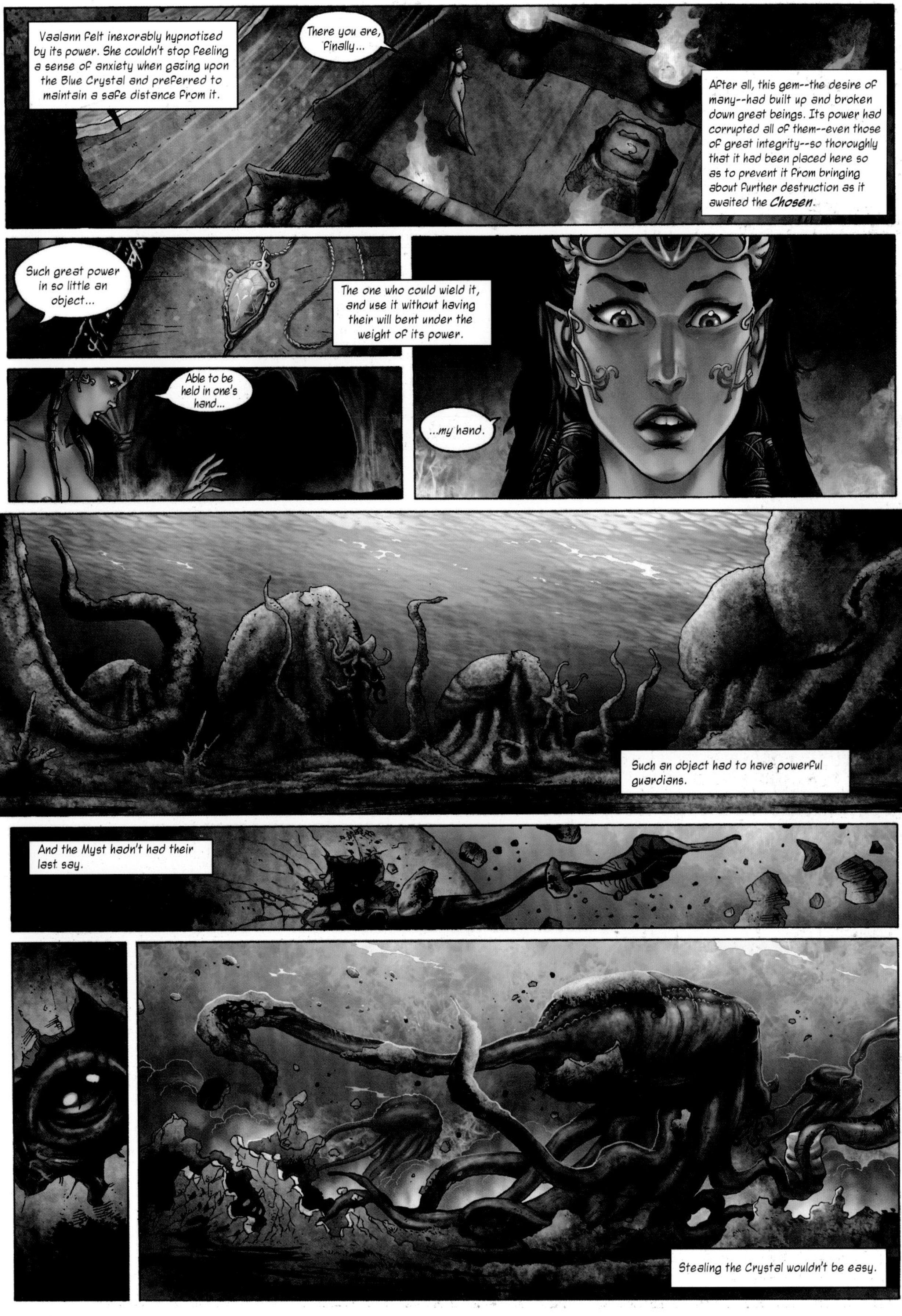
Vaalann felt inexorably hypnotized by its power. She couldn't stop feeling a sense of anxiety when gazing upon the Blue Crystal and preferred to maintain a safe distance from it.
There you are, finally...
After all, this gem--the desire of many--had built up and broken down great beings. Its power had corrupted all of them--even those of great integrity--so thoroughly that it had been placed here so as to prevent it from bringing about further destruction as it awaited the Chosen.
Such great power in so little an object...
The one who could wield it, and use it without having their will bent under the weight of its power.
Able to be held in one's hand...
...my hand.
Such an object had to have powerful guardians.
And the Myst hadn't had their last say.
Stealing the Crystal wouldn't be easy.

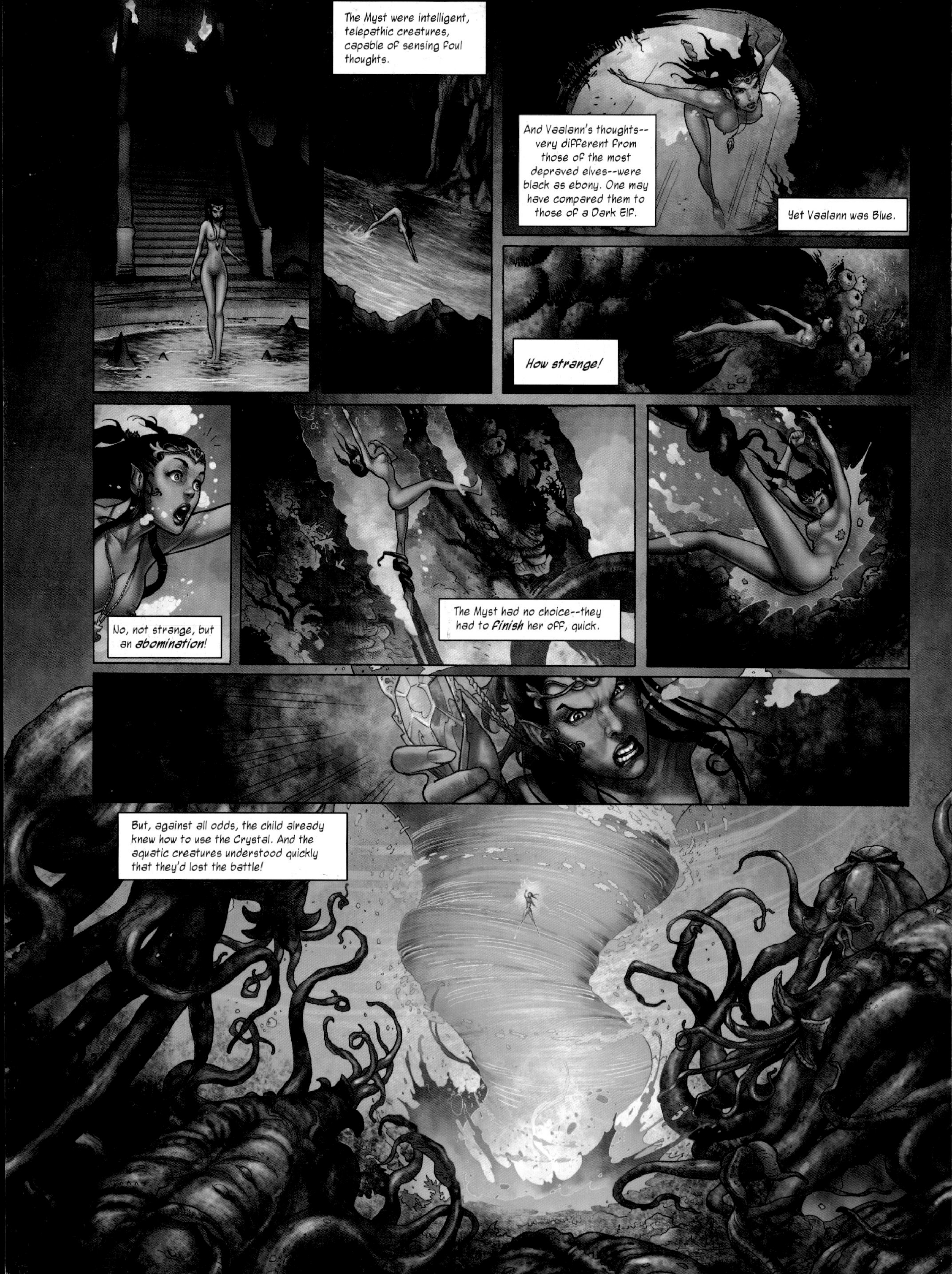
The Myst were intelligent, telepathic creatures, capable of sensing foul thoughts.
And Vaalann's thoughts--very different from those of the most depraved elves--were black as ebony. One may have compared them to those of a Dark Elf.
Yet Vaalann was Blue.
How strange!
No, not strange, but an abomination!
The Myst had no choice--they had to finish her off, quick.
But, against all odds, the child already knew how to use the Crystal. And the aquatic creatures understood quickly that they'd lost the battle!

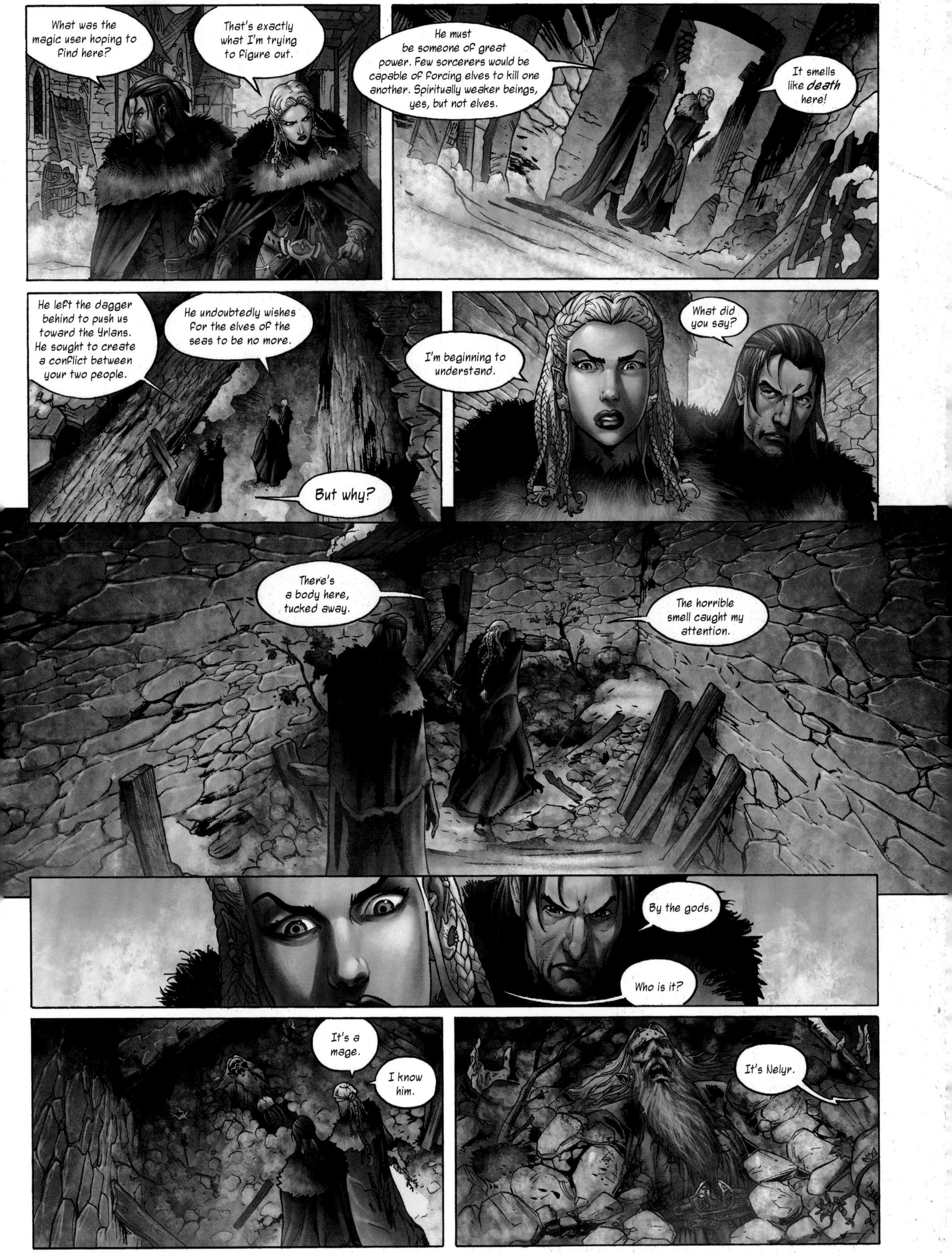
What was the magic user hoping to find here?
That's exactly what I'm trying to figure out.
He must be someone of great power. Few sorcerers would be capable of forcing elves to kill one another. Spiritually weaker beings, yes, but not elves.
It smells like *death* here!
He left the dagger behind to push us toward the Yrlans. He sought to create a conflict between your two people.
He undoubtedly wishes for the elves of the seas to be no more.
But why?
I'm beginning to understand.
What did you say?
There's a body here, tucked away.
The horrible smell caught my attention.
By the gods.
Who is it?
It's a mage.
I know him.
It's Nelyr.

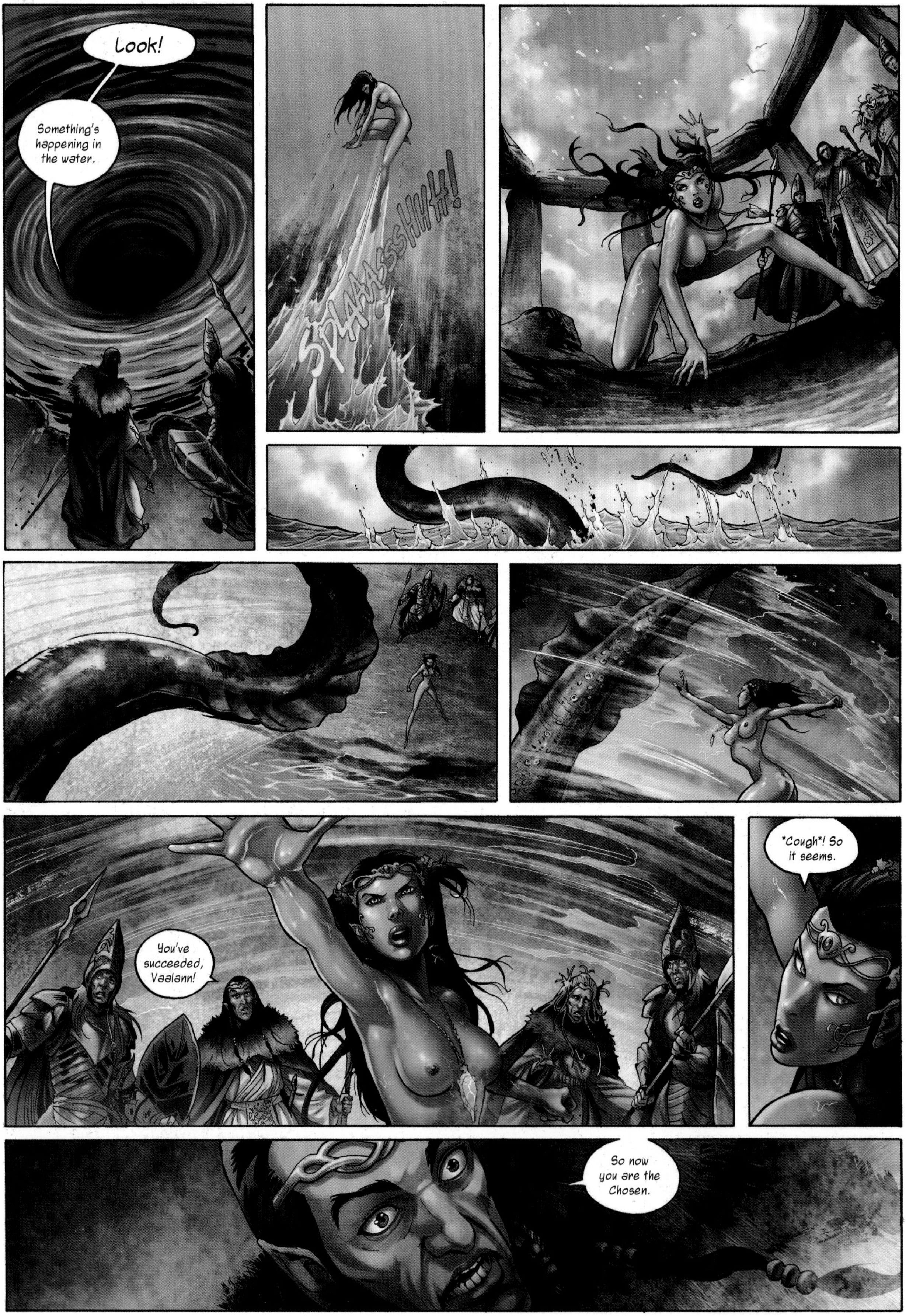

Look!
Something's happening in the water.
SPLAAASSSHHH!
You've succeeded, Vaalann!
Cough! So it seems.
So now you are the Chosen.

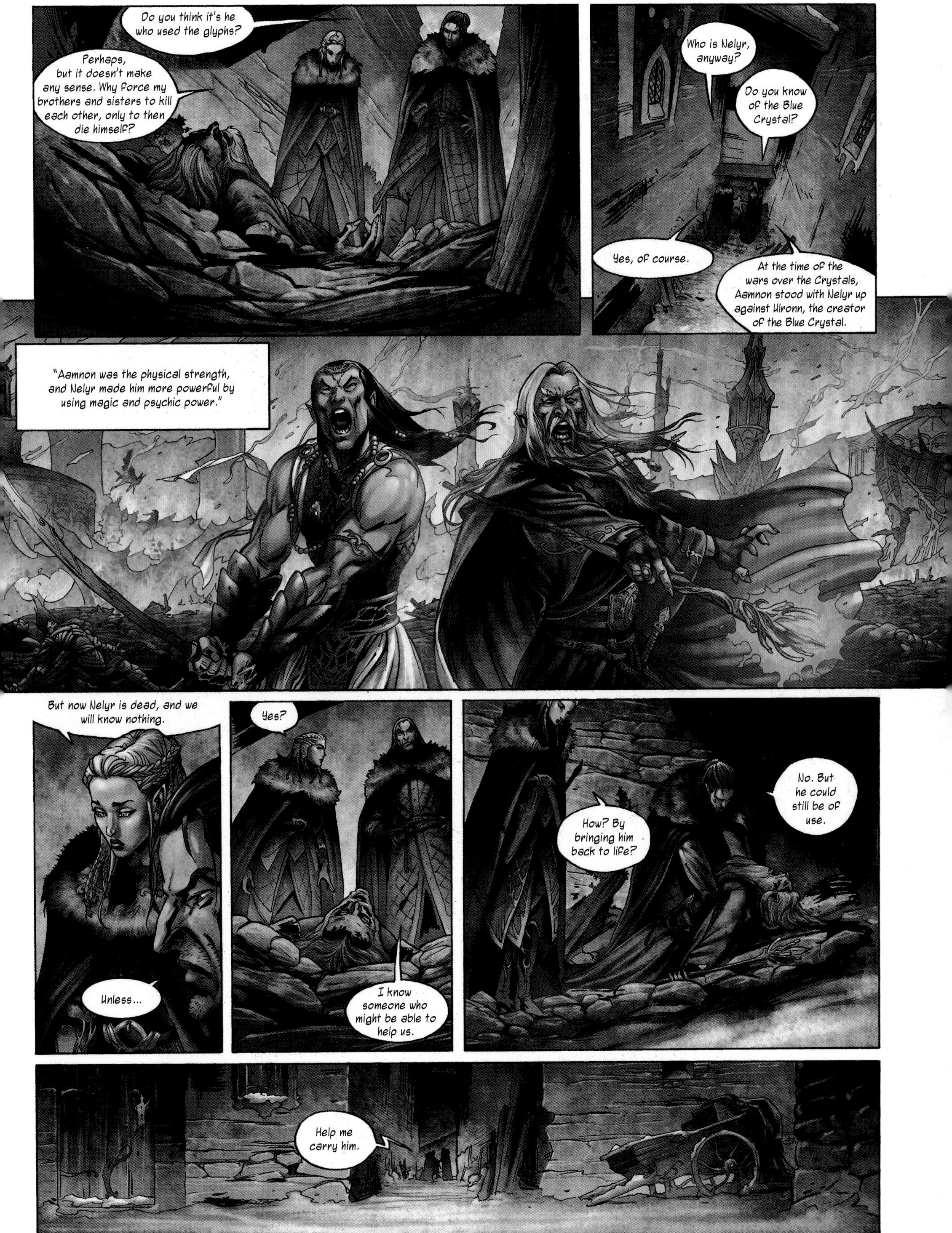
Do you think it's he who used the glyphs?
Perhaps, but it doesn't make any sense. Why force my brothers and sisters to kill each other, only to then die himself?
Who is Nelyr, anyway?
Do you know of the Blue Crystal?
Yes, of course.
At the time of the wars over the Crystals, Aamnon stood with Nelyr up against Ulronn, the creator of the Blue Crystal.
"Aamnon was the physical strength, and Nelyr made him more powerful by using magic and psychic power."
But now Nelyr is dead, and we will know nothing.
Unless...
Yes?
I know someone who might be able to help us.
How? By bringing him back to life?
No. But he could still be of use.
Help me carry him.

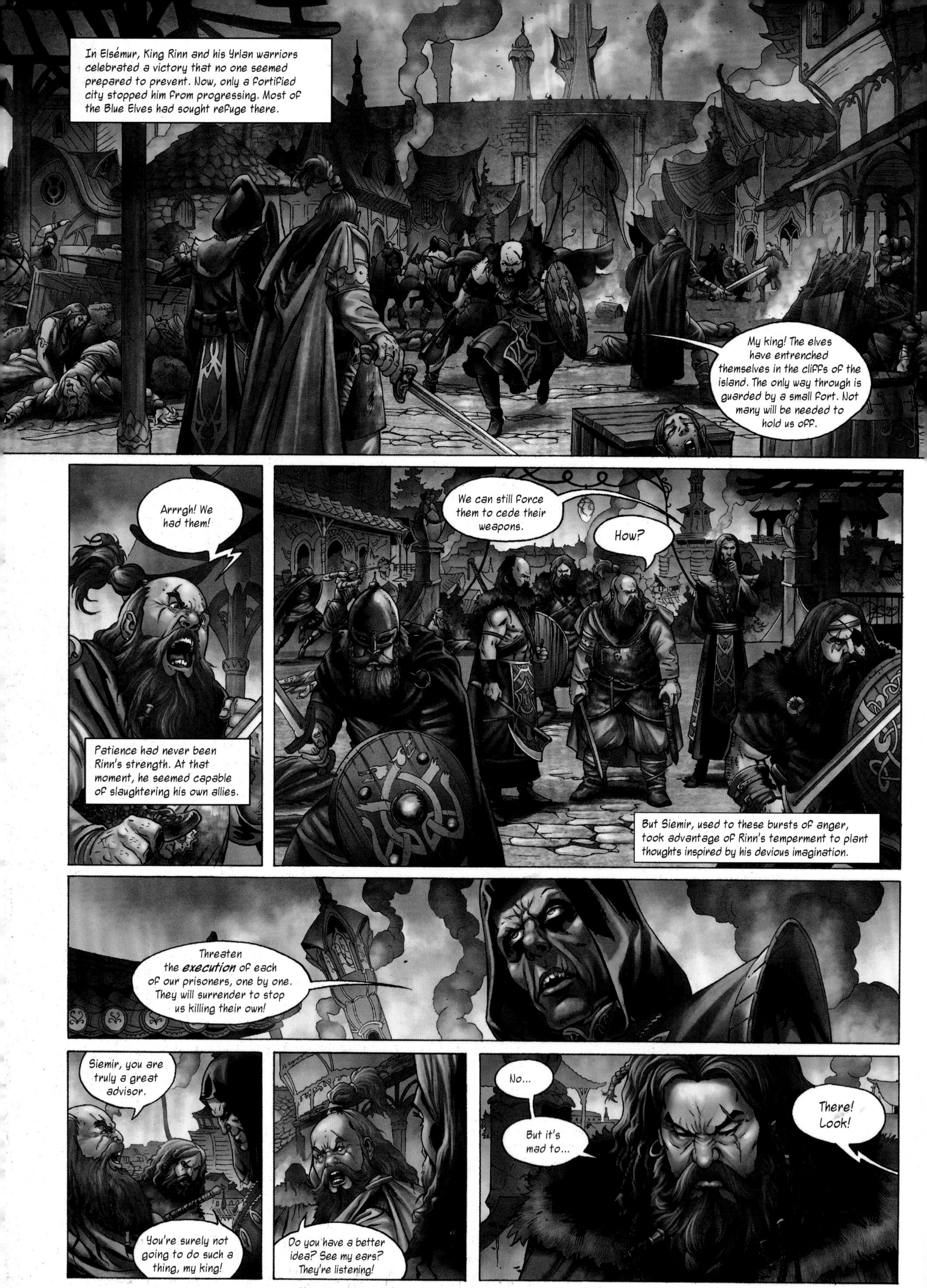
In Elsémur, King Rinn and his Yrlan warriors celebrated a victory that no one seemed prepared to prevent. Now, only a fortified city stopped him from progressing. Most of the Blue Elves had sought refuge there.
My king! The elves have entrenched themselves in the cliffs of the island. The only way through is guarded by a small fort. Not many will be needed to hold us off.
Arrrgh! We had them!
Patience had never been Rinn's strength. At that moment, he seemed capable of slaughtering his own allies.
We can still force them to cede their weapons.
How?
But Siemir, used to these bursts of anger, took advantage of Rinn's temperment to plant thoughts inspired by his devious imagination.
Threaten the *execution* of each of our prisoners, one by one. They will surrender to stop us killing their own!
Siemir, you are truly a great advisor.
You're surely not going to do such a thing, my king!
Do you have a better idea? See my ears? They're listening!
No...
But it's mad to...
There! Look!

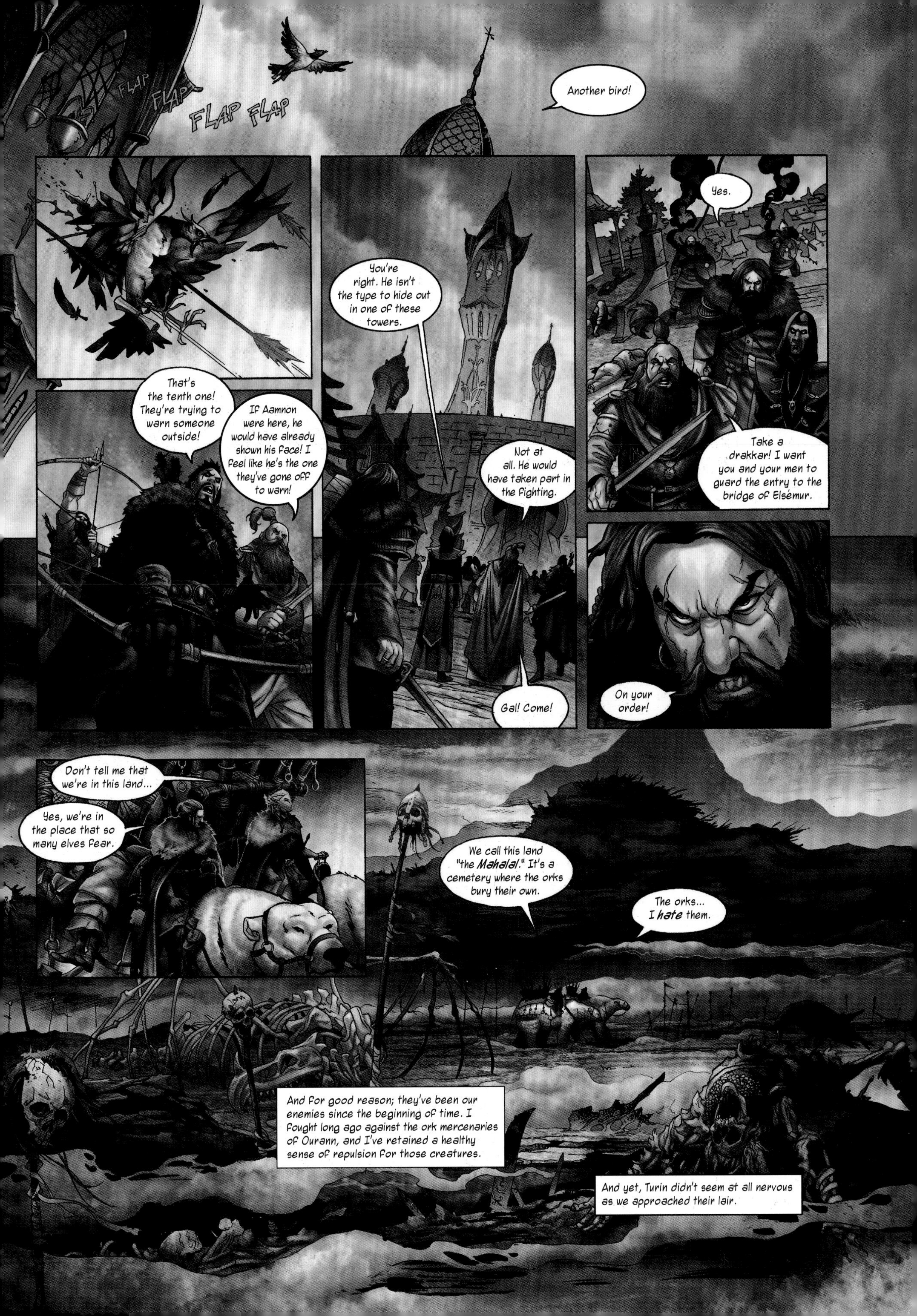
FLAP
FLAP
FLAP FLAP
Another bird!
That's the tenth one! They're trying to warn someone outside!
If Aamnon were here, he would have already shown his face! I feel like he's the one they've gone off to warn!
You're right. He isn't the type to hide out in one of these towers.
Not at all. He would have taken part in the fighting.
Gal! Come!
Yes.
Take a drakkar! I want you and your men to guard the entry to the bridge of Elsémur.
On your order!
Don't tell me that we're in this land...
Yes, we're in the place that so many elves fear.
We call this land "the Mahalal." It's a cemetery where the orks bury their own.
The orks... I hate them.
And for good reason; they've been our enemies since the beginning of time. I fought long ago against the ork mercenaries of Ourann, and I've retained a healthy sense of repulsion for those creatures.
And yet, Turin didn't seem at all nervous as we approached their lair.

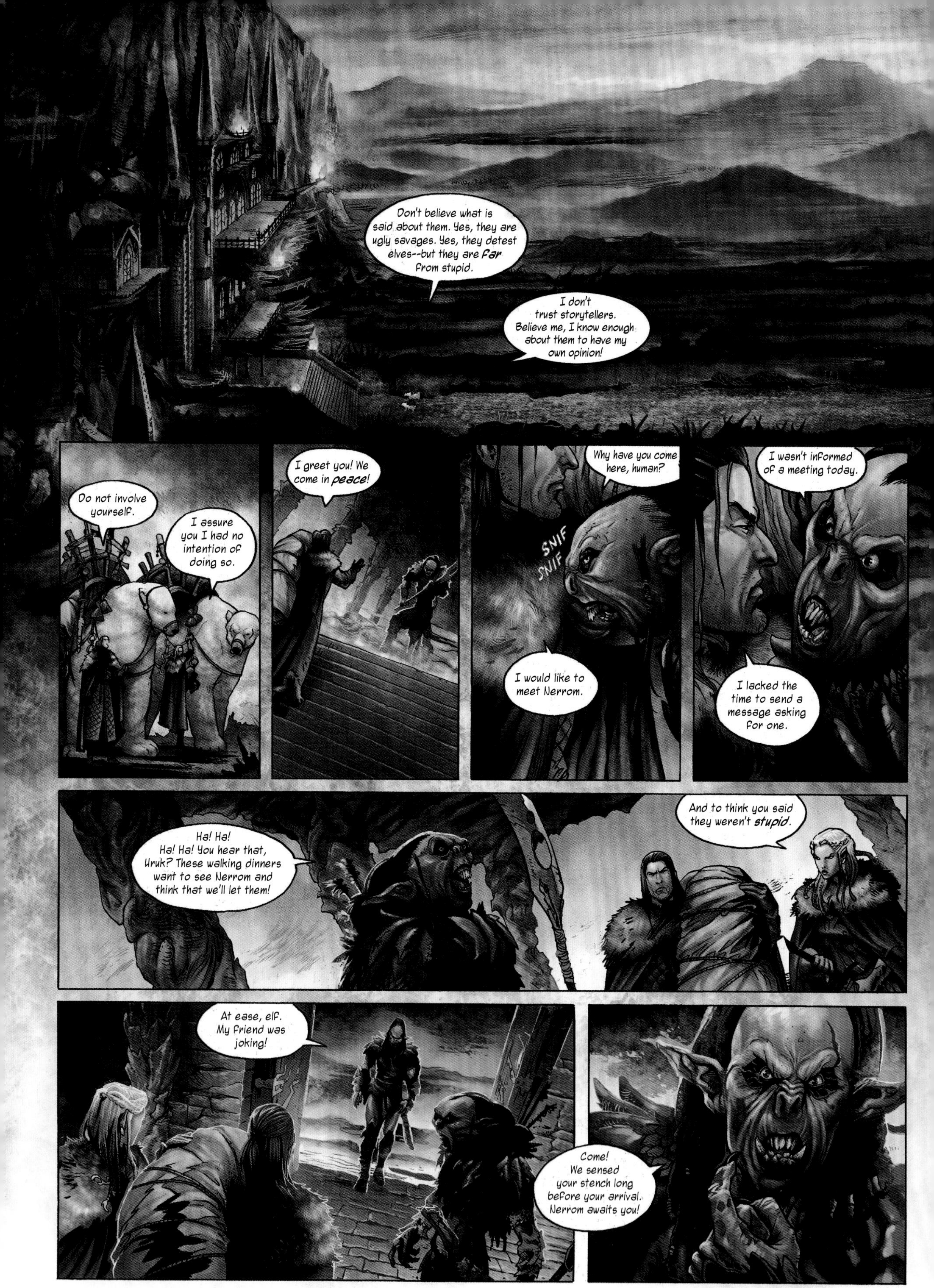

Don't believe what is said about them. Yes, they are ugly savages. Yes, they detest elves--but they are far from stupid.
I don't trust storytellers. Believe me, I know enough about them to have my own opinion!
Do not involve yourself.
I assure you I had no intention of doing so.
I greet you! We come in peace!
Why have you come here, human?
SNIF SNIF
I would like to meet Nerrom.
I wasn't informed of a meeting today.
I lacked the time to send a message asking for one.
Ha! Ha! Ha! Ha! You hear that, Uruk? These walking dinners want to see Nerrom and think that we'll let them!
And to think you said they weren't stupid.
At ease, elf. My friend was joking!
Come! We sensed your stench long before your arrival. Nerrom awaits you!

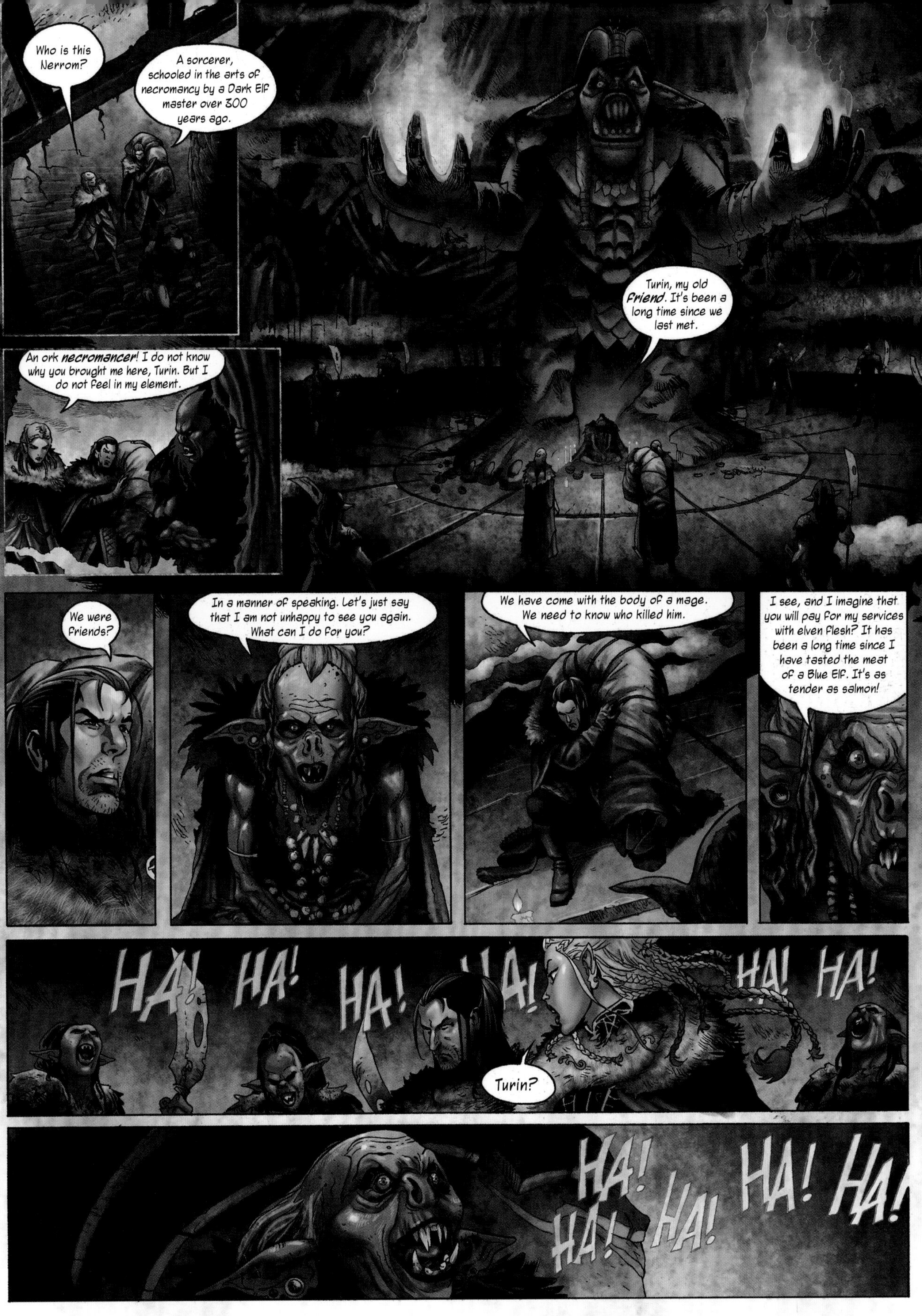
Who is this Nerrom?
A sorcerer, schooled in the arts of necromancy by a Dark Elf master over 300 years ago.
An ork necromancer! I do not know why you brought me here, Turin. But I do not feel in my element.
Turin, my old friend. It's been a long time since we last met.
We were friends?
In a manner of speaking. Let's just say that I am not unhappy to see you again. What can I do for you?
We have come with the body of a mage. We need to know who killed him.
I see, and I imagine that you will pay for my services with elven flesh? It has been a long time since I have tasted the meat of a Blue Elf. It's as tender as salmon!
HA! HA! HA! HA! HA! HA!
Turin?
HA! HA! HA! HA! HA! HA!

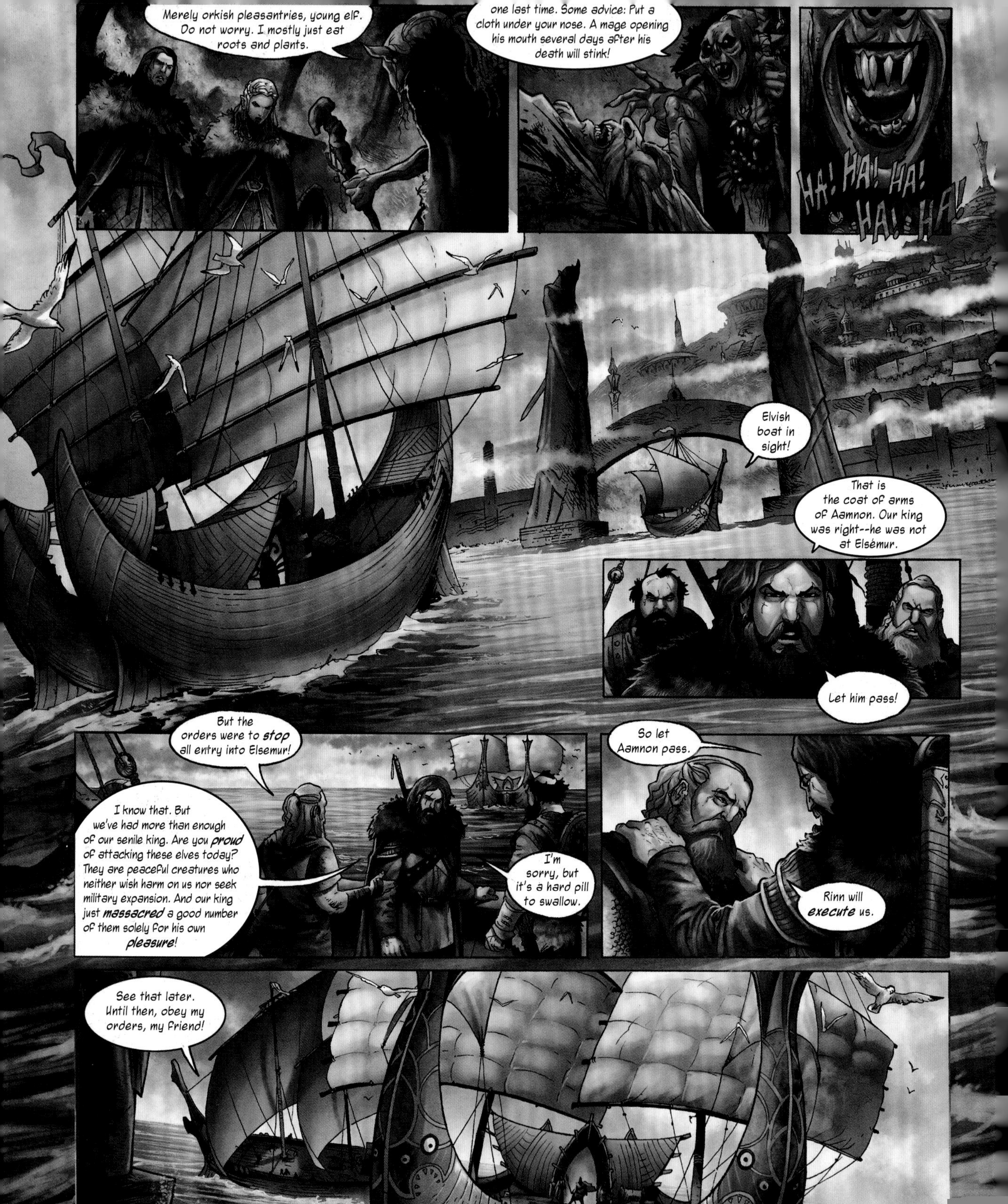

Merely orkish pleasantries, young elf. Do not worry. I mostly just eat roots and plants.
one last time. Some advice: Put a cloth under your nose. A mage opening his mouth several days after his death will stink!
HA! HA! HA! HA! HA!
Elvish boat in sight!
That is the coat of arms of Aamnon. Our king was right--he was not at Elsémur.
Let him pass!
But the orders were to *stop* all entry into Elsemur!
I know that. But we've had more than enough of our senile king. Are you *proud* of attacking these elves today? They are peaceful creatures who neither wish harm on us nor seek military expansion. And our king just *massacred* a good number of them solely for his own *pleasure*!
I'm sorry, but it's a hard pill to swallow.
So let Aamnon pass.
Rinn will *execute* us.
See that later. Until then, obey my orders, my friend!

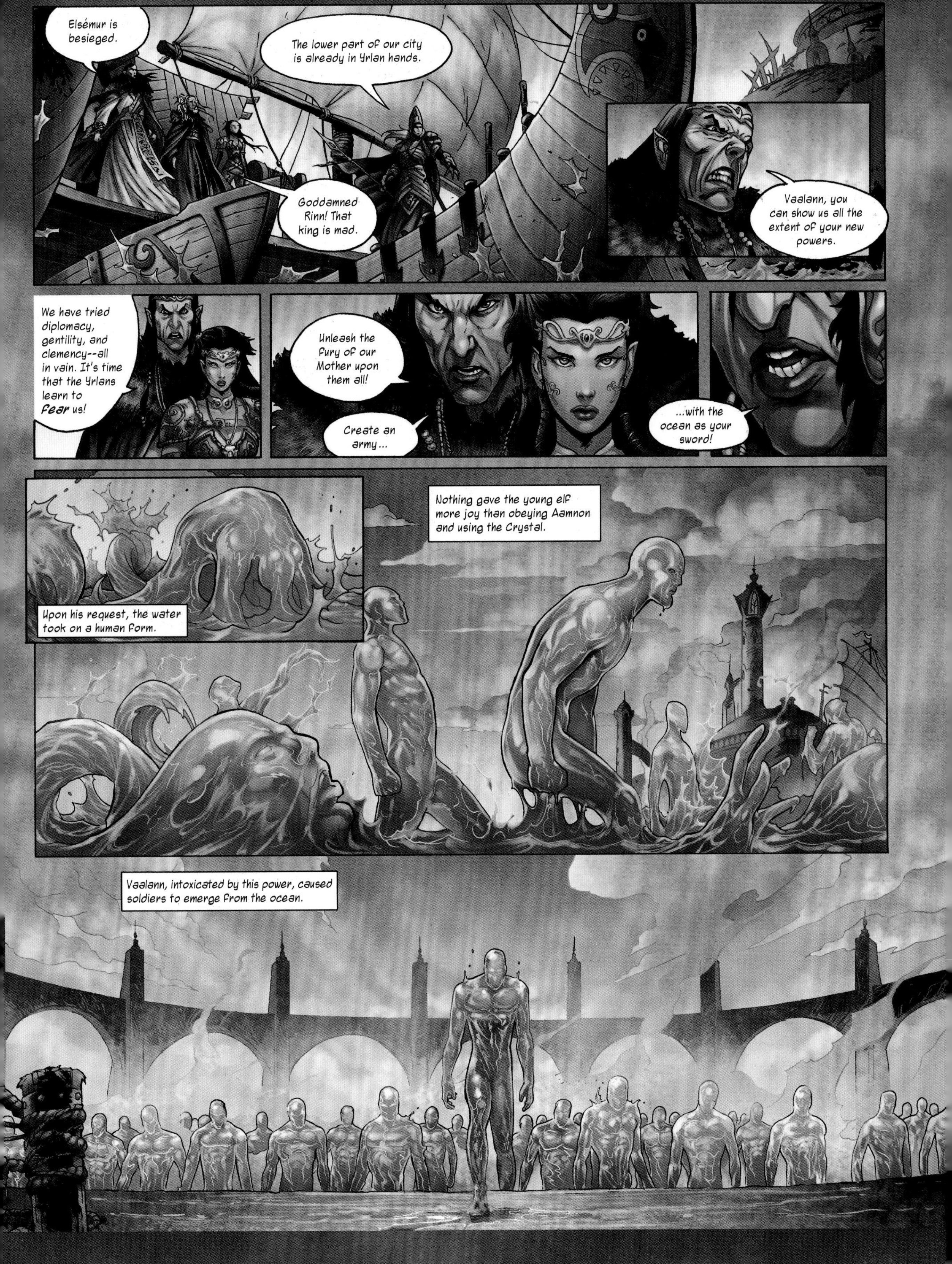
Elsémur is besieged.
The lower part of our city is already in Yrlan hands.
Goddamned Rinn! That king is mad.
Vaalann, you can show us all the extent of your new powers.
We have tried diplomacy, gentility, and clemency--all in vain. It's time that the Yrlans learn to **fear** us!
Unleash the fury of our Mother upon them all!
Create an army...
...with the ocean as your sword!
Nothing gave the young elf more joy than obeying Aamnon and using the Crystal.
Upon his request, the water took on a human form.
Vaalann, intoxicated by this power, caused soldiers to emerge from the ocean.

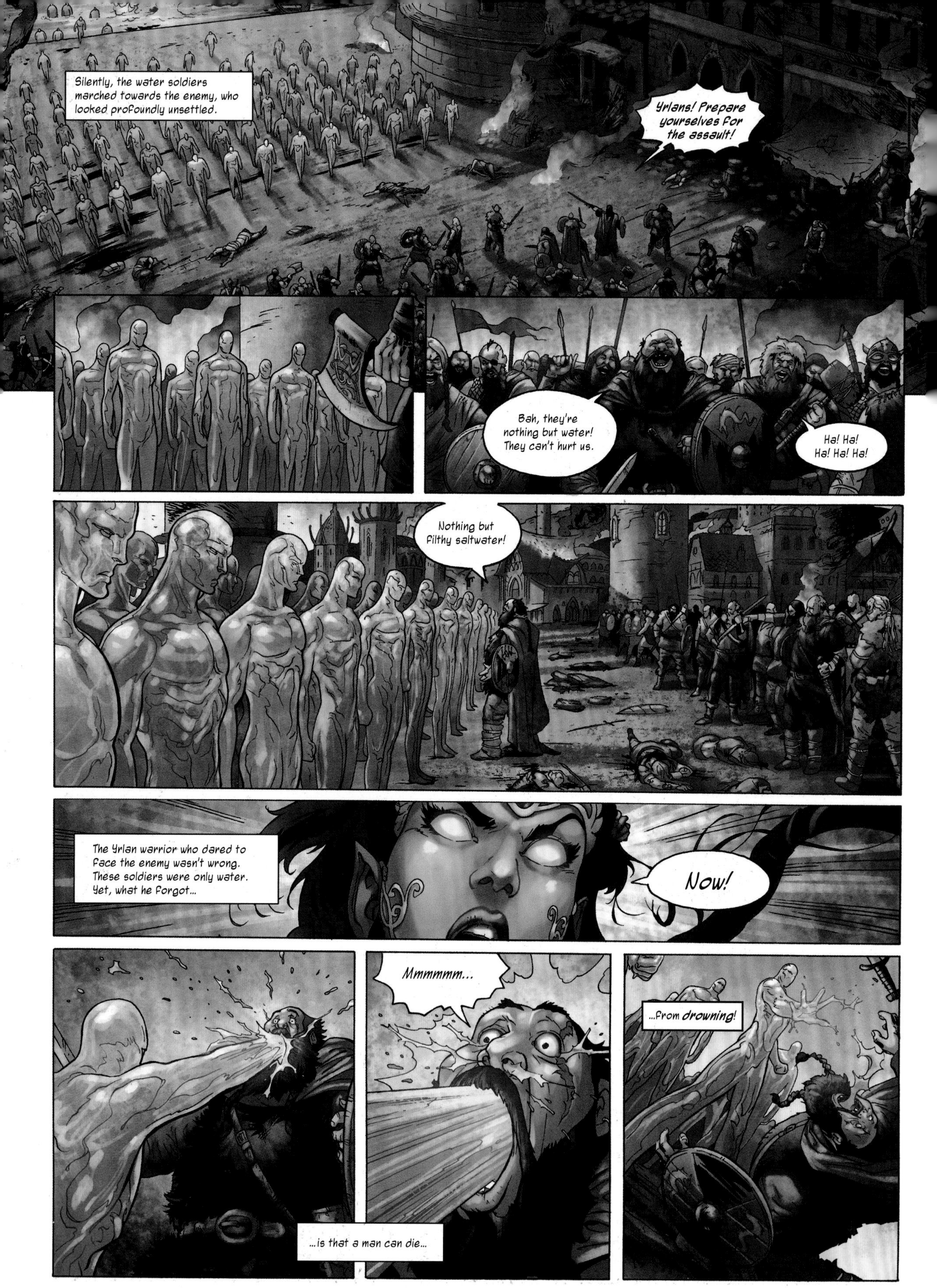
Silently, the water soldiers marched towards the enemy, who looked profoundly unsettled.
Yrlans! Prepare yourselves for the assault!
Bah, they're nothing but water! They can't hurt us.
Ha! Ha! Ha! Ha! Ha!
Nothing but filthy saltwater!
The Yrlan warrior who dared to face the enemy wasn't wrong. These soldiers were only water. Yet, what he forgot...
Now!
Mmmmmm...
...is that a man can die...
...from drowning!

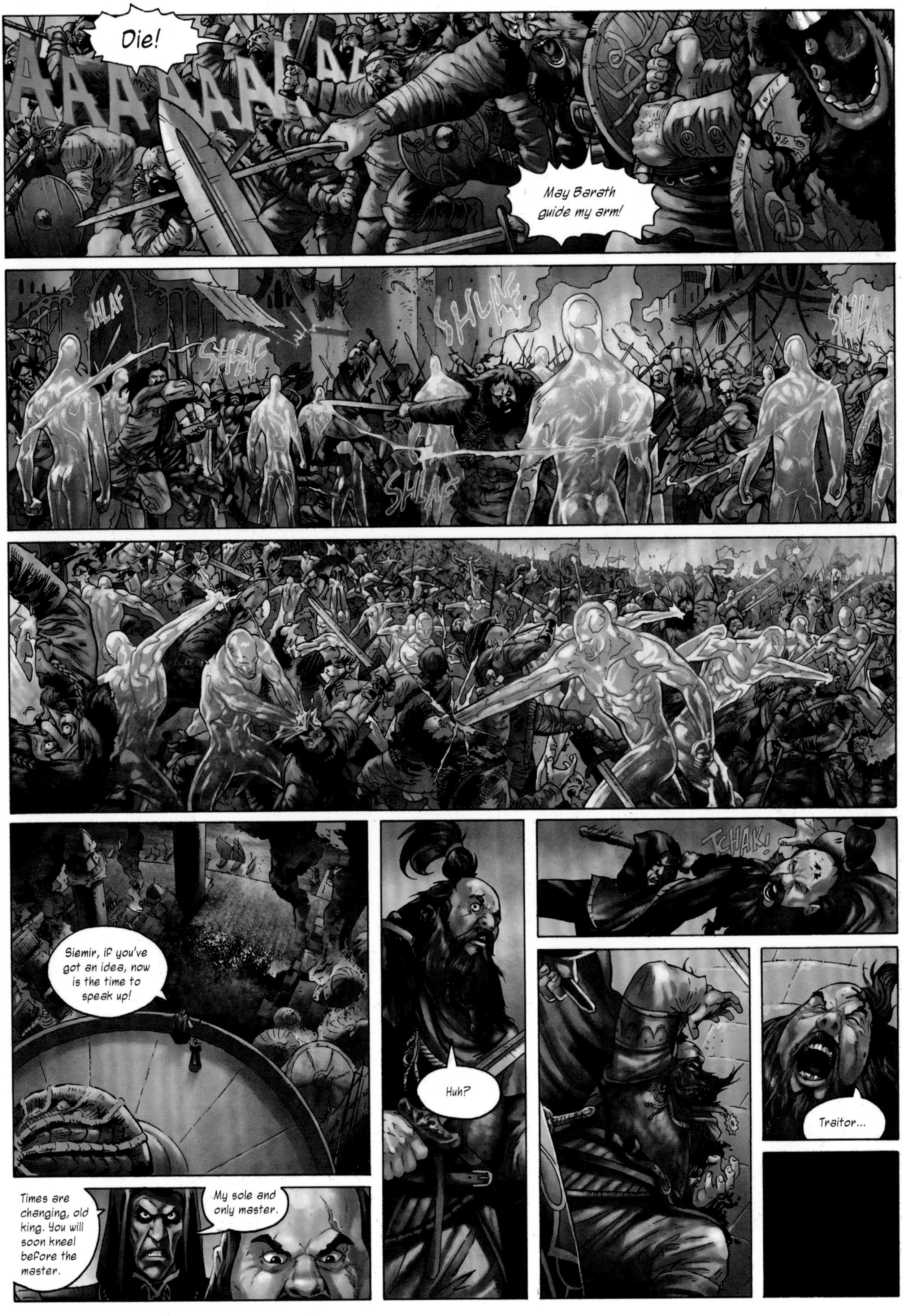
Die!
AAAAAAAA
May Barath guide my arm!
SHLAF
SHLAF
SHLAF
SHLAF
Siemir, if you've got an idea, now is the time to speak up!
Times are changing, old king. You will soon kneel before the master.
My sole and only master.
Huh?
TCHAK!
Traitor...

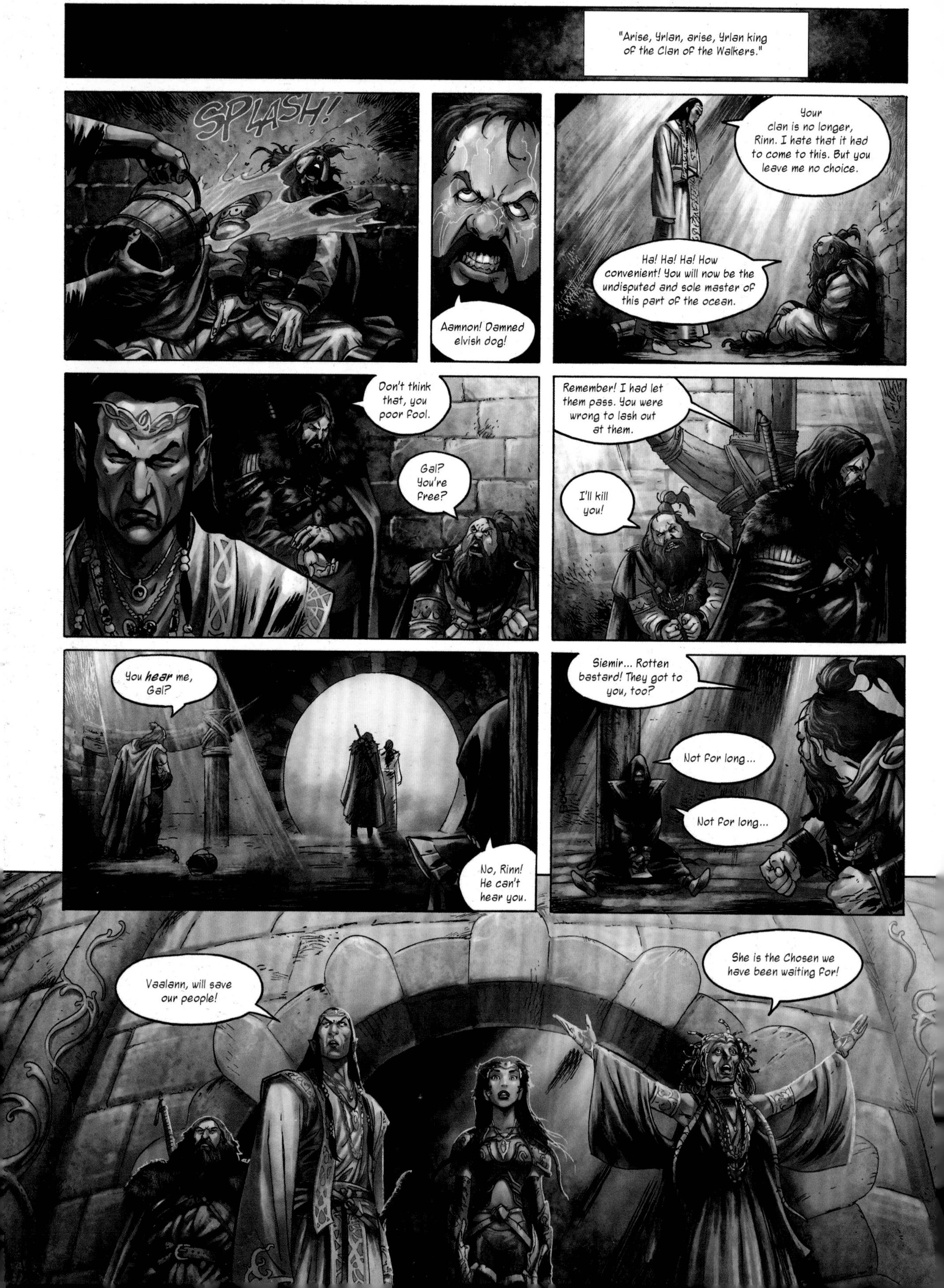
"Arise, Yrlan, arise, Yrlan king of the Clan of the Walkers."
SPLASH!
Aamnon! Damned elvish dog!
Your clan is no longer, Rinn. I hate that it had to come to this. But you leave me no choice.
Ha! Ha! Ha! How convenient! You will now be the undisputed and sole master of this part of the ocean.
Don't think that, you poor fool.
Gal? You're free?
Remember! I had let them pass. You were wrong to lash out at them.
I'll kill you!
You *hear* me, Gal?
No, Rinn! He can't hear you.
Siemir... Rotten bastard! They got to you, too?
Not for long...
Not for long...
Vaalann, will save our people!
She is the Chosen we have been waiting for!

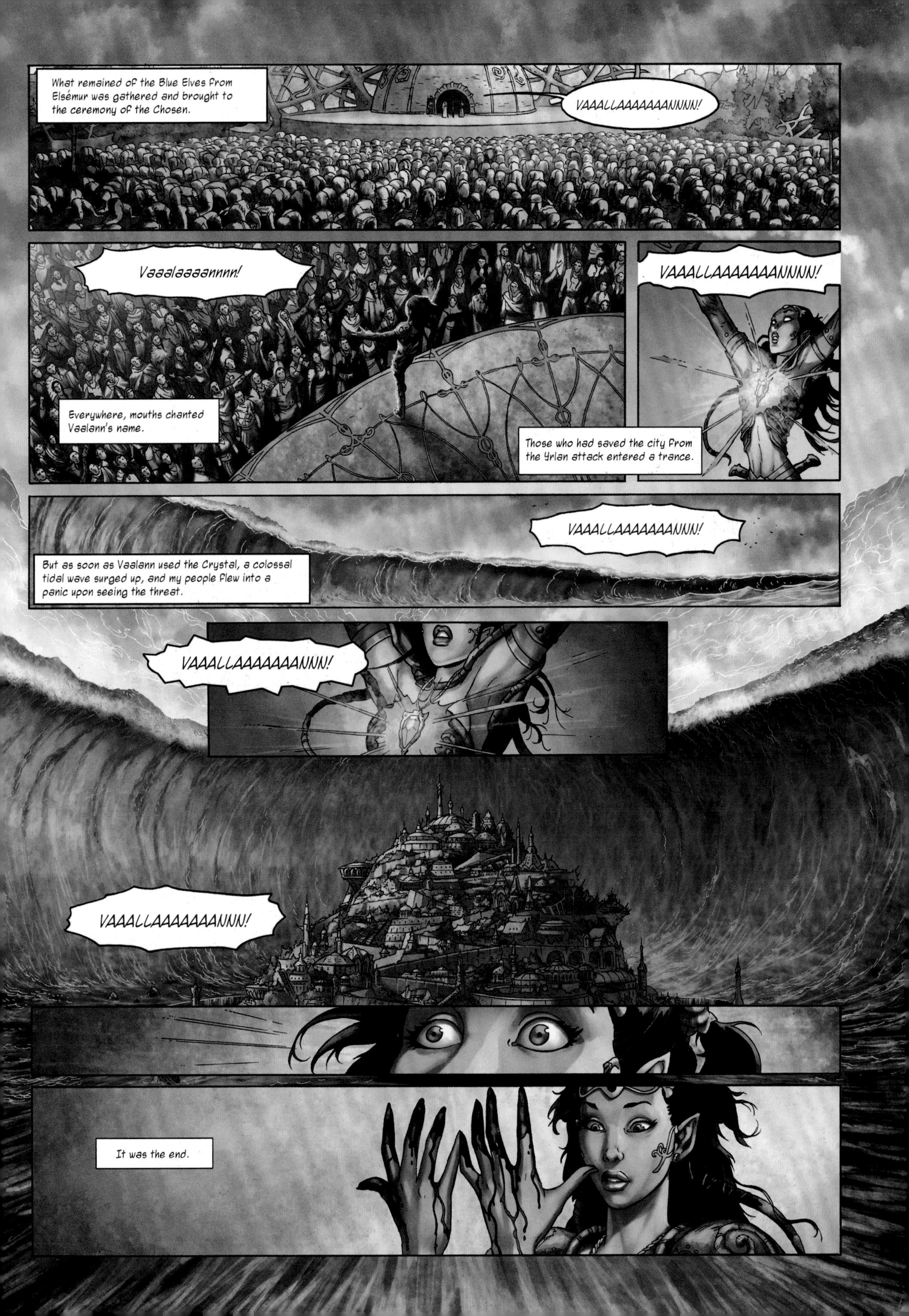
What remained of the Blue Elves from Elsémur was gathered and brought to the ceremony of the Chosen.
VAAALLAAAAAAANNNN!
Vaaalaaaannnn!
Everywhere, mouths chanted Vaalann's name.
VAAALLAAAAAAANNNN!
Those who had saved the city from the Yrlan attack entered a trance.
VAAALLAAAAAAANNNN!
But as soon as Vaalann used the Crystal, a colossal tidal wave surged up, and my people flew into a panic upon seeing the threat.
VAAALLAAAAAAANNN!
VAAALLAAAAAAANNN!
It was the end.

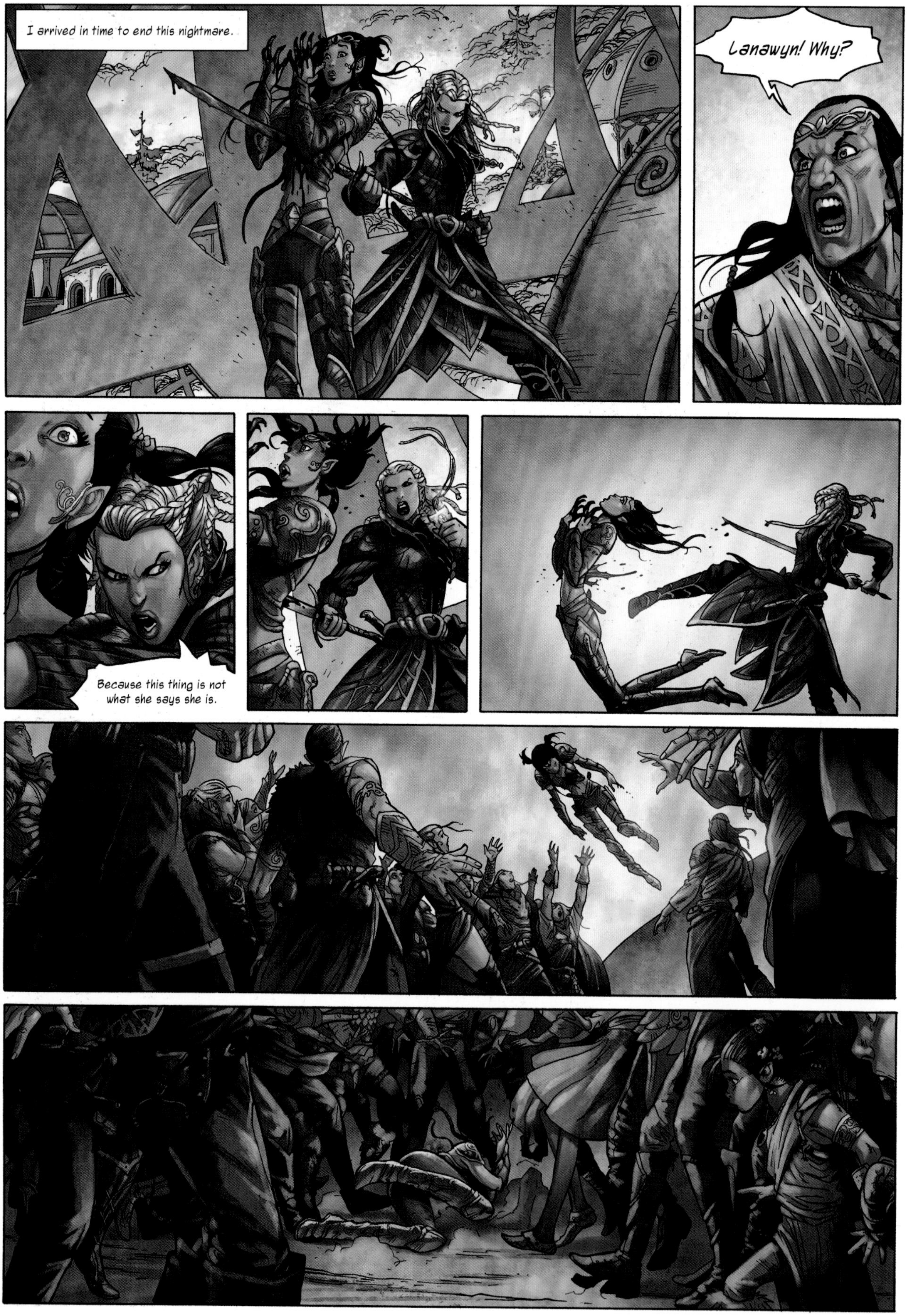
I arrived in time to end this nightmare.
Lanawyn! Why?
Because this thing is not what she says she is.

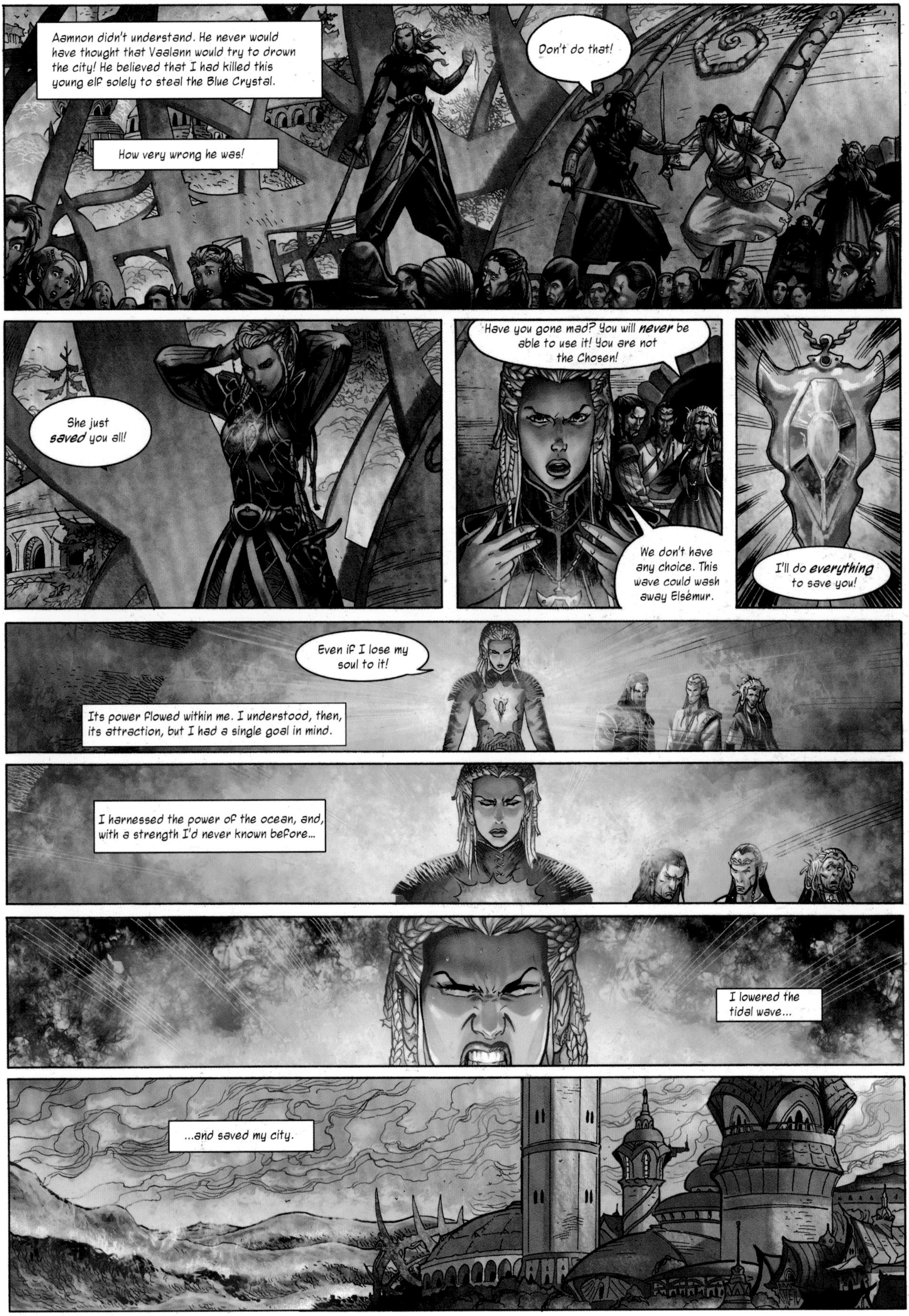
Aamnon didn't understand. He never would have thought that Vaalann would try to drown the city! He believed that I had killed this young elf solely to steal the Blue Crystal.
How very wrong he was!
Don't do that!
She just *saved* you all!
Have you gone mad? You will ***never*** be able to use it! You are not the Chosen!
We don't have any choice. This wave could wash away Elsémur.
I'll do ***everything*** to save you!
Even if I lose my soul to it!
Its power flowed within me. I understood, then, its attraction, but I had a single goal in mind.
I harnessed the power of the ocean, and, with a strength I'd never known before...
I lowered the tidal wave...
...and saved my city.

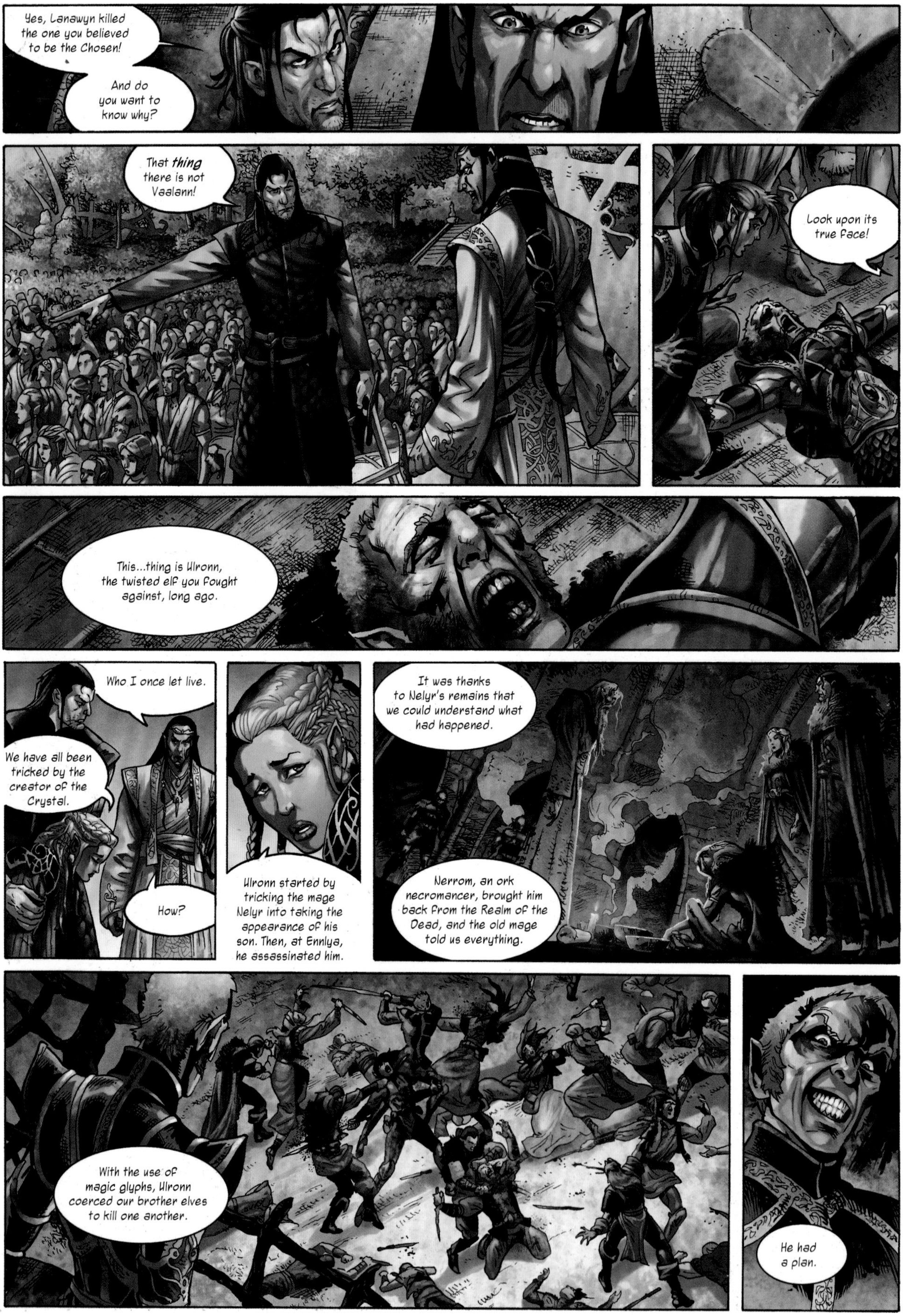
Yes, Lanawyn killed the one you believed to be the Chosen!
And do you want to know why?
That *thing* there is not Vaalann!
Look upon its true face!
This...thing is Ulronn, the twisted elf you fought against, long ago.
Who I once let live.
We have all been tricked by the creator of the Crystal.
How?
Ulronn started by tricking the mage Nelyr into taking the appearance of his son. Then, at Ennlya, he assassinated him.
It was thanks to Nelyr's remains that we could understand what had happened.
Nerrom, an ork necromancer, brought him back from the Realm of the Dead, and the old mage told us everything.
With the use of magic glyphs, Ulronn coerced our brother elves to kill one another.
He had a plan.

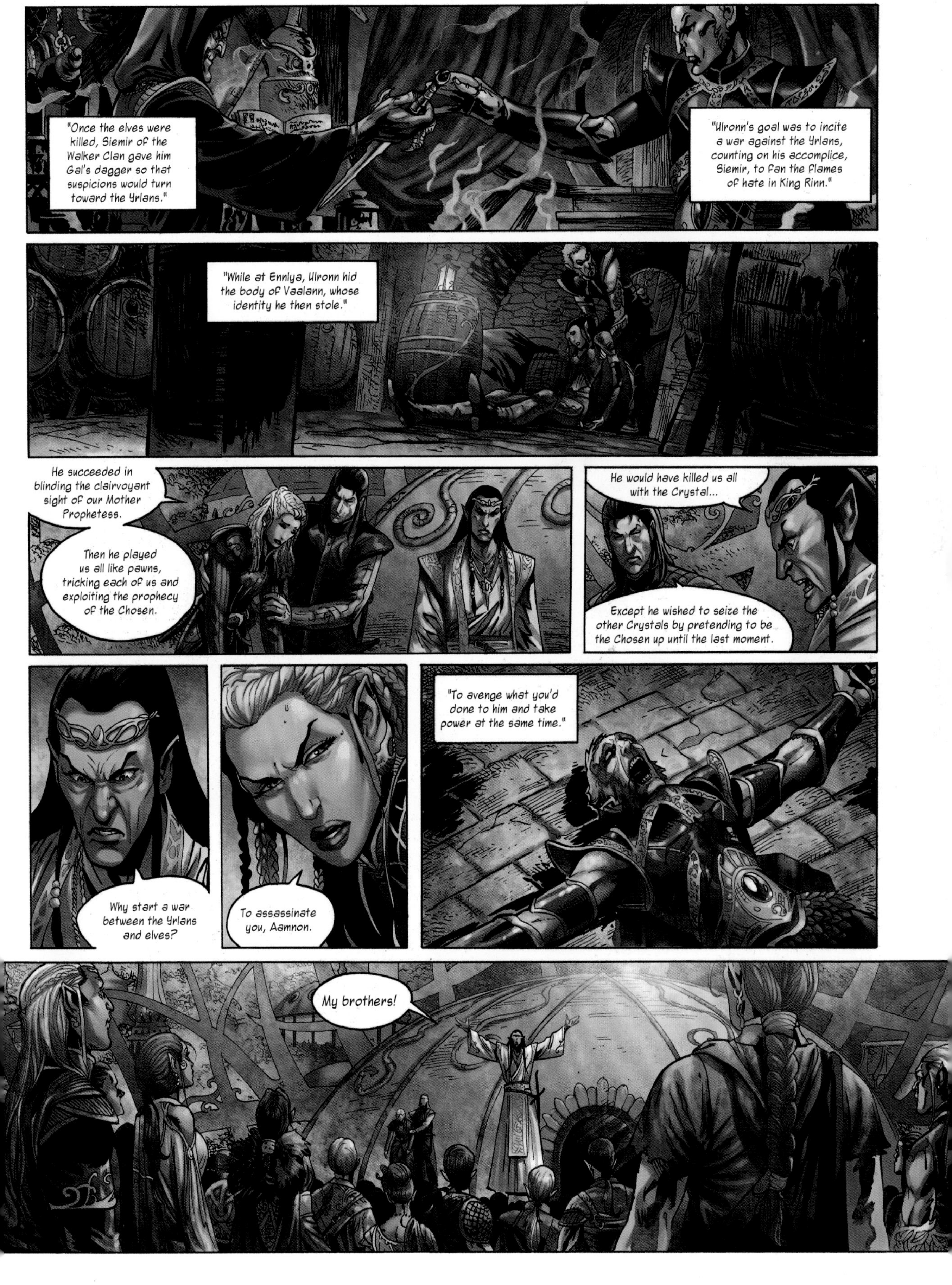
"Once the elves were killed, Siemir of the Walker Clan gave him Gal's dagger so that suspicions would turn toward the Yrlans."
"Ulronn's goal was to incite a war against the Yrlans, counting on his accomplice, Siemir, to fan the flames of hate in King Rinn."
"While at Ennlya, Ulronn hid the body of Vaalann, whose identity he then stole."
He succeeded in blinding the clairvoyant sight of our Mother Prophetess.
Then he played us all like pawns, tricking each of us and exploiting the prophecy of the Chosen.
He would have killed us all with the Crystal...
Except he wished to seize the other Crystals by pretending to be the Chosen up until the last moment.
Why start a war between the Yrlans and elves?
To assassinate you, Aamnon.
"To avenge what you'd done to him and take power at the same time."
My brothers!

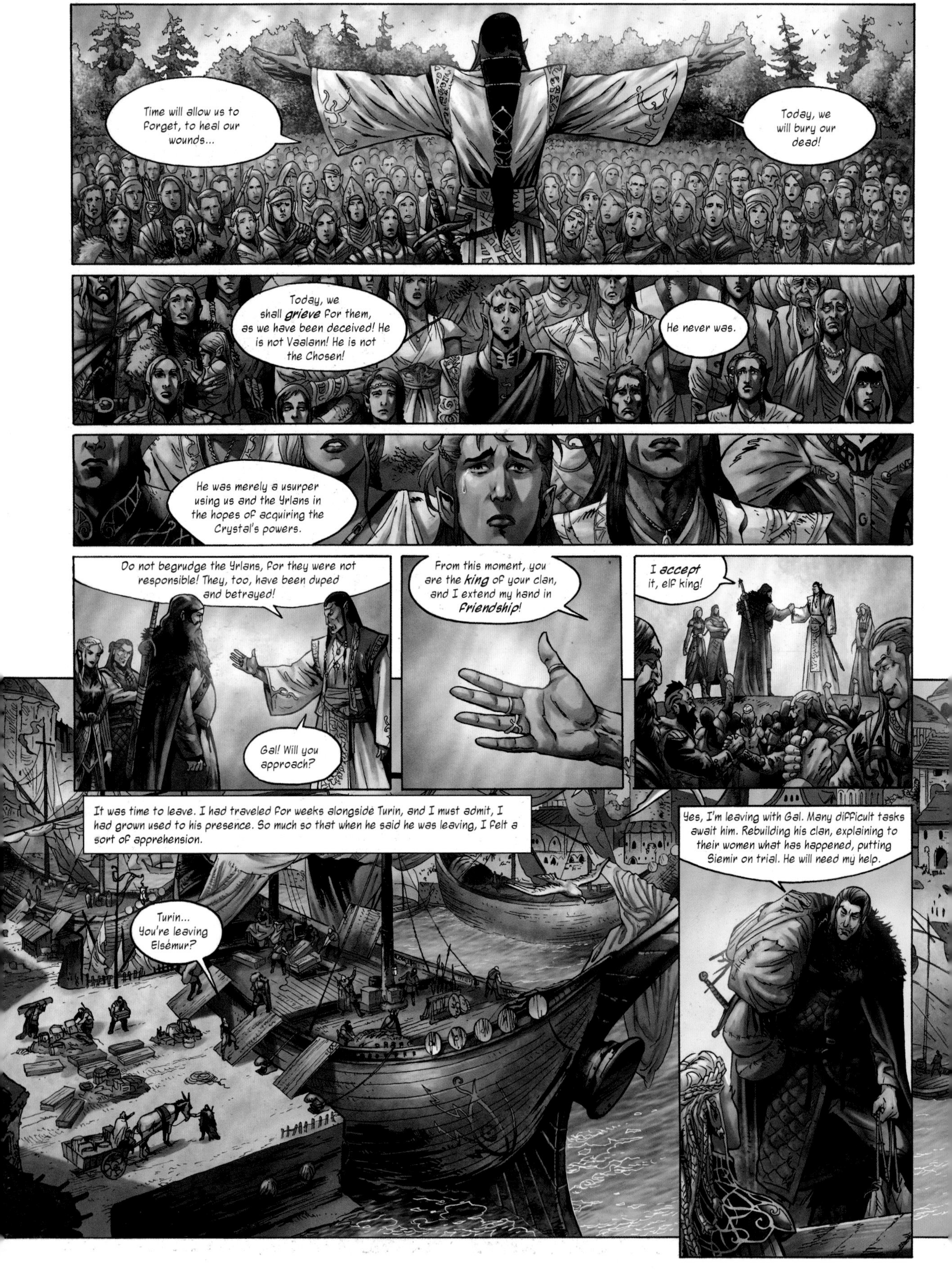
Time will allow us to forget, to heal our wounds...
Today, we will bury our dead!
Today, we shall grieve for them, as we have been deceived! He is not Vaalann! He is not the Chosen!
He never was.
He was merely a usurper using us and the Yrlans in the hopes of acquiring the Crystal's powers.
Do not begrudge the Yrlans, for they were not responsible! They, too, have been duped and betrayed!
Gal! Will you approach?
From this moment, you are the king of your clan, and I extend my hand in friendship!
I accept it, elf king!
It was time to leave. I had traveled for weeks alongside Turin, and I must admit, I had grown used to his presence. So much so that when he said he was leaving, I felt a sort of apprehension.
Turin... You're leaving Elsémur?
Yes, I'm leaving with Gal. Many difficult tasks await him. Rebuilding his clan, explaining to their women what has happened, putting Siemir on trial. He will need my help.

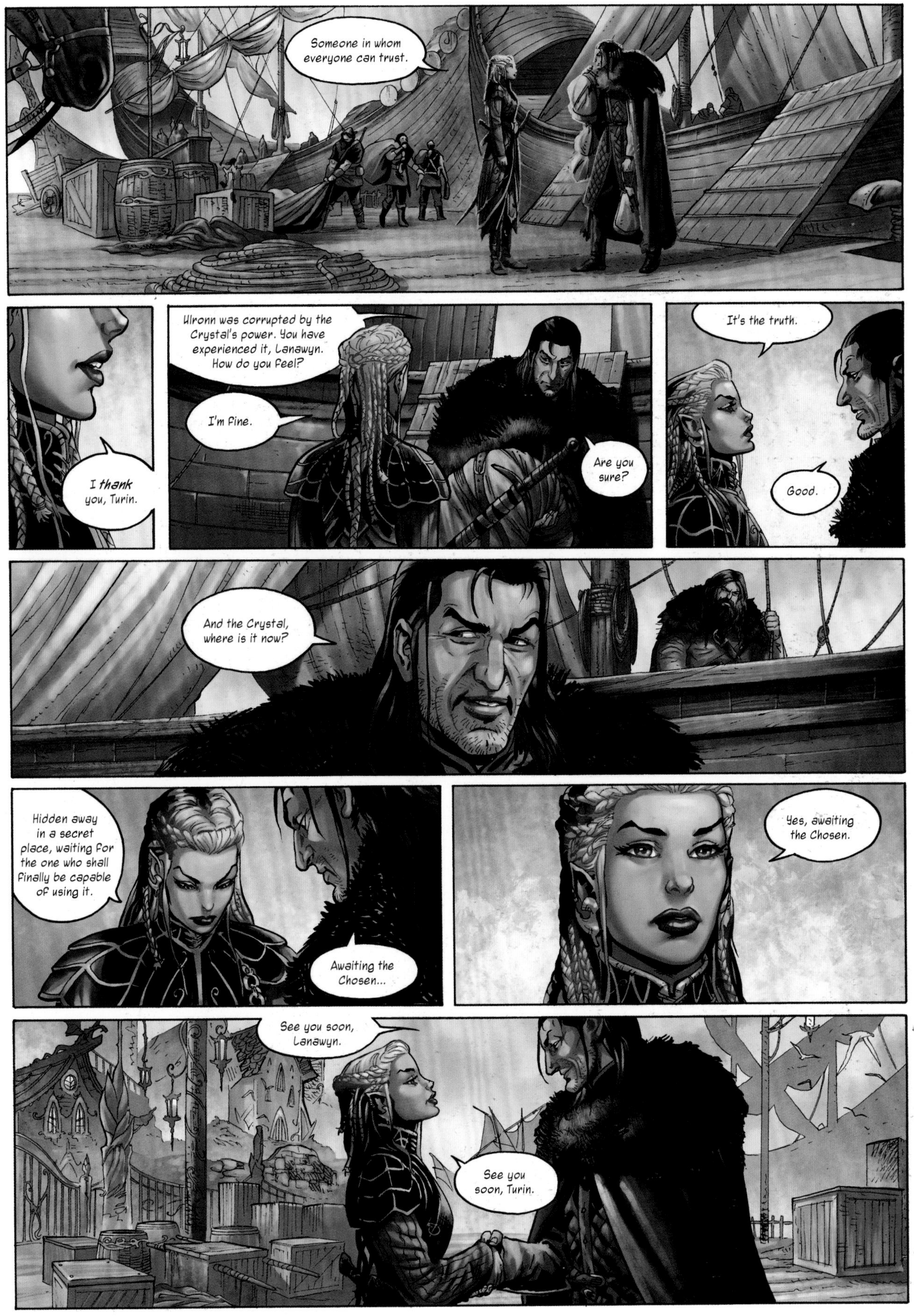
Someone in whom everyone can trust.
I *thank* you, Turin.
Ulronn was corrupted by the Crystal's power. You have experienced it, Lanawyn. How do you feel?
I'm fine.
Are you sure?
It's the truth.
Good.
And the Crystal, where is it now?
Hidden away in a secret place, waiting for the one who shall finally be capable of using it.
Awaiting the Chosen...
Yes, awaiting the Chosen.
See you soon, Lanawyn.
See you soon, Turin.

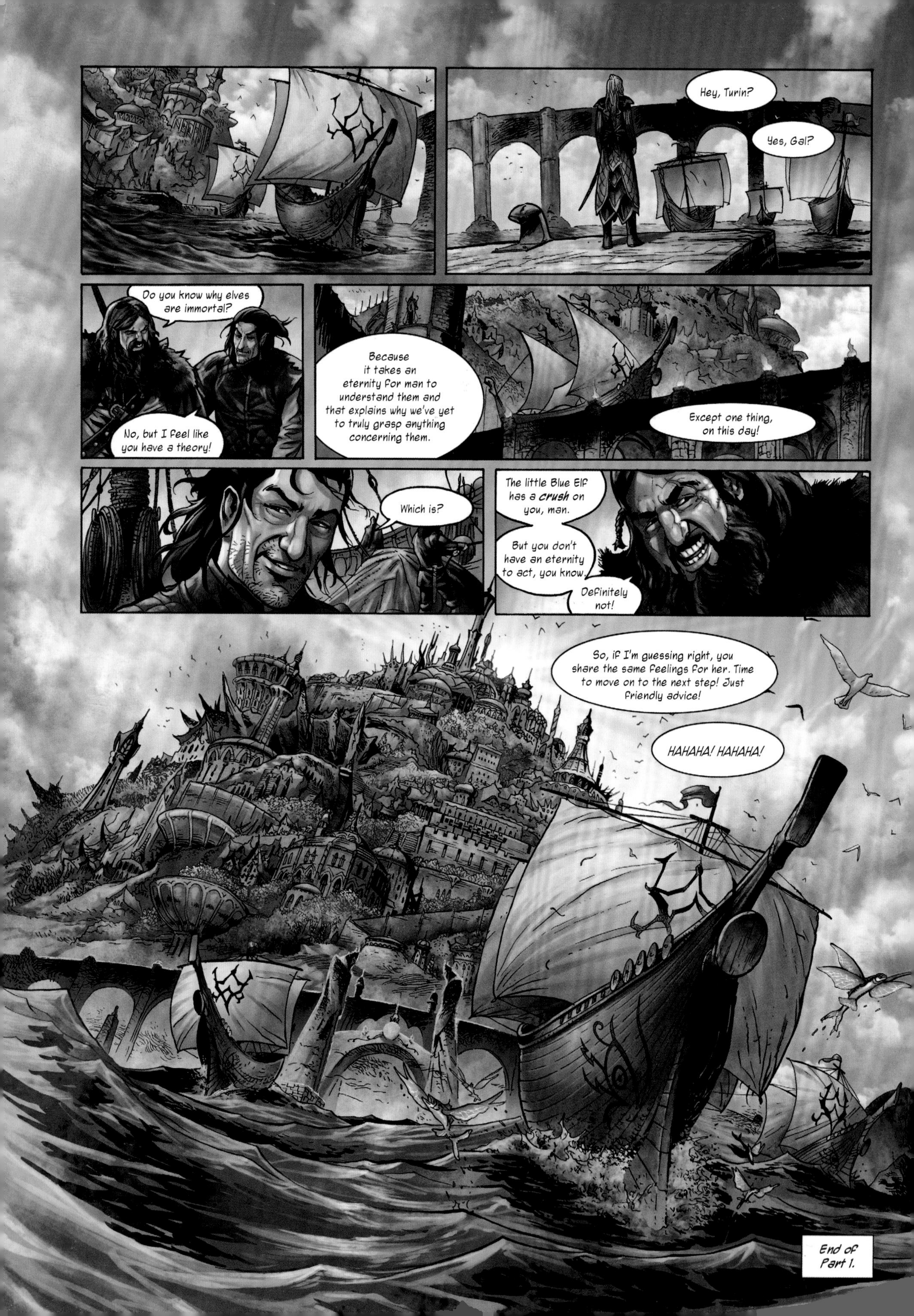
Hey, Turin?
Yes, Gal?
Do you know why elves are immortal?
No, but I feel like you have a theory!
Because it takes an eternity for man to understand them and that explains why we've yet to truly grasp anything concerning them.
Except one thing, on this day!
Which is?
The little Blue Elf has a **crush** on you, man.
But you don't have an eternity to act, you know.
Definitely not!
So, if I'm guessing right, you share the same feelings for her. Time to move on to the next step! Just friendly advice!
HAHAHA! HAHAHA!
End of Part 1.

ELVES

PART 2
THE HONOR OF THE SYLVAN ELVES

BY JARRY AND MACONI

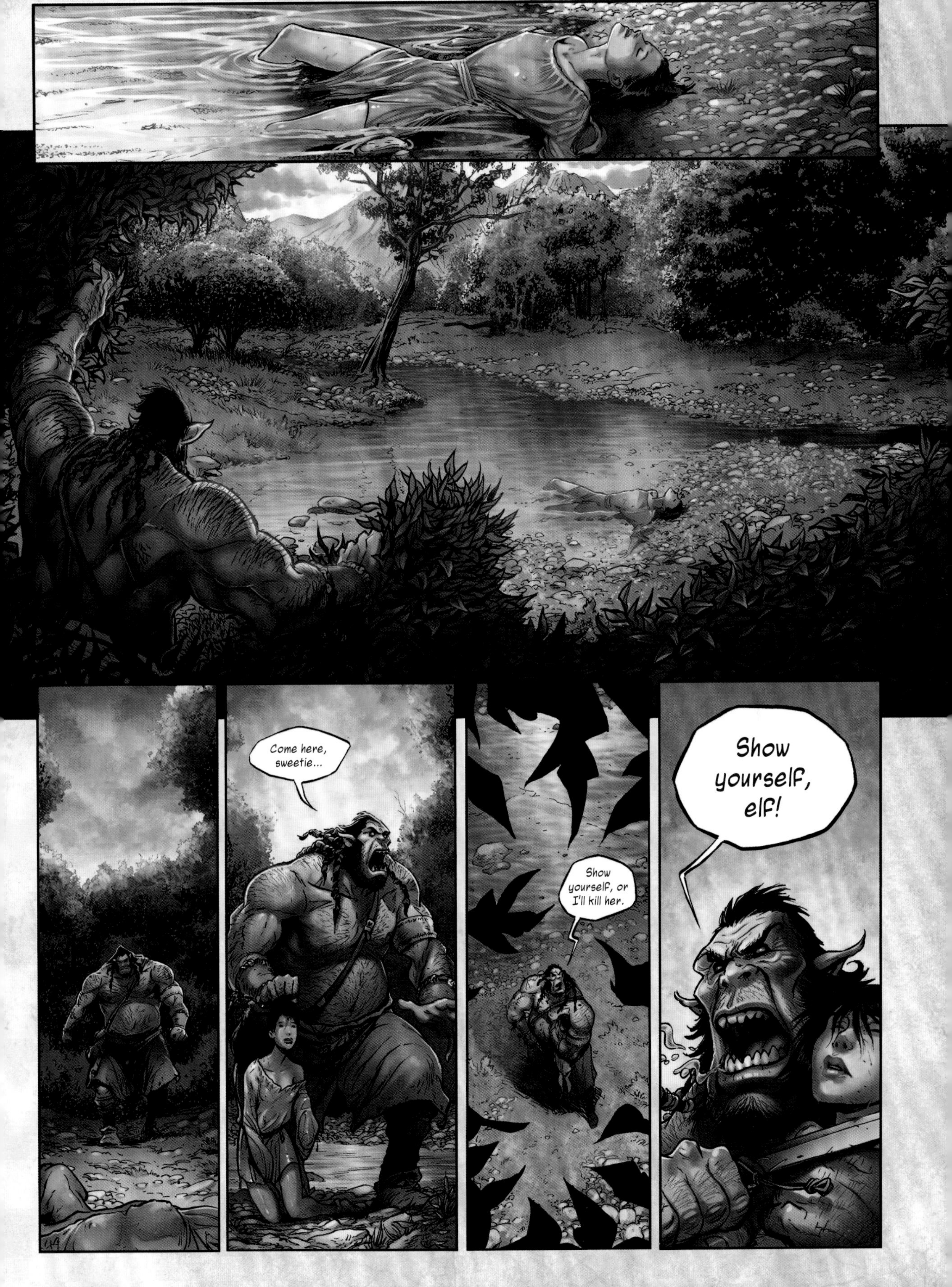
Come here, sweetie...
Show yourself, or I'll kill her.
Show yourself, elf!

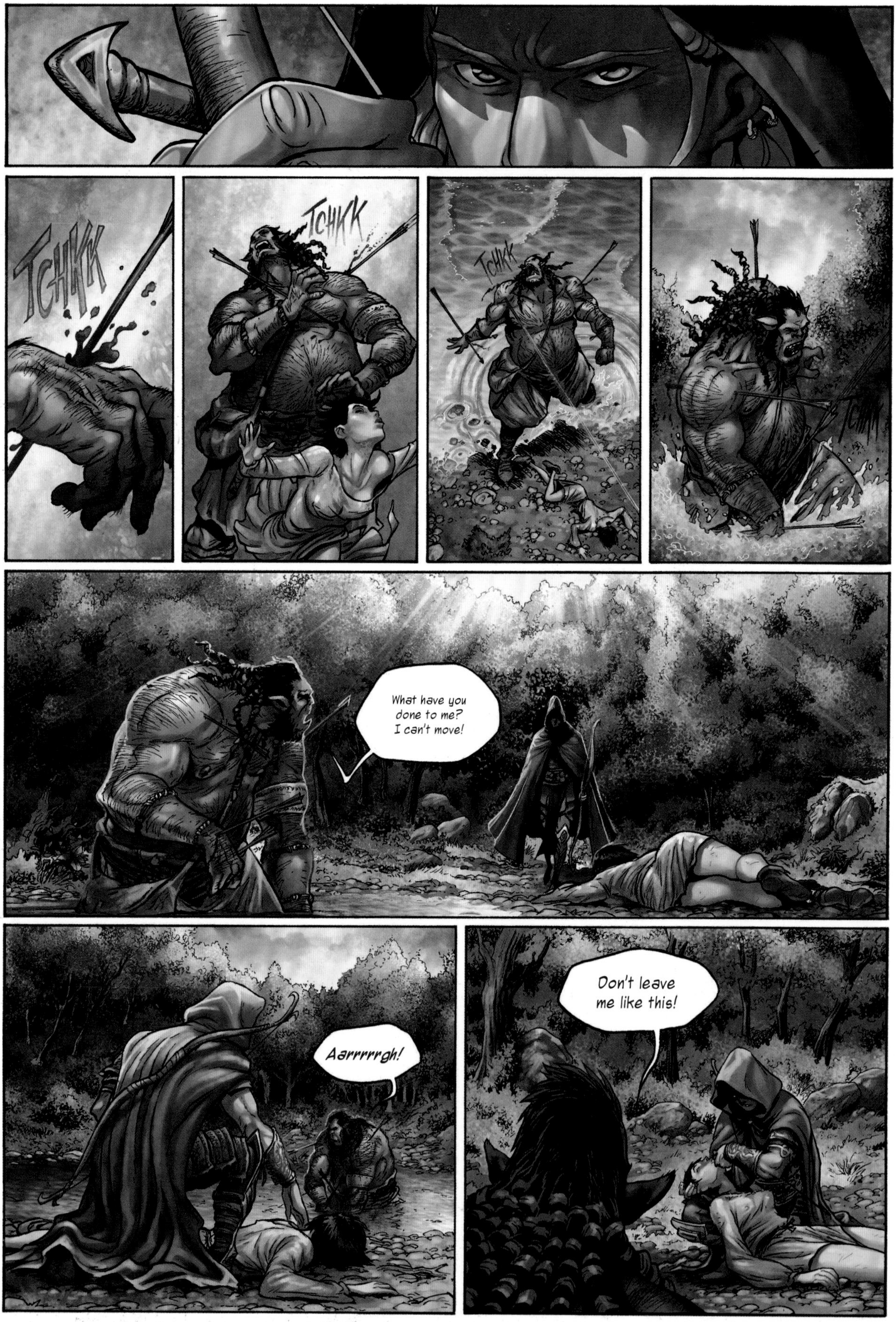
TCHKK
TCHKK
TCHKK
What have you done to me? I can't move!
Aarrrrrgh!
Don't leave me like this!

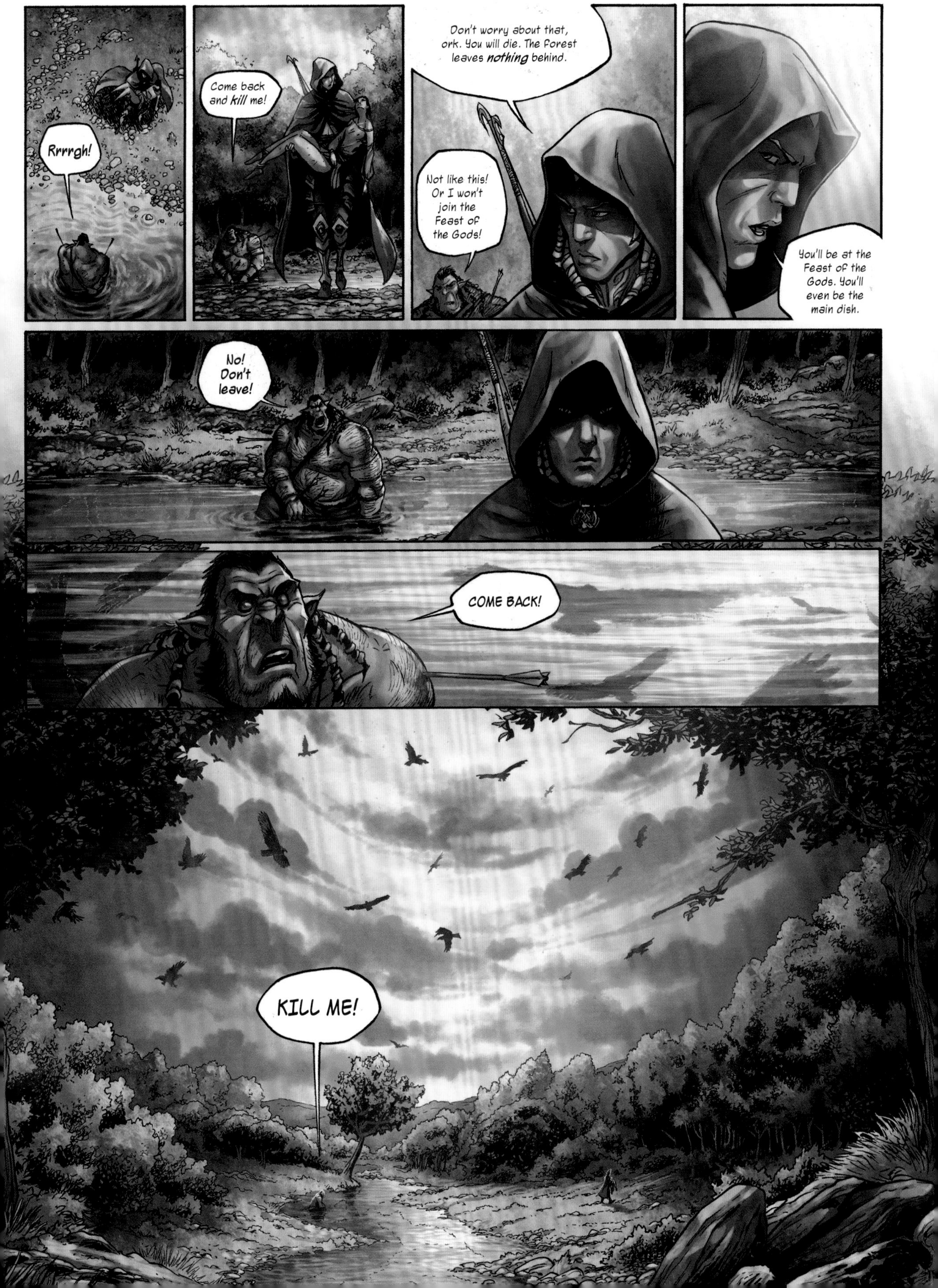
Rrrrgh!
Come back and *kill* me!
Don't worry about that, ork. You will die. The Forest leaves ***nothing*** behind.
Not like this! Or I won't join the Feast of the Gods!
You'll be at the Feast of the Gods. You'll even be the main dish.
No! Don't leave!
COME BACK!
KILL ME!

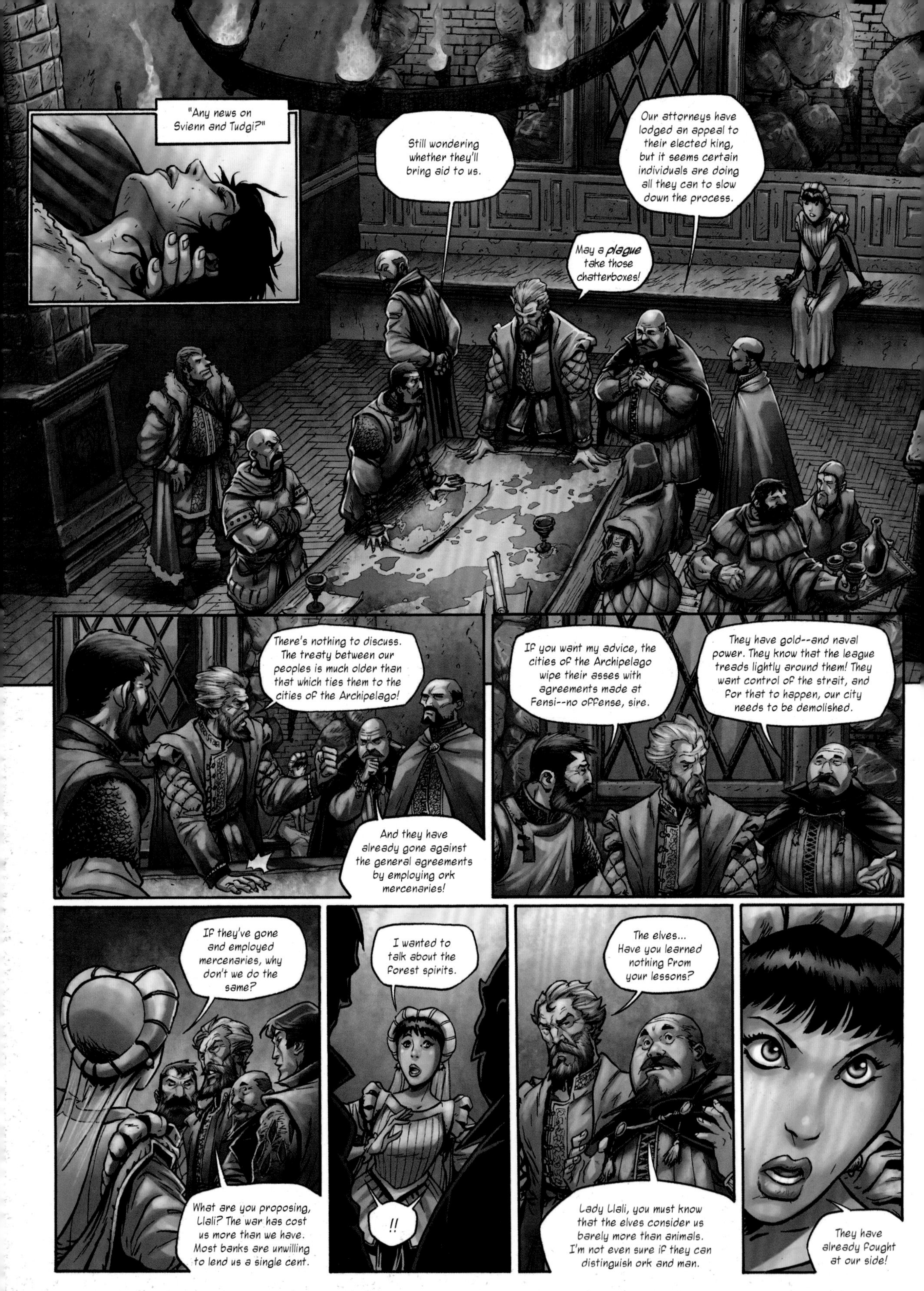

"Any news on Svienn and Tudgi?"
Still wondering whether they'll bring aid to us.
Our attorneys have lodged an appeal to their elected king, but it seems certain individuals are doing all they can to slow down the process.
May a *plague* take those chatterboxes!
There's nothing to discuss. The treaty between our peoples is much older than that which ties them to the cities of the Archipelago!
And they have already gone against the general agreements by employing ork mercenaries!
If you want my advice, the cities of the Archipelago wipe their asses with agreements made at Fensi--no offense, sire.
They have gold--and naval power. They know that the league treads lightly around them! They want control of the strait, and for that to happen, our city needs to be demolished.
If they've gone and employed mercenaries, why don't we do the same?
What are you proposing, Llali? The war has cost us more than we have. Most banks are unwilling to lend us a single cent.
I wanted to talk about the forest spirits.
!!
The elves... Have you learned nothing from your lessons?
Lady Llali, you must know that the elves consider us barely more than animals. I'm not even sure if they can distinguish ork and man.
They have already fought at our side!

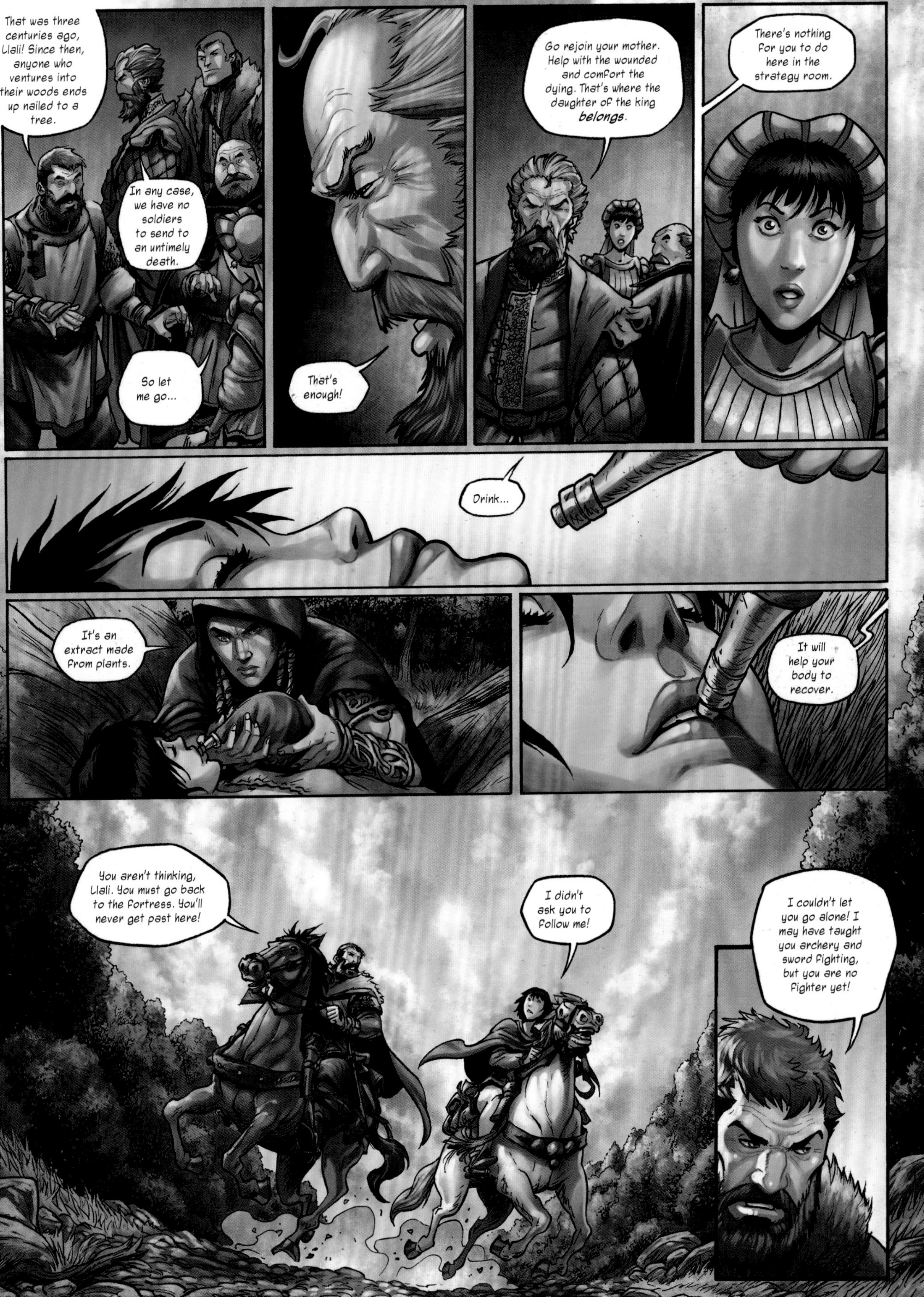
That was three centuries ago, Llali! Since then, anyone who ventures into their woods ends up nailed to a tree.
In any case, we have no soldiers to send to an untimely death.
So let me go...
That's enough!
Go rejoin your mother. Help with the wounded and comfort the dying. That's where the daughter of the king *belongs*.
There's nothing for you to do here in the strategy room.
Drink...
It's an extract made from plants.
It will help your body to recover.
You aren't thinking, Llali. You must go back to the fortress. You'll never get past here!
I didn't ask you to follow me!
I couldn't let you go alone! I may have taught you archery and sword fighting, but you are no fighter yet!

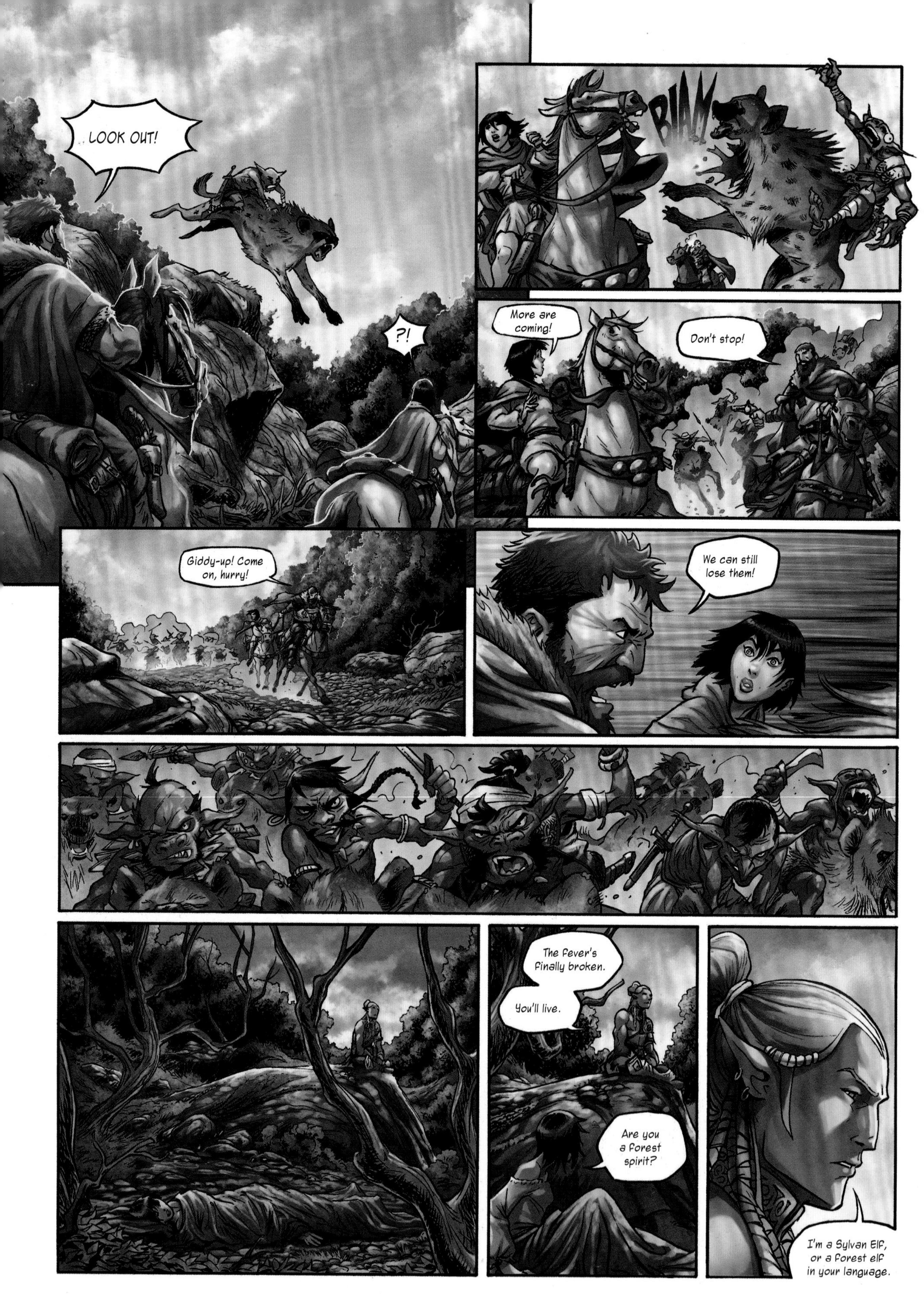
..LOOK OUT!
?!
BIAM
More are coming!
Don't stop!
Giddy-up! Come on, hurry!
We can still lose them!
The fever's finally broken.
You'll live.
Are you a forest spirit?
I'm a Sylvan Elf, or a forest elf in your language.

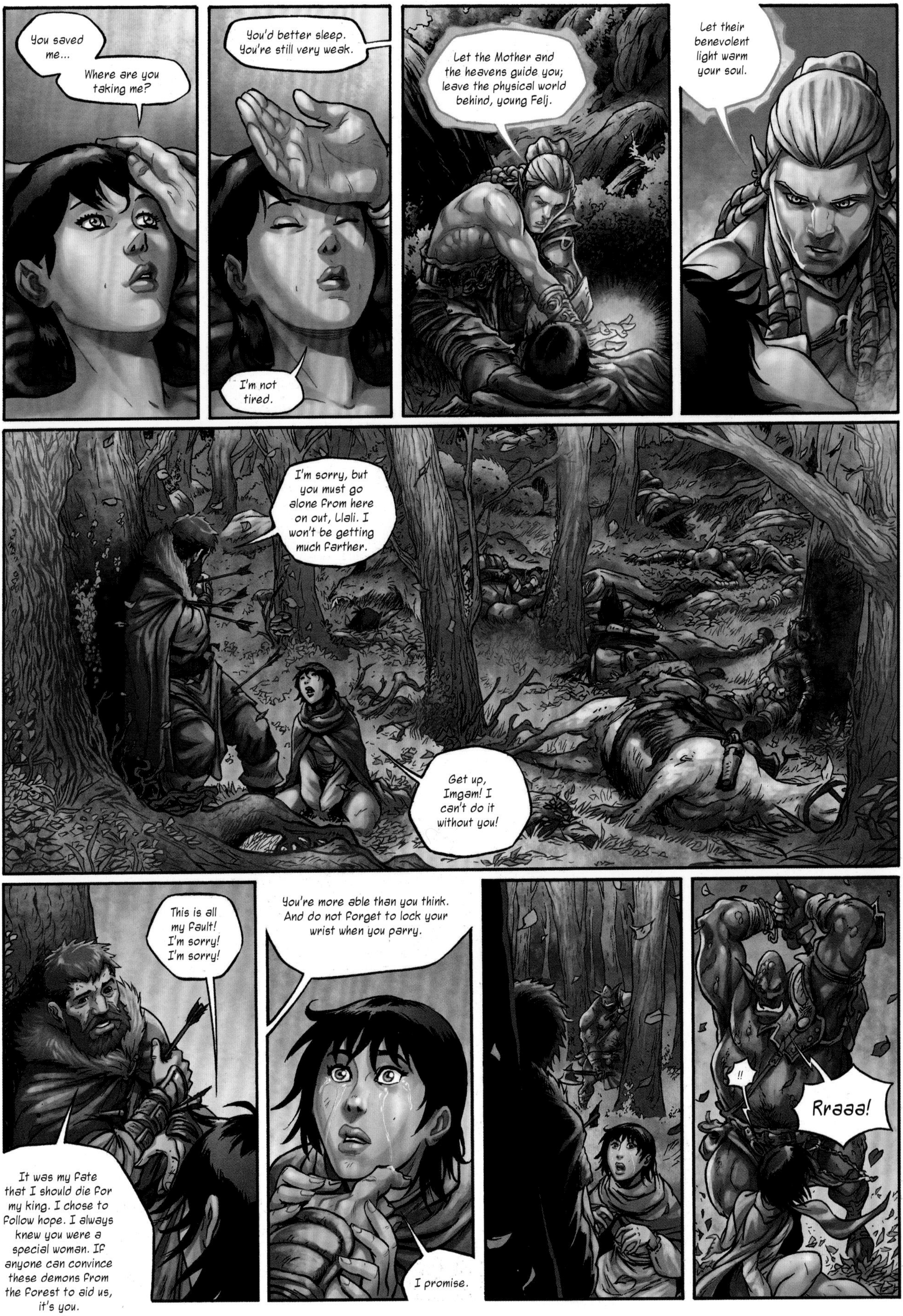
You saved me...
Where are you taking me?
You'd better sleep. You're still very weak.
I'm not tired.
Let the Mother and the heavens guide you; leave the physical world behind, young Felj.
Let their benevolent light warm your soul.
I'm sorry, but you must go alone from here on out, Llali. I won't be getting much farther.
Get up, Imgam! I can't do it without you!
This is all my fault! I'm sorry! I'm sorry!
It was my fate that I should die for my king. I chose to follow hope. I always knew you were a special woman. If anyone can convince these demons from the forest to aid us, it's you.
You're more able than you think. And do not forget to lock your wrist when you parry.
I promise.
!!
Rraaa!

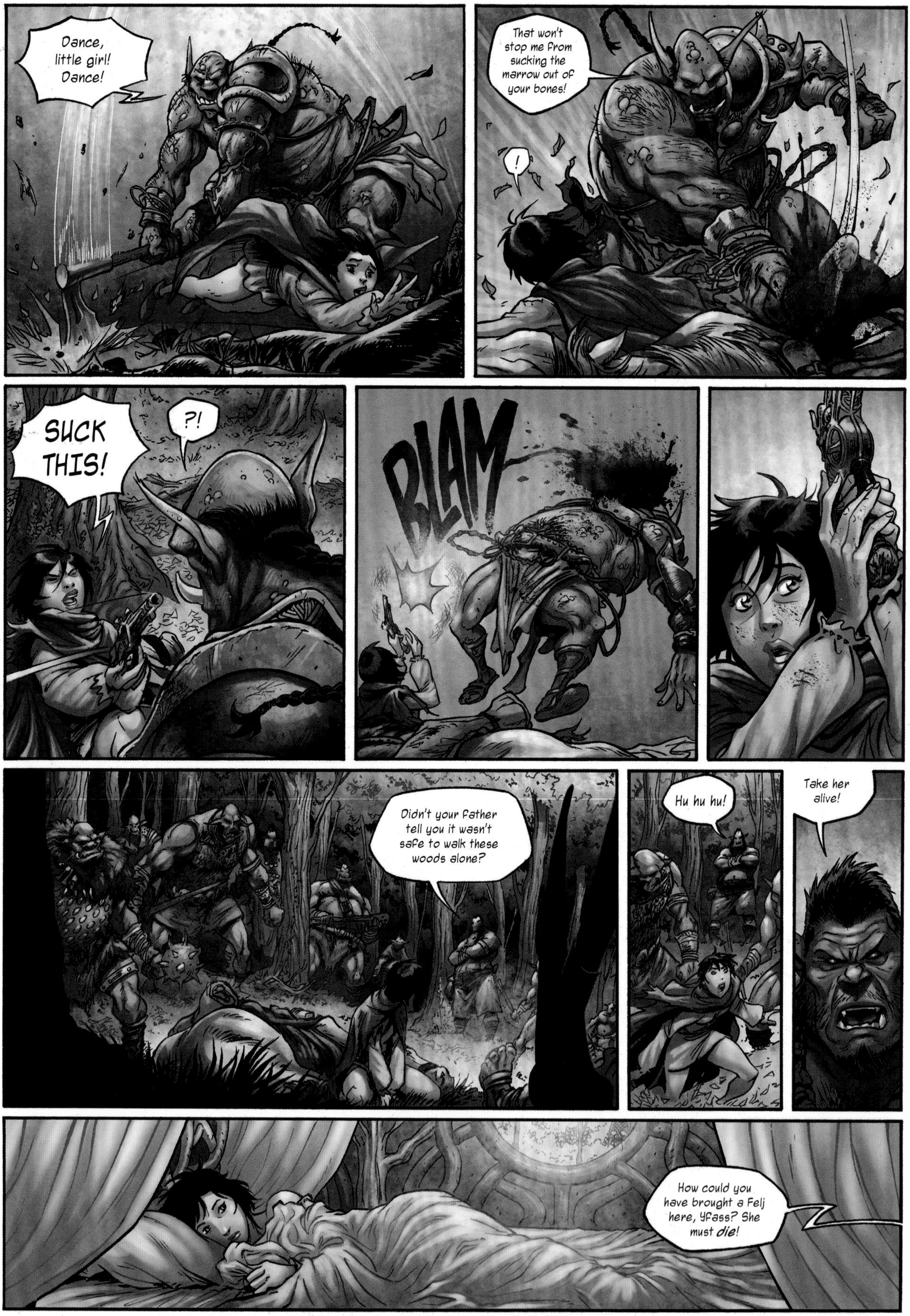
Dance, little girl! Dance!
That won't stop me from sucking the marrow out of your bones!
!
SUCK THIS!
?!
BLAM
Didn't your father tell you it wasn't safe to walk these woods alone?
Hu hu hu!
Take her alive!
How could you have brought a Felj here, Yfass? She must *die*!

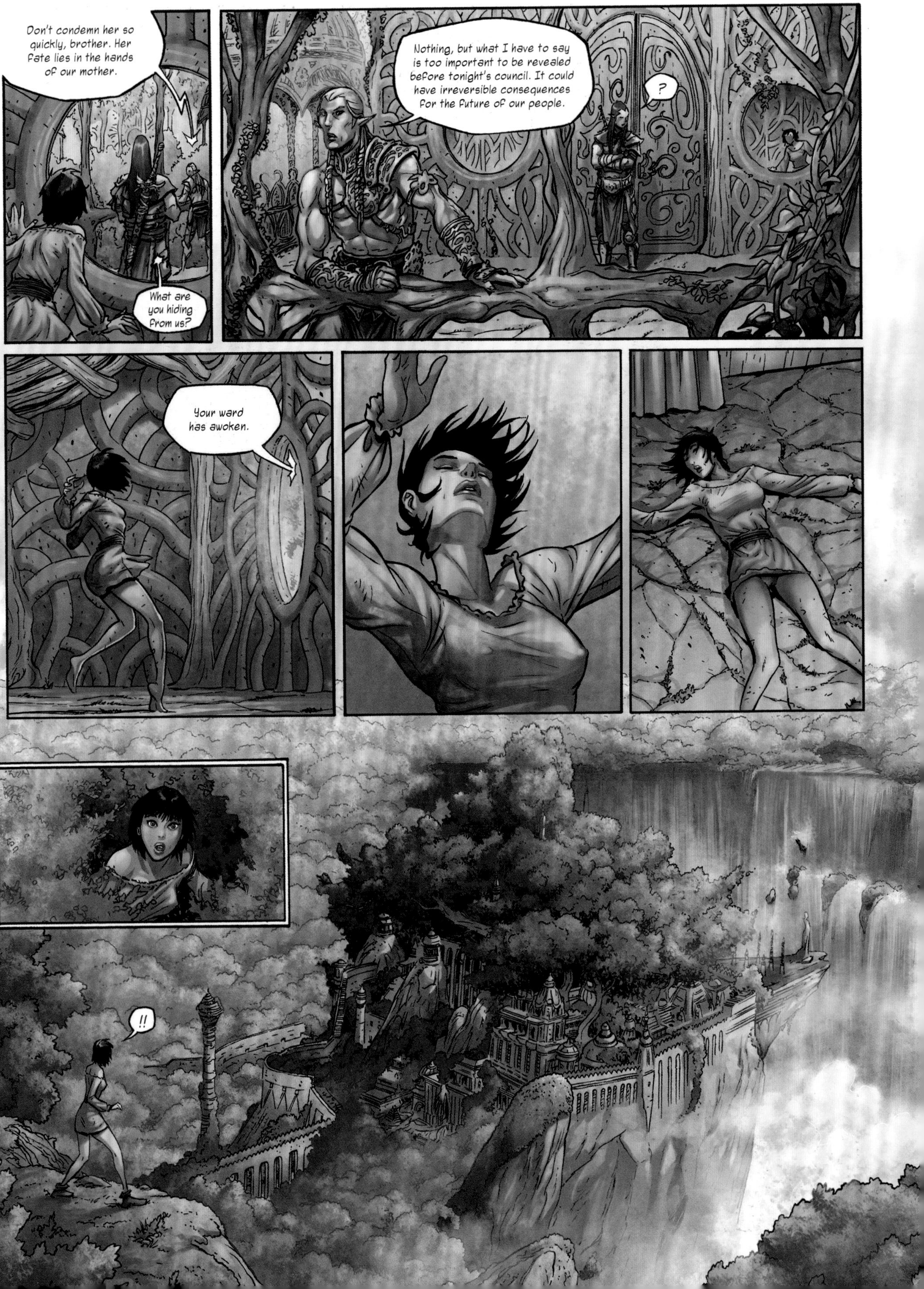

Don't condemn her so quickly, brother. Her fate lies in the hands of our mother.
What are you hiding from us?
Nothing, but what I have to say is too important to be revealed before tonight's council. It could have irreversible consequences for the future of our people.
?
Your ward has awoken.
!!

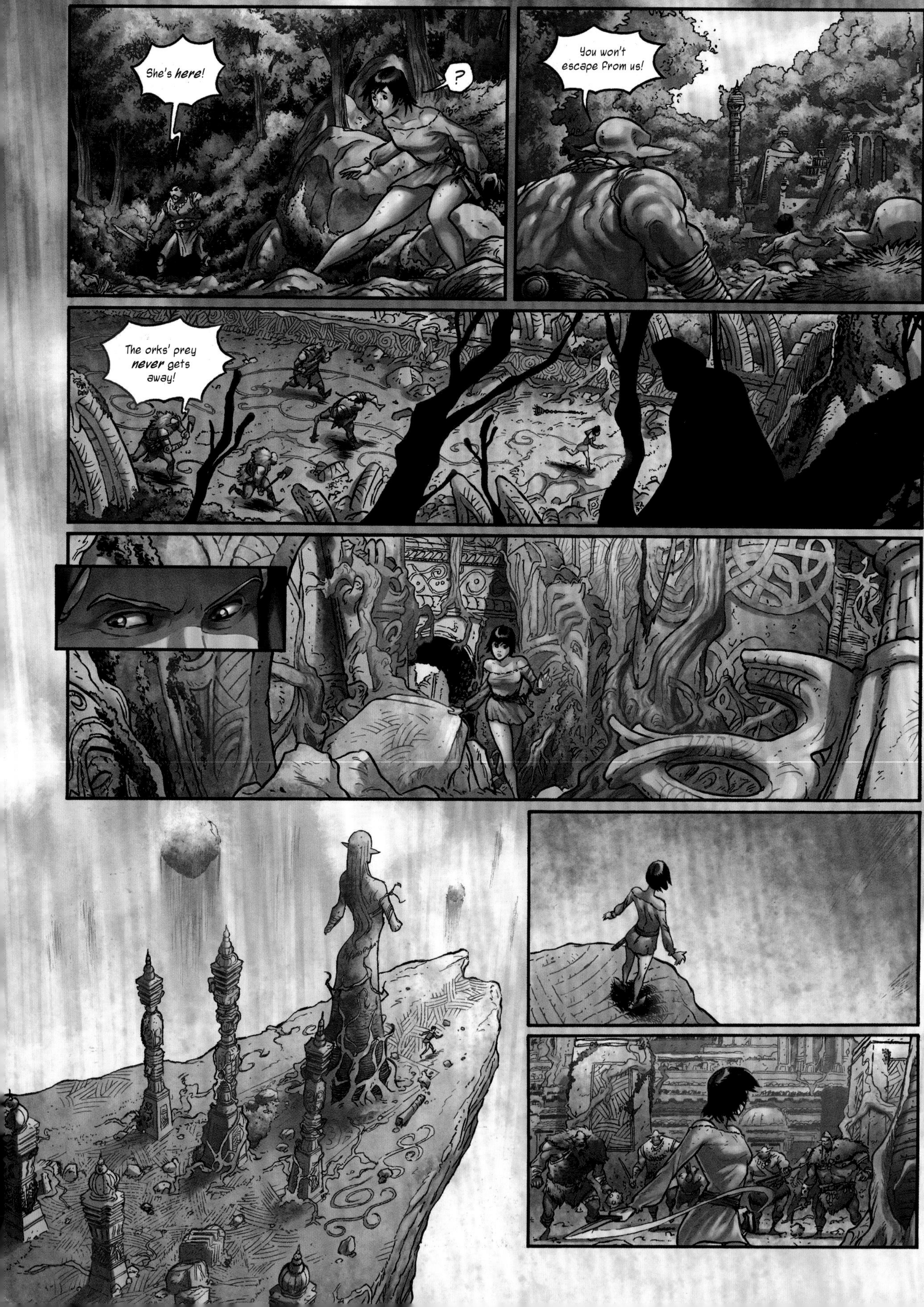
She's **here**!
?
You won't escape from us!
The orks' prey **never** gets away!

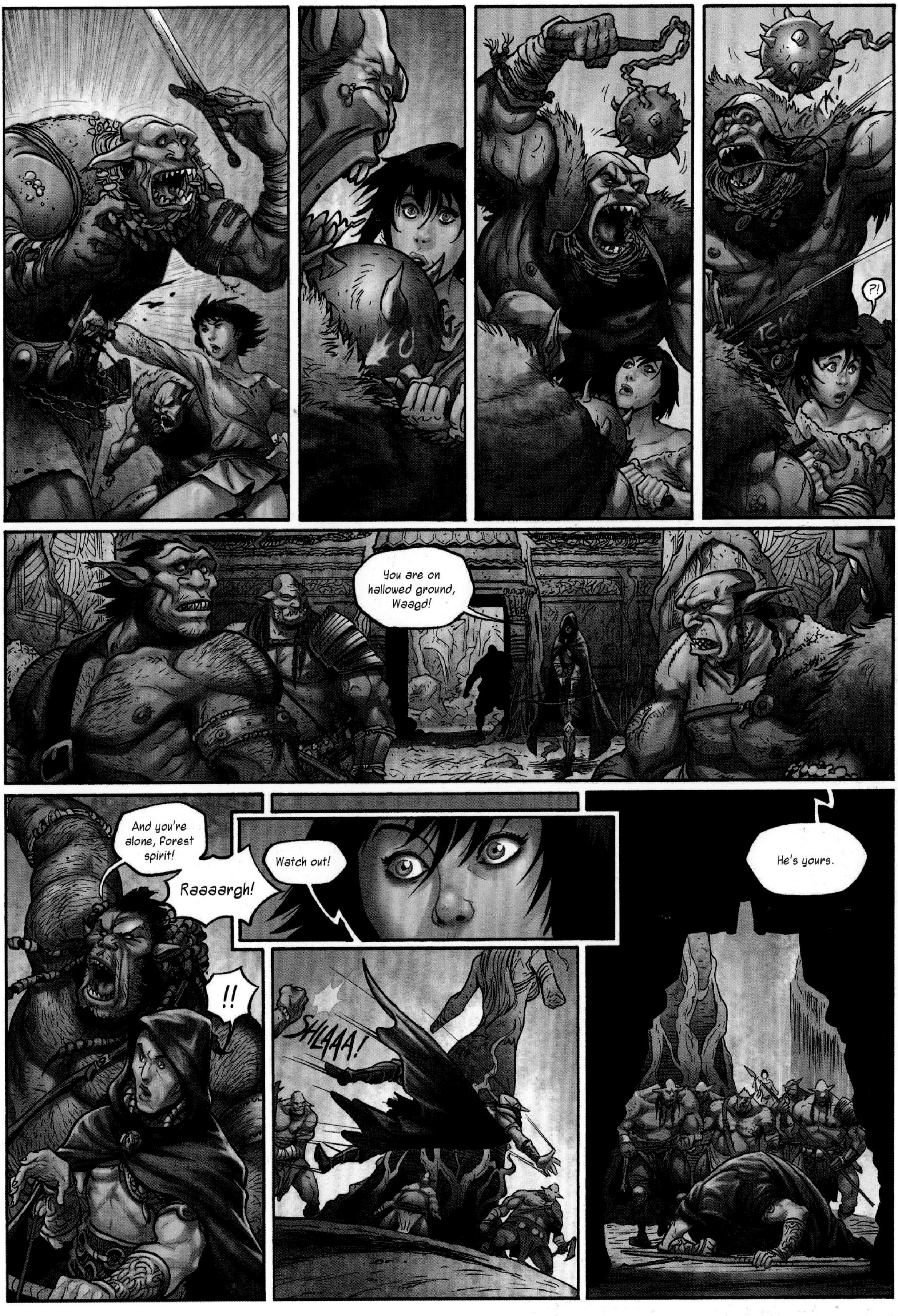

?!
You are on hallowed ground, Waagd!
And you're alone, forest spirit!
Raaaargh!
Watch out!
!!
SHLAAA!
He's yours.

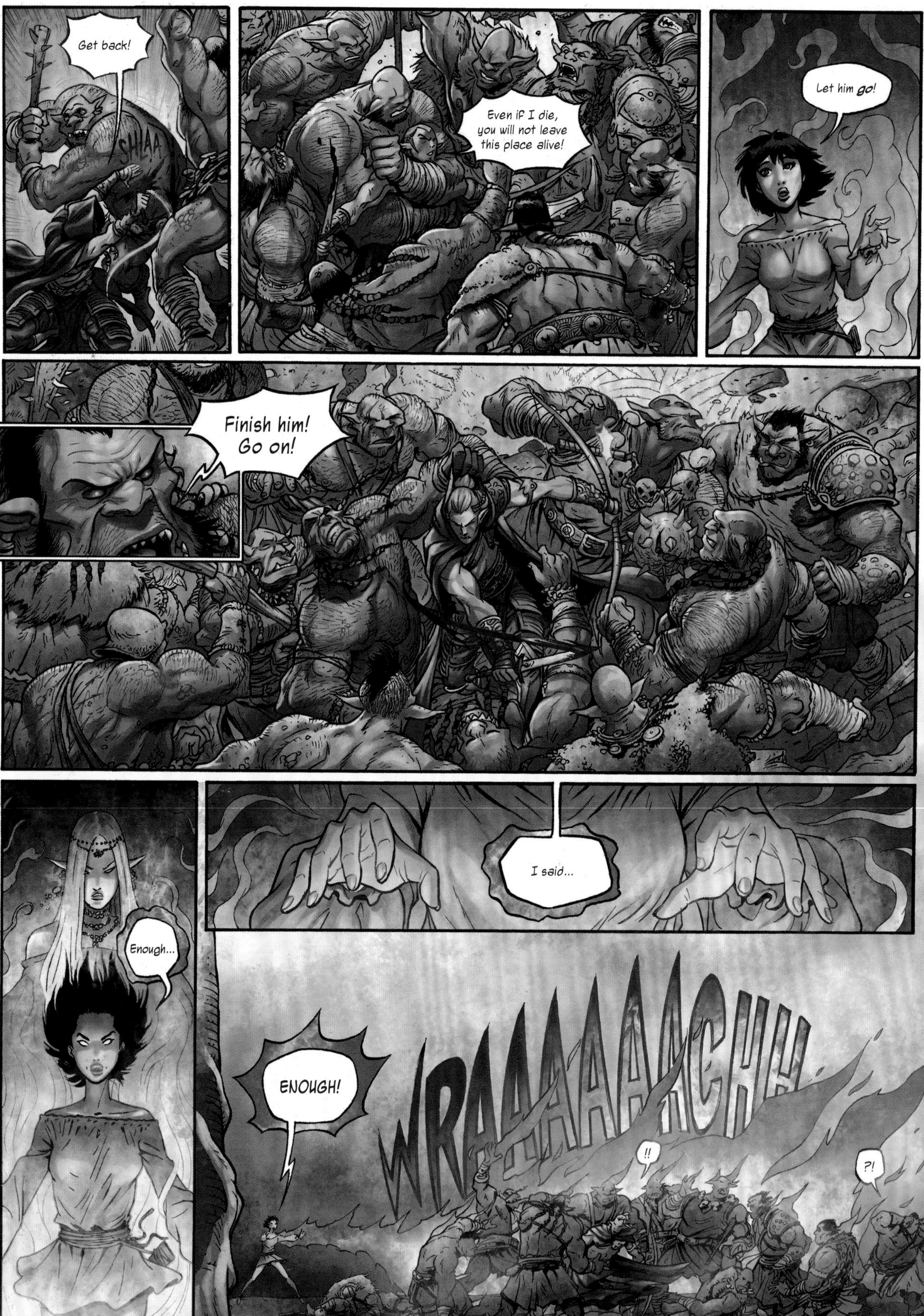
Get back!
SHIAA
Even if I die, you will not leave this place alive!
Let him go!
Finish him! Go on!
I said...
Enough...
ENOUGH!
WRAAAAAACHH
!!
?!

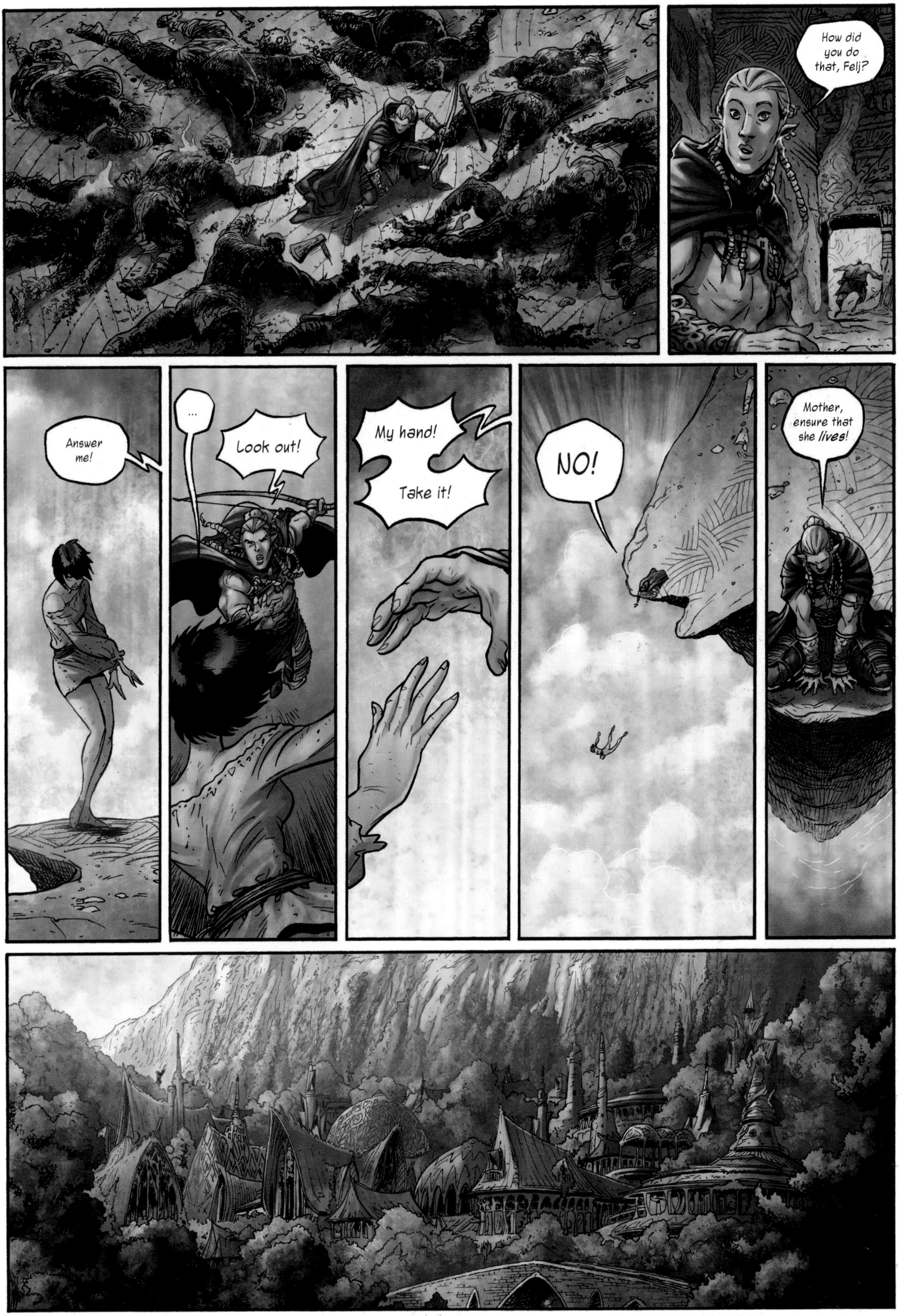
How did you do that, Felj?
Answer me!
...
Look out!
My hand!
Take it!
NO!
Mother, ensure that she *lives*!

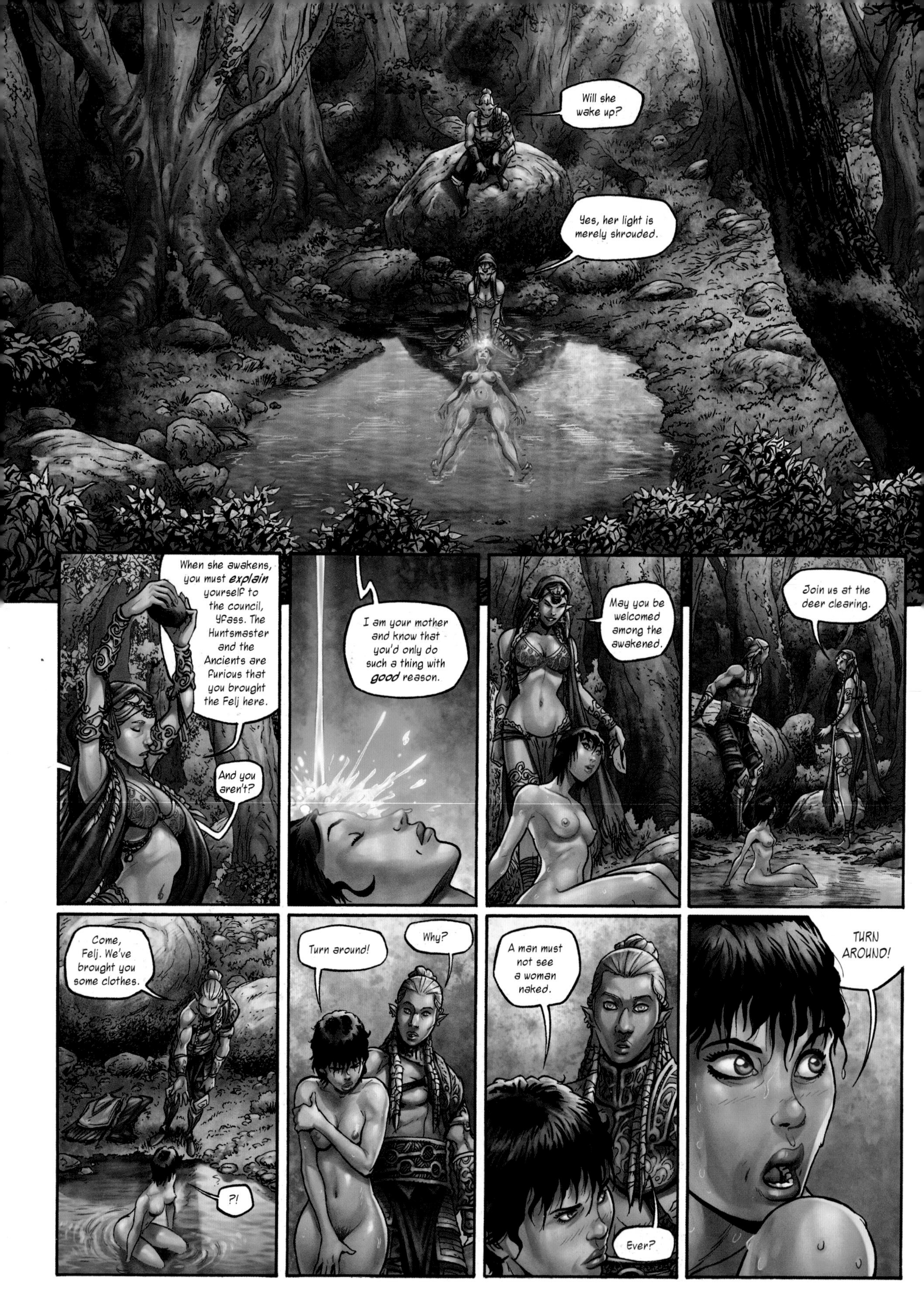

Will she wake up?
Yes, her light is merely shrouded.
When she awakens, you must *explain* yourself to the council, Yfass. The Huntsmaster and the Ancients are furious that you brought the Felj here.
And you aren't?
I am your mother and know that you'd only do such a thing with *good* reason.
May you be welcomed among the awakened.
Join us at the deer clearing.
Come, Felj. We've brought you some clothes.
?!
Turn around!
Why?
A man must not see a woman naked.
Ever?
TURN AROUND!

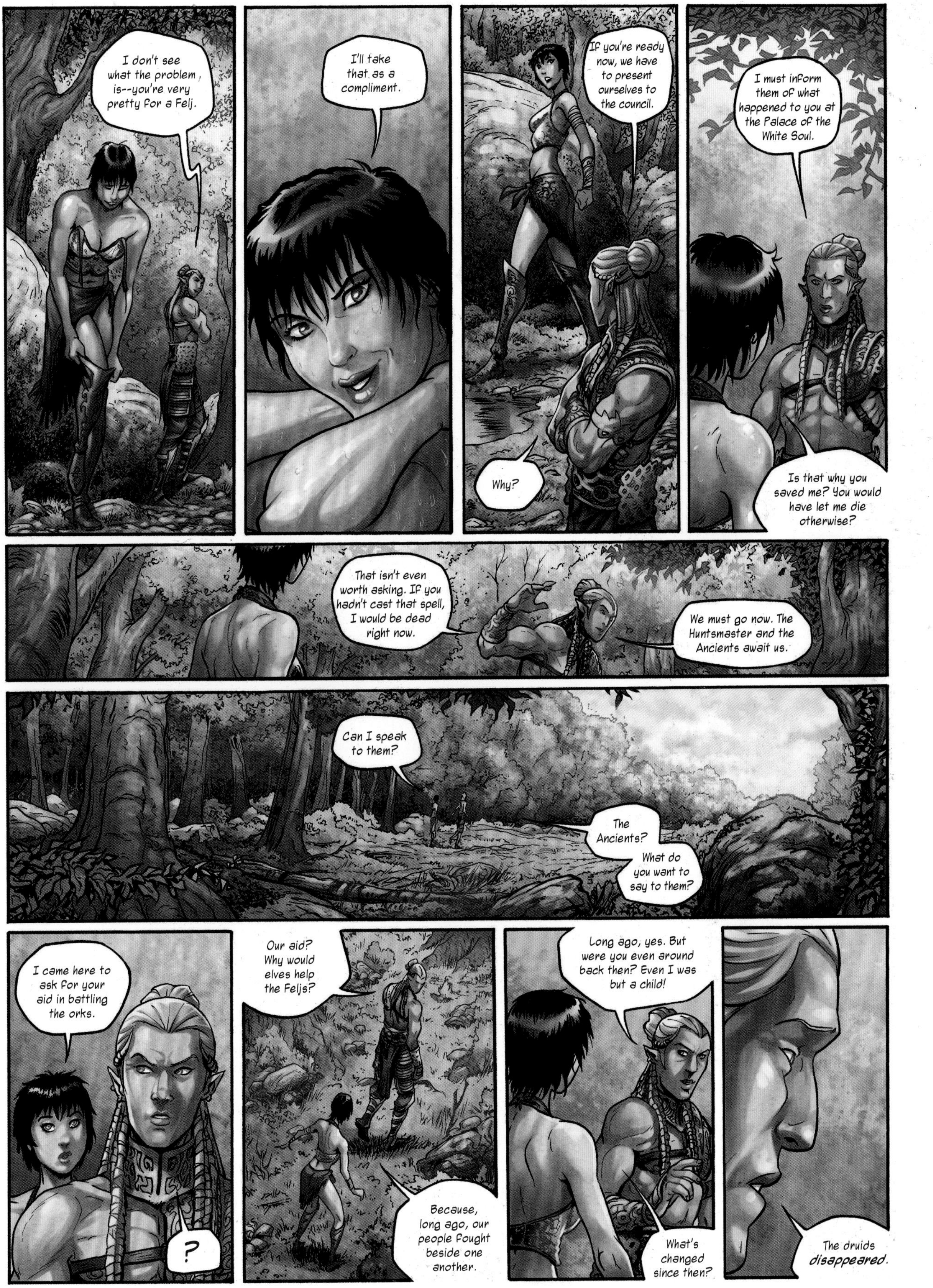
I don't see what the problem is--you're very pretty for a Felj.
I'll take that as a compliment.
If you're ready now, we have to present ourselves to the council.
Why?
I must inform them of what happened to you at the Palace of the White Soul.
Is that why you saved me? You would have let me die otherwise?
That isn't even worth asking. If you hadn't cast that spell, I would be dead right now.
We must go now. The Huntsmaster and the Ancients await us.
Can I speak to them?
The Ancients?
What do you want to say to them?
I came here to ask for your aid in battling the orks.
?
Our aid? Why would elves help the Feljs?
Because, long ago, our people fought beside one another.
Long ago, yes. But were you even around back then? Even I was but a child!
What's changed since then?
The druids *disappeared*.

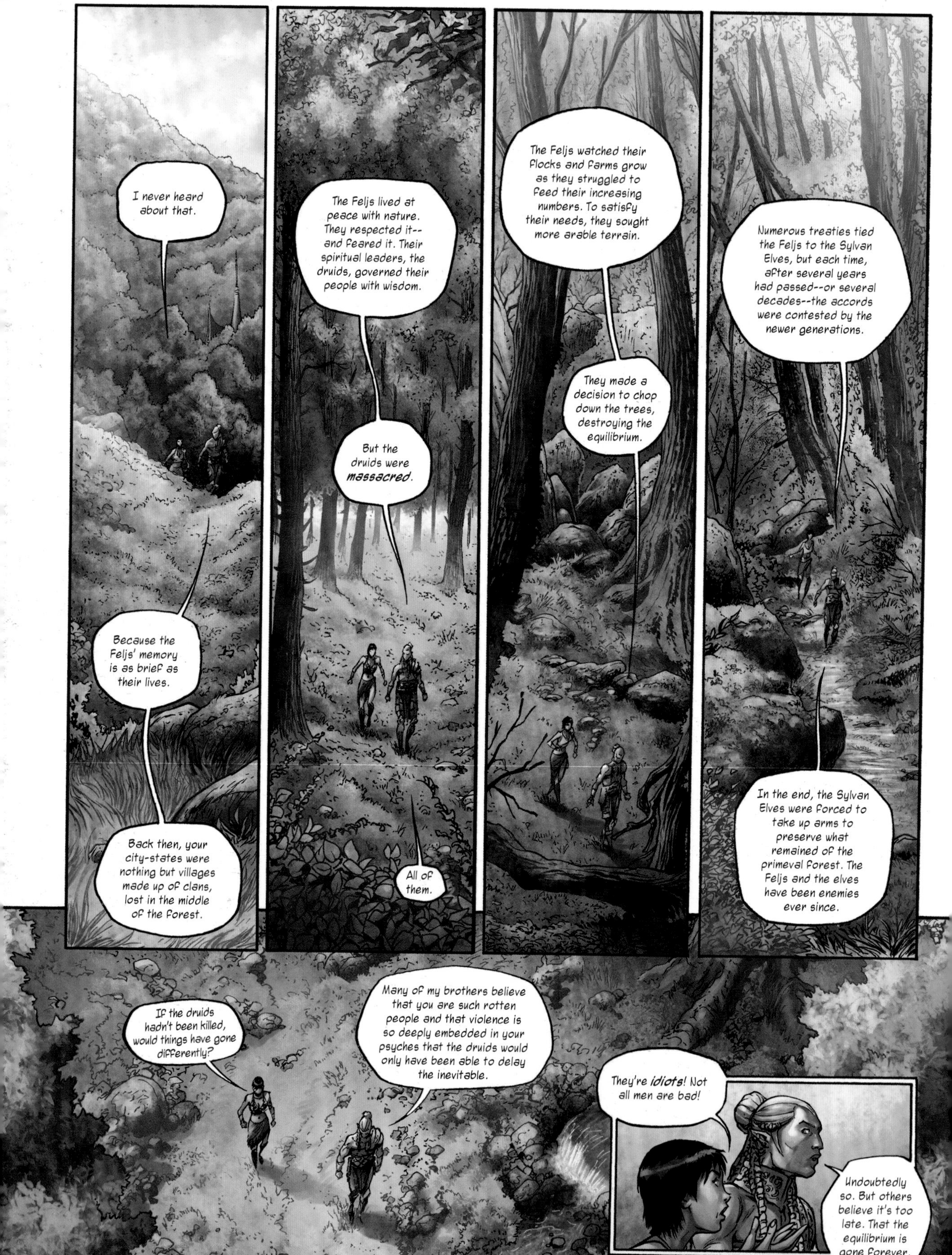
I never heard about that.
Because the Feljs' memory is as brief as their lives.
Back then, your city-states were nothing but villages made up of clans, lost in the middle of the forest.
The Feljs lived at peace with nature. They respected it--and feared it. Their spiritual leaders, the druids, governed their people with wisdom.
But the druids were *massacred*.
All of them.
The Feljs watched their flocks and farms grow as they struggled to feed their increasing numbers. To satisfy their needs, they sought more arable terrain.
They made a decision to chop down the trees, destroying the equilibrium.
Numerous treaties tied the Feljs to the Sylvan Elves, but each time, after several years had passed--or several decades--the accords were contested by the newer generations.
In the end, the Sylvan Elves were forced to take up arms to preserve what remained of the primeval forest. The Feljs and the elves have been enemies ever since.
If the druids hadn't been killed, would things have gone differently?
Many of my brothers believe that you are such rotten people and that violence is so deeply embedded in your psyches that the druids would only have been able to delay the inevitable.
They're *idiots*! Not all men are bad!
Undoubtedly so. But others believe it's too late. That the equilibrium is gone forever.

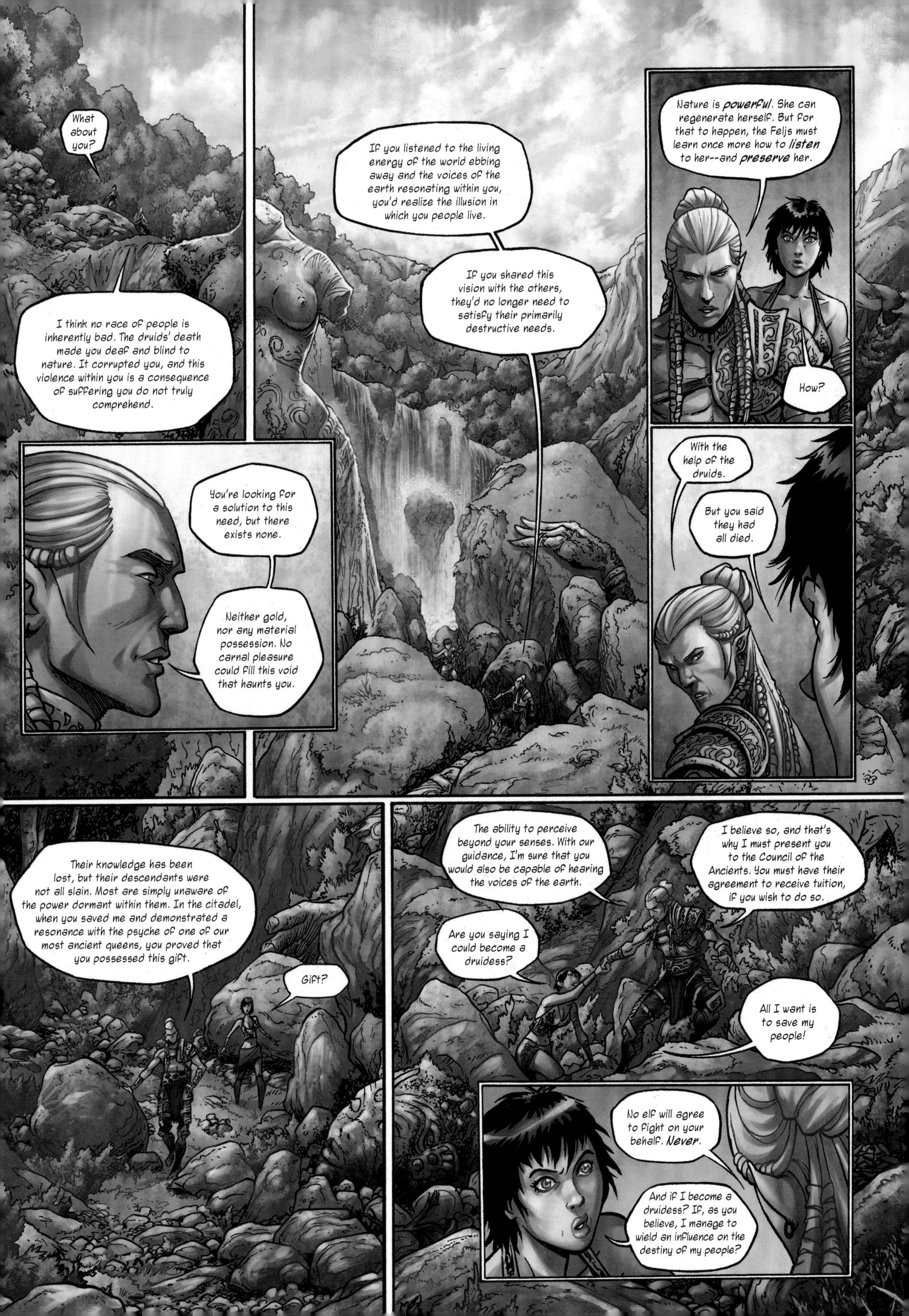
What about you?
I think no race of people is inherently bad. The druids' death made you deaf and blind to nature. It corrupted you, and this violence within you is a consequence of suffering you do not truly comprehend.
You're looking for a solution to this need, but there exists none.
Neither gold, nor any material possession. No carnal pleasure could fill this void that haunts you.
If you listened to the living energy of the world ebbing away and the voices of the earth resonating within you, you'd realize the illusion in which you people live.
If you shared this vision with the others, they'd no longer need to satisfy their primarily destructive needs.
Nature is powerful. She can regenerate herself. But for that to happen, the Feljs must learn once more how to listen to her--and preserve her.
How?
With the help of the druids.
But you said they had all died.
Their knowledge has been lost, but their descendants were not all slain. Most are simply unaware of the power dormant within them. In the citadel, when you saved me and demonstrated a resonance with the psyche of one of our most ancient queens, you proved that you possessed this gift.
Gift?
The ability to perceive beyond your senses. With our guidance, I'm sure that you would also be capable of hearing the voices of the earth.
Are you saying I could become a druidess?
I believe so, and that's why I must present you to the Council of the Ancients. You must have their agreement to receive tuition, if you wish to do so.
All I want is to save my people!
No elf will agree to fight on your behalf. Never.
And if I become a druidess? If, as you believe, I manage to wield an influence on the destiny of my people?

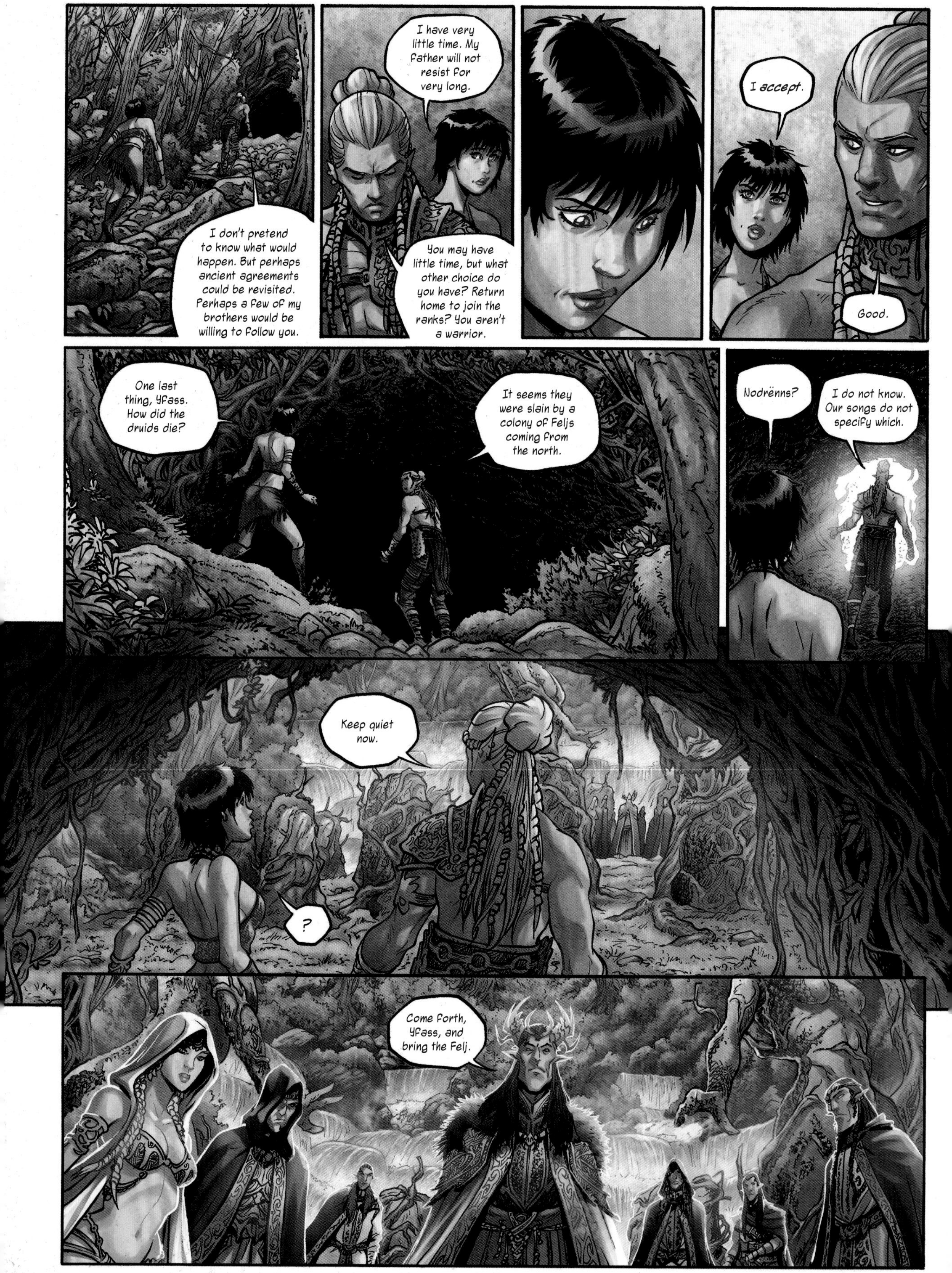

I don't pretend to know what would happen. But perhaps ancient agreements could be revisited. Perhaps a few of my brothers would be willing to follow you.
I have very little time. My father will not resist for very long.
You may have little time, but what other choice do you have? Return home to join the ranks? You aren't a warrior.
I accept.
Good.
One last thing, Yfass. How did the druids die?
It seems they were slain by a colony of Feljs coming from the north.
Nodrënns?
I do not know. Our songs do not specify which.
Keep quiet now.
?
Come forth, Yfass, and bring the Felj.

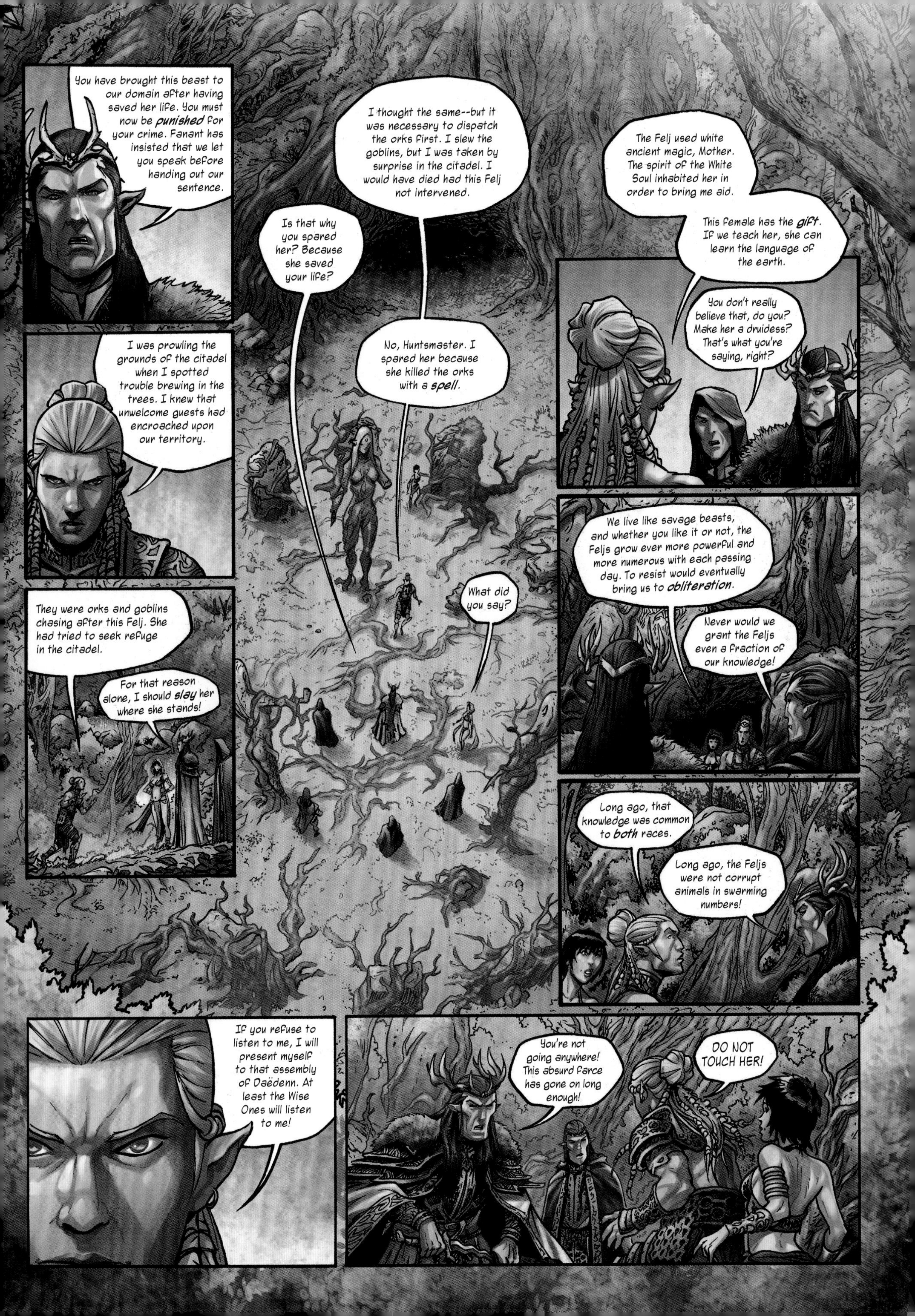

You have brought this beast to our domain after having saved her life. You must now be *punished* for your crime. Fanant has insisted that we let you speak before handing out our sentence.
I was prowling the grounds of the citadel when I spotted trouble brewing in the trees. I knew that unwelcome guests had encroached upon our territory.
They were orks and goblins chasing after this Felj. She had tried to seek refuge in the citadel.
For that reason alone, I should *slay* her where she stands!
Is that why you spared her? Because she saved your life?
I thought the same--but it was necessary to dispatch the orks first. I slew the goblins, but I was taken by surprise in the citadel. I would have died had this Felj not intervened.
No, Huntsmaster. I spared her because she killed the orks with a *spell*.
What did you say?
The Felj used white ancient magic, Mother. The spirit of the White Soul inhabited her in order to bring me aid.
This female has the *gift*. If we teach her, she can learn the language of the earth.
You don't really believe that, do you? Make her a druidess? That's what you're saying, right?
We live like savage beasts, and whether you like it or not, the Feljs grow ever more powerful and more numerous with each passing day. To resist would eventually bring us to *obliteration*.
Never would we grant the Feljs even a fraction of our knowledge!
Long ago, that knowledge was common to *both* races.
Long ago, the Feljs were not corrupt animals in swarming numbers!
If you refuse to listen to me, I will present myself to that assembly of Daëdenn. At least the Wise Ones will listen to me!
You're not going anywhere! This absurd farce has gone on long enough!
DO NOT TOUCH HER!

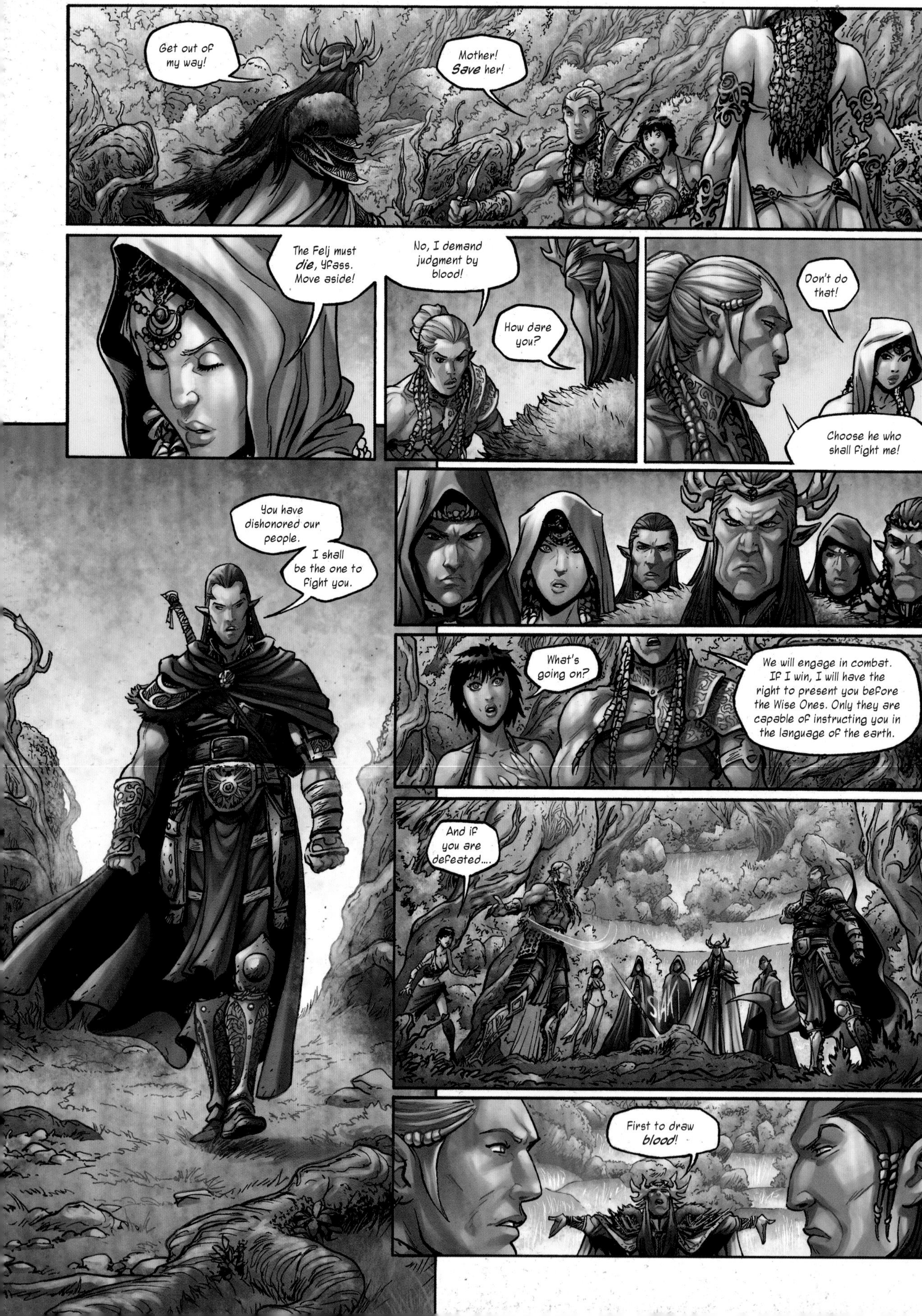

Get out of my way!
Mother! *Save* her!
The Felj must *die*, Yfass. Move aside!
No, I demand judgment by blood!
How dare you?
Don't do that!
Choose he who shall fight me!
You have dishonored our people.
I shall be the one to fight you.
What's going on?
We will engage in combat. If I win, I will have the right to present you before the Wise Ones. Only they are capable of instructing you in the language of the earth.
And if you are defeated....
First to draw *blood*!

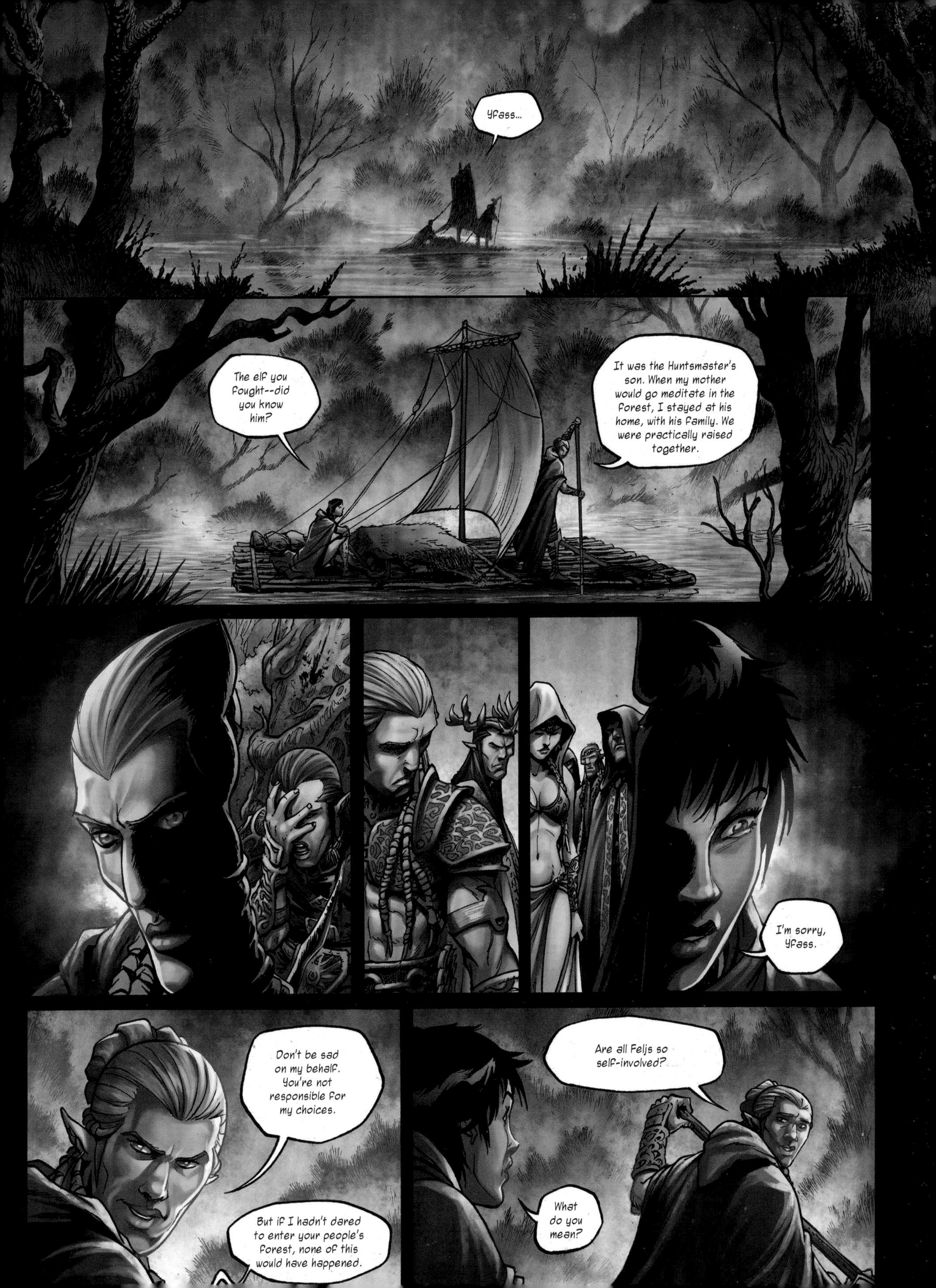
Yfass...
The elf you fought--did you know him?
It was the Huntsmaster's son. When my mother would go meditate in the forest, I stayed at his home, with his family. We were practically raised together.
I'm sorry, Yfass.
Don't be sad on my behalf. You're not responsible for my choices.
But if I hadn't dared to enter your people's forest, none of this would have happened.
Are all Feljs so self-involved?
What do you mean?

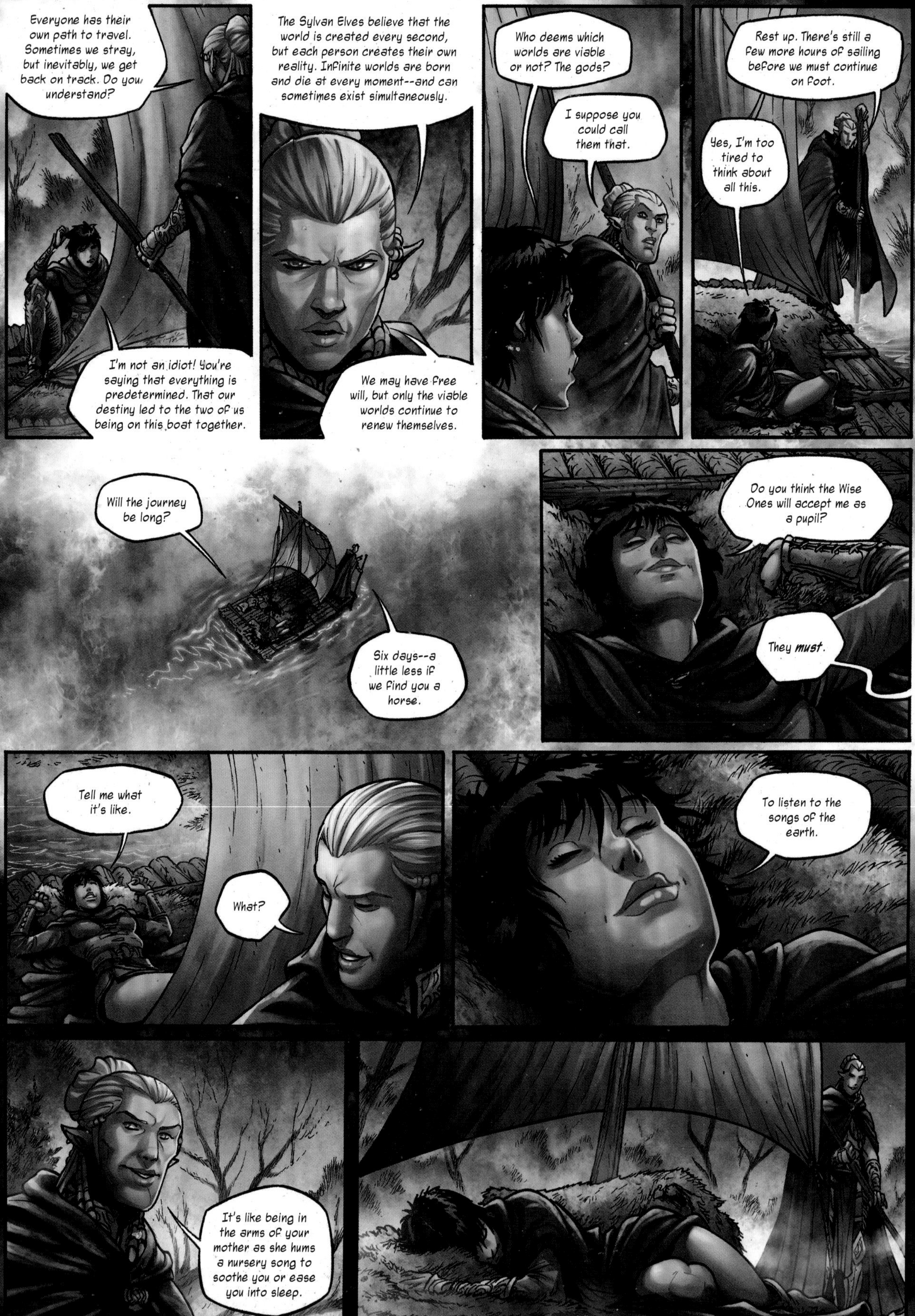
Everyone has their own path to travel. Sometimes we stray, but inevitably, we get back on track. Do you understand?
I'm not an idiot! You're saying that everything is predetermined. That our destiny led to the two of us being on this boat together.
The Sylvan Elves believe that the world is created every second, but each person creates their own reality. Infinite worlds are born and die at every moment--and can sometimes exist simultaneously.
We may have free will, but only the viable worlds continue to renew themselves.
Who deems which worlds are viable or not? The gods?
I suppose you could call them that.
Rest up. There's still a few more hours of sailing before we must continue on foot.
Yes, I'm too tired to think about all this.
Will the journey be long?
Six days--a little less if we find you a horse.
Do you think the Wise Ones will accept me as a pupil?
They *must*.
Tell me what it's like.
What?
To listen to the songs of the earth.
It's like being in the arms of your mother as she hums a nursery song to soothe you or ease you into sleep.

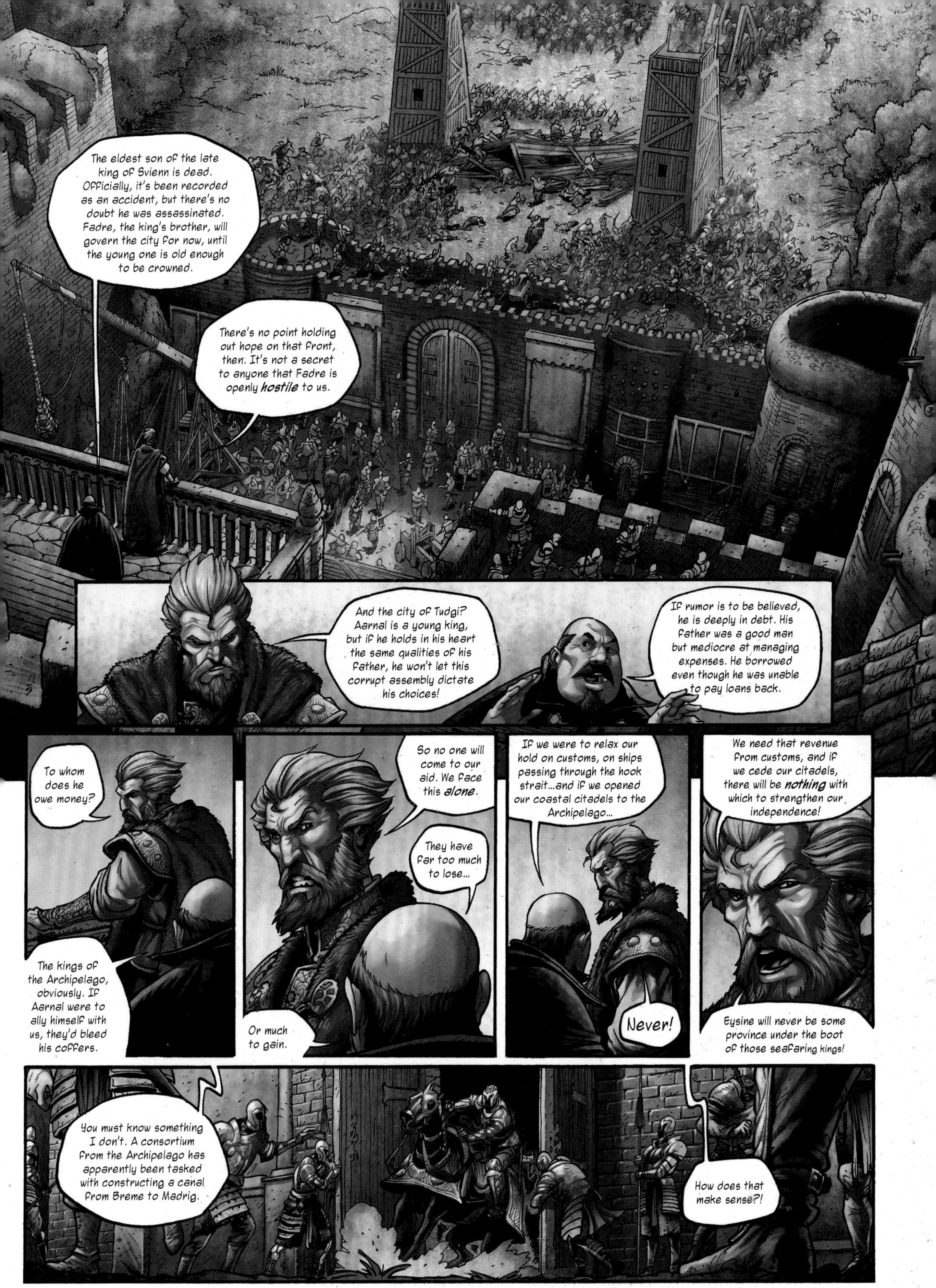

The eldest son of the late king of Svienn is dead. Officially, it's been recorded as an accident, but there's no doubt he was assassinated. Fadre, the king's brother, will govern the city for now, until the young one is old enough to be crowned.
There's no point holding out hope on that front, then. It's not a secret to anyone that Fadre is openly *hostile* to us.
And the city of Tudgi? Aarnal is a young king, but if he holds in his heart the same qualities of his father, he won't let this corrupt assembly dictate his choices!
If rumor is to be believed, he is deeply in debt. His father was a good man but mediocre at managing expenses. He borrowed even though he was unable to pay loans back.
To whom does he owe money?
The kings of the Archipelago, obviously. If Aarnal were to ally himself with us, they'd bleed his coffers.
So no one will come to our aid. We face this *alone*.
They have far too much to lose...
Or much to gain.
If we were to relax our hold on customs, on ships passing through the hook strait...and if we opened our coastal citadels to the Archipelago...
Never!
We need that revenue from customs, and if we cede our citadels, there will be *nothing* with which to strengthen our independence!
Eysine will never be some province under the boot of those seafaring kings!
You must know something I don't. A consortium from the Archipelago has apparently been tasked with constructing a canal from Breme to Madrig.
How does that make sense?!

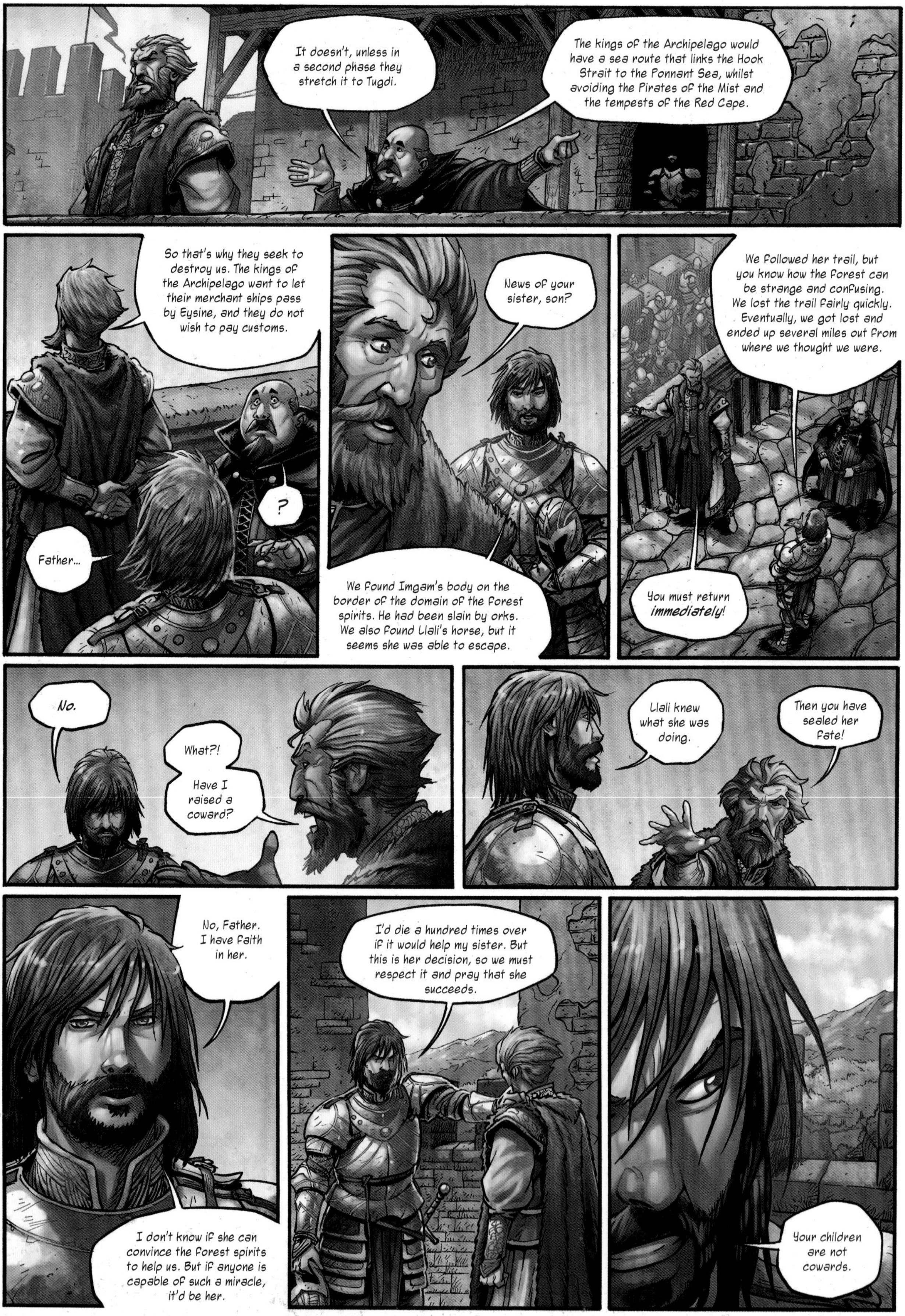

It doesn't, unless in a second phase they stretch it to Tugdi.
The kings of the Archipelago would have a sea route that links the Hook Strait to the Ponnant Sea, whilst avoiding the Pirates of the Mist and the tempests of the Red Cape.
So that's why they seek to destroy us. The kings of the Archipelago want to let their merchant ships pass by Eysine, and they do not wish to pay customs.
?
Father...
News of your sister, son?
We found Imgam's body on the border of the domain of the Forest spirits. He had been slain by orks. We also found Llali's horse, but it seems she was able to escape.
We followed her trail, but you know how the forest can be strange and confusing. We lost the trail fairly quickly. Eventually, we got lost and ended up several miles out from where we thought we were.
You must return *immediately*!
No.
What?!
Have I raised a coward?
Llali knew what she was doing.
Then you have sealed her fate!
No, Father. I have faith in her.
I don't know if she can convince the forest spirits to help us. But if anyone is capable of such a miracle, it'd be her.
I'd die a hundred times over if it would help my sister. But this is her decision, so we must respect it and pray that she succeeds.
Your children are not cowards.

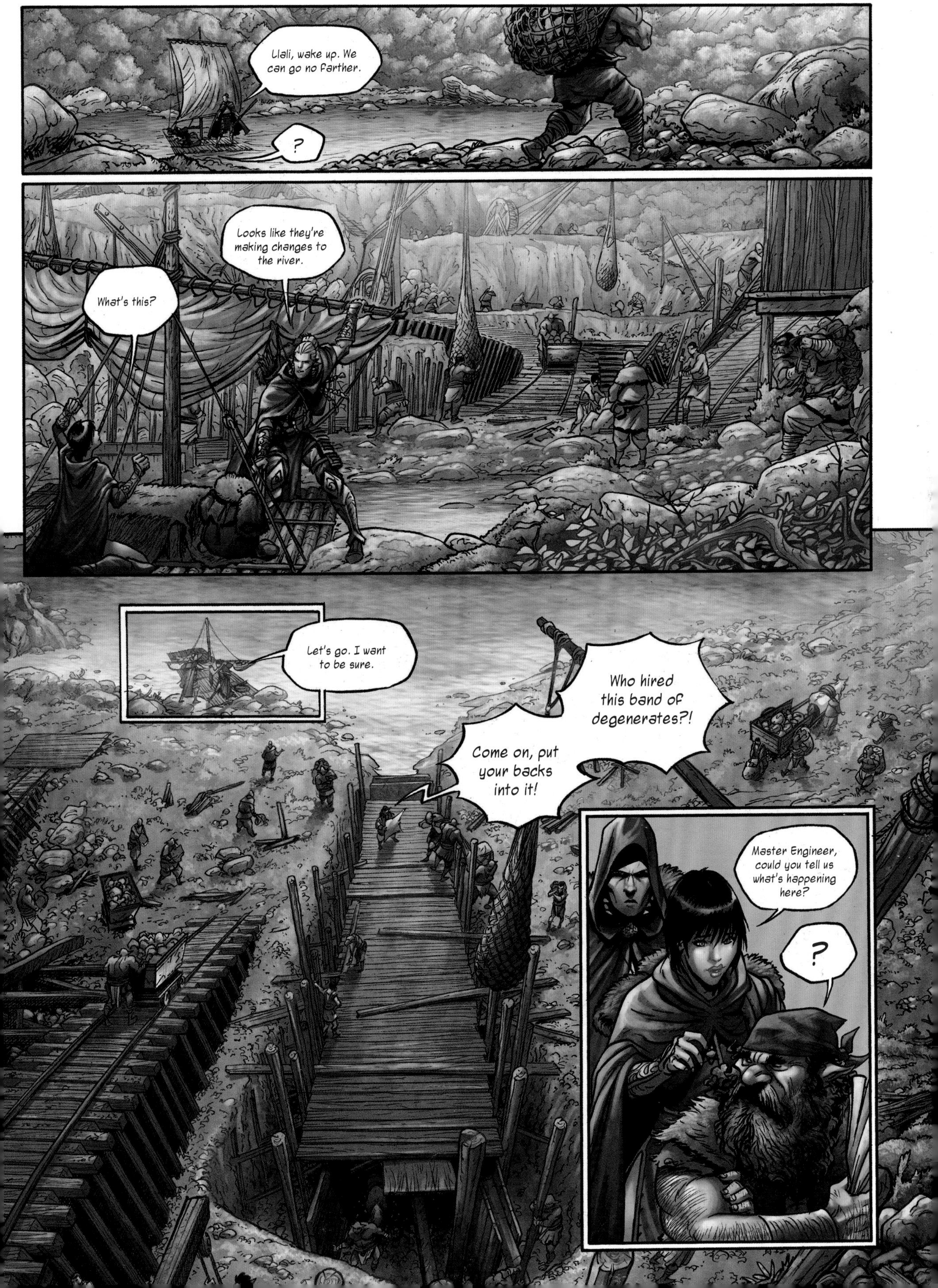
Llali, wake up. We can go no farther.
?
What's this?
Looks like they're making changes to the river.
Let's go. I want to be sure.
Who hired this band of degenerates?!
Come on, put your backs into it!
Master Engineer, could you tell us what's happening here?
?

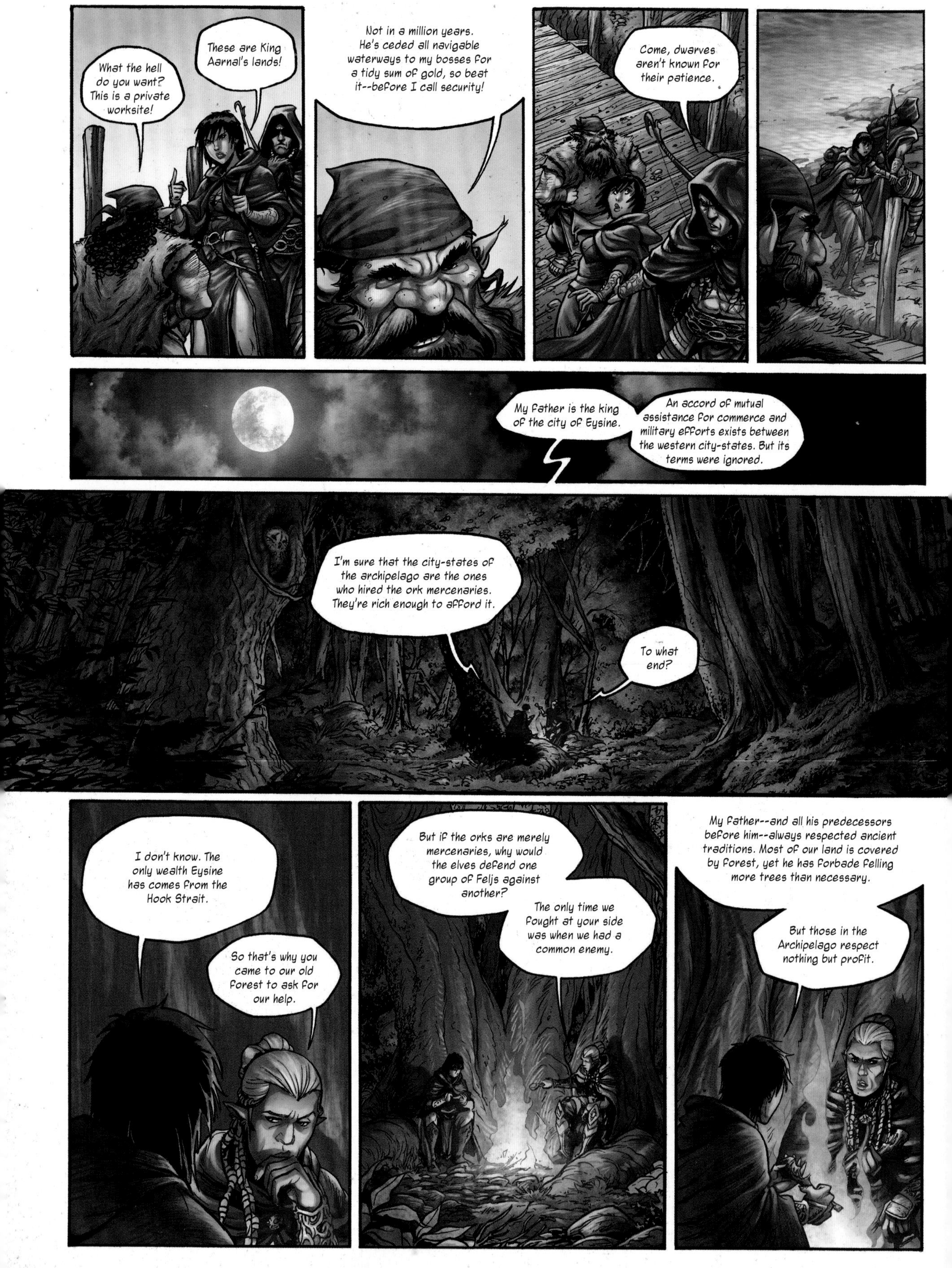

What the hell do you want? This is a private worksite!
These are King Aarnal's lands!
Not in a million years. He's ceded all navigable waterways to my bosses for a tidy sum of gold, so beat it--before I call security!
Come, dwarves aren't known for their patience.
My father is the king of the city of Eysine.
An accord of mutual assistance for commerce and military efforts exists between the western city-states. But its terms were ignored.
I'm sure that the city-states of the archipelago are the ones who hired the ork mercenaries. They're rich enough to afford it.
To what end?
I don't know. The only wealth Eysine has comes from the Hook Strait.
So that's why you came to our old forest to ask for our help.
But if the orks are merely mercenaries, why would the elves defend one group of Feljs against another?
The only time we fought at your side was when we had a common enemy.
My father--and all his predecessors before him--always respected ancient traditions. Most of our land is covered by forest, yet he has forbade felling more trees than necessary.
But those in the Archipelago respect nothing but profit.

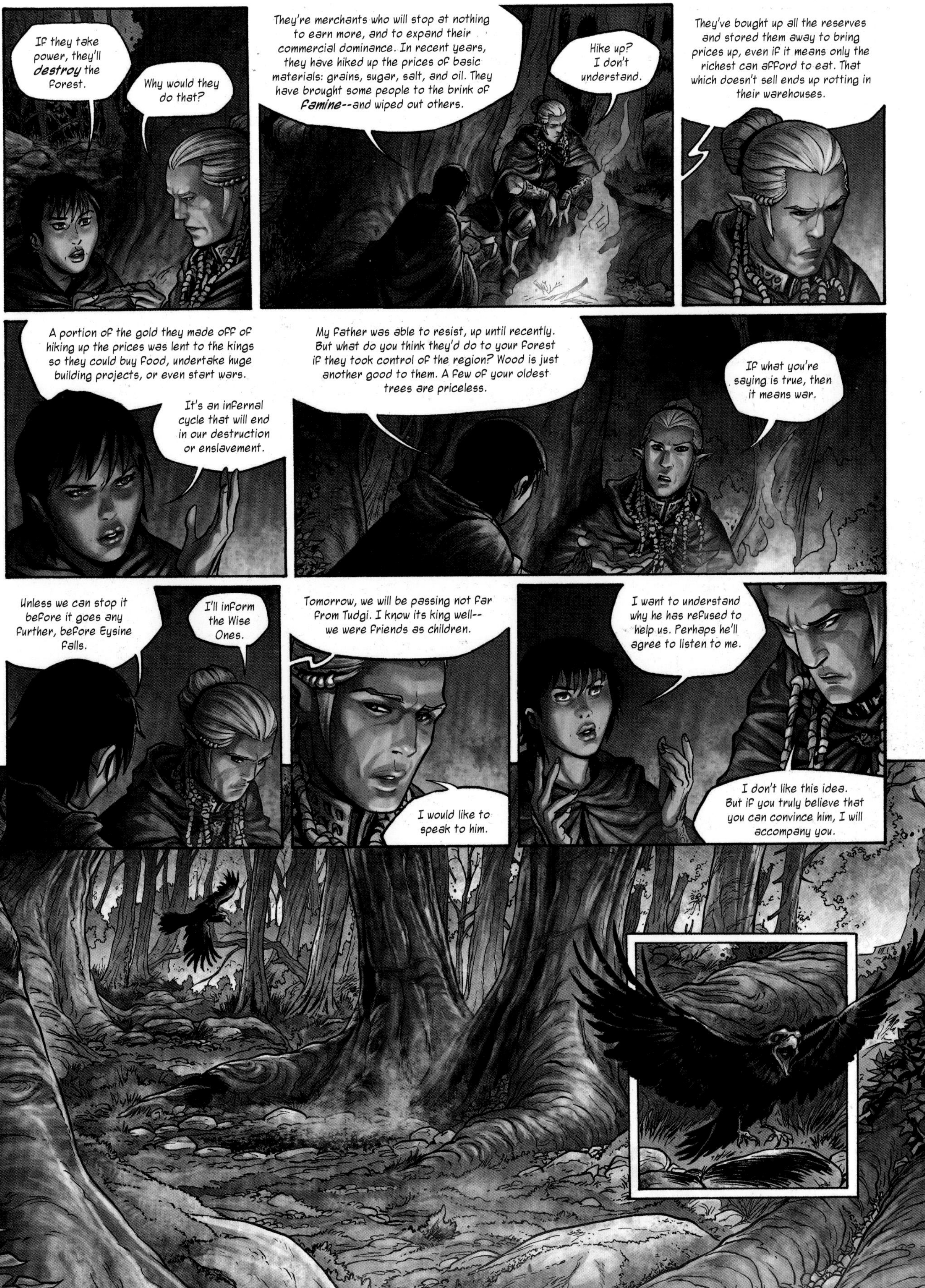

If they take power, they'll destroy the forest.
Why would they do that?
They're merchants who will stop at nothing to earn more, and to expand their commercial dominance. In recent years, they have hiked up the prices of basic materials: grains, sugar, salt, and oil. They have brought some people to the brink of famine--and wiped out others.
Hike up? I don't understand.
They've bought up all the reserves and stored them away to bring prices up, even if it means only the richest can afford to eat. That which doesn't sell ends up rotting in their warehouses.
A portion of the gold they made off of hiking up the prices was lent to the kings so they could buy food, undertake huge building projects, or even start wars.
It's an infernal cycle that will end in our destruction or enslavement.
My father was able to resist, up until recently. But what do you think they'd do to your forest if they took control of the region? Wood is just another good to them. A few of your oldest trees are priceless.
If what you're saying is true, then it means war.
Unless we can stop it before it goes any further, before Eysine falls.
I'll inform the Wise Ones.
Tomorrow, we will be passing not far from Tudgi. I know its king well-- we were friends as children.
I would like to speak to him.
I want to understand why he has refused to help us. Perhaps he'll agree to listen to me.
I don't like this idea. But if you truly believe that you can convince him, I will accompany you.

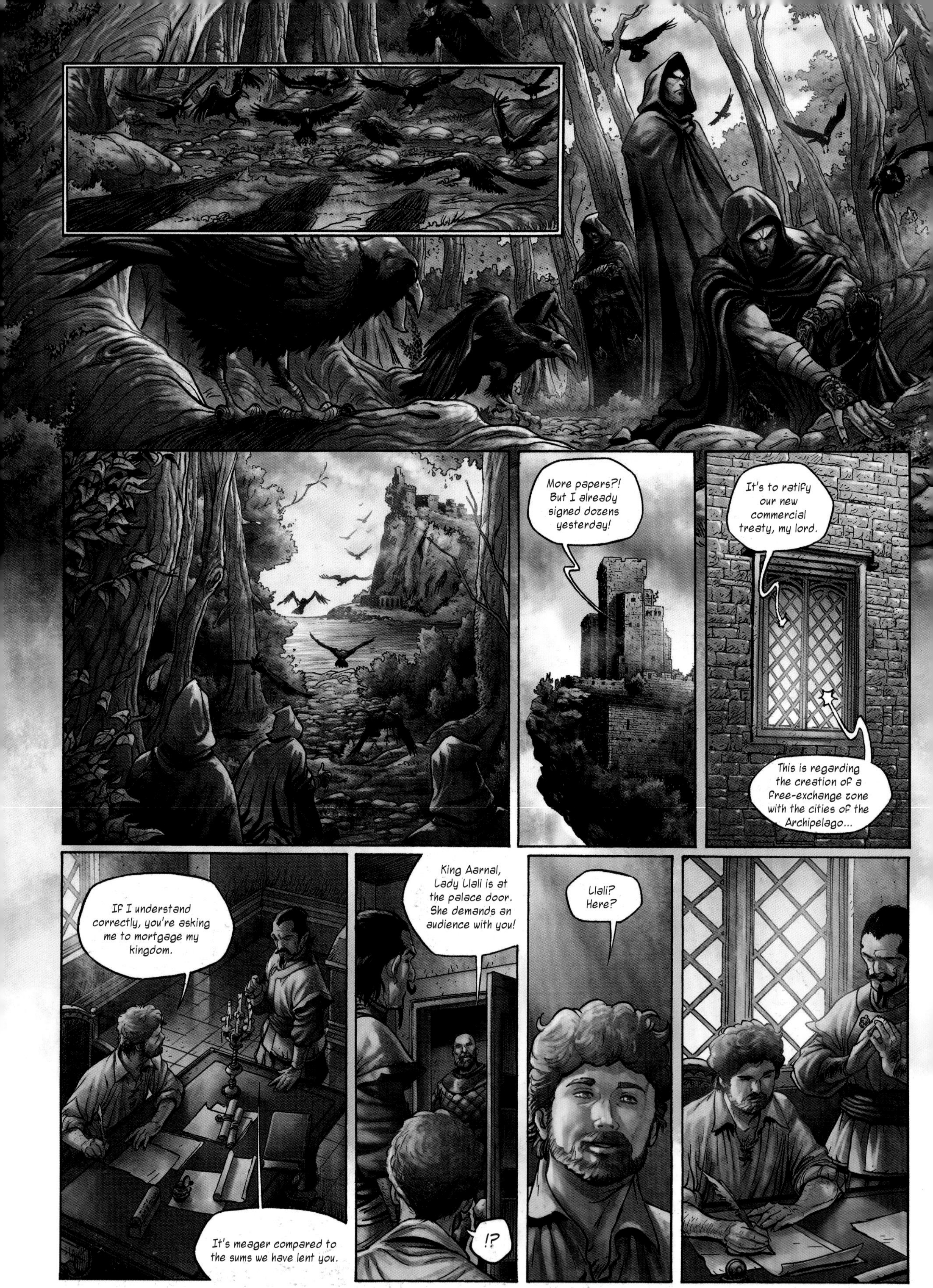
More papers?! But I already signed dozens yesterday!
It's to ratify our new commercial treaty, my lord.
This is regarding the creation of a free-exchange zone with the cities of the Archipelago...
If I understand correctly, you're asking me to mortgage my kingdom.
It's meager compared to the sums we have lent you.
King Aarnal, Lady Llali is at the palace door. She demands an audience with you!
!?
Llali? Here?

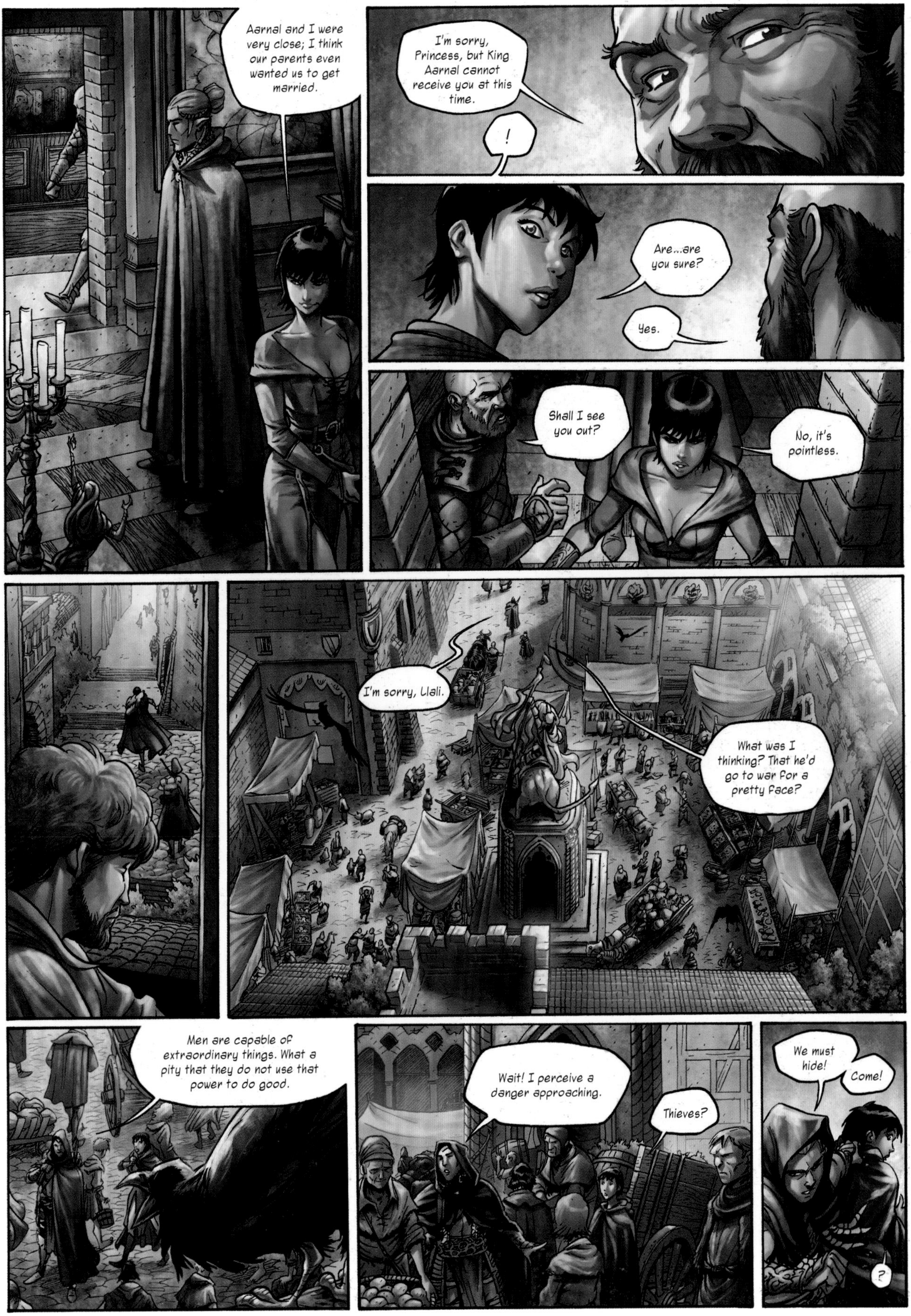
Aarnal and I were very close; I think our parents even wanted us to get married.
I'm sorry, Princess, but King Aarnal cannot receive you at this time.
!
Are...are you sure?
Yes.
Shall I see you out?
No, it's pointless.
I'm sorry, Ulali.
What was I thinking? That he'd go to war for a pretty face?
Men are capable of extraordinary things. What a pity that they do not use that power to do good.
Wait! I perceive a danger approaching.
Thieves?
We must hide!
Come!
?

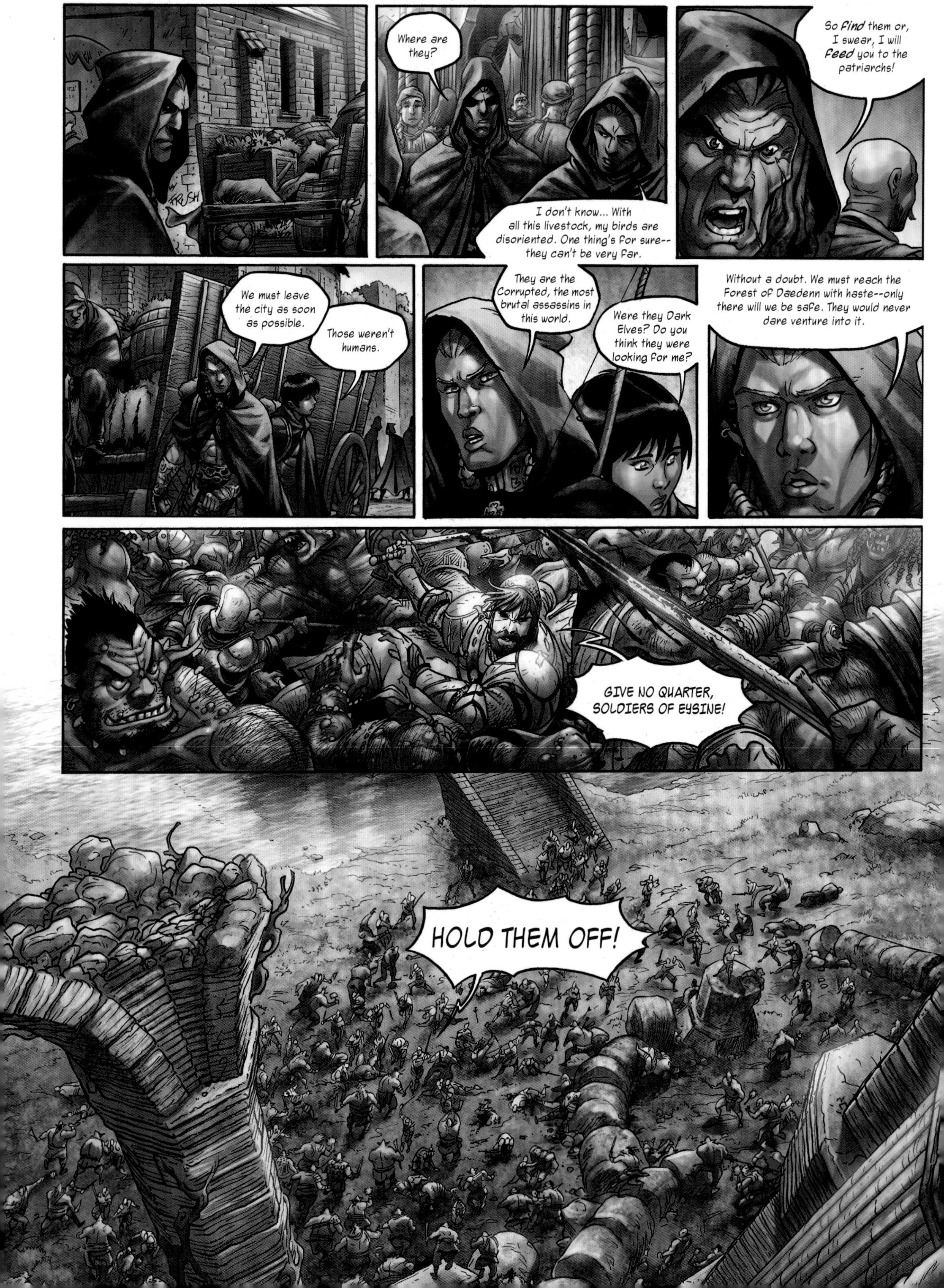
FRUSH
Where are they?
I don't know... With all this livestock, my birds are disoriented. One thing's for sure--they can't be very far.
So find them or, I swear, I will feed you to the patriarchs!
We must leave the city as soon as possible.
Those weren't humans.
They are the Corrupted, the most brutal assassins in this world.
Were they Dark Elves? Do you think they were looking for me?
Without a doubt. We must reach the Forest of Daedenn with haste--only there will we be safe. They would never dare venture into it.
GIVE NO QUARTER, SOLDIERS OF EYSINE!
HOLD THEM OFF!

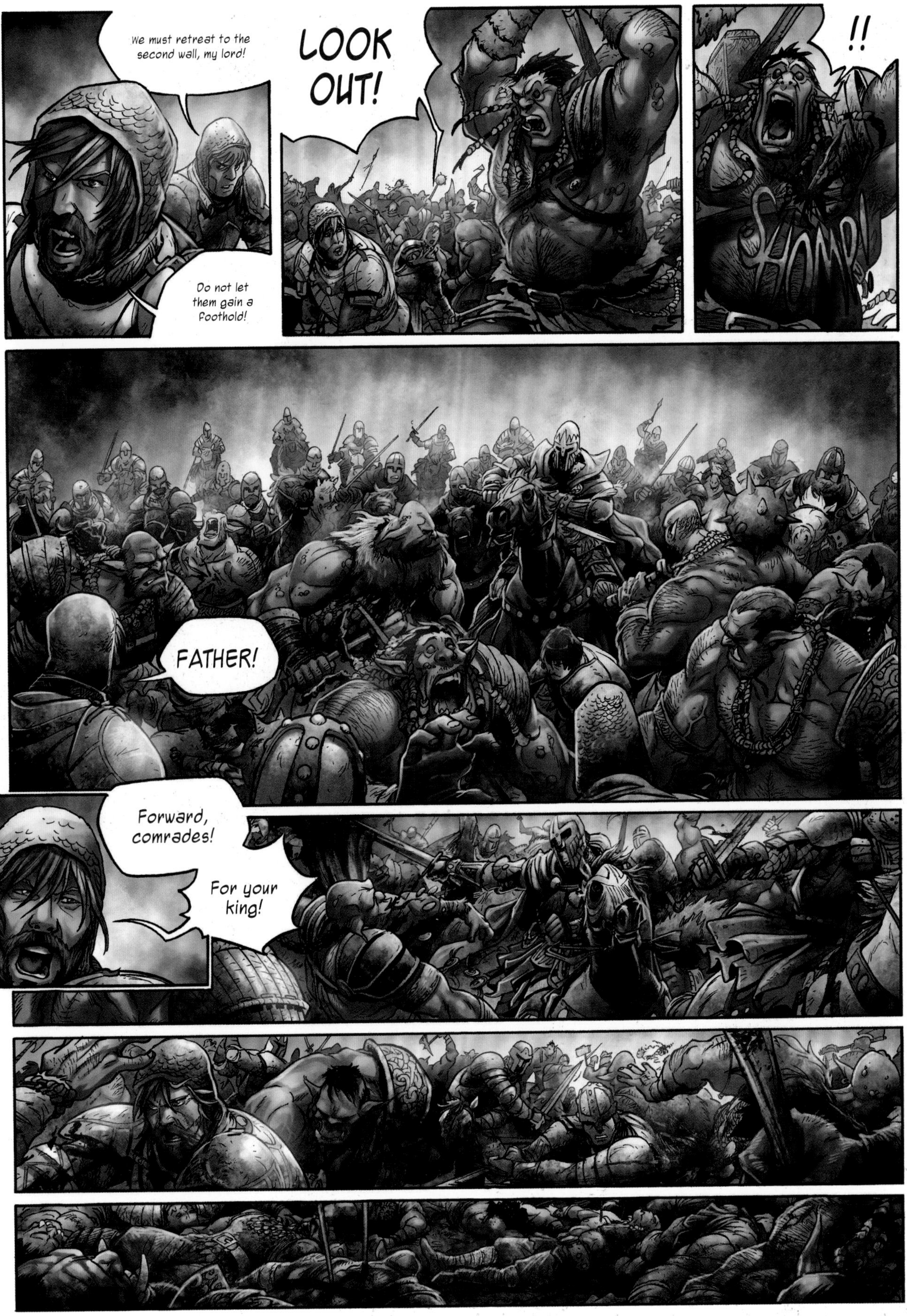
We must retreat to the second wall, my lord!
Do not let them gain a foothold!
LOOK OUT!
!!
SHOMP!
FATHER!
Forward, comrades!
For your king!

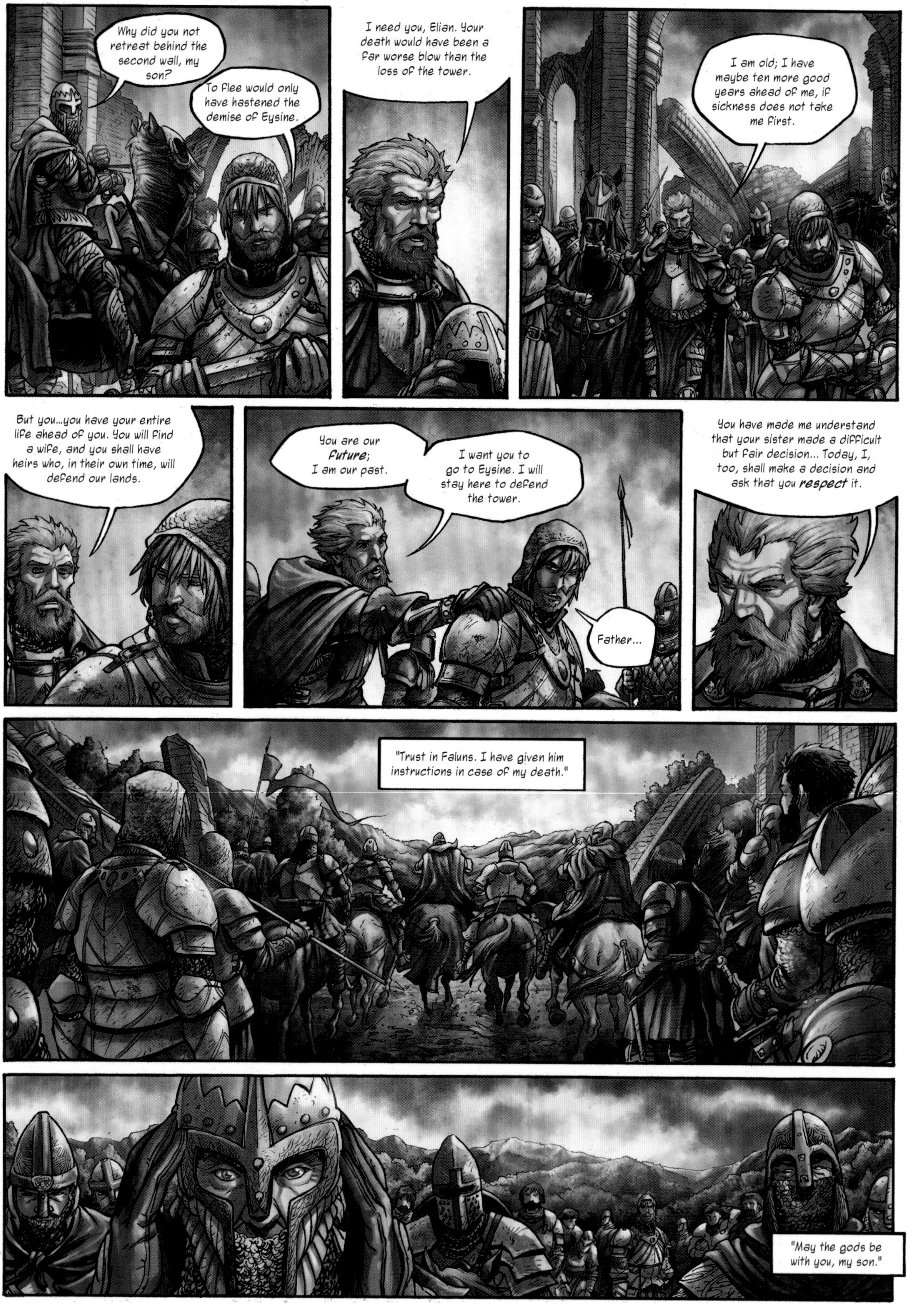
Why did you not retreat behind the second wall, my son?
To flee would only have hastened the demise of Eysine.
I need you, Elian. Your death would have been a far worse blow than the loss of the tower.
I am old; I have maybe ten more good years ahead of me, if sickness does not take me first.
But you...you have your entire life ahead of you. You will find a wife, and you shall have heirs who, in their own time, will defend our lands.
You are our *future*; I am our past.
I want you to go to Eysine. I will stay here to defend the tower.
Father...
You have made me understand that your sister made a difficult but fair decision... Today, I, too, shall make a decision and ask that you *respect* it.
"Trust in Faluns. I have given him instructions in case of my death."
"May the gods be with you, my son."

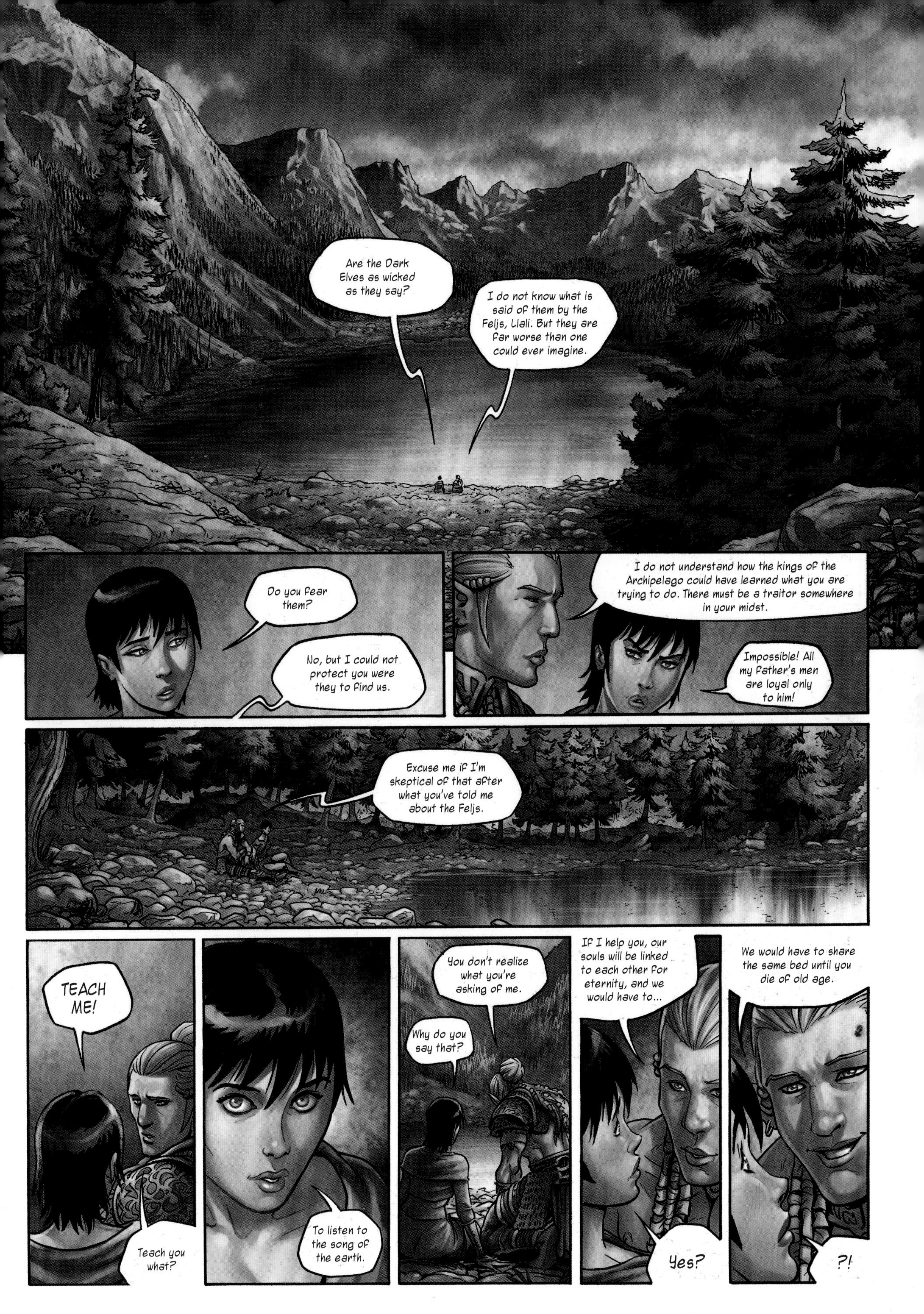
Are the Dark Elves as wicked as they say?
I do not know what is said of them by the Feljs, Llali. But they are far worse than one could ever imagine.
Do you fear them?
No, but I could not protect you were they to find us.
I do not understand how the kings of the Archipelago could have learned what you are trying to do. There must be a traitor somewhere in your midst.
Impossible! All my father's men are loyal only to him!
Excuse me if I'm skeptical of that after what you've told me about the Feljs.
TEACH ME!
Teach you what?
To listen to the song of the earth.
You don't realize what you're asking of me.
Why do you say that?
If I help you, our souls will be linked to each other for eternity, and we would have to...
Yes?
We would have to share the same bed until you die of old age.
?!

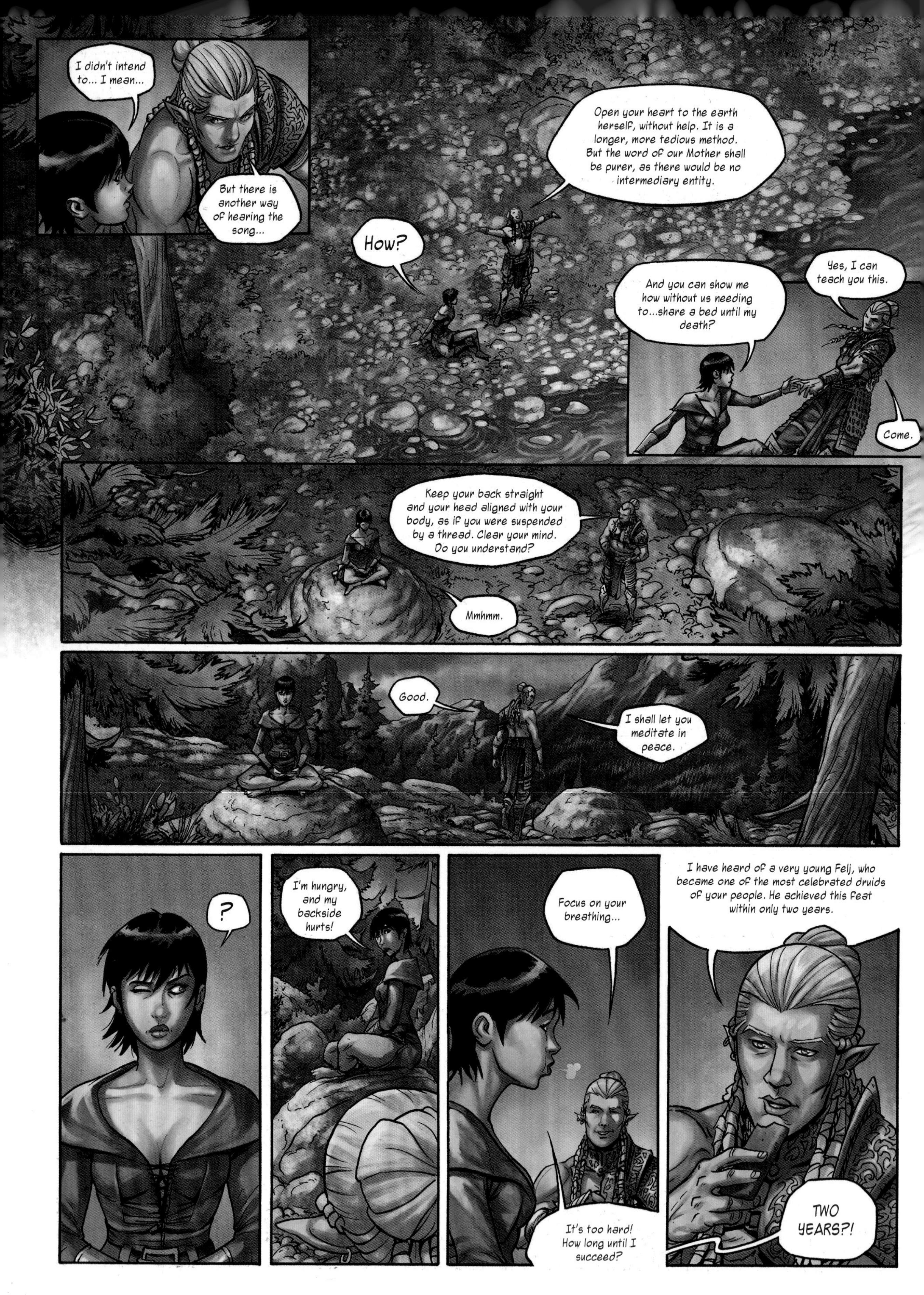
I didn't intend to... I mean...
But there is another way of hearing the song...
Open your heart to the earth herself, without help. It is a longer, more tedious method. But the word of our Mother shall be purer, as there would be no intermediary entity.
How?
And you can show me how without us needing to...share a bed until my death?
Yes, I can teach you this.
Come.
Keep your back straight and your head aligned with your body, as if you were suspended by a thread. Clear your mind. Do you understand?
Mmhmm.
Good.
I shall let you meditate in peace.
?
I'm hungry, and my backside hurts!
Focus on your breathing...
It's too hard! How long until I succeed?
I have heard of a very young Felj, who became one of the most celebrated druids of your people. He achieved this feat within only two years.
TWO YEARS?!

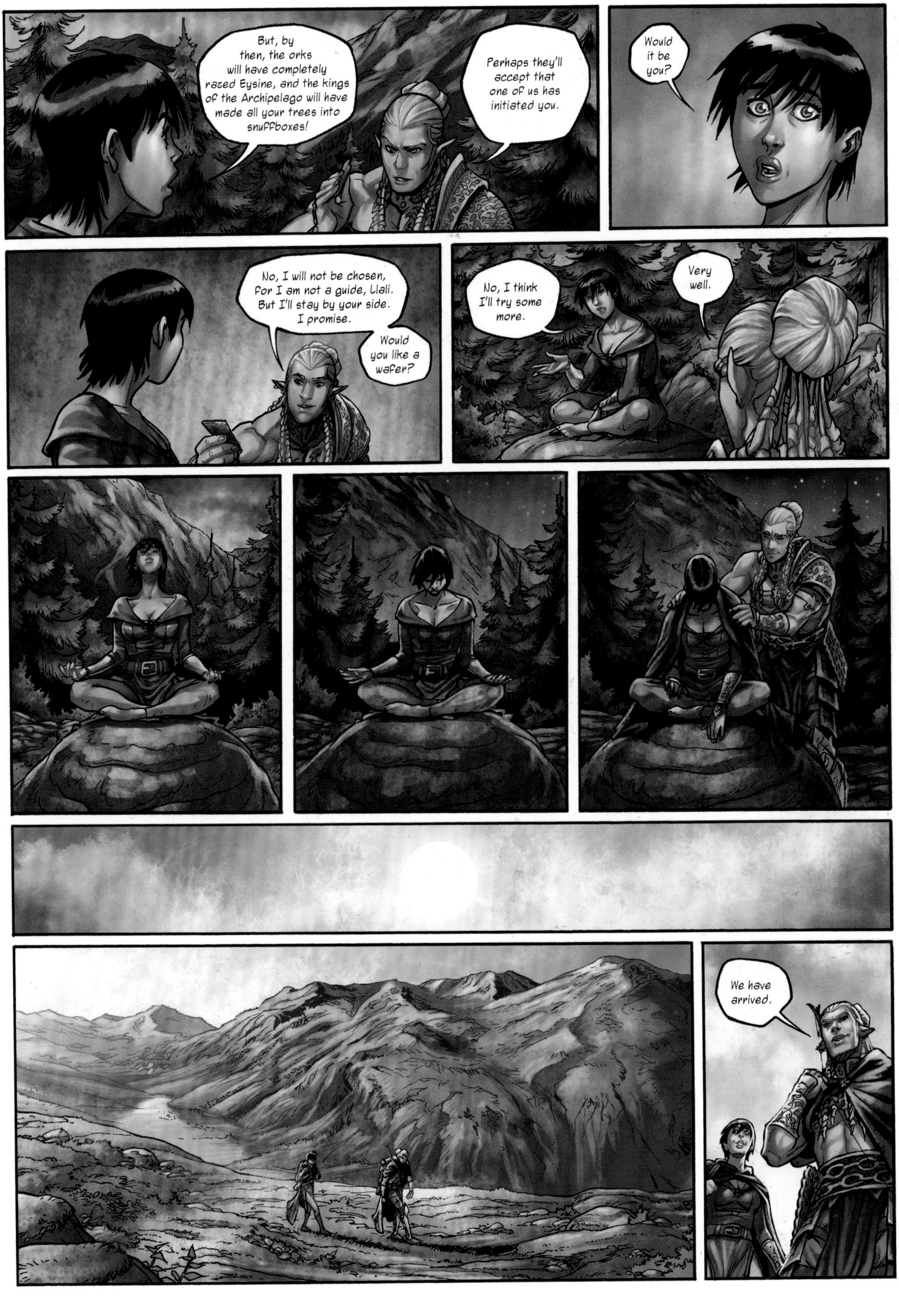
But, by then, the orks will have completely razed Eysine, and the kings of the Archipelago will have made all your trees into snuffboxes!
Perhaps they'll accept that one of us has initiated you.
Would it be you?
No, I will not be chosen, for I am not a guide, Llali. But I'll stay by your side. I promise.
Would you like a wafer?
No, I think I'll try some more.
Very well.
We have arrived.

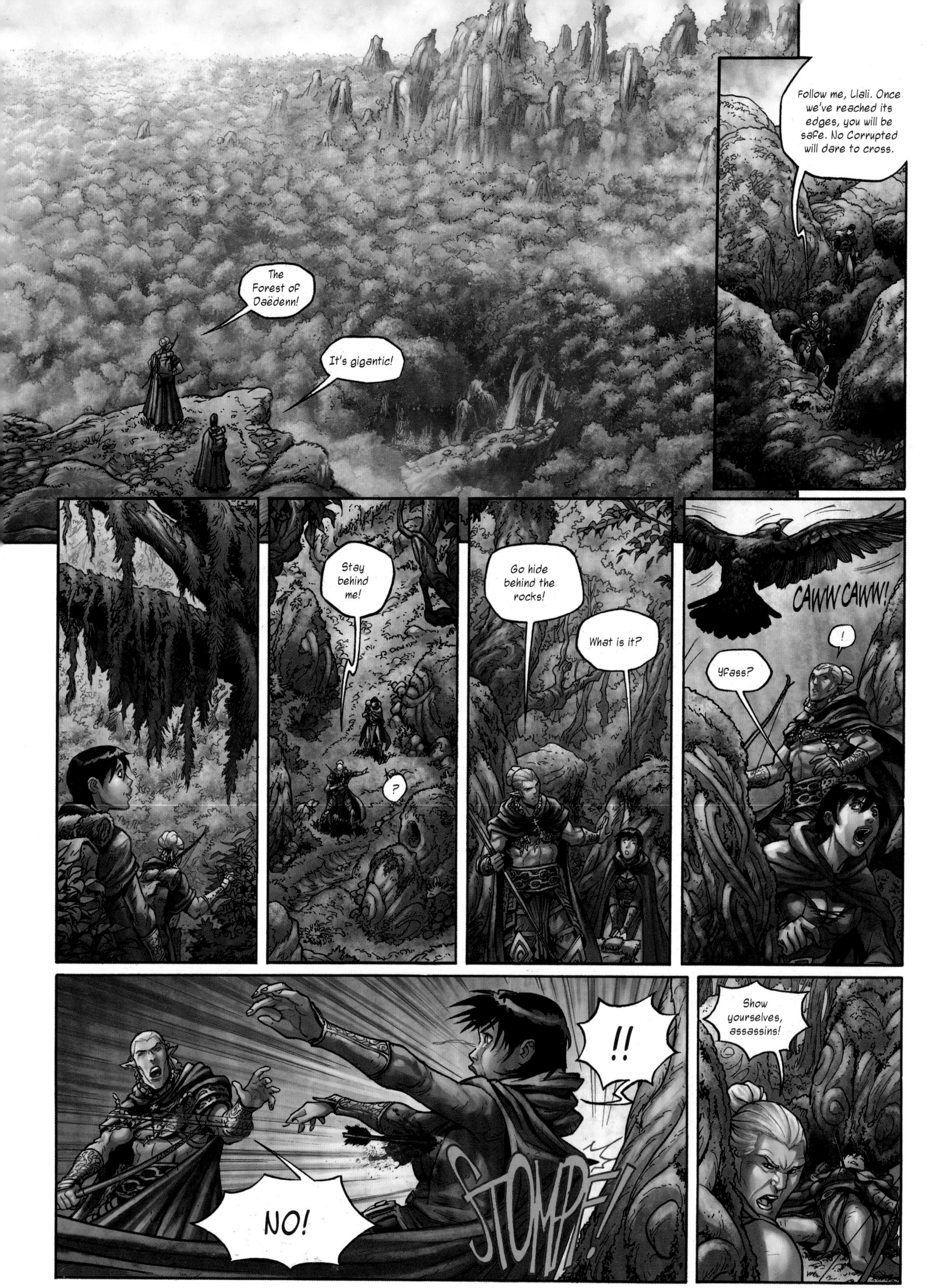
The Forest of Daëdenn!
It's gigantic!
Follow me, Llali. Once we've reached its edges, you will be safe. No Corrupted will dare to cross.
Stay behind me!
?
Go hide behind the rocks!
What is it?
CAWW CAWW!
!
Yfass?
!!
NO!
STOMPF!
Show yourselves, assassins!

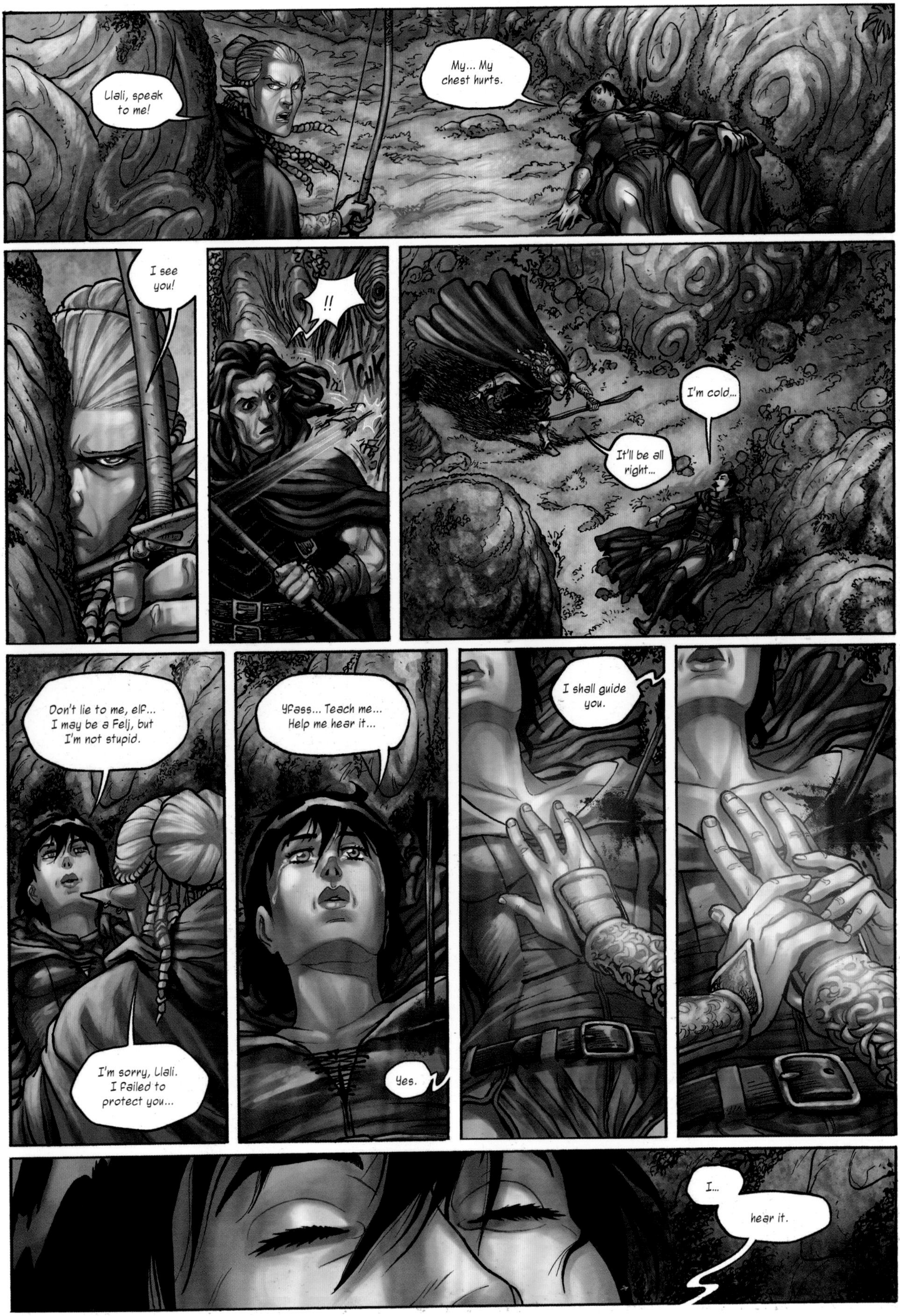
Llali, speak to me!
My... My chest hurts.
I see you!
!!
TCHK
I'm cold...
It'll be all right...
Don't lie to me, elf... I may be a Felj, but I'm not stupid.
I'm sorry, Llali. I failed to protect you...
Yfass... Teach me... Help me hear it...
Yes.
I shall guide you.
I...
hear it.

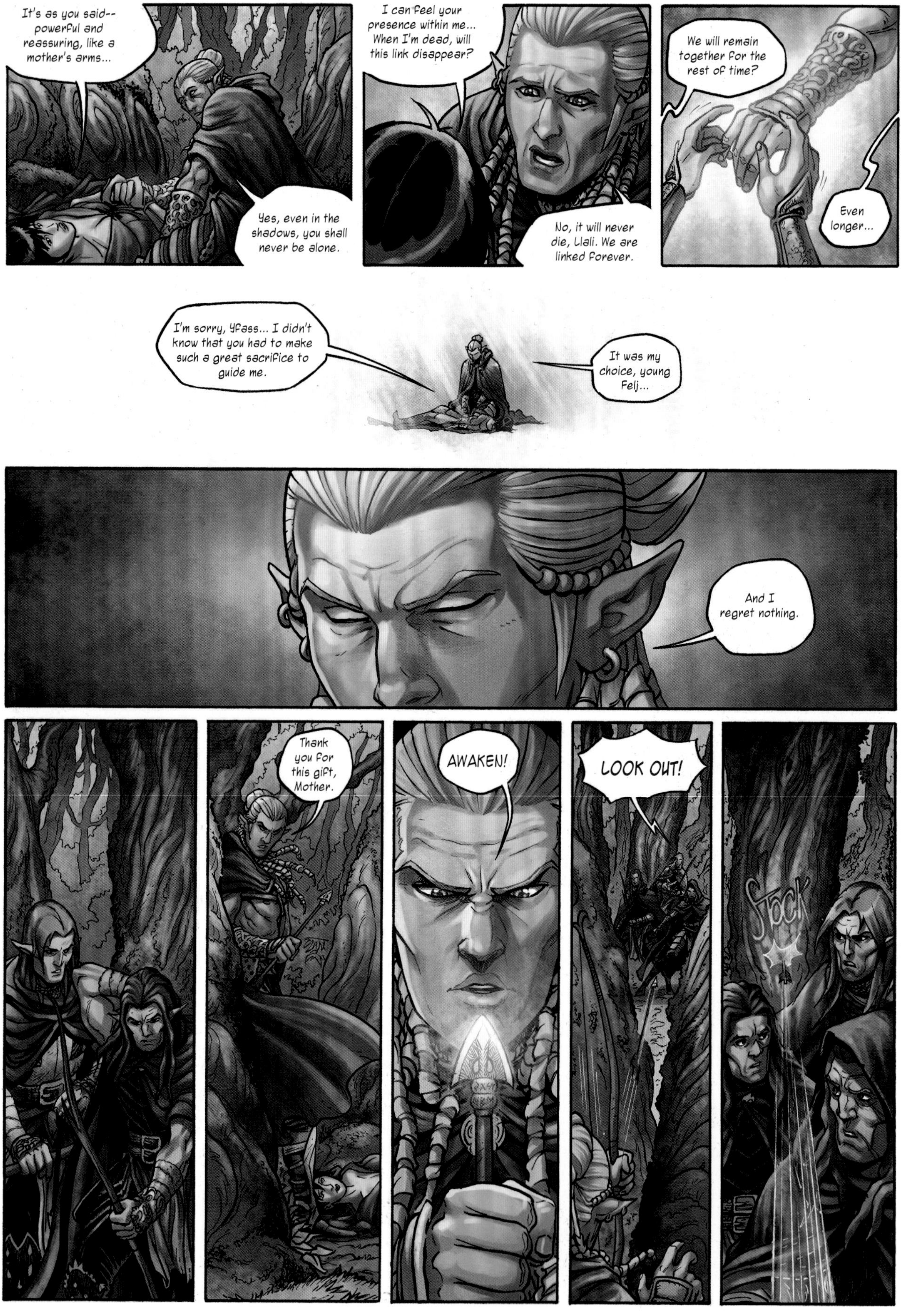
It's as you said-- powerful and reassuring, like a mother's arms...
Yes, even in the shadows, you shall never be alone.
I can feel your presence within me... When I'm dead, will this link disappear?
No, it will never die, Llali. We are linked forever.
We will remain together for the rest of time?
Even longer...
I'm sorry, Yfass... I didn't know that you had to make such a great sacrifice to guide me.
It was my choice, young Felj...
And I regret nothing.
Thank you for this gift, Mother.
AWAKEN!
LOOK OUT!
STOCK

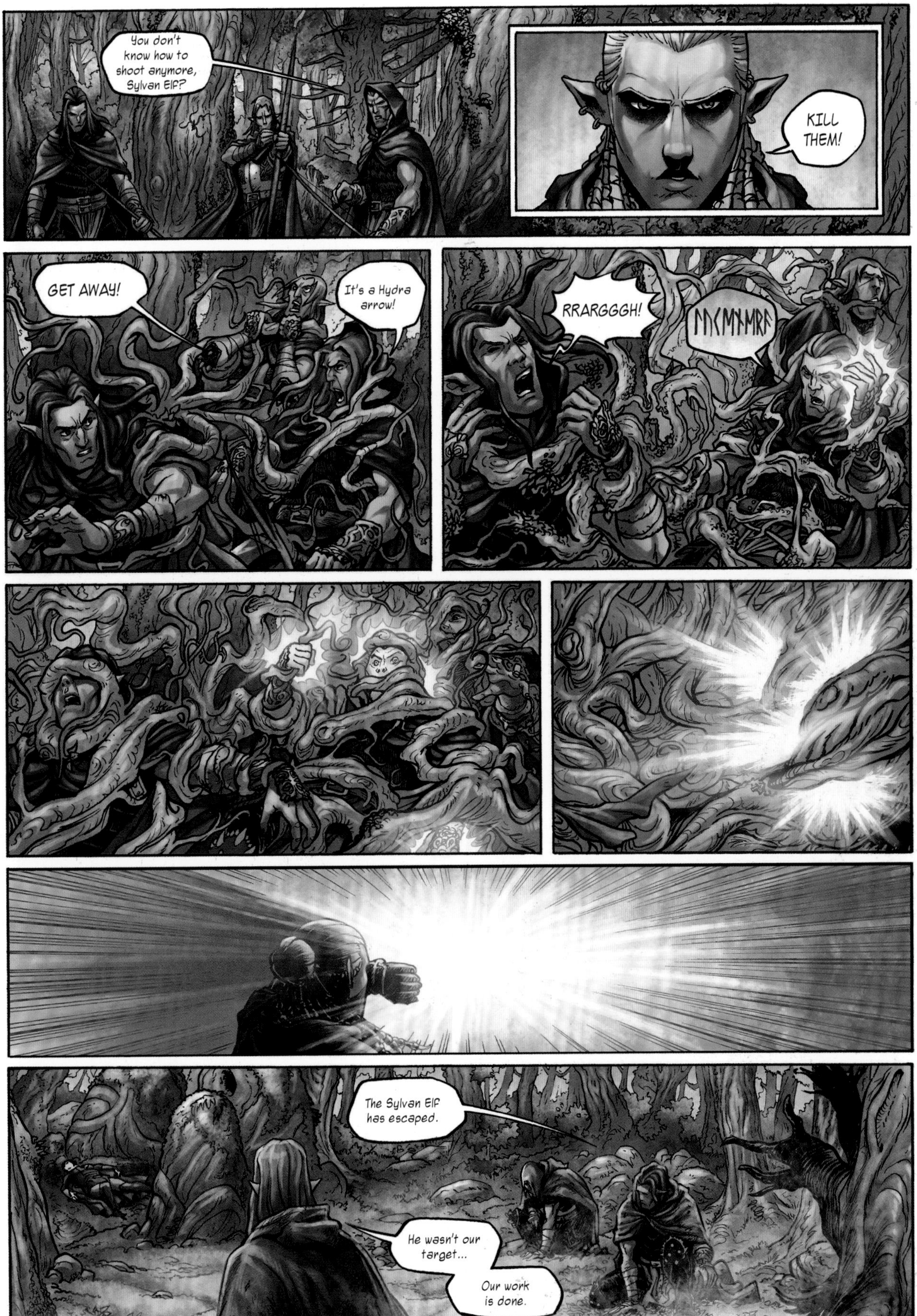
You don't know how to shoot anymore, Sylvan Elf?
KILL THEM!
GET AWAY!
It's a Hydra arrow!
RRARGGGH!
The Sylvan Elf has escaped.
He wasn't our target...
Our work is done.

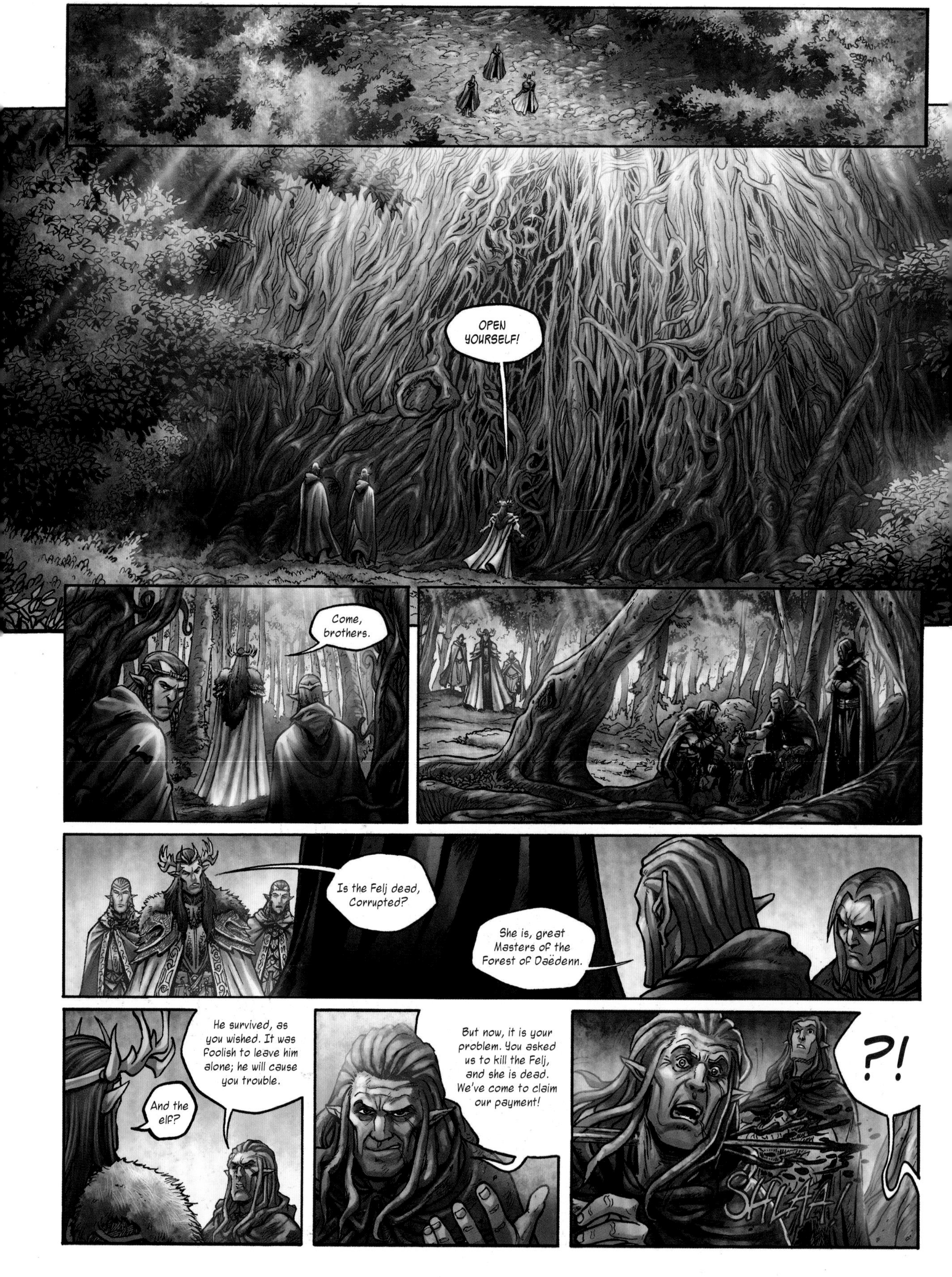
OPEN YOURSELF!
Come, brothers.
Is the Felj dead, Corrupted?
She is, great Masters of the Forest of Daëdenn.
And the elf?
He survived, as you wished. It was foolish to leave him alone; he will cause you trouble.
But now, it is your problem. You asked us to kill the Felj, and she is dead. We've come to claim our payment!
?!
SHLAA!

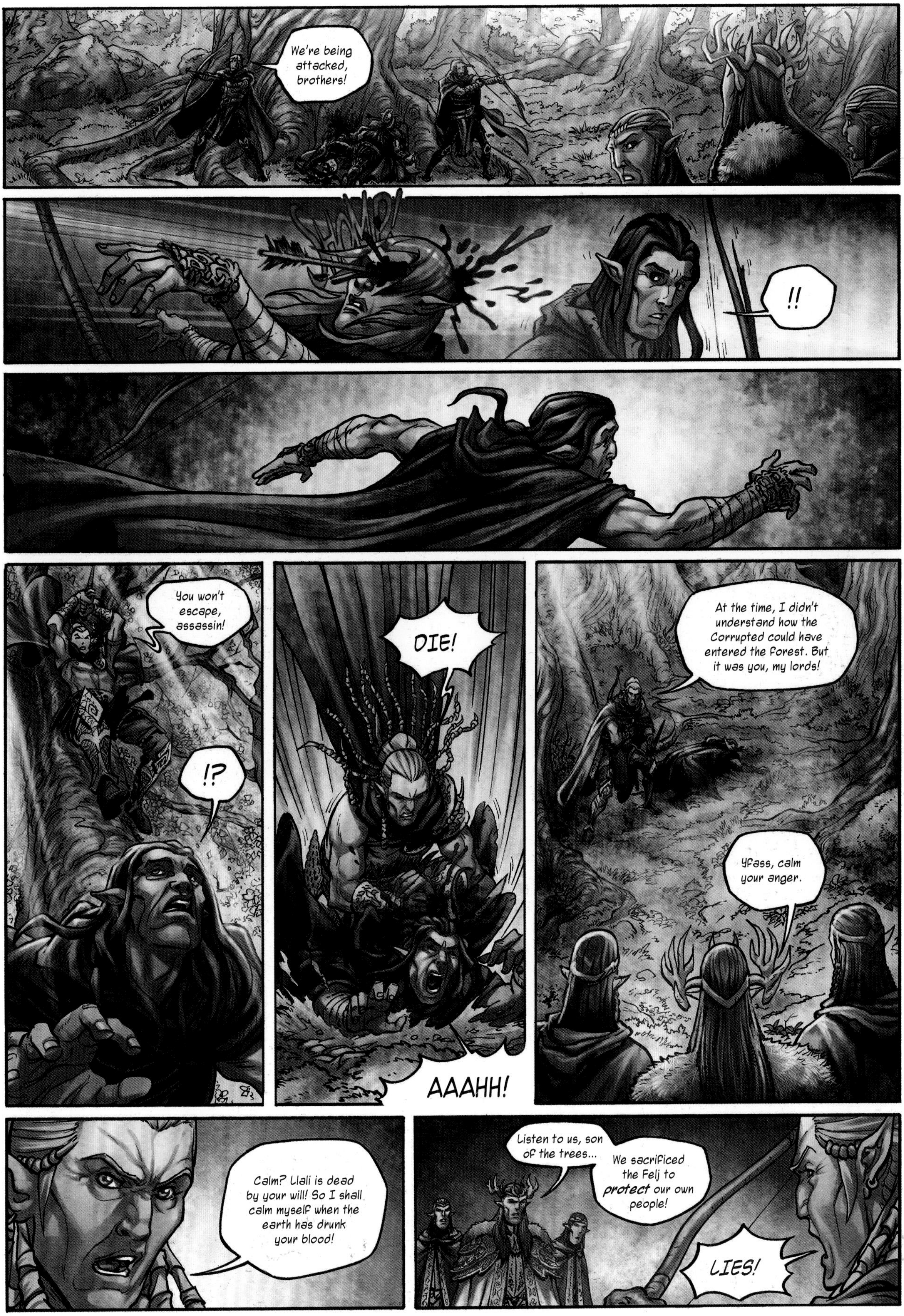
We're being attacked, brothers!
SHOMP!
!!
You won't escape, assassin!
!?
DIE!
AAAHH!
At the time, I didn't understand how the Corrupted could have entered the Forest. But it was you, my lords!
Yfass, calm your anger.
Calm? Llali is dead by your will! So I shall calm myself when the earth has drunk your blood!
Listen to us, son of the trees...
We sacrificed the Felj to *protect* our own people!
LIES!

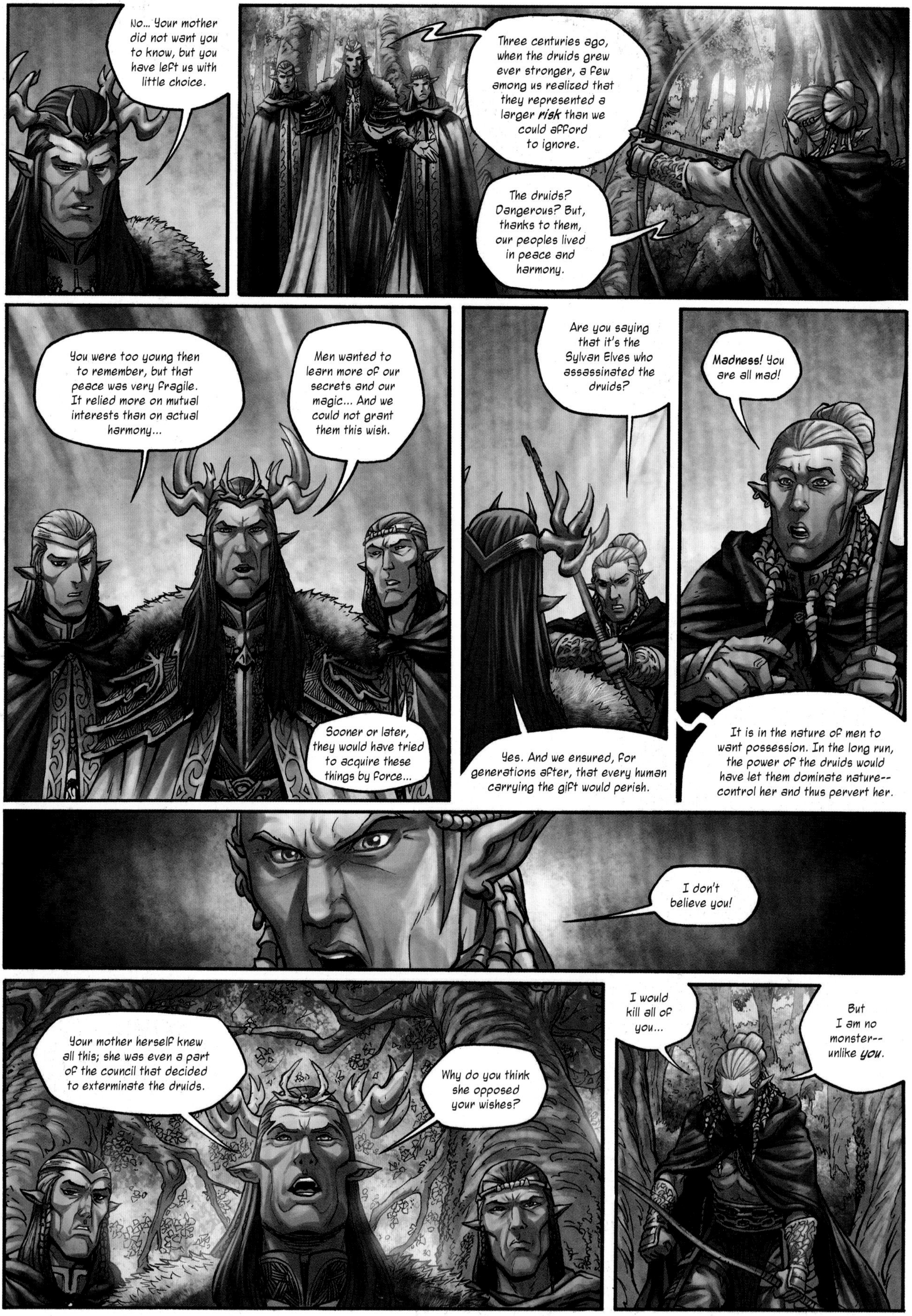
No... Your mother did not want you to know, but you have left us with little choice.
Three centuries ago, when the druids grew ever stronger, a few among us realized that they represented a larger risk than we could afford to ignore.
The druids? Dangerous? But, thanks to them, our peoples lived in peace and harmony.
You were too young then to remember, but that peace was very fragile. It relied more on mutual interests than on actual harmony...
Men wanted to learn more of our secrets and our magic... And we could not grant them this wish.
Sooner or later, they would have tried to acquire these things by force...
Are you saying that it's the Sylvan Elves who assassinated the druids?
Yes. And we ensured, for generations after, that every human carrying the gift would perish.
Madness! You are all mad!
It is in the nature of men to want possession. In the long run, the power of the druids would have let them dominate nature-- control her and thus pervert her.
I don't believe you!
Your mother herself knew all this; she was even a part of the council that decided to exterminate the druids.
Why do you think she opposed your wishes?
I would kill all of you...
But I am no monster-- unlike you.

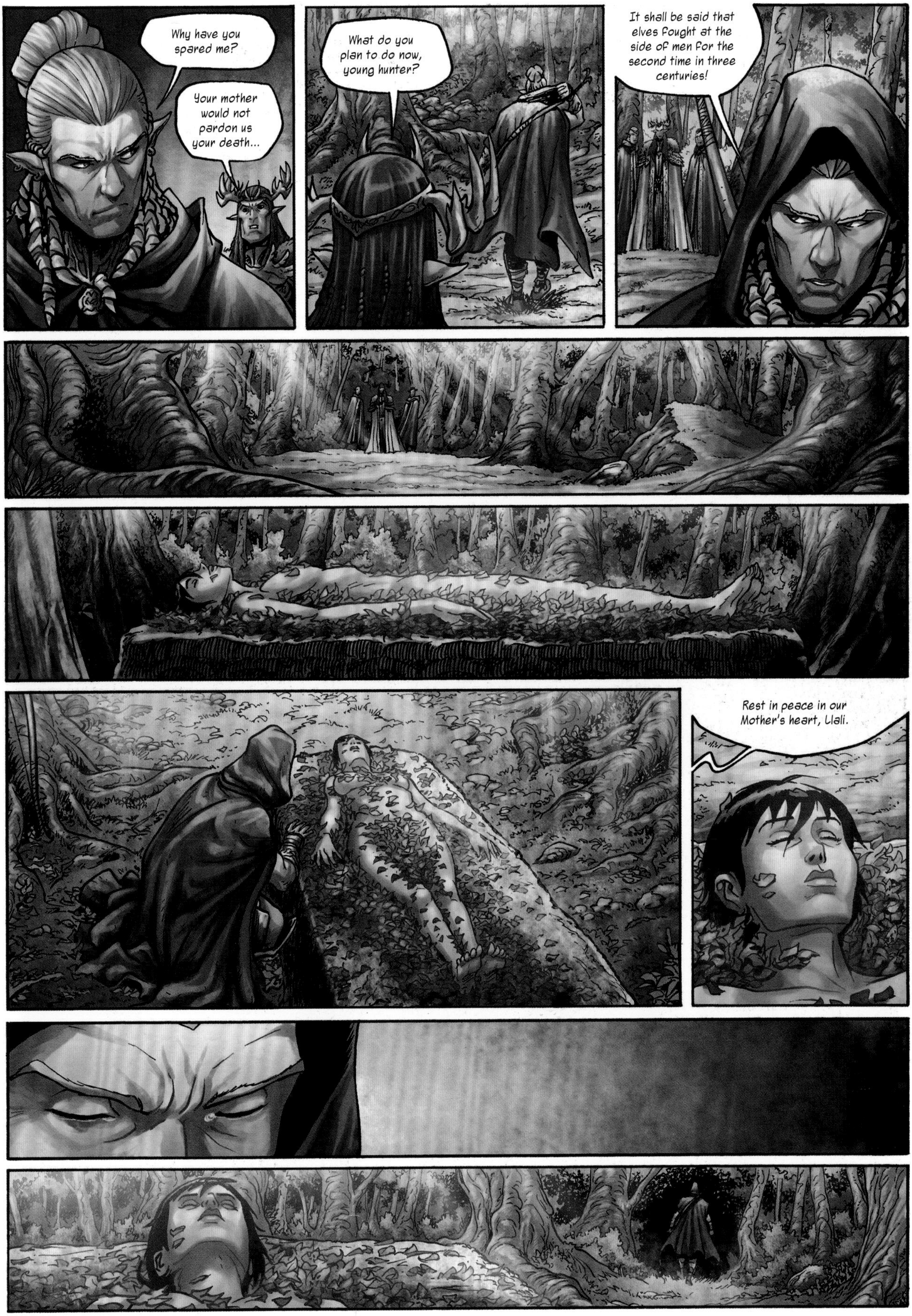
Why have you spared me?
Your mother would not pardon us your death...
What do you plan to do now, young hunter?
It shall be said that elves fought at the side of men for the second time in three centuries!
Rest in peace in our Mother's heart, Llali.

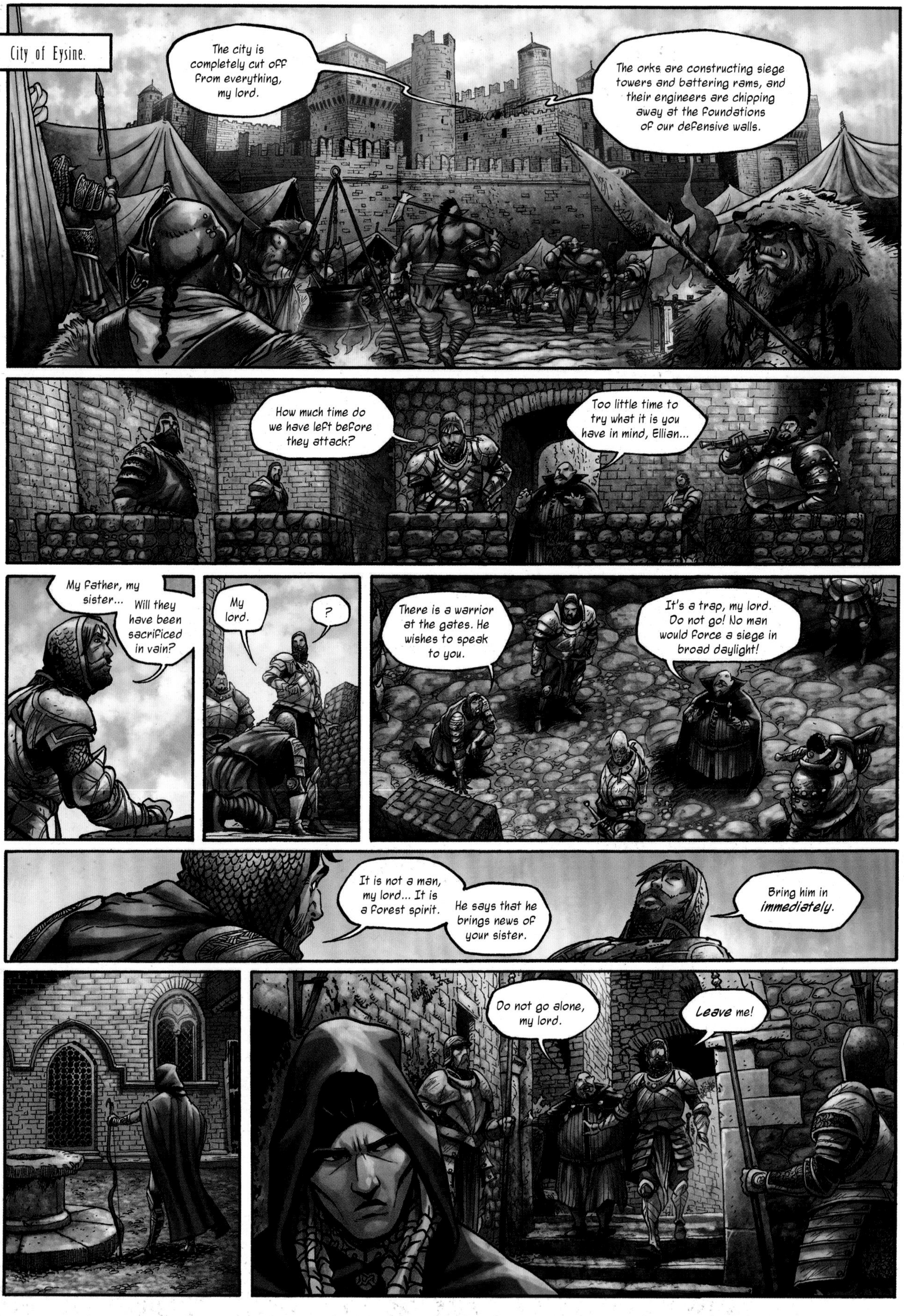
City of Eysine.
The city is completely cut off from everything, my lord.
The orks are constructing siege towers and battering rams, and their engineers are chipping away at the foundations of our defensive walls.
How much time do we have left before they attack?
Too little time to try what it is you have in mind, Ellian...
My father, my sister...
Will they have been sacrificed in vain?
My lord.
?
There is a warrior at the gates. He wishes to speak to you.
It's a trap, my lord. Do not go! No man would force a siege in broad daylight!
It is not a man, my lord... It is a forest spirit.
He says that he brings news of your sister.
Bring him in *immediately*.
Do not go alone, my lord.
Leave me!

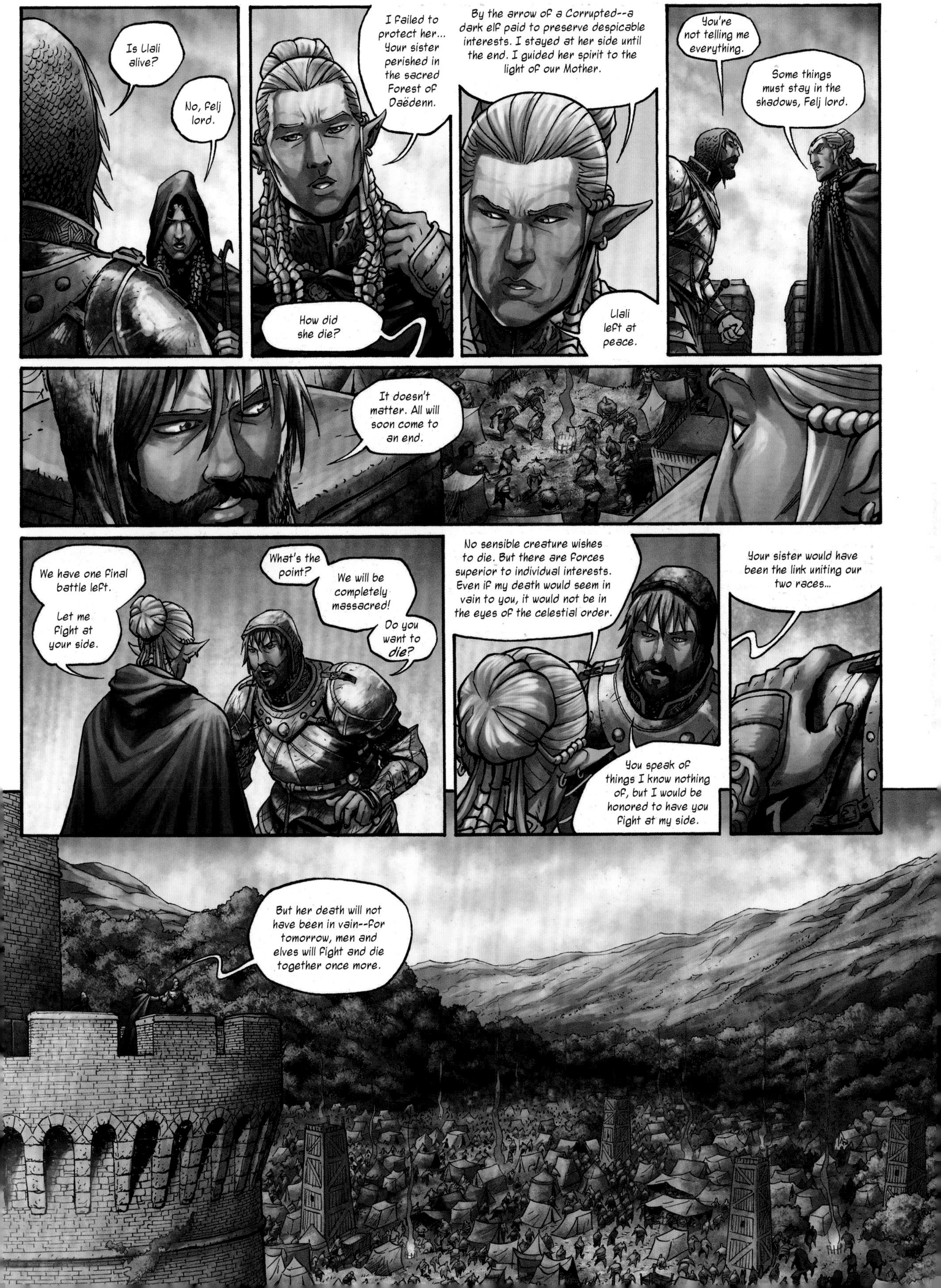

Is Llali alive?
No, Felj lord.
I failed to protect her... Your sister perished in the sacred Forest of Daëdenn.
How did she die?
By the arrow of a Corrupted--a dark elf paid to preserve despicable interests. I stayed at her side until the end. I guided her spirit to the light of our Mother.
Llali left at peace.
You're not telling me everything.
Some things must stay in the shadows, Felj lord.
It doesn't matter. All will soon come to an end.
We have one final battle left.
Let me fight at your side.
What's the point?
We will be completely massacred!
Do you want to *die*?
No sensible creature wishes to die. But there are forces superior to individual interests. Even if my death would seem in vain to you, it would not be in the eyes of the celestial order.
You speak of things I know nothing of, but I would be honored to have you fight at my side.
Your sister would have been the link uniting our two races...
But her death will not have been in vain--for tomorrow, men and elves will fight and die together once more.

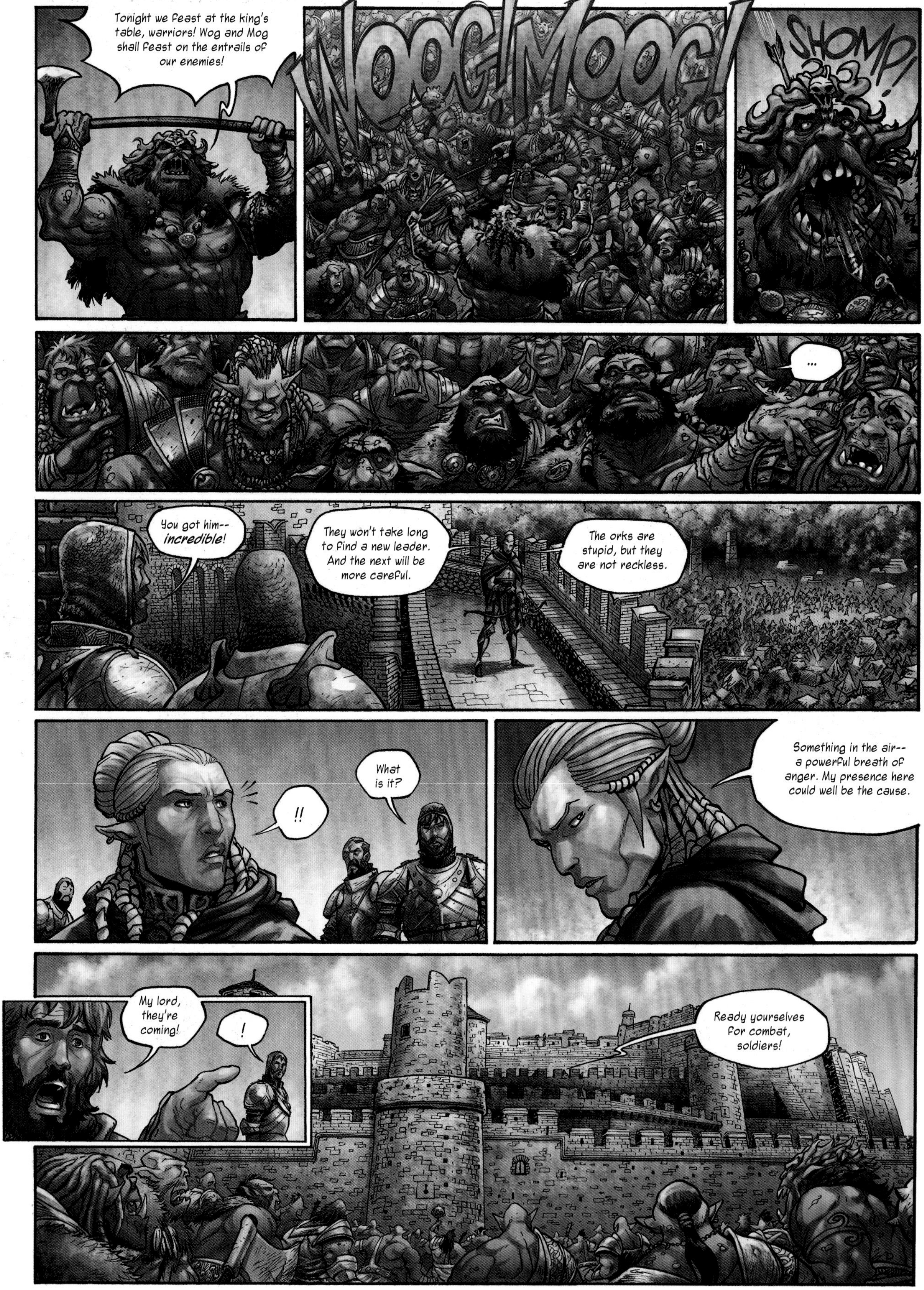
Tonight we feast at the king's table, warriors! Wog and Mog shall feast on the entrails of our enemies!
WOOG! MOOG!
SHOMP!
...
You got him-- *incredible*!
They won't take long to find a new leader. And the next will be more careful.
The orks are stupid, but they are not reckless.
!!
What is it?
Something in the air-- a powerful breath of anger. My presence here could well be the cause.
My lord, they're coming!
!
Ready yourselves for combat, soldiers!

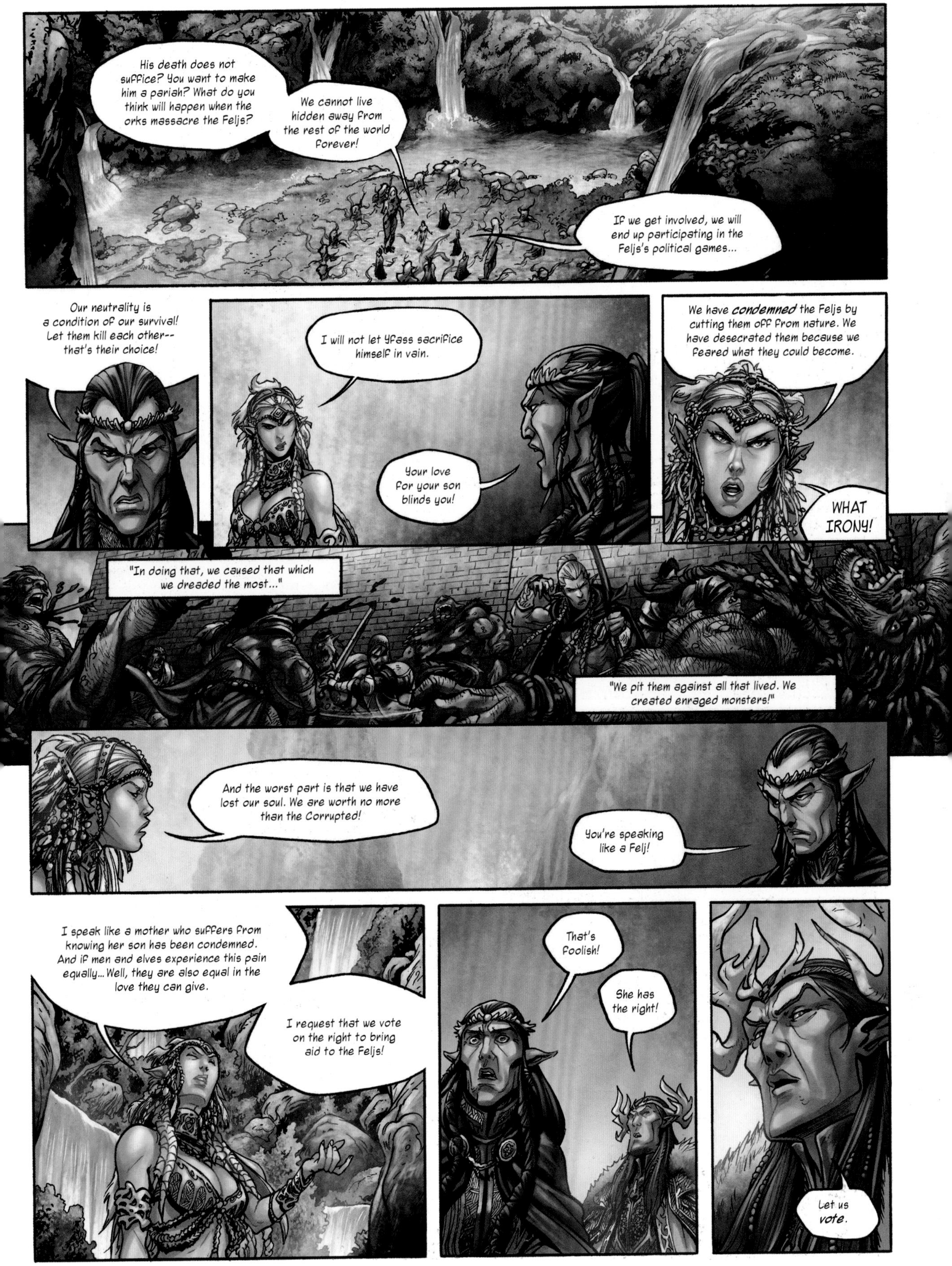

His death does not suffice? You want to make him a pariah? What do you think will happen when the orks massacre the Feljs?
We cannot live hidden away from the rest of the world forever!
If we get involved, we will end up participating in the Feljs's political games...
Our neutrality is a condition of our survival! Let them kill each other-- that's their choice!
I will not let Yfass sacrifice himself in vain.
Your love for your son blinds you!
We have *condemned* the Feljs by cutting them off from nature. We have desecrated them because we feared what they could become.
WHAT IRONY!
"In doing that, we caused that which we dreaded the most..."
"We pit them against all that lived. We created enraged monsters!"
And the worst part is that we have lost our soul. We are worth no more than the Corrupted!
You're speaking like a Felj!
I speak like a mother who suffers from knowing her son has been condemned. And if men and elves experience this pain equally... Well, they are also equal in the love they can give.
I request that we vote on the right to bring aid to the Feljs!
That's foolish!
She has the right!
Let us *vote*.

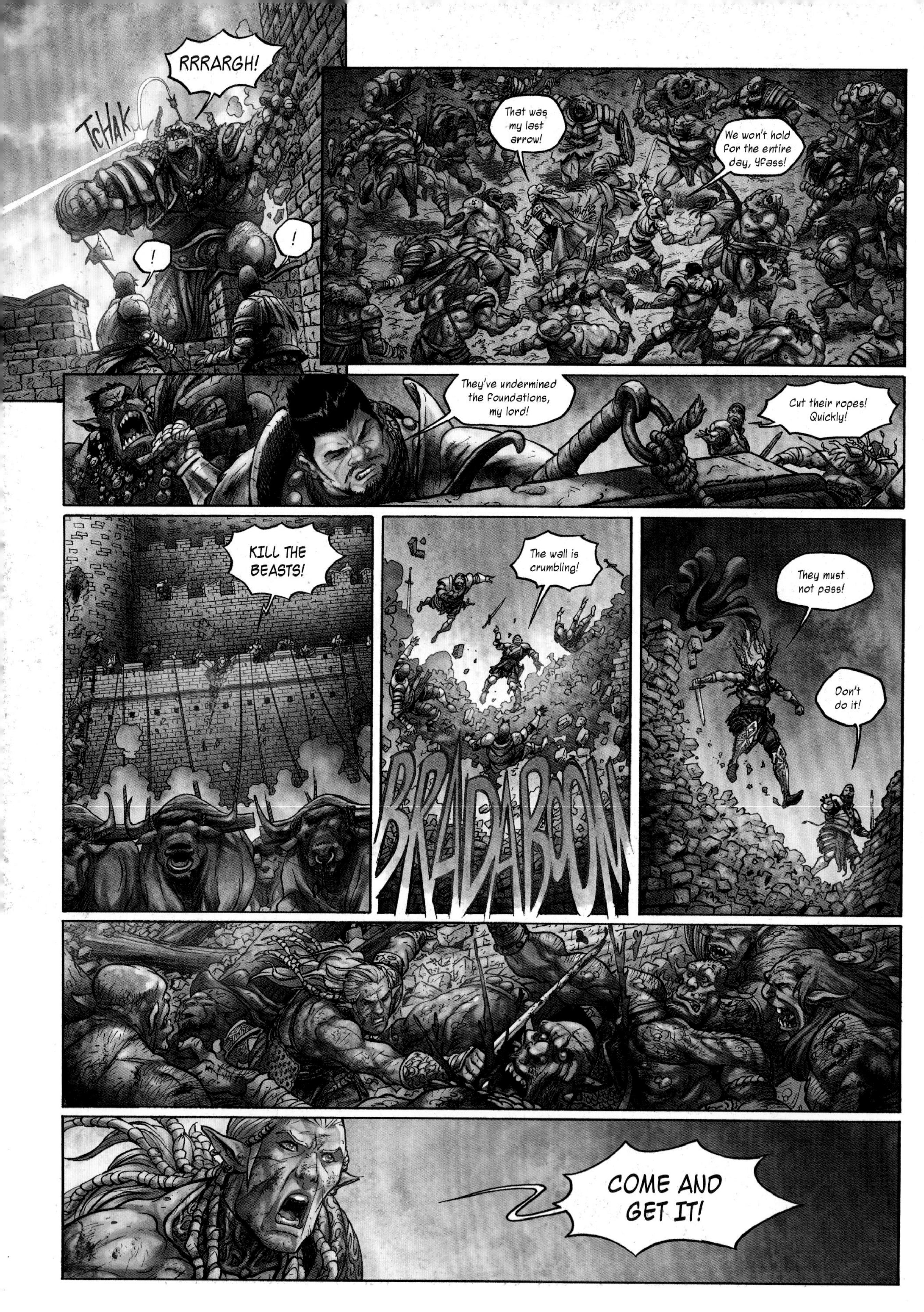
RRRARGH!
TCHAK
!
!
That was my last arrow!
We won't hold for the entire day, Yfass!
They've undermined the foundations, my lord!
Cut their ropes! Quickly!
KILL THE BEASTS!
The wall is crumbling!
BRADABOOM
They must not pass!
Don't do it!
COME AND GET IT!

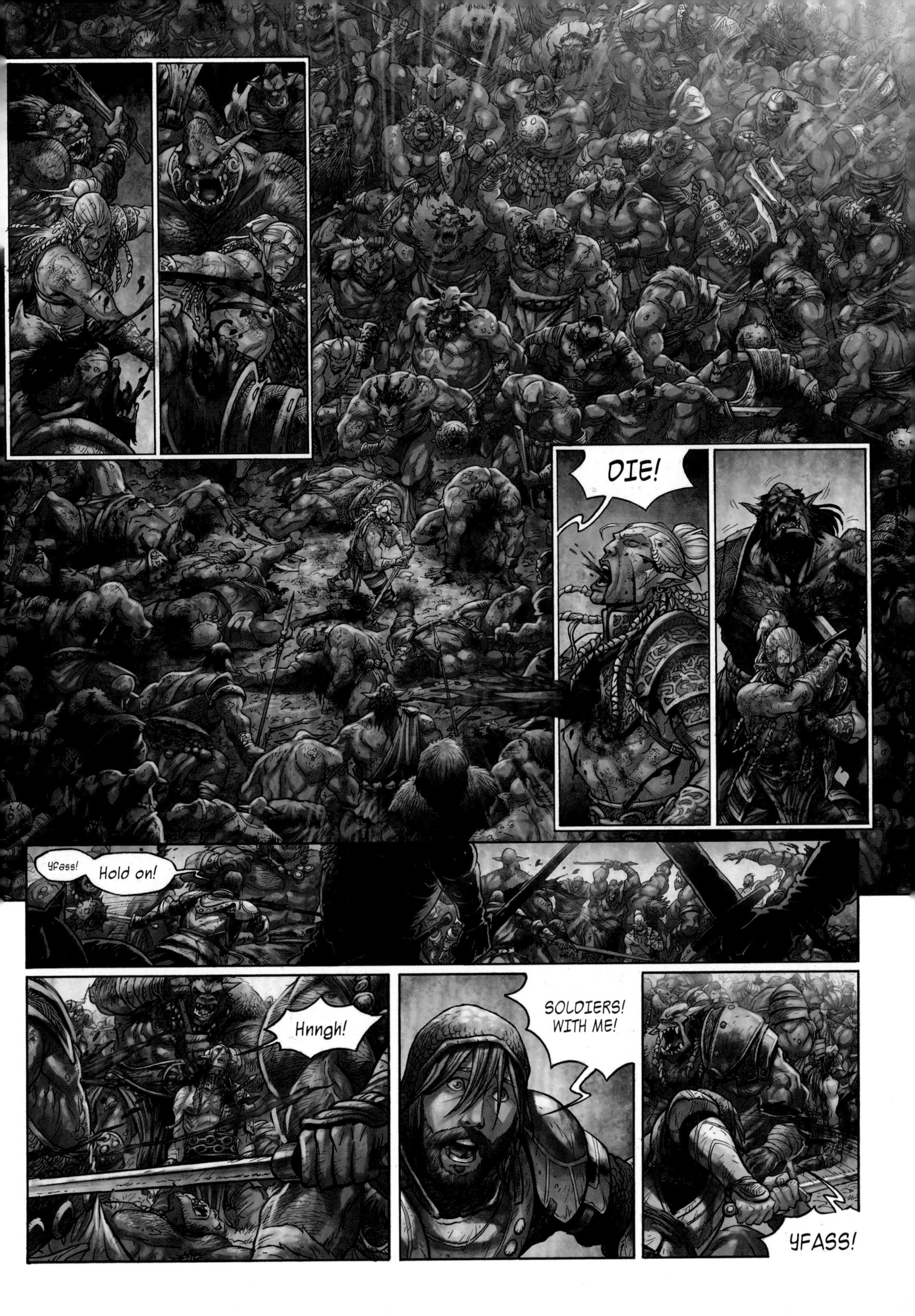
DIE!
Yfass!
Hold on!
Hnngh!
SOLDIERS! WITH ME!
YFASS!

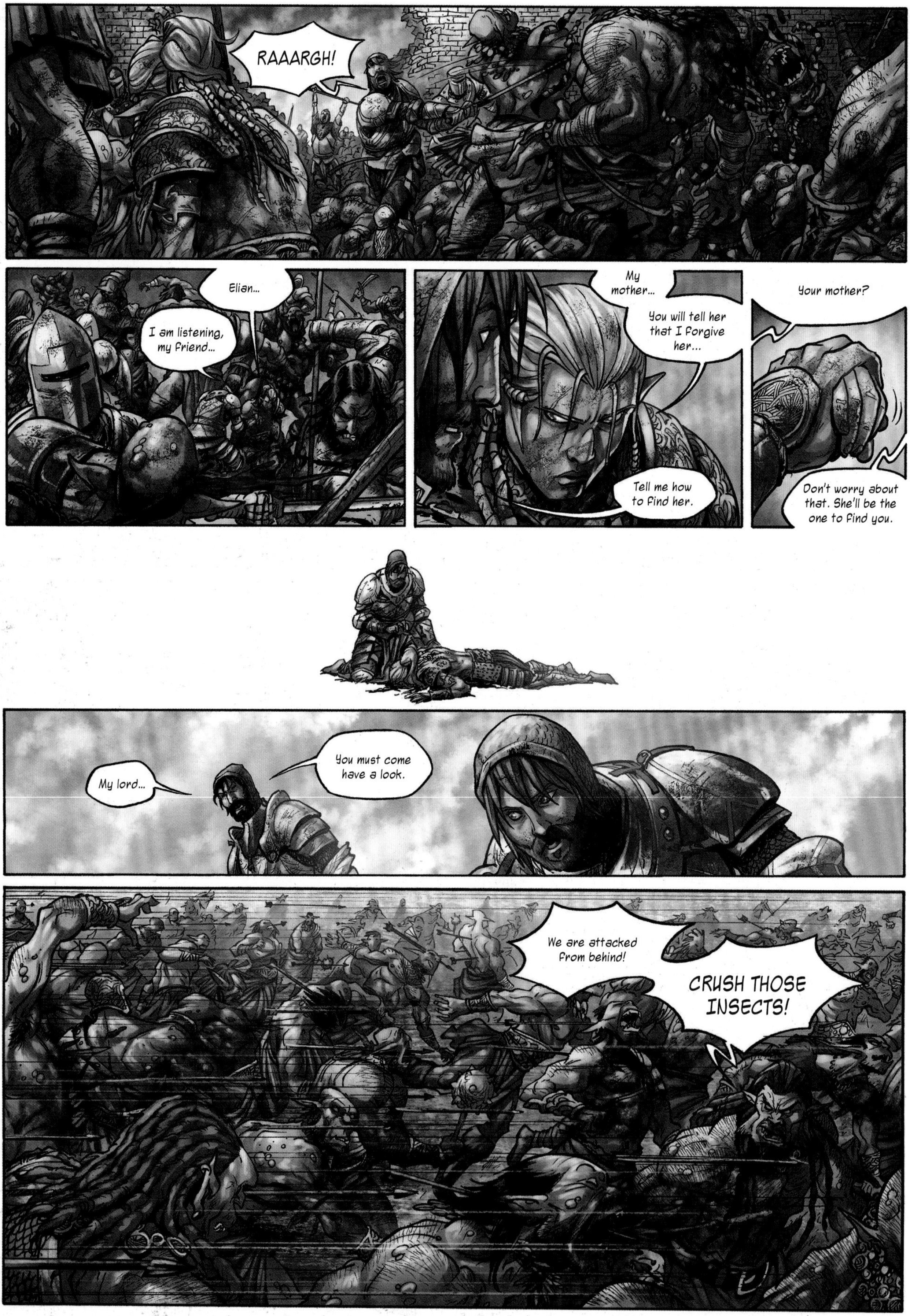
RAAARGH!
Elian...
I am listening, my friend...
My mother...
You will tell her that I forgive her...
Tell me how to find her.
Your mother?
Don't worry about that. She'll be the one to find you.
My lord...
You must come have a look.
We are attacked from behind!
CRUSH THOSE INSECTS!

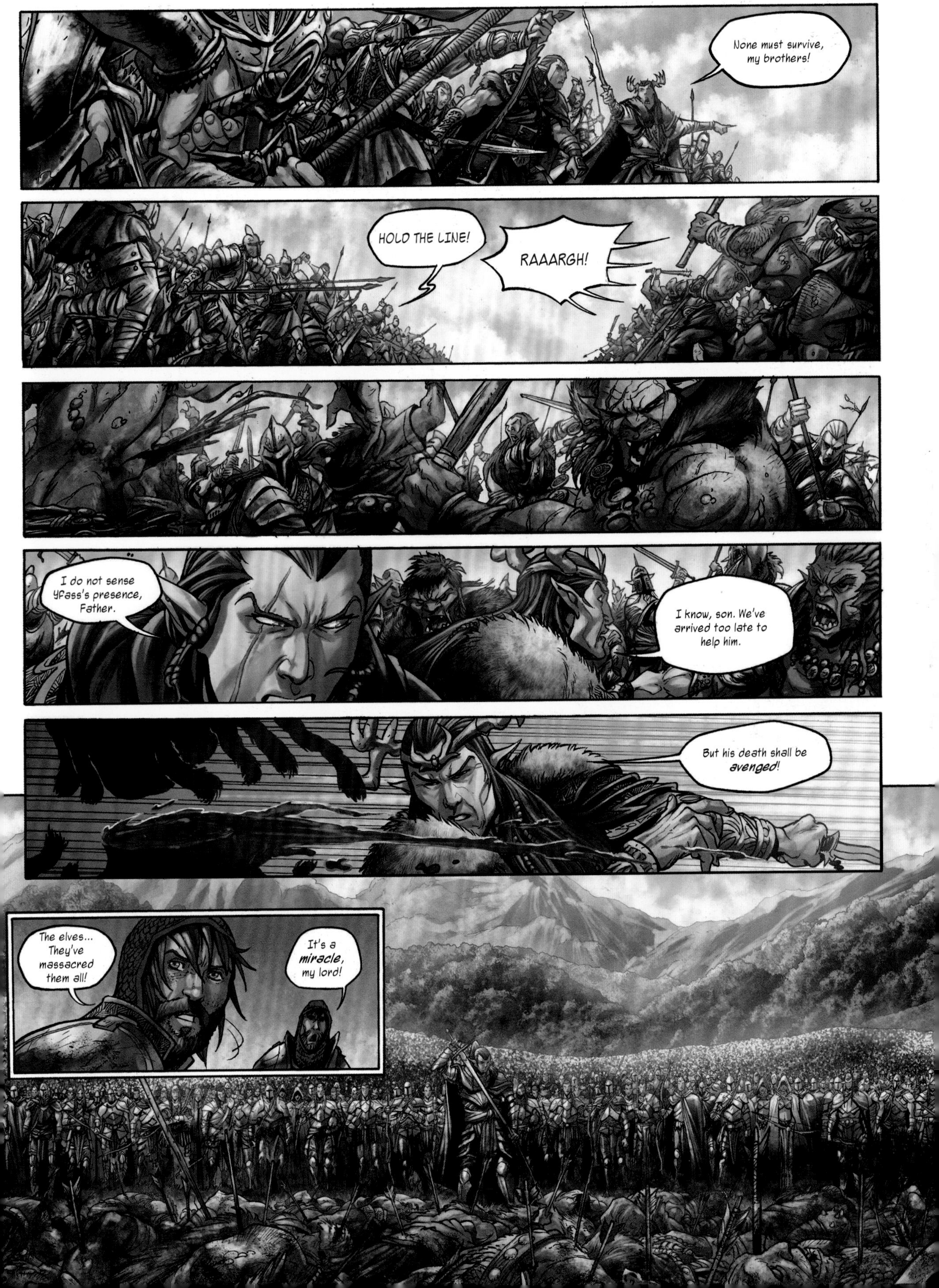
None must survive, my brothers!
HOLD THE LINE!
RAAARGH!
I do not sense Yfass's presence, Father.
I know, son. We've arrived too late to help him.
But his death shall be *avenged*!
The elves... They've massacred them all!
It's a *miracle*, my lord!

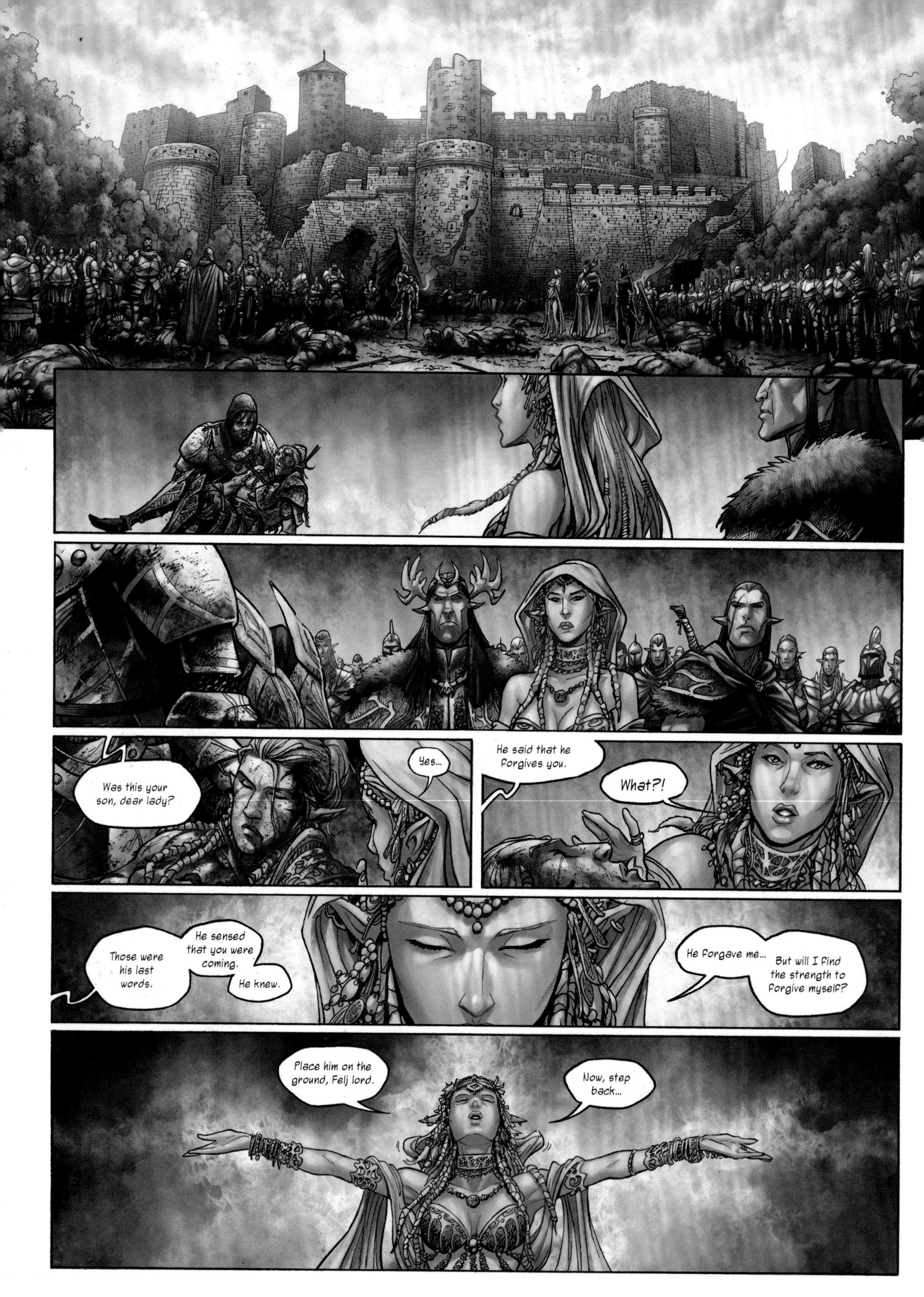
Was this your son, dear lady?
Yes...
He said that he forgives you.
What?!
Those were his last words.
He sensed that you were coming.
He knew.
He forgave me...
But will I find the strength to forgive myself?
Place him on the ground, Felj lord.
Now, step back...

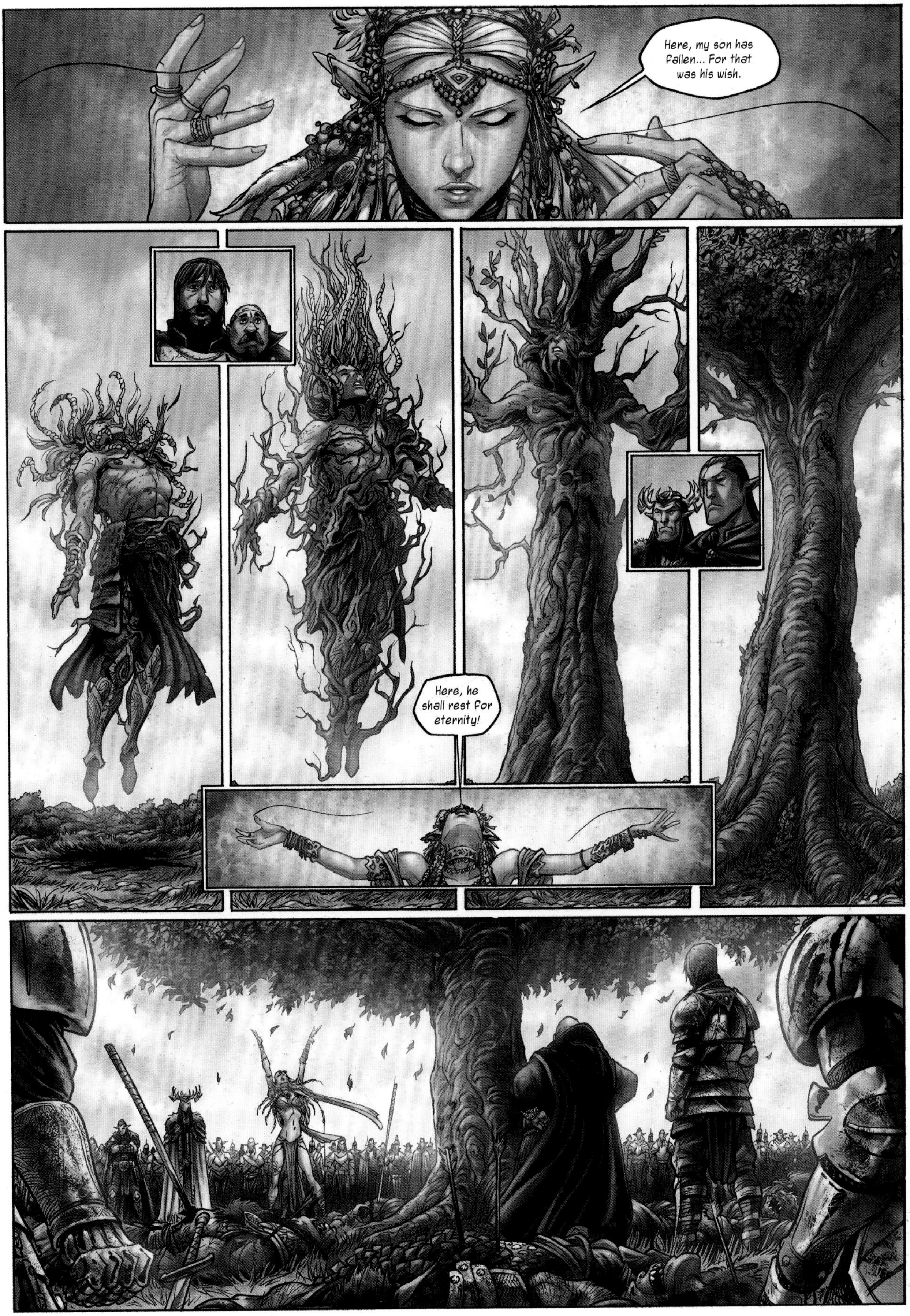
Here, my son has fallen... For that was his wish.
Here, he shall rest for eternity!

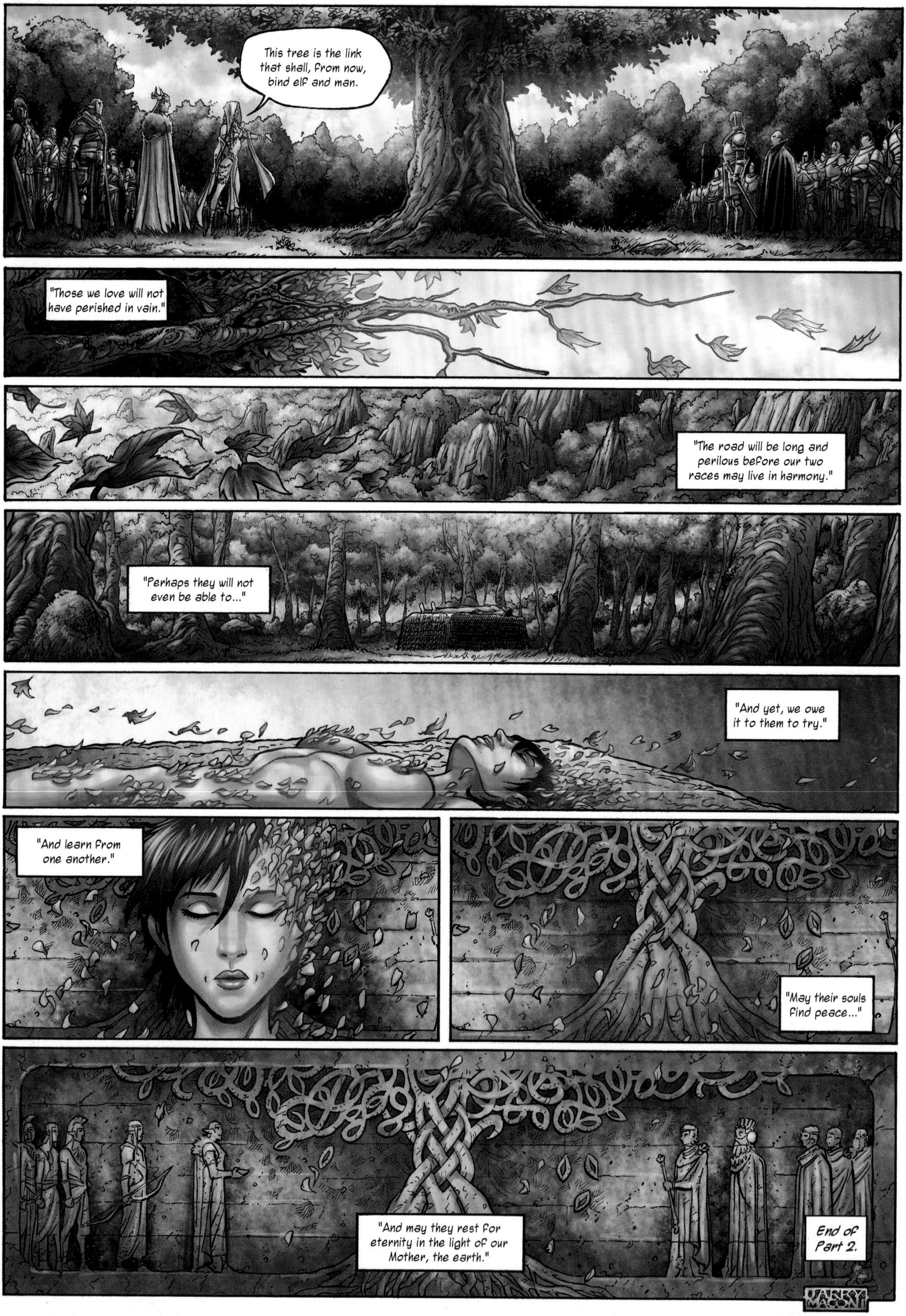
This tree is the link that shall, from now, bind elf and man.
"Those we love will not have perished in vain."
"The road will be long and perilous before our two races may live in harmony."
"Perhaps they will not even be able to..."
"And yet, we owe it to them to try."
"And learn from one another."
"May their souls find peace..."
"And may they rest for eternity in the light of our Mother, the earth."
End of Part 2.

To Be Continued...

WWW.INSIGHTCOMICS.COM

Find us on Facebook: www.facebook.com/InsightEditionsComics

Follow us on Twitter: @InsightComics

Follow us on Instagram: Insight_Comics

All rights reserved. First published in the United States in 2017 by Insight Editions. Originally published in French in two volumes as *Elfes* by Editions Soleil, France, in 2013. English translation by Christina Cox-De Ravel. English translation © 2017 Insight Editions.

Elfes, volume 1 by Istin and Duarte
Elfes, volume 2 by Jarry and Maconi
© Editions Soleil – 2013

Library of Congress Cataloging-in-Publication Data available.

ISBN: 978-1-60887-877-2

PUBLISHER: RAOUL GOFF
EXECUTIVE EDITOR: VANESSA LOPEZ
EDITORS: MARK IRWIN, WARREN BUCHANAN, AND KELLY REED
ART DIRECTOR: CHRISSY KWASNIK
MANAGING EDITOR: ALAN KAPLAN
PRODUCTION EDITOR: ELAINE OU
PRODUCTION MANAGER: ALIX NICHOLAEFF
PRODUCTION ASSISTANTS: PAULINE KERKHOVE SELLIN AND SYLVESTER VANG

ROOTS of PEACE   REPLANTED PAPER

Insight Editions, in association with Roots of Peace, will plant two trees for each tree used in the manufacTuring of this book. Roots of Peace is an internationally renowned humanitarian organization dedicated to eradicating land mines worldwide and converting war-torn lands into productive farms and wildlife habitats. Roots of Peace will plant two million fruit and nut trees in Afghanistan and provide farmers there with the skills and support necessary for sustainable land use.

Manufactured in Hong Kong by Insight Editions

10 9 8 7 6 5 4 3 2